WAKING
LIONS

AYELET GUNDAR-GOSHEN

WAKING
LIONS

Translated from the Hebrew
by Sondra Silverston

PUSHKIN PRESS
LONDON

Pushkin Press
71–75 Shelton Street
London WC2H 9JQ

Published by arrangement with The Institute for
the Translation of Hebrew Literature

Waking Lions was first published in Israel as *Leha'ir Arajot*

This edition first published by Pushkin Press in 2016

0 0 1

ISBN 978 1 782271 56 7

Set in Monotype Baskerville by Tetragon, London,
printed and bound by TJ International Ltd, Padstow, PL28 8RW

www.pushkinpress.com

For Yoav

H<small>E'S THINKING THAT THE MOON</small> is the most beautiful he has ever seen when he hits the man. For the first moment after he hits him he's still thinking about the moon, and then he suddenly stops, like a candle that has been blown out. He hears the door of the SUV open and knows that he's the one opening it, that he's the one getting out now. But that knowledge is connected to his body only loosely, like a tongue skimming over gums shortly after a Novocain injection: it's all there, but different. His feet tread the desert gravel and the crunching sound he hears confirms that he's walking. Somewhere beyond the next step the man he hit is waiting for him; he can't see him from here, but he's there, another step and he's there. He slows down, tries to delay that final step, after which he'll have no choice but to look at the man lying on the side of the road. If only he could freeze that step, but of course he can't, just as he can't freeze the previous moment, the exact moment he ran him down, the moment a man driving an SUV ran down a man walking on the road. Only the next step will reveal whether that man is still a man or is now – something else. The mere thought of the word paralyzes him because when he takes that last step, he might discover that the man is no longer a man, but the cracked, empty shell of one. And if the man lying there is no longer a man, he cannot imagine what will become of the man standing there, shaking, unable to complete one simple step. What will become of him.

PART ONE

1

THE DUST WAS EVERYWHERE. A thin white layer, like the icing on a birthday cake no one wants. It had accumulated on the palm tree fronds in the central square, mature trees that had been trucked in and planted in the ground because no one believed that young seedlings could take hold there. It covered the local campaign posters still fluttering on apartment balconies three months after the election: balding, mustached men observing a crowd of voters from beneath the dust, some smiling authoritatively, some looking grave, each following the advice of his latest media consultant. Dust on advertising billboards; dust on bus stops; dust on the bougainvillaea straggling along the edge of the sidewalk, faint with thirst; dust everywhere.

And yet no one appeared to notice. The residents of Beersheba had grown accustomed to the dust, just as they had grown accustomed to all the rest – unemployment, crime, public parks strewn with broken bottles. The people of the city continued to wake up to dust-filled streets, went to their dusty jobs, had sex under a layer of dust and produced children whose eyes reflected the dust. He sometimes wondered which of the two he hated more – the dust or the residents of Beersheba. Apparently the dust. The residents of Beersheba weren't spread over his SUV in the morning. The dust was. A thin white layer that dulled the blazing red of the SUV, turning it to faded pink. Angrily, Eitan ran a finger over the windshield and wiped away some of the disgrace. It remained on his hand even after he rubbed it on his trousers, and he knew he would have to wait until he scrubbed in at Soroka before he'd feel really clean again. Fuck this city.

When he got into the car he was careful to keep his dirty finger from touching anything, as if it wasn't part of his body but rather a tissue sample he was holding and would momentarily place in front of Prof. Zakai so they could examine it together avidly – tell us who you are! But Prof. Zakai was many kilometers away from here now, waking to a dustless morning in the leafy green streets of Raanana, sitting in the comfort of his silver Mercedes as it made its way to the hospital through the traffic jams of the highly populated center of the country.

Racing through the empty streets of Beersheba, Eitan wished Prof. Zakai at least an hour and a quarter of sweaty waiting at the Geha intersection, with the air conditioner broken. But he knew very well that Mercedes air conditioners didn't break and that the traffic jams at Geha were nothing more than a sweet reminder of what Eitan had left behind when he moved here – the big city. Granted, there are no traffic jams in Beersheba, something he mentioned in every conversation he had with people from the Tel Aviv area. But when he did – a serene smile on his face, the clear-eyed look of a desert aristocrat – he always had the thought that there were no traffic jams in cemeteries either, but he wouldn't make his home in one. The buildings along Rager Boulevard really did remind him of a cemetery. A faded, uniform row of stone blocks that had once been white and were now bordering on gray. Giant headstones with the tired, dusty face of one apparition or another occasionally appearing in their windows.

In the Soroka Hospital parking lot he met Dr Zandorf, who gave him a broad smile and asked, "And how is Dr Green today?" He dredged up a battered smile, did his best to spread it across his face and replied, "Fine." They entered the hospital together, replacing the climate and time that nature had imposed upon them with the insolent defiance of an air conditioning and lighting system that guaranteed them eternal morning and endless spring. Eitan parted from Dr Zandorf at the entrance to the department and had begun a prolonged scrubbing at the sink when a young nurse walked by and remarked that he had a pianist's hands. That's true, he thought, he did have a musician's fingers. Women always told him that. But the only strings he strummed were damaged, truncated neurons.

A strange instrument, the brain. You never really know what sound you'll get when you press one key or another. Of course, if you stimulate the occipital lobe with a mild electric shock, the man sitting in front of you will most likely report that he sees colors, just as pressing on neurons in the temporal lobe will probably lead to the illusion of sounds. But while science is extremely partial to general, uniform rules, people are partial to being distinguished from one another. Two patients with damage to their orbitofrontal cortex will never have the courtesy to coordinate their side effects. One will behave crudely and the other will become obsessively cheerful. One will make tasteless sexual remarks and the other will feel an uncontrollable need to pick up every object in his path. Randomness, that seductive little whore, dances among the department beds, spits on the doctors' lab coats and tickles the exclamation marks of science until they bow their heads and become rounded into question marks.

"So how can we ever know anything at all?!" he once blurted out in the lecture hall. Fifteen years had passed since then and he still remembered the anger that had risen in him on that sleepy afternoon when he realized that the profession he was training for was no more certain than any other. A student who had fallen asleep beside him was startled awake by his cry and gave him a hostile look. The rest of the class was waiting for the remainder of what the senior lecturer had to say, which would most likely contain material for their exam. The only person who did not consider the question an annoyance was Prof. Zakai himself, who shot him an amused glance over the lecturer's podium. "And what is your name?"

"Eitan. Eitan Green."

"The only way to know something, Eitan, is to investigate death. Death teaches you everything you need to know. Take, for example, the case of Henry Molaison. In 1953 he underwent an innovative surgical resection of the areas responsible for his epilepsy, among them the hippocampus. You know what happened afterwards?"

"He died?"

"Yes and no. Henry Molaison didn't die because he woke up after the surgery and continued to live. But in another sense, Henry Molaison did die because from the moment he woke up after the surgery, he was incapable of creating even a single new memory. He couldn't fall in love or hold a grudge or be exposed to a new idea for longer than two minutes because after two minutes the object of his love or grudge was simply erased. He was twenty-seven when the surgery was performed, and even though he didn't die until he was eighty-two, he actually remained twenty-seven for ever. You see, Eitan, only after the hippocampus was removed did they discover that it was in fact responsible for encoding long-term memories. We have to wait for something to be destroyed in order to understand what had previously functioned properly. That is, in fact, the most basic method of brain research – you cannot simply dismantle parts of people's brains and see what happens; you wait for the case to do it for you. And then, like a guild of scavengers, scientists swoop down on what remains after the case has done its job and try to arrive at what you desire so fervently – knowing something."

Was that where the bait had been laid, in that lecture hall? Had Prof. Zakai known then that his diligent, fascinated student would follow him like a loyal dog wherever he went? As he donned his lab coat, Eitan laughed at his naivety. He, who didn't believe in God, who even as a child had refused to listen to any story that contained the slightest hint of the supernatural, had transformed that lecturer into a living god. And when the faithful dog refused to play dead, to play deaf-dumb-blind, the living god poured out all his wrath on him and drove him from the Tel Aviv Garden of Eden to this wilderness, to Soroka Hospital.

"Dr Green?"

The young nurse stopped beside him and reported on the night's events. He was suitably attentive, then went to make himself some coffee. Walking along the corridor, he glanced quickly at the patients' faces – a young woman choked with quiet weeping. A middle-aged Russian man trying to do a Sudoku puzzle with a palsied hand. Four members of a Bedouin family staring with glazed eyes at a TV set high on the wall. Eitan looked up at the screen – a determined cheetah was vigorously chewing up the bits of flesh left over from what had once been – according to the voiceover – a red-tailed fox. The fact that all of life is destined to be annihilated was never alluded to in hospital corridors, and yet here it was, openly presented on a TV screen. If Dr Eitan Green were to walk through the concrete jungle known as Soroka Hospital and actually speak about death, the patients would go mad. There would be crying, shouting, attacks on the medical staff. Countless times he had heard impassioned patients call them "angels in white". And though he knew that under their lab coats they were not angels but flesh-and-blood people, he didn't nitpick. If people needed angels, who was he to prevent them from having them? So what if a nurse had escaped a negligence suit by the skin of her teeth after pouring a medication meant for one parched throat down a different parched throat? Even angels make mistakes sometimes, especially if

16

they haven't slept for twenty-three hours. And when family members, stricken with grief and anger, attacked a frightened intern or a terrified specialist, Eitan knew that they would have attacked real angels the same way, would have torn the feathers from their wings so they couldn't fly off to the golden kingdom of heaven while their beloved relative was being dispatched into the darkness of the earth. And now all those people who could not bear even a fleeting glance at the face of death were watching it serenely, even eagerly, as it spread fear on the African savannah. Because now it wasn't only the Bedouins staring at the screen – the Russian man had put down his Sudoku and raised his head, and even the weeping woman was watching the scene through tear-soaked lashes. The cheetah energetically chewed the remaining flesh of the red-tailed fox. The narrator spoke about drought. In the absence of rain, the animals on the savannah would begin to eat their young. Everyone at the neurosurgery department desk was riveted by the rare description, given by the narrator, of an African lion devouring its cubs, and Eitan Green knew with all his heart that it wasn't for morphine that he had to thank the gods of science, but for the 33-inch Toshiba.

Four years earlier, a bald woman patient had called him a cynic and spat in his face. He could still remember the sensation of the saliva running down his cheek. She was a young woman, not especially attractive. But she walked around the department with a certain majesty, other patients and nurses unconsciously moving aside to let her pass. One day, when he visited her on morning rounds, she called him a cynic and spat in his face. He tried in vain to understand what had caused her to do that. During earlier examinations, his questions had been matter-of-fact and her replies brief. She had never spoken to him in the corridor. And it was because he could find no reason that the incident upset him. Against his will, he was drawn into magical thinking about blind people who see clearly, bald women whose approaching death equips them with a sort of sixth sense. That night, in the double bed whose sheets smelled of semen, he had asked Liat, "Am I a cynic?"

She had laughed, and he was hurt.

"That bad?"

"No," she said, and kissed the tip of his nose, "no more than anybody else."

And he truly wasn't a cynic. No more than anybody else. Dr Eitan Green didn't grow more – or less – tired of his patients than doctors in the department usually did. And yet he had been banished beyond the sea to a land of dust and sand, driven from a hospital in the bustling heart of the country to the desolate concrete wilderness of Soroka. "You idiot," he whispered to himself as he struggled to revive the wheezing air conditioner in his office, "You naive idiot." Because what else but idiocy would push a medical prodigy into a head-on confrontation with his boss? What else but sheer idiocy would lead him to insist that he was right when his boss had warned him to watch his step? What new forms of idiocy had the medical prodigy invented when he banged on the desk in a pale imitation of assertiveness and said, "It's bribery, Zakai, and I'm going to blow the whistle on it." And when he went to the hospital director and told him about the envelopes of money and unscheduled emergency operations that followed, had he really been stupid enough to believe the expression of surprise in his eyes?

And worst of all, he would do it again. All of it. In fact, he had almost given a repeat performance when he found out, two weeks later, that the only action the hospital director had taken was to arrange his transfer.

"I'm going to the media," he had told Liat. "I'll make so much noise that they won't be able to bury it."

"Fine," she said, "right after we pay for Yaheli's nursery school, the car and the apartment."

Later, she'd say that it was his decision to make, that she would support him in whatever path he chose. But he remembered how the brown of her eyes had turned instantly from honey to hard chestnut, remembered how she had tossed and turned in bed that entire night, struggling in her dreams with horrors whose nature he could guess at. The next morning he went into the hospital director's office and agreed to the transfer.

And three months later, here he was, in the whitewashed house in Omer. Yaheli and Itamar played on the grass. Liat considered where to hang the pictures. And he stood and looked at the bottle of whiskey the department members had given him as a farewell present, not knowing whether to laugh or cry.

In the end, he had taken the bottle to the hospital with him and put it on the shelf among his diplomas. After all, like them, it symbolized something. An era that had come to an end, a lesson he had learned. If he was lucky enough to enjoy a few moments of peace between patients, he took the bottle off the shelf and studied it, dwelling on the card. "To Eitan, Good Luck." The words seemed to mock him. He knew Prof. Zakai's handwriting very well, small Braille scribbles which, during Eitan's time in medical school, had brought students to tears. "Could you explain what you wrote?" "I prefer that you, young lady, learn to read." "But it's not clear." "Science, ladies and gentlemen, is an unclear subject." And everyone would bend their heads and write, storing up their anger for particularly venomous end-of-year feedback forms, which never changed anything. The following year, Prof. Zakai returned to stand in the lecture hall, his handwriting on the blackboard a series of indecipherable pigeon droppings. The only person happy to see him was Eitan. Slowly, painstakingly, he learned to puzzle out Prof. Zakai's scrawl, but the professor's character remained an enigma to him

"To Eitan, Good Luck." The card hung on the neck of the whiskey bottle in an eternal embrace that sickened Eitan. Several times he had contemplated tearing it up and throwing it into the waste basket, perhaps even ridding himself of the bottle altogether. But he always stopped himself at the last minute, concentrating on Prof. Zakai's words exactly as he'd concentrated on solving a complicated equation when he was a schoolboy.

He was working too much that night, and he knew it. His muscles ached. The cups of coffee lost their effect after half an hour. Behind his hand, the yawns threatened to swallow up the entire waiting room. At eight o'clock he called to say goodnight to his kids, and he was so tired and irritable that he hurt Yaheli's feelings. The boy asked him to make horse sounds and he said, "Not now" in a tone that frightened both of them. Then Itamar took over the conversation, asked how things were at work and whether he'd be home late, and Eitan had to remind himself that his perceptive older son wasn't even eight yet. While speaking to Itamar, he heard Yaheli sniffing in the background, probably trying to keep his big brother from hearing that he was crying. After the conversation, Eitan was even more tired than before, and feeling very guilty.

He almost always felt guilty when he thought about his children. No matter what he did, it felt like too little. There was always a chance that it would be this particular conversation, in which he adamantly refused to make horse sounds, that Yaheli would remember years later. After all, it was exactly that kind of thing he himself remembered from the time he was Yaheli's age – not all the hugs he'd received, but the ones he hadn't. Like the time he burst into tears during a tour of his father's lab at Haifa University and his mother simply stood there with all the other visitors and whispered that he should be ashamed of himself. Or perhaps she had actually hugged him later. Or taken a five-shekel note out of her wallet as a substitute for a hug and sent him to buy a popsicle as consolation. It didn't matter. He didn't remember that. Just as he didn't remember all the times he'd jumped off the tree in the yard and the ground had received him gladly, but only the one time he'd landed on it with a crash and broken his leg.

Like all fathers, he knew that it was inevitable, that he was destined to disappoint his son. But like all fathers, he harbored a secret hope that perhaps not. Perhaps that wouldn't happen with them. Perhaps he would manage to give Itamar and Yaheli exactly what they needed. Yes, children cry sometimes, but with him they would cry only when they really had to, because they had failed, not because he had.

He walked down the department corridor, under the frozen flames of the fluorescent lights, and tried to think about what was happening at home now. Itamar was in his room, lining up dinosaurs according to size. Yaheli had most likely calmed down by now. That child was like Liat, heated up quickly and cooled down just as fast. Not like Eitan, whose anger was like a Sabbath hotplate: you turn it on and don't turn it off for two days. Yes, Yaheli had already calmed down and was sitting on the couch now watching *March of the Penguins* on TV for the thousandth time. Eitan knew that film by heart. The narrator's jokes, the musical theme, even the order of the final credits. And he knew Yaheli's reactions equally well: when he would laugh, when he would recite a favorite punchline along with the narrator, when he would peer at the screen from behind a pillow. The funny parts made him laugh every time, and the scary parts scared him every time, and that was strange, because how many times can you laugh at a joke you already know, and how scared can you be at the sight of a sea lion's ambush if you already know for sure that in the end the penguin will outwit the sea lion and escape? And yet, the moment the sea lion appeared, Yaheli dived behind the pillow, where he observed from a distance what was happening to the penguin. And Eitan would watch him watching the penguin, wondering when he would finally tire of that video, wondering when children stop asking for the familiar all the time and begin to ask for something new.

On the other hand, how much fun and how comfortable it was to know already halfway through the film just how it was going to end. The dangerous storm at the 32nd minute became so much more bearable when you knew that it would die down at the 43rd minute. Not to mention the sea lions, the seagulls and all the other evil creatures that stared covetously at the egg laid by the penguin queen but never managed to get it. And when the sea lion's ambush finally failed, as he knew it would, Yaheli would cheer, emerge from behind the pillow and say – Daddy, can I have some chocolate milk?

Of course you can. In the purple cup – he wouldn't drink from any other. Three teaspoons of Chocolit powder, mix well so there are no lumps, remind Yaheli that if he drinks it now, there won't be any chocolate milk later because it's not healthy. Knowing that in two hours he'd wake up and ask for it again. And there was a good chance that he'd get it, because Liat couldn't cope with that crying of his. He asked himself why he actually could. Was it because he was such a brilliant educator, such an authoritative and consistent father, or was it something else?

He had fallen in love with Itamar right after he was born. With Yaheli, it took time. He didn't talk about it. It wasn't the sort of thing you say about your children. About women, yes. For example: we've been dating for a month and I still haven't fallen in love with her. But when it's your child, you're supposed to love him right then and there. Even if you don't know him yet. With Itamar, it really was like that. Even before they washed him, before he saw his face clearly, he had already made room in his heart for him. Perhaps because during the weeks preceding the birth, all he did was make room for him. Room in the closet for his clothes, room in the cabinets for his toys, room on the shelves for his diapers. And when Itamar finally arrived, he slipped into that place as naturally as possible, settled in there and didn't move.

Or at least that's how it was for Eitan. It had been a bit more difficult for Liat. They agreed that it was because of the pain and the drop in her hormone levels, and that if she didn't stop crying within ten days they would see a doctor. She stopped crying in less than ten days, but it took time for her to begin smiling. They didn't talk about it because there was nothing to talk about, but they both knew that Eitan had loved Itamar immediately and Liat had joined him two weeks later. And that with Yaheli it had been the opposite. But the question always remained: did the parent who joined later, with a slight delay, catch up with the other parent's love in a guilty, panting run? Did that parent really walk at the same pace now, or was he still lagging behind?

*

Six hours later, when they finally managed to stabilize the injured victims of a road accident in the Arava, he was able to take off his lab coat at last.

"You look wiped out," the young nurse said. "How about sleeping here?"

Eitan was too tired to contemplate the hidden meaning that did or didn't lie behind her words. He thanked her politely, washed his face and went out into the night air. With the very first step, he felt what nineteen hours of air conditioning had made him forget: oppressive, dusty desert heat. The gentle humming in the hospital corridors – a muted symphony of beeping monitors and pinging elevators – was abruptly replaced by Beersheba night sounds. The crickets were too hot to chirp. The alley cats were too dry to mew. Only the radio in an apartment across the street doggedly screeched a familiar pop song.

Through the hospital gate Eitan could see an empty parking lot, and he dared to hope that someone had stolen his suv. Liat would be furious, of course. She'd start pulling strings, curse the Bedouins in her inimitable fashion. Then the insurance money would arrive and she'd demand that he buy a new one. But this time, he'd tell her no, the "no" he hadn't had the courage to say then, when she'd insisted on getting him a special treat to celebrate his transfer. She'd said "treat", not "compensation", but they both knew it was the same thing. "We'll plow through the dunes around Beersheba in it," she'd said, "you'll do a doctorate in all-terrain driving." It sounded almost right when she said it, and during the first few days of packing up he still consoled himself with thoughts of sharp inclines and steep slopes. But when they arrived in Beersheba Liat became immersed in her new job, and Saturday suv outings seemed further away than ever. At first, he'd still tried to persuade Sagi and Nir to join him, but after he left the hospital they spoke less and less, until the very idea of spending time together began to seem strange. The red suv quickly grew accustomed to its shift from wild wolf to domesticated poodle, and apart from the slight growl it emitted when he accelerated suddenly on the way out of Omer, it was like any other standard suburban car. Eitan hated it more from week to week, and now – seeing it behind the guard's booth – he could barely control his urge to kick the bumper.

When he opened the door, he was astonished to realize that he was wide awake. His last reserve of noradrenaline began to pump now from some forgotten shelf in his brain, sending a new, unexpected spurt of energy through his body. The full moon above him glowed with the whiteness of promise. When he started the suv, the engine growled a question. Perhaps tonight?

He jerked the wheel to the right instead of the left and sped toward the hills south of the city. A week before the move, he had read on the Internet about a particularly challenging suv track not far from Kibbutz Tlalim. At this hour, with the roads wide open, he'd be there in twenty minutes. He could hear the engine's purr of pleasure as the speedometer crossed the 120-kilometer mark. For the first time in weeks, Eitan found himself smiling. The smile turned into actual happiness when, eighteen minutes later, he saw that the track's reputation was well deserved. The enormous moon washed over the white ground and the SUV's tires sped forward into the depths of the desert. Four hundred meters later, his brakes squealed to a stop. An extremely large porcupine stood on the road. Eitan was convinced it would run off, but the animal simply stood there and looked at him. It didn't even bother to raise its quills. He had to tell Itamar about this. He hesitated for a moment, unable to decide if he should take out his phone and snap a picture, but he knew it would only detract from the story. The porcupine in front of him was less than a meter long, and the porcupine he'd describe to Itamar would be at least a meter and a half. This porcupine did not have raised quills, but that one would be shooting quills out in every direction. This porcupine wasn't uttering a sound, but the one in his story would ask, "Excuse me, but do you happen to know what time it is?"

Imagining Itamar's laughter, Eitan smiled to himself. Who knows, maybe he'd repeat the story to his classmates. But Eitan knew that it would take much more than a desert porcupine to break down the glass wall between his son and the other children. He never understood where Itamar's introversion had come from. And although Liat always said there was no point in digging around for reasons, that's what made him happy, Eitan was not at all sure it was the boy's choice. It wasn't that he was shunned. He had one friend, Nitai. But that was it. (Which is fine, Liat kept saying – some children like to be part of groups and others feel better with more intimate relationships.)

Perhaps she was right. There were no signs that Itamar was suffering in school. And yet he worried. Because he, Eitan, was not like that. Because when all the boys had gone to hang out in the square on Friday nights, he'd been there. Not in the center of things, but there. His son wasn't. And even though it shouldn't have mattered to him, it did.

Outside the suv, the porcupine turned its back and continued on its way. Slow, haughty, its quills tagging along behind it. He watched as it vanished among the dark rocks. The road in front of him was once again empty, inviting. Suddenly, he felt as if that stop had only clarified for him how hungry he was for movement. How much he wanted to surge forward. But hold on, a good sprint needs a soundtrack. He took a minute trying to choose between Janis Joplin and Pink Floyd, but decided that, for this sort of nocturnal journey, nothing could compare to Joplin's tormented screams. And she really did scream, at full volume, and the engine screamed as well, and shortly after that even Eitan joined in, screaming exuberantly on the wild descent, screaming defiantly as he took the steep rise, screaming with total abandon as he careened around the curve near the hill. Then he was quiet (Janis Joplin continued; that woman's vocal cords were incredible) and kept driving, occasionally joining her when she sounded particularly lonely. It had been years since he had enjoyed himself so much alone, with no other eyes to share the wonder with him, with no one else to echo his joy. He glanced at the enormous, majestic moon through the rearview mirror.

He was thinking that the moon was the most beautiful he had ever seen when he hit the man. For the first moment after he hit him, he was still thinking about the moon, and then he suddenly stopped, like a candle that had been blown out.

At first, all he could think about was how much he needed to defecate. An urgent, total need that he could just barely contain. It was as if his stomach had plummeted all at once and in another second he'd lose control and everything would pour out of him. And then all at once his body disconnected. His brain shifted to automatic pilot. He no longer felt the need to defecate. He no longer wondered if he would ever reach his next breath.

He was Eritrean. Or Sudanese. Or God knows what. A man of about thirty, maybe forty; he could never determine with any certainty how old those people were. At the end of the safari in Kenya, he had given the driver a tip. Flattered by the man's gratitude, he'd added a few bland questions with an amiability which, at the time, he believed was sincere. He had asked the man what his name was, how many children he had and how old he was. His name was Husu, he had three children, and he was the same age as Eitan, though he looked a decade older. Those people were born old and died young, and the in-between wasn't much to speak of. When he asked him what his exact date of birth was, he learned that they had been born a day apart. It didn't mean anything, but still… Now here was this man, thirty or maybe forty years old, lying on the road, his head crushed.

Janis Joplin begged him to take another little piece of her heart, but he knelt on the ground and put his head close to the Eritrean's cracked lips. A doctor at Soroka who finished work at two in the morning after a nineteen-hour shift. Instead of driving home to sleep, he decided to check out his suv's performance. In the dark. At high speed. How many years do you get for something like that? Eitan looked imploringly at the hole in the man's head, but the two sides of the split skull showed no intention of miraculously uniting. At the end of their fifth-year examination, Prof. Zakai had asked them what to do when a patient comes to them with an open skull. Pens were chewed, whispers were exchanged, and still, everyone failed. "Your problem is that you assume that something can be done," Prof. Zakai had said when the objections began to pile up on his desk. "When the calvarium is crushed and there is extensive neurosurgical damage, the only thing you can do is have a cup of coffee." And yet Eitan took the man's pulse, which was thready, examined his capillary filling, which was remarkably slow, and also checked with ludicrous precaution that his airways were unimpeded. Damn it, he couldn't just sit there and watch the man die.

"Twenty minutes," Zakai's voice reverberated serenely. "Not a minute longer. Unless you've begun to believe in miracles." Eitan examined the Eritrean's head wound again. It would take much more than a miracle to recover the gray matter that showed under the hair: naked, exposed neurons that glowed in the moonlight. Blood trickled from the man's ears, bright and watery because of the cerebrospinal fluid, which had already begun to leak from the cracked skull. None the less, Eitan stood up, hurried to the suv, returned with a first-aid kit and had already opened the package of bandages when he suddenly froze. What was the point? This man was going to die.

And when it finally appeared, the explicit word, he suddenly felt his internal organs become sheathed in ice. A layer of white frost spread from his liver to his stomach, from his stomach to his intestines. Unfolded, the small intestine is eight meters long. More than three times a person's height. Its diameter is almost three centimeters, but the size is not uniform at all ages. The small intestine is divided into the duodenum, the jejunum and the ileum. Eitan drew a strange sense of tranquility from that knowledge, frozen white tranquility. He lingered on the small intestine. He examined it. Its internal surface, for example, is enlarged by finger-like projections called villi. Those structures increase the interior surface area of the small intestine by 500 times to about 250 square meters. Incredible. Simply incredible. Now he truly appreciated his studies. A wall in the shape of knowledge that stood between him and that filthy verb, "to die". This man was going to die.

You have to call the hospital, he said to himself, and have them send an ambulance. Prepare an operating room. Get hold of Prof. Tal.

Call the police.

Because that's what they'd do. That's what they always do when they receive a report of a road accident. The fact that the doctor attending to the patient happened to be the driver who hit him wouldn't change anything. They'd call the police and the police would come and he would explain to them that it had been dark. That he hadn't been able to see anything. That there had been no reason to expect that someone would be walking on the side of the road at that hour. Liat would help him. He wasn't married to a senior detective in the Israeli police for no reason. She'd explain to them and they would understand. They would have to understand. True, he was driving way over the speed limit, and yes, he hadn't slept for more than twenty hours, but the irresponsible party here was the Eritrean; Eitan had no reason to assume that anyone would be here.

And did the Eritrean have a reason to expect anyone to be here?

Liat's voice was cold and matter-of-fact. He'd already heard her speak that way, but always to others. To the cleaner who had finally admitted that she had stolen her pearl earrings, to the guy who renovated their house and confessed that he had inflated his prices. How much he had loved to imagine her at work, giving the suspect sitting opposite her a distant, amused look, a languid lioness toying with her prey for a bit before pouncing on it. But now he saw her in front of him, her brown eyes fixed on the man lying on the ground, then rising to stare at him.

He looked at the Eritrean again. Blood flowed from his head, staining his shirt collar. If he was lucky, the judge would give him only a few months. But he wouldn't be able to do surgery anymore. That was for certain. No one would hire a doctor convicted of manslaughter. And then there was the media and Yaheli and Itamar and Liat and his mother and the people he happened to meet on the street.

And the Eritrean kept bleeding as if he were doing it deliberately.

Suddenly he knew he had to go. Now. He couldn't save this man. At least he'd try to save himself.

The possibility stood in the night air, clear and simple: get into the SUV and get the hell out of here. Eitan contemplated that possibility from a distance, tensely following its movements. Now it leaped up and grasped him, all of him, the choking icy fear that screamed in his ears – get into the SUV. Now.

But right then, the Eritrean opened his eyes. Eitan froze once again. The air grew thinner and his tongue felt like sandpaper in his mouth. At his feet, right beside the shoes with the orthopaedic inner soles he'd bought in the duty-free shop, the Eritrean whose skull had been crushed lay with wide open eyes.

He didn't look at Eitan, merely lay there and stared at the sky, stared at it with such concentration that Eitan couldn't help stealing an upward glance at the spot the Eritrean was focused on. Perhaps there might actually be something there. There was nothing there. Only the spectacular moon in a glittering indigo sky, as if someone had Photoshopped them. When he returned his gaze to the ground, the Eritrean's eyes were closed, his breathing calm. Eitan's breathing, however, was loud and rapid, and his entire body shook. How could he drive away if the man's eyes were still open, still liable to open. On the other hand, open eyes meant nothing, while the cerebrospinal fluid now leaking not only from his ears, but from his nose too, foaming from his mouth, meant a great deal. The Eritrean's limbs were stiff and shrunken, the decorticate posture. Even if he had wanted to, there was not even a sliver of life to fight for. Truly.

And truly, the Eritrean appeared to be reconciled to his situation with that well-known African complaisance, because the fact was that he was kind enough to keep his eyes shut and breathe quietly with a grimace on his face that wasn't very different from a smile. Eitan looked at him again before going to the SUV. Now he was sure that the Eritrean was smiling at him, his closed eyes signaling his approval.

2

H E SLEPT WELL THAT NIGHT. More than well – he slept really well. A deep, solid sleep that continued even after the sun rose. After the children got out of bed. After Liat had shouted at them to get a move on. He slept when Yaheli screamed about a toy that frustrated him. He slept when Itamar turned on the TV at full volume. He slept when the front door closed and the car carrying his entire family drove away. He slept and slept and slept, and then he slept some more, until the moment came when he could absolutely sleep no more – and then he woke up.

The midday sun shone through the shutters and danced on the bedroom walls. A bird sang outside. A small, brave spider dared to defy Liat's obsessive cleanliness and labored vigorously to spin a web in the corner above the bed. Eitan watched the spider for a while before the blessed fog of sleep faded, leaving one simple truth: last night he had run a man over and driven away. Every cell of his body woke to that clear, unalterable reality. He had run a man over. He had run a man over and driven away. He kept repeating the words to himself, trying to connect the vowels and the consonants into something that made sense. But the more he said them, the more they fell apart in his mind until they totally lost substance.

Now he spoke the words aloud, allowing the sounds to take shape in the room. I ran a man over. I ran a man over and drove away. The more he repeated the words, first in a whisper and then more loudly, the more unreal, even stupid, they sounded, as if he were talking about something he'd read in the newspapers or seen in a bad TV show. Nor did the spider or the bird help him: you would expect birds to refrain from singing at the window of someone who had run a man over and driven away, and spiders to refuse to build their homes over the bed of such a person. Even the sun – instead of shifting its angle – persisted in shining through the shutters and painting truly breathtaking splashes of light on the wall.

Suddenly, Eitan simply had to study them carefully. Spots of light on a white wall at the same angle at the same time every morning. Because that which hath been is that which shall be, and today, like yesterday, the earth would carry on rotating on its axis with the same slow, sleepy movement that rocked Eitan as if he were a baby. If the earth suddenly rotated in the other direction, Eitan would stumble and fall.

Though he was already completely awake, he continued to lie in bed, unmoving. How could he dare to stand on his feet after running a man over and driving away? The ground would surely fall away beneath him.

Or would it, a cold, dark, smiling voice asked, would it fall away? After all, it continued to support Prof. Zakai's feet quite nicely.

That thought caused Eitan to sit up in bed and place one bare foot on the marble floor. And then the other. He took three steps toward the kitchen before a quick flash of the dead man's face stopped him in his tracks. It was one thing to tell yourself over and over again that you ran a man over and drove away, but something else to see that man's face right in front of you. With great effort he pushed the image to the back of his mind and kept walking. In vain. Before he reached the door, the image, sharper than ever, struck him again: the Eritrean's eyes opened to slits, the pupils frozen in an eternal expression of incredulity. This time he pushed the image away more forcefully. Get back there. Get back to the same dark room where all those other images are stored – the corpses they had dissected in their first year of medical school, the hideous photographs of amputated, scorched, acid-burned limbs that the trauma lecturer had shown them with such obvious pleasure in his third year, delighting in every groan of revulsion coming from the class. "You have weak stomachs," she'd say when one of the students mumbled a pathetic excuse and ran out into the fresh air for a few minutes, "and people with weak stomachs don't become doctors." The memory of Prof. Reinhart's stern face helped to ease his agitation somewhat.

Now he reached the kitchen. So clean. As if it had never been the scene of cornflakes wars, as if coffee had never been spilled in it. How did Liat manage to keep this house looking like a display in a furniture shop?

He looked through the large window at the suv in the driveway. Not a scratch on it. Not for no reason had the car salesman called it "a Mercedes tank". Nevertheless, he had examined it for a long time yesterday, kneeling in front of the bumper, straining his eyes in the pale glow of the flashlight of his cell phone. It wasn't possible to hit a person that way without leaving a sign. A dent in the tin, a kink in the bumper, some indication that something had indeed occurred. Proof that it had not only driven through air, but had hit a body, a mass, a cause of friction. But the SUV stood in the driveway intact and unchanged, and Eitan turned away from the window and filled the kettle with a shaking hand.

Flashes of the dead man's face assailed him again as he made himself coffee, but they were less intense. The smell of lemon-scented detergent that filled the air of the kitchen and the almost sterile gleam of the work counter pushed away images of the previous night the way doormen in Tel Aviv restaurants block the way of beggars trying to get inside. Eitan ran a grateful hand over the stainless-steel surface. Three months ago, when Liat had insisted on buying it, he'd objected to the extravagance. So much money for a kitchen he was hoping to leave behind in less than two years, when his forced exile to the heart of the desert would come to an end. But Liat had already made up her mind and he was forced to consent, though he reserved the right to look angrily at the needless expense every time he went into the kitchen. Now he looked at it gratefully because there was nothing like a shiny stainless-steel surface to obliterate dark images. He was convinced that nothing bad would happen to him between the ultra-modern dishwasher and the top-quality cooker hood. True, he almost dropped the coffee mug when he picked it up because the memory of the dead man's hand attacked him mercilessly, but he managed to push it away and steady the mug before it could fall. And even if it did fall – that wasn't a problem. He would take a rag and clean the marble floor. Because it had to be acknowledged – cups would fall in the days to come. There would be moments of distraction. Nightmares, perhaps. But he would pick up the pieces, clean the floor and get on with his life. He would have to get on with his life. Even if the coffee tasted stale and bitter in his mouth, even if his hands were sweating despite the desert chill, even if he had to restrain himself from falling to the floor weeping with guilt, he would keep walking, the mug of coffee in his hand, to the armchair in the living room. The pain would have to pass in the end. It would take two weeks or a month or five years, but would pass in the end. The new stimulus was causing the neurons in his brain to transmit electrical signals with enormous speed. But as time passed, the pace of the transmission would slow down until it stopped completely. Habituation. The gradual loss of sensitivity. "You walk into a room," Prof. Zakai had told them, "and there's a terrible smell of garbage. You think you're going to vomit. The molecules of the smell stimulate the olfactory epithelium, which sends urgent signals to the amygdala and the cerebral cortex. Your neurons scream for help. But you know what happens after a few minutes? They stop. They get tired of screaming. And suddenly someone else comes into the room and says, 'It stinks here,' and you have no idea what he's talking about."

Sitting in the armchair, the mug of coffee in his hand almost empty, Eitan looked at the dark residue at the bottom of the mug. His first argument with Liat had taken place three weeks after they met when she told him that her grandmother read coffee grounds.

You mean, she thinks she reads coffee grounds.

No, Liat had insisted, she really reads coffee grounds. She looks at them and knows what's going to happen.

Like the fact that the sun will rise tomorrow? That we're all going to die eventually?

No, you idiot, things that not everyone knows. Let's say – if the husband of the woman who drank the coffee is cheating on her. Or whether she'll be able to get pregnant.

Liat, how the hell can coffee beans picked by an eight-year-old kid in Brazil and sold for an outrageous price in the supermarket predict whether some stupid woman in the godforsaken town of Or Akiva will get pregnant?

She told him he was being condescending, and that was true. She told him that there was nothing wrong with Or Akiva, and that too was apparently true. She told him that guys who put down the grandmothers of girls they were dating would quickly stoop to putting down the girls themselves, which sounded fine but wasn't necessarily true. Finally she told him that they probably shouldn't see each other again, and that frightened him so much that the next day he appeared at her house and suggested that they go immediately to visit her grandmother in Or Akiva so she could read his coffee grounds. Liat's grandmother welcomed them warmly, made excellent, if somewhat tepid coffee, took a quick look at the grounds and said that they were going to get married.

That's what you see in the grounds? he asked with all the awe he could muster.

No, Liat's grandmother laughed, it's what I see in your eyes. You never read people's coffee grounds, you read their eyes, their body language, the way they ask the question. But if you tell them that, they'll feel naked, which is not pleasant for anyone and also not polite, so instead, you read their coffee grounds. Do you understand, child?

Now he tilted the mug to the side and examined the coffee residue. Black and thick, like yesterday. It seemed that, like the birds, the spiders and the sunbeams, the coffee grounds saw no reason to deviate from their routine just because yesterday he'd run somebody over and driven away. Habituation. The Eritrean's face grew dimmer in his mind, the way the images of a bad dream fade gradually as the day progresses, until all that remains is a general feeling of unease. Unease is not pain, he told himself. People live entire lives with some measure or another of unease. Those words felt so right that he repeated them in his mind several more times, so focused on the liberating new insight that at first he didn't hear the knock on the door.

The woman at the door was tall, thin and very beautiful, but Eitan didn't notice any of those details. Two others captured his full attention: she was Eritrean and she was holding his wallet in her hand.

(And once again, he felt as if he had to empty his bowels, even more than he had the previous day. His stomach plummeted suddenly, pulling all his internal organs with it, and he knew clearly that this time he would not be able to control it. He'd run to the bathroom or relieve himself right there, on the threshold of the front door, in front of this woman.)

But he remained where he was, barely breathing, and looked at her as she showed him the wallet.

This is yours, she said in Hebrew.

"Yes," Eitan said. "It's mine."

And immediately regretted it because, who knew, perhaps he could persuade her that the wallet didn't belong to him at all, but rather to someone else – a twin brother, let's say – who had flown somewhere yesterday, Canada for example, or Japan, somewhere far away. Perhaps he could simply ignore her and close the door, or threaten to call the immigration police. Possible courses of action filled his head like colorful soap bubbles, bursting at the first touch of reality. To fall on his knees and beg her forgiveness. To pretend he had no idea what she was talking about. To accuse of her of being crazy. To claim that the man was already dead when he hit him. After all, he should know. He was a doctor.

The woman did not take her eyes off him. The hysterical voices in his head were replaced by a different, icy voice: she'd been there.

And as if to confirm those words, the woman looked at the whitewashed house in Omer and said, *Your house is lovely*.

"Thank you."

The yard is lovely too.

The woman looked at the toy car he'd bought for Yaheli. On Saturday he'd raced it back and forth along the length of the lawn, shouting and cheering, until another toy caught his eye and the car was left upside-down on the pathway to the house. Now the red plastic wheels were turned to the sky like damning evidence.

"What do you want?"

I want to talk.

He could hear the Dor family's Mazda sliding into its parking spot behind the stone wall. The slamming of the doors as Anat Dor and her children got out of the car. The tired reprimands as they walked toward the house. Thank God for the stone wall, for the wonderful suburban alienation that had managed to seep into communities like Omer. If not for that alienation, he'd be standing across from Anat Dor's curious look now because she would certainly rather forget her own troubles for a brief moment to wonder why her doctor neighbor was standing in his yard with a black woman. But the consolation of the stone wall was dwarfed by the knowledge that Anat Dor was merely the first robin to herald not spring, but the arrival of an entire flock of cars making its way toward the street at that very moment. And in each one sat a tiny chick asking what there was for lunch. In another few minutes – two? three? – Liat and his chicks would arrive. This woman had to leave.

*

"Not now," he told her, "I can't talk now."

So when?

"Tonight. Let's talk tonight."

Here?

Was that a glimmer of sarcasm he saw in her eyes as she pointed to the pine chairs on the porch?

"No," he said, "not here."

At the deserted garage outside of Tlalim. Turn right 200 meters after the turnoff to the access road. I'll be there at ten.

And suddenly he knew for certain that she had planned this encounter down to the smallest detail. The arrival a moment before the children were picked up at nursery school. The nerve-wracking lingering at the front door. The cold emanating from her eyes. For the first time since he had opened the door and found her standing there, he actually looked at her: tall, thin and very beautiful. And she, as if she understood that only now was he actually seeing her, nodded and said:

I am Sirkit.

He didn't bother to answer. She knew his name. If she hadn't known it, she wouldn't be standing on his lawn, an ecological marvel of reclaimed water irrigation, telling him where to be at ten that night.

"I'll be there," he said, then turned around and went inside. His mug of coffee was where he'd left it, on the table beside the armchair. The stainless-steel kitchen gleamed as usual. The sun continued to dance on the wall in truly breathtaking splashes of light.

3

LESS THAN TWENTY MINUTES after the woman left and he went back into the house, he felt he had never met her at all. He studied the yard through the half-open shutters: the rosemary bush, the manicured lawn, Yaheli's upside-down toy car. It was difficult to believe that less than half an hour ago a woman named Sirkit had stood right there on the path. Her existence grew even fainter when Liat and the children came home. Itamar and Yaheli ran around the yard in what might have been either a game or a life-and-death struggle. The clatter of their feet easily blotted out the memory of the Eritrean woman, and he gave her no more thought than someone sitting on a bus would give to the person who had occupied the seat before him. An hour and a half later, he could almost persuade himself that the visit had never taken place at all.

"The things our brain is prepared to do in order to protect us..." Prof. Zakai leaned on the lecturers' podium as he spoke, his smile wavering between mockery and affection until it finally settled on mockery. "Denial, for example. Yes, that's the psychologists' word. But don't be too quick to toss it into the garbage. Because what's the first thing a person will say after you've told him he has a brain tumor?"

It can't be.

"Right, 'it can't be'. But of course it absolutely can. In fact, it's happening right now: anaplastic astrocytomas are reproducing themselves over and over again, spreading from one hemisphere of the brain to the other through the corpus callosum. In less than a year, that entire system will collapse. Already now there are headaches, vomiting, hemiplegia. And yet that sick brain, that non-functioning bundle of neurons, is still capable of doing one thing: denying reality. You show the patient the test results. You repeat the prognosis three times in the clearest manner you can, but the man sitting across from you, who will soon turn into a lump of chemotherapy and side effects, manages to push away everything you tell him. And it doesn't matter how intelligent he is. Hell, he could be a doctor himself. But all those years of medical training become meaningless in the face of the brain's persistent refusal to look at what's staring it in the face."

Prof. Zakai was right. As usual. Like a silver-haired prophet of wrath he would stand on the lecturer's dais and roll out the future for them. In their fifth year of medical school it was easy to believe that his words were merely cynical anecdotes, but from the moment they were pushed out of the academic womb into the real world, his prophecies came true, one after the other. It *can* be, Eitan said to himself. It's happening. And if you want it to stop, you need to pull your head out of the desert sand and drive straight over to the bank.

All the way there, he fantasized about courteous, automatic service, a walking robot that would follow his instructions without any unnecessary words. But when he told the teller what he wanted, she raised her nose above her computer monitor and said, "Wow, that's a whole lot of money."

Three more tellers peered over the glass partitions that separated them, eager to know the exact amount of that "wow, that's a whole lot of money" and the identity of the man who was about to carry it off into the unknown. Eitan didn't react, hoping that cold disregard would suffice to shut the mouth of the teller whose name he could see now on the nametag pinned to her shirt as she lifted her head to look at him: Ravit. But Ravit wasn't fazed by his coldness. On the contrary. The intransigence of the man standing in front of her, the scornful look in his eyes served only to give her special pleasure as she raised her voice and said, "So you're buying a house?"

She continued working as she spoke, of course, counting the notes once, then counting them once again to make sure she was actually holding 70,000 shekels in cash in her hand. She counted a third time to prolong the feel of the notes on her fingers because she earned barely that amount for an entire year's work. Eitan looked at the gorgeous nail enhancements that lay on his money. Plastic gemstones tripped pleasurably along the length of the growing pile of 200-shekel notes. As Ravit continued to be amazed at the amount, Eitan was growing anxious that it might not be enough. The Eritrean woman might ask for 200,000. Or 300,000. Or even half a million. What was the price of silence? What was the price of a man's life?

When he left the bank he called Liat and told her he'd be at a department get-together, a spontaneous gathering one of the doctors had suggested. Everyone had loved the idea and he felt uncomfortable being the only one to pass on it. They'd be going out for a beer at ten and he'd try to duck out by 11:30. "It's important that you go," she said, "and it's important that they don't see on your face that you're suffering." He had never lied to Liat like that, and it both relieved and frightened him that it was so easy.

At ten that night, Eitan turned off the engine of the suv at the entrance to an abandoned garage near Kibbutz Tlalim. Half an hour earlier, he had driven along the access road to the garage and checked out the dark building. There was no movement visible inside. He considered waiting for the woman at the garage door, but decided against it. He didn't want the smell of that place, the smell of that dusty earth, to adhere to him. With the press of a button, all four windows closed. With the press of another button, the radio turned on. The outside air and the night sounds were left to smash against the chrome cover of the suv. But by ten o'clock, Eitan knew that he could wait no longer. Reluctantly, his sweaty hand reached for the handle of the door that separated the interior of the hot suv, saturated with the Beatles and Led Zeppelin, and the cool, quiet desert air. Now he was outside, the noise of his footsteps on the gravel grating in his ears, audible for miles, making a mockery of all his efforts to be discreet.

He had barely taken two steps when he saw the Eritrean woman emerge from the garage. Her dark skin blended into the darkness of the night. Only the whites of her eyes glittered and two black pupils fixed on him as she said, *Come*. Though his feet began to move almost of their own volition in response to this quiet order, he stopped himself.

"I brought you money."

But the words seemed to have no effect on the woman, who didn't react to them, but simply repeated, *Come*. And once again, Eitan felt that his feet instantly wanted to obey the hushed order, the soft voice commanding him to walk. The garage in front of them now looked darker than before and he couldn't help but ask himself about other people who might be inside, resentful dark-skinned people who now had been given the opportunity to hurt the person who had hurt them. Though he hadn't hurt them, but had hurt *him*, the man who didn't have even a name, it could easily have been any one of them. Hell, it could have been the woman standing beside him now, a look of urgency in her eyes. If he had run *her* over, would he have gone to the police that same night? The next morning?

When he didn't move, the woman reached out and took his hand, pulling him behind her toward the garage. The vestiges of resistance he still felt (she'll drag you inside and they'll beat the living daylights out of you. They're hiding behind the door and they'll kill you) fell away the moment her hand touched his. Again, he could do nothing but walk behind her, descending to the dark netherworld of the garage.

*

49

He felt the presence of another person even before he saw him. The acrid smell of sweat. The rapid breathing. The silhouette of a man in the dark. And he suddenly realized that this was a death trap. The late hour. The abandoned garage. He would never get out of this place. Then Sirkit turned on the light and he found himself standing at a rusty metal table with a half-naked Eritrean man on it.

At first he thought it was *him*, the Eritrean he had hit the previous night. And for a brief moment he was filled with happiness because if this was the condition of the man he'd run over, then everything was fine, really fine. But a second later he realized that he was deluding himself. The man he had hit yesterday was now completely dead, while this man, though his features perfectly resembled those of the other man, suffered only from a severely infected right arm. Despite himself, his gaze was drawn to the Eritrean's wound. A spectacular mosaic of red and purple, dappled here and there with a fleck of yellow or a dot of green. And to think that this rainbow of colors owed its existence to a simple cut caused, for example, by barbed wire or a pair of scissors. Five centimeters into the flesh, perhaps even less than that. But without an antiseptic… several hours of blazing sun, a bit of dust, the slightest contact with a filthy rag and within a week, your path to death was paved.

Help him.

He heard those two words dozens of times a day. Pleading, hopeful, in high sopranos and deep baritones. But he had never heard them spoken like this: with not an iota of obsequiousness. Sirkit wasn't asking him to help the man on the table.

She was ordering him to do it. And that was exactly what he did. He hurried to the suv and returned with his first-aid kit. The man moaned in a language Eitan didn't know as the needle of the syringe of cefazolin penetrated his muscle. Sirkit muttered something in response. He worked quite a while disinfecting the wound, the man mumbling and Sirkit replying, and Eitan was surprised to discover that although he didn't understand a word, he understood everything. Pain and consolation sound the same in every language. He spread an antibiotic salve on the cut and explained with his hands that the man should apply it three times a day. The man stared at him with inscrutable eyes, and Sirkit muttered something else. Now the man's eyes lit up and he began to nod enthusiastically, his head going up and down like the bobblehead bulldog on the dashboard of the suv.

"And tell him to wash it before he applies the salve. With soap." Sirkit nodded and spoke again to the Eritrean, who also nodded after several seconds. Then the patient launched into a speech that was at least a minute long, and though it was spoken entirely in Tigrinya, the message it conveyed was clear: gratitude. Sirkit listened but didn't translate. The man's gratitude stopped with her, did not move on to the doctor who, under normal circumstances, would consider himself deserving of it.

"What is he saying?"

He's saying that you saved his life. That you are a good man. That not every doctor would be willing to come in the middle of the night to a garage to treat a refugee. He's calling you an angel, he—

"Stop."

She fell silent. After a few moments, the patient fell silent as well. Now he was looking in bewilderment from Sirkit to Eitan as if he sensed, through his wound, what stood between them. Sirkit turned away from the rusty metal table and walked toward the entrance. Eitan followed her.

"I've brought you money," he said. She straightened her arched back and remained silent. "Seventy thousand."

A moment later, when her back remained straight and her mouth closed, he added, "I'll bring you more if necessary." He reached for his bag and took out the notes he'd been given by the teller Ravit, whose remodeled nose he had managed to forget completely. But Sirkit stood there unmoving, arms folded, and looked at the offering. Though the night was cool, Eitan's hands began to sweat, staining the pinkish 200-shekel notes with embarrassing dampness. Despite himself, he found himself speaking: yes, he knows that there can be no price on a man's life. And that's why he is so grateful for… this opportunity that has been given him today to save a life in place of the one he took. And perhaps this combination of, well, a large sum of money and, no less importantly, dedicated medical treatment can atone, if only a little, for what he regrets with all his heart and soul.

Sirkit's silence continued even after he'd finished his stammering speech. He asked himself whether she'd actually understood what he'd said. He'd spoken quickly, perhaps too quickly, and the words had sounded so hollow in his ears.

Asum was my husband.

He almost asked her who Asum was, had already opened his mouth to speak before he stopped himself with a grating squeal of brakes. Idiot, didn't it occur to you that he had a name; did you think that everyone called him *him*, the Eritrean, the illegal immigrant? His name was Asum and he was her husband.

But if he was her husband, why did she look so calm now, so poised? Less than twenty-four hours had passed since she'd buried him, if she had buried him. She didn't look very much like a woman who had lost her husband. The spark in her eyes, the unnatural glow of her skin, the black hair that seemed to dance in the desert night wind. Sirkit remained silent and Eitan knew that it was his turn to speak now. He didn't know what he could say, so he said the first thing that came to mind – he said that he was sorry. That he would feel guilty for the rest of his life. That not a day would go by when he didn't think about…

During the day, you can do whatever you want, she interrupted him, *but you will keep your nights free.*

Eitan looked at her questioningly and she explained slowly, the way you explain to a child: she would take the money. But not only the money. The people here needed a doctor. They were too afraid to go to the hospital. That's why she was asking the esteemed doctor to kindly give her his phone number – she hadn't found it in his wallet last night – so she could call for help whenever she needed it. And since the local community had been living without continuous medical assistance for a long time, she would most likely need it a great deal, at least for the first few weeks.

So that's how it is, he thought, the Eritrean bitch has decided to extort me. There was no reason to assume she'd stop with 70,000 and a few weeks of work. What began with medical treatment would probably end up with his paying for the sick leave of half the members of the Eritrean diaspora in the Negev. Damn it, what doctor would agree to treat patients on a rusty table in an abandoned garage? He could imagine dozens of lawyers competing for the right to file the malpractice suit of the decade. No, you black-eyed Che Guevara, that's not going to happen.

Then, as if reading his mind, she smiled and said, *Not that you really have a choice.*

And that was true. He really didn't have a choice. Though he walked off angrily and slammed the SUV door without saying a word, they both knew he would return to the abandoned garage tomorrow for his second night of patient rounds.

*   *   *

Everyone is looking, but her eyes are dry. She has no tears for him. Everyone's ready to say the nice words, but if you want to get nice words, you must give tears. Just as you must give money if you want to get bread; you can't just take a loaf without giving anything in return. But when she goes into the caravan, her eyes are dry, so they keep the nice words to themselves, along with the possibility of a hand on her shoulder. She doesn't care. All she wants is for them to stop looking at her. The caravan door is open all night to let the air in, and the gas-station lights color everything pale yellow. In the silence of the night, she hears them listening hard – maybe she's crying in bed. And in the morning they'll examine the mattress looking for signs of tears, wetness that will prove she was truly devoted to that man. Just as once, in another place, on another mattress, they looked for signs of blood that would prove she had not already given herself to another man.

She turns onto her back and looks at the ceiling, and on the other side of the ceiling there are either clouds or stars, it doesn't matter. She runs her hand up and down along the scar on her forearm. An old scar without a history, so old that she has no idea who or what caused it, and there is no longer anyone to ask now. Her fingers travel the length of the scar, faint and pleasant to the touch. Pleasant because it's faint. Other scars come with memories, and then it's not faint and not pleasant, and who wants to touch them at all? But it's nice to move her fingers over this one, back and forth, two centimeters of a different texture that, even now in the dark, she knows is lighter than the rest of her skin.

The caravan is quiet and the people who looked at her are lying in bed asleep. As asleep as they can be, because after what happened, they don't really remember how to sleep with their entire bodies – there is always some part of them that remains awake. And the opposite is also true – when they're awake, it's never total. Something remains asleep. It's not that they do their jobs less well because of it. None of them forgets to take the chips out of the oil in the restaurant, or to wash the floor before sweeping it. The sleeping part of them doesn't interfere with their work. Maybe it even helps. And the awake part doesn't interfere with their sleep. Just the opposite. None of the people here would dare to fall asleep without it. But tonight, the awake part of her is extremely awake, and though the movement of her fingers along her scar has soothed her for as long as she can remember, the blood is still flowing very fast through her body; she has already forgotten that blood could flow so fast. And even though she knows it must stop, that she needs to sleep, that she has a long day tomorrow, a small part of her doesn't want it to stop. Doesn't want it to thicken again in her veins. Doesn't want to fall asleep.

But it happens of its own accord. The minutes pass and her blood slows down. And her fingers abruptly stop moving up and down along the scar and spread out on the mattress. She turns onto her side. Sees eyes white in the darkness and turns onto her other side before she has time to see reproach in them. What kind of woman are you. Why don't you cry. And maybe it isn't the reproach that makes her turn around, but the other possibilities that might be in the open eyes of a man looking at you in the middle of the night. Her husband is lying in the ground now instead of watching out for her, and she must be careful. And on the other side of her – the wall. She closes her eyes. Inhales the damp, moldy smell coming from the places where the paint is peeling. Even through the dampness and mold she can smell the body of the woman on the mattress next to her. She has smelled it for so many nights that she has no doubt she would recognize her even if they didn't see each other again for years. She'd walk down the street, inhale, turn around to her and say, I remember you; it was ten years ago and even then you were sweet-and-sour from the sun.

Her blood has slowed down, but not completely, and when she remembers what happened it begins to race once more and she begins to think that she will never sleep again. That strikes her as funny, because she's old enough to remember all the previous times she thought the same thing, and how she always fell asleep in the end. When she was a little girl, the nights seemed as long as years and the years as long as eternity and if you couldn't fall asleep, you'd lie there and listen to the sound of grass growing and you'd go mad. Later, the nights became less long and the years shorter, but there were still nights that stretched out far beyond what was logical. The night when blood flowed from her down there for the first time, and not long after that the night she slept with him for the first time, and the night before the morning they set out on their way. And now this night, which might end in a moment or might never end at all, and a part of her would give everything to fall asleep, her head hurt and her muscles were tense, but another part of her was actually smiling, looking at the peeling walls of the caravan and the sleeping people, saying: why not.

In her sleep Liat feels the blanket being lifted as Eitan gets into bed. He hugs her from behind, his nose against her neck, his hand on hers, his leg on her thigh, his stomach pressed to her back. And though tonight is not the slightest bit different from all other nights – their bodies are intertwined in precisely the same way – something is nevertheless registered in the flutter of eyelids. Nose to neck, hand to hand, leg to thigh, stomach to back, but this time with an urgency, a desire to flee – the man who got into bed is a man running away. All that is registered in the flutter of Liat's eyelids, and all that is erased when her eyelids open four hours later and she awakes to her day.

*   *   *

Every morning Victor Balulo would get out of bed, cook an egg in its shell for exactly two and a half minutes and eat it as he listened to the radio. While broadcasters talked about inflation and Cabinet meetings, Victor Balulo would mop up the yellow yolk with a slice of challah and think about how another ill-fated chick was entering his body. Victor Balulo knew very well that chicks weren't born from the eggs sold in the grocery store. But that thought about the chick, though it made him slightly uncomfortable, was also somewhat pleasurable because it meant that he, Victor Balulo, generally considered an inconsequential person, still had the power to bring about a disaster of such great proportions. One egg, two and a half minutes, every morning. That added up to 363 chicks a year, if you leave out Yom Kippur and Tisha b'Av, the two fasting days on which Victor Balulo didn't eat eggs or any other food. Taking into account Victor Balulo's age, excluding his first year when his diet consisted mainly of mother's milk, you reach the extraordinary number of 13,431 eggs, which means that a huge yellow flock waddled after Victor Balulo wherever he went.

Victor Balulo ruminated about that flock of chicks as he washed the challah crumbs and yolk off his plate and then went to dress. The label on his shirt collar told him that it was made in China, that it was first-quality and that it should not be washed in water hotter than 20 degrees centigrade. Victor Balulo paid hardly any attention, if at all, to that information, despite the fact that China was a country of 1.4 billion inhabitants, and a world power to boot.

When he finished buttoning his shirt but still hadn't put on his pants, Victor Balulo usually went to the bathroom. Gravely and with quite a lot of apprehension, he sat on the toilet and waited to see what the day would bring. He never thought about the fact that the toilet seat he was sitting on was made in India, which shared a border with China, along with a menu in which rice played a large role. When he finished his business on the toilet, Victor Balulo would press the small metal handle and dispatch his faeces from the familiar area in which they were created into the sewage pipes of the city of Beersheba, and from there along some unknown path to the sea. In fact, Beersheba faeces are never sent to the sea – which is many kilometers away from it – but rather are channeled by pipes and machines to a cesspit in the Soreq River area. Nevertheless, in some sense all rivers flow to the sea, even the ones that are only seasonal streams. This belief was particularly important to Victor Balulo, because despite the discomfort he felt when he thought about his faeces polluting the magnificent ocean depths, he none the less took some pleasure in the knowledge that he, Victor Balulo, a man few people gave a thought to – even he himself sometimes forgot the fact of his existence – had created something that was presently sailing around the vast ocean.

After eating, putting on his shirt and moving his bowels, Victor Balulo would get organized quickly and leave his house, scolding himself for the late hour. When he had covered the streets that separated him from his destination, he would stop and wait. After a while, when a woman appeared on the street, he would take a deep breath and roar: Fucking cunt!

Sometimes they froze. Sometimes they jumped in fear. Most of them walked more rapidly, some even breaking into a run. Others screamed at him or laughed at him or sprayed him with pepper spray. Some returned a short time later with a male friend or a husband who beat him for varying lengths of time. And through all of it the women looked at him, either in disgust or fear, with compassion or repugnance. But never, ever with indifference. Victor Balulo would stand for days at a time on the streets of Beersheba waiting for women to come. Short or tall, pretty or ugly, Ethiopian or Russian. All of them intended to walk past him without a second glance, to go on with their lives as if Victor Balulo wasn't a man but a plant, a rock or a stray cat. But Victor Balulo fought their indifference courageously, Beersheba tiger that he was, took a deep breath and roared: Fucking cunt!

On good days, when luck was with him as he stood on a corner that was busy enough, he would return home with a raw throat and a body tingling from having been looked at so much. He would make himself a cup of lemon tea, sit down on the armchair and recall the wonderful things that had happened to him: the shocked expression on the face of the girl soldier with the ponytail. The red-haired woman's look of utter disgust. The marvelous cold contempt that wafted toward him from the face of an elderly woman in a striped blouse. On those rare good days, Victor Balulo would go to bed with a smile on his face.

Every now and then, instead of going home and sipping lemon tea, Victor Balulo would be picked up and taken to the police station. There too the looks darkened his skin, but he would feel a bit anxious, afraid that they would make him spend the night in a cell. If that happened, he wouldn't be able to eat his egg cooked in water for exactly two and a half minutes the next morning. So he did his best to behave well and be released quickly.

But that morning, his luck turned bad and he was put in a chair across from a woman detective. Her acorn eyes were the color of the acorns he used to gather long ago in a distant city that people called Nazareth and he called home. He used to bring them from the grove to their tin shack to cheer his mother, who refused to be cheered, and when she died, the oak trees died, or at least they should have. When Victor Balulo saw the detective's brown eyes he was filled with such anger that his mother had died and the acorns hadn't that he roared, "Fucking cunt!" more loudly than ever before. And the detective, instead of being frightened by his shout, instead of getting irate, reprimanding him or calling one of her fellow cops, simply sat there and looked at him indifferently. So Victor Balulo raised the volume to the absolutely highest he could muster and screamed "Fucking cunt", but to no avail. He screamed and screamed until he felt his strength begin to ebb, and he was terrified that the detective might succeed where three psychiatrists and five social workers had failed, where threats and beatings had not helped. With the indifference in her eyes, with her exhausting composure, the woman detective tore his scream right out of him.

But then they called Liat and she hurried out with a sense of relief because though that Balulo guy really was good for a laugh, that screaming of his hurt her eardrums. The commander, who was standing in the corridor, said, "The body of an Eritrean, hit and run," and Liat nodded. Then they got into the cruiser and headed south. The commander drove 150 kilometers an hour and turned on the siren, as if getting to the scene faster would make the Eritrean less dead. He looked at Liat every few minutes, checking to see that she was suitably impressed by his driving skills, and Liat was forced to be impressed, because what else could she do? They reached the scene faster and discovered that the Eritrean had been dead for more than a day and he smelled to high heaven. The commander took out a handkerchief and offered it to Liat, who said it was okay, she was fine. Flies drunk with joy swarmed around the Eritrean's cracked skull and the commander told Liat that she could wait in the cruiser. Liat replied that it was okay, she was fine. Several of the flies grew tired of the Eritrean's dried blood and moved house to the beads of sweat on the commander's forehead. The commander slapped them away with a nervous hand and said, "Let's go, I see you're having a hard time here. We'll drive over to see the guy who found him."

His name was Guy Davidson and he had the biggest feet Liat had ever seen. After nine years in the Israeli police, she'd had her fair share of experience with unnatural-looking bodies – cracked skulls, stab wounds, even a headless corpse that washed up onto the Ashdod beach and gave her her first promotion. But she had never seen anything as unnatural, as bizarre as Guy Davidson's feet. They were beyond large, gigantic really, and the ankles they were connected to were thin, almost flimsy, as if the slightest pressure would cause those feet to rebel against the body that bore them and take off on a trip around the world without it. But at the moment they were in place, wrapped in a pair of enormous sandals that Liat assumed were made to order for him. Davidson definitely looked like a person who could demand that a shoe company make his sandals to order without raising the price. There was something determined and self-assured about him, a sort of bear-like quality some kibbutzniks have that caused the commander to tense slightly in his uniform and Liat to recoil slightly in hers.

"He didn't show up at the restaurant yesterday. I thought maybe he was sick. But this morning one of the tractor guys saw him." He spoke decisively, sharply and Liat said to herself that he probably fucks that way too, decisively and sharply. But to Davidson she said, "Did you see any cars here?"

Davidson's lips opened, revealing teeth that the kibbutz's cheap unfiltered cigarettes had devastated. "Cars? On these dirt roads? No, sweetheart, the only thing you'll see here is either a camel – or an suv."

Liat gave an embarrassed smile, even though she wasn't really embarrassed at all, and certainly didn't feel like smiling. She always smiled in embarrassment when she was called sweetheart, and after nine years in the Israeli police she'd been called sweetheart quite a few times. By bankers, farmers, lawyers, building contractors, ceos, divorced men, married men. She let them call her sweetheart, and later, when she placed their confessions in front of them to be signed for the final time after an interrogation they hadn't foreseen, couldn't have foreseen, she no longer seemed like a sweetheart to them at all.

"Sorry. Did you see an suv here?"

Davidson shook his head. "On the weekends, all those little rich boys from Herzliya come down here with their new suvs, raise dust and leave. But during the week, it's dead here."

"And kibbutz suvs?"

A shadow crossed Davidson's eyes. "None of our members would hit a man like that and take off."

"What was his name?

"Asum."

"Asum what?"

"I'll be damned if I remember every Eritrean who passes through here."

"How long did he work for you?"

"A year and a half, something like that."

"A year and a half and you don't know his last name?"

"Let me get this straight, you know the last name of every cleaning woman who ever worked for you? Do you know how many workers I have here in this restaurant? And that's not counting the gas station."

A heavy silence filled the room and Liat noted that Davidson's right foot was moving uneasily in its sandal, like an animal in a cage. The commander, who had been listening to the conversation without speaking until then, cleared his throat. "Let's go back for a minute to the other Eritreans. Did you ask them if they saw anything?"

Davidson shook his head. "I told you, no one saw anything." And a moment later, "Maybe a Bedouin who came here to steal hit him and took off."

The commander stood up. So did Liat. Davidson was the last to rise, his enormous feet making the caravan floor shake slightly.

At the door of the cruiser, Davidson extended a large, bear-like and surprisingly smooth hand to her. "You have to catch the shit who did this," he said to both of them, but looked directly at Liat. "You don't run a guy over and drive away like it's just a fox."

Liat pressed his hand, somewhat surprised not only by the hand's smoothness, but mainly by the man's sensitivity.

On the way back, the commander didn't turn on the siren again. Nor did he hurry. The police report entitled "Hit and run. Illegal immigrant. Case closed due to lack of suspects" could definitely wait until tomorrow. The radio was playing a familiar pop song and Liat's voice stopped the commander just as he was about to hum the chorus. "Maybe there's a chance we can trace the suv," she said, "check the tire tracks on the ground."

The commander waited for the chorus to end – a truly great song – before saying that there was no point. A big hassle, a lot of manpower, and in the end they wouldn't find anything on such dry desert ground anyway so many hours after the incident. The song ended and a new one began, not as good as the previous one, but definitely worth listening to quietly instead of asking smug, annoying questions. The commander managed to listen to two entire verses before the new detective with the lioness eyes asked him again, "If it was a girl from the kibbutz who was run over like that, would the investigation be pointless then?"

They drove the rest of the way in silence. Song after song after the news after the weather forecast of sandstorms in the Negev. Elderly people and asthmatics are advised to avoid physical activity.

4

T HEY CAME EN MASSE. The rumor about secret, unre-
corded medical treatment spread faster than any viral
infection. They came from the deserts and wadis, the restaurants and construction sites, the half-paved roads in Arad and
the central bus station where they worked as cleaners. Small
cuts made life-threatening by dust and dirt. Genital fungi that
didn't threaten life but certainly made it miserable. Intestinal
infections caused by poor nutrition. Stress fractures resulting
from endless walking. Dr Eitan Green, up-and-coming neu-
rologist, treated them all.

And how much he hated them. Tried to stop, but couldn't.
Reminded himself that they weren't the ones extorting him,
she was. That in the end, they were people who had crowded
together here awaiting the touch of his hand. But the smell
did him in. The contamination. The rotting pus of cuts they
still carried with them from the Sinai, the sour, foreign sweat
of men who worked for days in the sun and women who
went weeks without a shower. Despite himself, he loathed
them, although the guilt of the hit and run was still growing.
Even though, during his first year in medical school, he had
sworn to treat all people and had meant it. But something as
close, as intimate as a doctor's contact with a patient becomes

unbearable the moment you are coerced into it. Since he had been coerced into helping his patients, he hated them at least as much as he hated himself. Repulsed by the stench. The bodily fluids. The hair. The bits of peeling skin and scars on filthy fingers. One lifted his shirt and another took off his pants; one opened her mouth and another bent over to show him. One after the other, they exposed their bodies to him, filled the garage with that monstrous physicality, skin and limbs, wrath and enmity and messengers of evil. However much he wanted to feel compassion for them, he couldn't help recoiling from them. Not only their smell and bodily fluids, but also their faces – alien, staring, filled with undying gratitude. He didn't speak their language and they didn't speak his, so they communicated with waving hands and facial expressions. Without language, without the ability to exchange a single sentence the way people do – one speaks, the other listens and vice versa – without words, only flesh remained. Stinking. Rotting. With ulcers, excretions, inflammations, scars. Perhaps this was how a veterinarian felt.

Nausea seized him in the SUV long before he entered the garage, a feeling of repugnance that choked his throat from the moment he turned onto the dirt road, growing a hundred times more intense when he stood in front of her. He hated her stance. Her voice. The way she said "Hello, Doctor." A profound loathing. Bottomless rancor. He should have felt guilty, but his guilt, like a flower that blooms for only one day, withered in the face of that blazing extortion. The ease with which she took possession of him, the undisputed authority she exercised over him left no room for anything but abhor-rence. Sometimes he suspected that his patients sensed it. Perhaps that was why they looked at him with such fear. But immediately they smiled submissively once again, leaving him alone with his rancor.

Clearly, there was guilt as well. Since that night, sleep had eluded him. In vain did he seek it with his tossing and turning, with the help of half a Lorivan. The dead man was coiled around his neck and would not release him. Squeezing him whenever he wanted to sleep. Only in the garage did he let go and leave room for the procession of pilgrims. Thin black faces that all looked the same to Eitan. Each patient resembled the previous one, and the one before that one in an endless backward movement to *that* patient, the first one. To the thin black face of the man he had killed.

He couldn't look at that face anymore. Couldn't bear the stench of the infected, diarrhoetic, broken bodies. Arms legs armpits stomachs pelvises nails nostrils teeth tongues pus ulcers rashes inflammations cuts hernias defects, one after the other and sometimes together, black eyes grateful, gauging as they entered and exited, displaying their black bodies in acquiescence or arrogance to Dr Eitan Green, who could no longer bear it, could no longer bear those people's limbs, who was drowning in a black sea of arms legs open your mouth let me touch does it hurt and when I press here what kind of pain is it, drowning in the horde that was engulfing him.

*

"Do you get it? He has no intention of investigating it!"

She was standing in the kitchen, strikingly beautiful with that regal anger of hers, and Eitan was standing beside her doing his best to look normal.

"And you know as clear as day that if it was a kid from the kibbutz or even just an air-conditioning technician from Yeruham, it wouldn't have ended like that."

"Why do you think so?"

He made a great effort to sound normal, managing to do a fairly decent job. "Think about it, Tuli, don't a lot of hit and runs end that way? You said yourself that there was no evidence, no leads at all."

"We could have asked the Eritreans to come in for questioning. Should I get you a rag?"

"No. I'll manage."

And a moment later, when he finished wiping up the coffee he'd spilled when the cup in his hand shook, he said, "Do they even speak Hebrew, the Eritreans?"

"We never even got to that stage. Marciano just said it would be a joke to bring thirty people to the precinct to ask them a question we already have the answer to. If I'd told him that we'd also have to pay an interpreter, he would have lost it completely."

Without his asking, without saying a word, she came and put a new cup of coffee in front of him in place of the one he'd spilled, and he thought about how much he loved her and ran his hand through her lovely brown hair when she turned back to the counter. Suddenly, without his even daring to hope she'd do it, she decided not to empty the dishwasher and sat in his lap instead, buried her head in his chest, and he buried his hand in her tangle of hair.

He knew that she'd taken a shower not too long ago because the hair close to her scalp was still slightly damp and the shampoo fragrance was very fresh. The faint scent of perfume rose from the back of her neck although he had pleaded endlessly with her to let him smell her as she was. The smell of her body drove him wild and embarrassed her, and was the subject of countless battles of wits. She tried to disguise and he insisted on discovering. She bought perfumed body lotion and he hid it. She took off her shirt and he lay in wait to grab her arms just as she raised them, to sniff her armpits despite her protests. She told him he was a pervert and he told her that there was nothing more normal than getting turned on by your wife's smell. And why would someone prefer the smell of soap to the smell of his wife. (He was prepared to accept a perfumed throat, but when she once came home with a jar of intimate gel wash, he exercised his right to veto. This was where he drew the line. She wouldn't steal the smell of her pussy from him.) Now she sat herself down in his lap in the kitchen, and he thought that on any other evening, if she had sat in his lap in the kitchen like this, her hair half wet and her feet bare, he would have begun immediately planning his moves. But today, right now, he was barely aware of her thigh rubbing against his. He simply ran his hand mechanically through her hair and waited for the nausea to pass. Waited to smell something, even perfume, even intimate gel wash, that wasn't overwhelmed by the stench in his mind.

"Maybe he's right," she said, her voice fainter as she pressed her mouth into the hollow of his neck. "Maybe it really is a waste of time." But then, just as his pulse was beginning its gradual return to the rate recommended for a man his age, she stood up and began walking around the kitchen again.

"I just don't understand how a person can let someone die that way, like a dog."

"Maybe he got scared. Maybe the Eritrean died right away and there was nothing he could do."

"The Eritrean took almost two hours to die. That's what the pathologist said."

Eitan almost replied that maybe the pathologist didn't know everything, but he stopped himself. When Liat finished emptying the dishwasher, he went and stood beside her to cut vegetables into small, precise cubes. The first time he had made a salad for her, when she finally agreed to sleep over in his apartment on Gordon Street, she had been so thrilled that she clapped her hands. "It's like you have a protractor in your fingers," she'd said.

"Not always, just when I'm stressed."

"Why are you stressed?"

Then he told her that before her, he had always been the one to explain gently that he couldn't fall asleep with someone else in bed, that it would be better if they spent the night in their own apartments. But ever since she'd come along two months ago, he hadn't been able to sleep, not because she didn't leave after sex, but because she didn't stay, and the night before, she had finally agreed, and now he was afraid that if breakfast wasn't perfect she wouldn't come back. Liat had smiled then with her cinnamon eyes, and the next night she had arrived with her toothbrush. Now she stood beside him in the kitchen looking at the cucumber that had been carved into neat little squares and asked, "Did something happen at work?"

"No," he said, reaching for the tomatoes, "I just thought I'd devote some time to you."

She kissed him on the cheek and said that cubing vegetables was his true calling, that medicine was just a pastime, and he allowed himself to hope that she'd finally left the Eritrean to die on the side of the road –

"But you know what Marciano's mistake is? He thinks it's a one-time thing. He doesn't understand that a person who can run over an Eritrean like that and drive away will run over a little girl someday and drive away."

Eitan put down the knife abruptly, leaving a slaughtered tomato on the cutting board.

"That's it?" Liat said smiling at him, "Half a job?"

"I'm on duty tonight. I want time to run before that."

Liat nodded, taking his place at the cutting board. "If this continues, you'll have to talk to Prof. Shakedi. He can't keep piling all this work on you. It's not right."

Wearing running shoes, his ear buds in place, Eitan walked out the front door. Though the desert night was chilly, his entire body was sweating. He wanted to run. Wanted to move from one point to another with the maximum speed his body could tolerate. Not because another point was so important, but because of the pituitary gland's blessed tendency to respond to that sort of effort by secreting endorphins, the only legal instant fix available to him. The faster he ran, the faster the hormone would flood his brain and mask his thoughts. And the faster he ran, the faster the oxygen in his brain would grow thinner. Emotions need oxygen. Guilt, for example, or self-loathing – it wasn't enough for them to stir; they required a certain amount of O_2 to reach the brain and be preserved. A poorly oxygenated brain is less efficient. A less efficient brain feels less. Therefore, Eitan increased his running speed, increased it and increased it and didn't stop, until a sharp pain pierced his stomach, telling him it was enough. Then he stopped abruptly, saw TV lights dancing like embers in the windows of the private homes, and walked back. A quick shower. A cup of coffee. A forty-minute drive to the abandoned garage at Tlalim, which wasn't really abandoned at all.

At the front door, Liat kissed him goodbye on the lips. A fleeting, routine kiss. A kiss that said nothing of sex, nothing of love, but merely: goodnight. And perhaps also: goodnight. I trust you to return so we can continue what we began, that is, our lives together. He kissed her back. Similarly, without sex or love, but merely: goodnight. I'm lying to you. In the narrow gap between our lips lies an entire world.

Later in the SUV, he asked himself why he was lying. Asked but didn't answer. Didn't answer because he knew.

He lied because he was unable to admit to her that he wasn't as good as she thought he was. He was unable to admit to her his fear that if she knew he wasn't as good as she thought, she would leave. Or worse than that – she'd stay and despise him. (The way his mother had despised him when he was in elementary school and she discovered that he hadn't told her about a math test he'd failed. She didn't shout at him, but her look killed him. A look that said: I thought you were better than that.) He himself knew, of course, that he was worse than that. But he was the only one who knew, and when you're the only one who knows something, that something has less of an existence. You look into people's eyes, into your wife's eyes, and see yourself reflected back at you, and there you are, clean and attractive. Almost beautiful. You can't destroy something like that.

Liat's eyes changed constantly. Sometimes they were cin-namon. Sometimes honey. The brown was always a different mixture, depending on the weather. And for almost fifteen years he had been judging himself by the scales of justice in those eyes. A measure of right and wrong unmatched in its precision. Only once had those scales erred, but even then, they had a reason. When he wanted to blow the business with Zakai wide open by filing a complaint against him with the Commission and she stopped him. He was so shocked that it didn't even occur to him to argue with her. The calm with which she accepted the fact of the bribery was no less, and perhaps even more staggering than the bribery itself. (It wasn't that she was a saint. She stole nuts from the supermarket display like everyone else did and called it "noshing" like everyone else did. Once she even agreed to sneak into a show when they arrived late at the club and there was no guard at the entrance. But she was one of those people who never, ever cheated on their income tax reports, even if they were sure they'd never be caught. The sort that finds a 100-shekel bill in the street and goes over to the nearby kiosk to ask the owners to call them if anyone comes asking about money they've lost on the street.)

The ease with which she'd been willing to let Zakai evade punishment had stunned him. But apparently, existential fears sometimes overcome moral imperatives, and their mortgage was undoubtedly an existential fear. Mainly for Liat, who knew very well what it meant to live on the minus side of your bank balance. "Settle for knowing that you at least did the right thing. The world might be corrupt, but it hasn't succeeded in corrupting you." She told him that with such trust after the business with Zakai, with such loving eyes. At the time he was flattered, but now he was angry at her. When she sanctified the good in him that way, she also unwittingly condemned the bad. She buried in unhallowed ground everything that didn't meet her moral criteria, that wasn't compatible with the man she thought he was. She censured entire pieces of him, and he, at that moment, had been happy to rid himself of them. To pretend to her, to himself, that he was the good man she saw. But he wasn't. Not only. The Eritrean knew.

But he still didn't understand how it was possible that at exactly the moment he had decided to shake the dust of that city off of him, exactly when he had tried to cleanse himself of an ugly layer of bitterness and boredom, when he had finally driven to the desert and raced his suv, when he had even sung (how absurd to think of that now, singing with Janis Joplin with what had seemed at the time to be pure truth and now felt like a bad joke) – how could that have been the moment when it happened to him. The moment he killed a man. Then he quickly corrected himself: it wasn't you who killed him, the suv did. Steel and iron, which have no anger or intention. Neutral, not personal force, a certain mass traveling at a certain speed which at a certain moment hit a person. Then he confirmed once again that it was absolutely not his anger that had gone amok there, that had erupted suddenly, uncontrollably. He always kept his anger firmly in check, placed on a shelf at room temperature: "To Eitan, Good Luck."

But if that was true, why did he lie? The answer was clear. As clear as the carcinogenic sun. As clear as the desert moon hanging in the sky, blazing long after night has passed: he lied for his sake and for hers. He lied so that she would never know how far he was from the man she thought he was. But when he lied, he merely distanced himself further and further away from that man, until in the end he saw him only as a caricature.

Filling his mind now was the she-devil waiting for him in the garage. Those two black eyes. And he was almost angry at himself for remembering, apart from the eyes, apart from the extortion, also the contours of the body beneath the loose cotton dress. Like someone about to fall into an abyss who takes the time to consider the flowers blossoming in the bottom of the wadi.

*   *   *

She always tried to guess what they were fighting about. A man and a woman at the gas pumps. An older woman and a young girl in line at the restaurant cash register. Two soldiers coming out of the bathroom. Sometimes the fights ignited suddenly and everyone looked to see who was shouting like that. And sometimes the fights were more subdued. A man and a woman speaking quietly, but the woman's eyes glistened with tears and the man checked the gas receipt as if it were the most interesting thing in the world. Two soldiers came out of the bathroom and although they walked to the same bus, they didn't speak. One of them said, "Cool," but didn't look at all pleased, and neither did his buddy. Sometimes the fights began in the gas station, and sometimes they brought them with them. You could already tell that something was wrong from the way they slammed the door when they got out of the car. And after that, they sat at the restaurant table without speaking. They read and reread the menu or looked at their cell phones, and were angry because the coffee wasn't hot enough.

She didn't pay much attention to it. She had a floor to wash and tables to clear. But sometimes, when there were a few moments of quiet, she looked at people's faces to see whether anyone was fighting and about what. It was much more complicated than guessing what they were laughing about. When a man and a woman roared with laughter over their chocolate cake and looked at each other as if they were about to do it right then and there on the table where their trays still lay, you didn't really have to make an effort to figure out what was going on between them. But when the man suddenly overturned the tray angrily, or the woman got up to take the tray away and her hands clutched the plastic as if she were about to fall and it was the only thing holding her up, then you could try to guess what was happening there. Then it became interesting.

Once she tried to talk about it with Asum. He washed dishes and she cleared tables, and in the middle of the day a woman came in and screamed into her phone so loudly that all the people waiting in line in front of her turned around and looked. Later, during their break behind the restaurant, Asum imitated the woman's screams in a shrill funny voice, and when she finished laughing, she asked him what he thought it was about. All at once his expression turned serious. "Who cares what she was screaming about."

"It's not a question of caring," she said. "It's like a game. It could be interesting." He smoked his cigarette and didn't reply, and she saw that she had annoyed him. Asum never looked at them unless he really had to. The others were like that too. It was a sort of unspoken rule: no one talked to you about it, it was simply clear. A few moments later, Asum finished his cigarette and they went inside. After that, she never spoke to him about it again, but she continued to look. Several days later the doctor ran him over and she noticed that now she looked even more than she had before, and maybe even enjoyed it more.

When darkness fell, she left quietly. Walked quickly. He would be here any minute. Deep inside the night dogs barked as if they were mad. Sirkit listened to the sound. If they kept on barking like that, people would be afraid to come. And maybe not. The fact was that she wasn't afraid. She had finished washing the restaurant floor, folded the rag neatly and walked into the darkness. For the first kilometer, the gas station lights lit her way. Then there was only the darkness and the dogs, and a tiny sliver of gray moon, a rag hanging in the middle of the sky.

She stopped a short distance from the garage. And opened her mouth.

Aaahhh.

The sound emerged from her mouth hesitantly. Unevenly. After hours of working in silence, her throat was a bit rusty. If she had washed dishes in the kitchen, she would have chatted with the others all day. But you wash floors in silence. It was only you and the ceramic tiles. Boring at first, but later your thoughts raced and it was nice. Then they stopped racing, leaving room for the silence of the detergent, and you float on the soap bubbles, becoming heavier and heavier, sinking. Like the chips they drop into the oil in the kitchen, like the roaches that float in dirty water in the corners of the restaurant and are swept away with the squeegee, like the clumps of hair caught in the broom, blond and black, long and short, the hair of women who came in and ate and drove onward.

Aaahhh.

He would be there any minute and she needed her throat. Needed to break through the silence of the detergent so she could once again command him.

*

After Eitan left, Liat sat down alone to eat a salad that was half cubed vegetables and half torn ones, a salad she thought was delicious. Sometimes, during exhausting interrogations, she asked herself what the first thing was that the people sitting across from her took off when they got home. With most people, it was their shoes. Eitan took off his shirt first. Itamar, unable to wait until he came into the house, tossed his schoolbag down in the yard, the way her grandmother used to unhook her bra the minute she came into the stairwell, saying that if the neighbors wanted to talk, let them talk, she didn't care. Liat opened the front door and first of all focused her eyes on the coat hooks.

Then she could take off her shoes, air out her breasts, which had been entrapped by steel wires and hooks, and slip from zippered trousers into sweatpants. But first her eyes. She made sure they didn't enter the house with all the mud and dirt from outside. There were bad people and terrible criminals out there. But inside, you didn't need those eyes, just as you didn't need your gun, and you'd better lock them both in a drawer. The house was familiar. There was no place in it for a gun or those looks. In the house, you pounded schnitzels on the table, put children to bed and folded laundry, all according to procedures known in advance. Known so well that there was no need to write them down; they came as easily to her as prayer came to the religious. And even if they sometimes didn't come easily and were done tiredly and reluctantly, even with a tiny bit of bitterness, she would still prevail like a lion the next morning. It wasn't that she loved housework.

But she loved the house itself, loved returning to it, clinging to the memory of its existence when her work day was at its busiest. And when she loaded the dishwasher in the middle of the night, it wasn't much different from shampooing her hair well in the shower: here I am, stopping everything so I will be clean. So everything in this entire kingdom – the hallway and living room and kitchen and bedrooms – will be clean and peaceful. Because you must have one place that is free of questions and doubts. Otherwise it is really sad.

The flow did not stop. If Eitan had harbored the hope that it was only a temporary job, several days of volunteer work and nothing more, then after two weeks it became clear to him that he had been mistaken. Most of the people he saw had never been to a doctor in their lives. They all had something. A specific trauma or chronic disease, a small injury that had developed complications or a serious problem that had been neglected, or both. The sterile operating room in Soroka was exchanged for an abandoned garage in the middle of the desert and a rusty table that creaked whenever he sat a patient on it. Despite the scandalous conditions, they thanked him with emotional speeches that were cut short when Sirkit hurried to bring over the next patient. He didn't ask her to translate for him again. He had learned that *hanza* meant pain and *harai* meant okay, and after a few days he had already tasted a few words on his own tongue, for the first time replying *batsha* when someone thanked him with the words *shukran* or *iknanilie,* ignoring the surprised expression of his taskmaster.

At work, he said he was sick. He spent his cancelled shifts in the garage. Whenever the phone rang at home, he leaped to answer it, frightened that someone from the department was calling to ask how he was, knowing that these days no one called home on a landline instead of a cell phone. He felt frightened, upset and guilty when he was home, and he tensed at every vibration of his phone from the moment he entered the garage. Every evening he made sure to call Liat, to let her hear the chatter of patients behind him. A plague of Eritreans, he told her, tons of work, and asked her to say goodnight to the kids for him.

Within a few days, the skin on his hands literally began to peel off. He washed them with soap after every patient, regardless of the fact that he wore gloves. Who knew what those people had brought with them from their hellholes? The constant rubbing with soap and water quickly led to stinging and itching. The redness of his fingers drove him mad. As did his muscle pain, which grew stronger with every sleepless night. But it was mainly the woman who drove him mad, parting from him every day at dawn with a commanding smile: *Thank you Doctor. We'll meet again tomorrow.*

After two weeks, he told her, "Enough. I have to get some rest."

You don't work on the Sabbath. She spoke the word "Sabbath" with a special intonation, and despite the darkness he knew she was smiling.

83

"They're asking questions in the department. Soon my wife will start. I need a few normal days."

Sirkit repeated his words slowly, contemplatively. *Normal days.*

And Eitan saw how his request, repeated by her, lost its simplicity and became immeasurably strange, astonishing, actually. He needed a few normal days. The man whose finger had been cut off by a lathe needed normal days. As did the cleaner who had fainted last night in the central bus station. But Eitan, he needed them more than anyone else. And so he would get them.

Monday, she finally said, *and don't forget to bring more medicine.*

He almost thanked her, but stopped himself. Instead, he went and put his head under the faucet in the corner of the garage. The water pounded his eyes, his cheeks, his eyelids. A wet, arousing kiss of coldness. It was enough to keep him awake until he reached home. He turned off the faucet and headed for the suv, accompanied by the emotional wave of a young man from whose foot he had just removed a two-centimeter rusty nail. He started the suv and drove toward the main road. On the way home, in the pale dawn light, he counted three dead animals on the side of the road.

Even after he turned off the engine, Eitan was in no hurry to get out of the suv. He studied the whitewashed house through the windshield. The walls inhaled and exhaled serenely behind the bougainvillaea. A small light curled through the furthest window on the right, silent proof of Yaheli's battle with his terror of the dark. The sun rose. The darkness retreated. Yaheli was victorious. The roses in the yard were beginning to stretch toward the morning. A gust of wind defeated the dew drops that had accumulated on the rosemary. They fell all at once. Rain in miniature. Only the SUV stank of forgotten coffee cups, of cardboard cartons with a line of dry grease marking the place where the pizza had been, of a tired, unbathed man. Eitan sat in the SUV, unable to bring himself to get out. Why should he defile the purity of the house with his presence?

He finally stepped out of the SUV, locked it, walked to the front door and opened it quietly. A quick look was enough to confirm what he already knew so well – that the house was tidy, clean, ready to begin the new day. And mainly, that the house knew nothing about the other houses, which also had four walls but no beds or hot water, twenty mattresses spread on the floor and tuberculosis covering the distance between them with small steps.

Now, standing in the entryway of the house in Omer, he asked himself how many mattresses he could fit into his parquet-floored living room. Twenty Eritreans could undoubtedly crowd into the space in relative comfort. Thirty, no. It was precisely because of such thoughts that he had preferred to stay in the SUV. He had allowed himself a moment to feel sorry for them and already his empathy had become uncontrollable, a monster of malignant guilt pursuing him relentlessly. When he entered the house, that herd of wolves entered with him. The ailing men and women he had seen that week devoured the house with their voracious looks.

The stainless-steel kitchen, the huge TV. Saliva drooled from their mouths onto the rug Liat had bought in Ikea, onto Yaheli's giant Lego house. Out, Eitan roared, out! But they refused to go. Twenty Eritrean witches danced around the dining-room table. The man from whose foot he had removed a two-centimeter nail jumped onto the white couch along with the one whose finger had been cut off. And standing in the midst of all that clamor was Sirkit, relaxed and serene, smiling seductively at him over a cup of espresso from the machine.

In despair, Eitan hurried to the bathroom. He'd brush his teeth and go to sleep. Brush his teeth and go to sleep and tomorrow he'd make inquiries about a move to the States. There were enough hospitals there that would be happy to take in a dedicated physician with minimal salary demands. But Sirkit asked him to give her the towel, and Eitan suddenly realized that the herd of wolves had not stopped in the living room and kitchen, but had invaded the bathroom as well.

She stood with her back to him, washing her hair, a black mane transformed by the water into a black snake that writhed down to her buttocks. Now she rubbed her armpits with Liat's organic soap and asked if he had a razor.

He fled to the bedroom.

And there – quiet. The tranquility of drawn curtains. Liat's breath through the blanket. Grateful, Eitan embraced his wife. A pleasant languor settled in his body. He was home.

5

"**B**UT I DON'T UNDERSTAND why you don't tell him!" They were sitting in the yard having what was supposed to be a leisurely Saturday breakfast. Except that it had stopped being a leisurely breakfast quite a while ago. It was a fight. The muted voices could not hide it. Somehow, Eitan thought, the muted voices were what gave it away. Witness the fact that Yaheli and Itamar, who had been chasing each other throughout breakfast, stopped their game shortly after he and Liat began speaking quietly. "Mommy, Daddy, why are you whispering?" To which Liat promptly gave her usual reply, "We don't want to bother you, sweetie. So you can play in peace."

He hated that answer. Not only because he hated to see Liat lie – after all, it had been her irresistible honesty that had drawn him to her in the first place – but because of what that answer said about Yaheli and Itamar. It assumed that his children were stupid. That they couldn't recognize the moment when ordinary quiet became fraught with tension. But they knew. It had absolutely nothing to do with age. Dogs feel it as well. And that was exactly what happened to the peace and quiet of their leisurely breakfast when Liat asked what his shift schedule was for the next week. "I'm off till Monday, and then two and a half night shifts, one on-call and a few after-hours surgeries."

"Tanni, it's insane! You have to talk to Prof. Shakedi!"

"Tul, I just started in the department. I'm not exactly in a position to make demands on my bosses. Amsalem is out on reserve duty, Beitan just had twins a month ago. Someone has to pick up the slack."

"But it's way too much, last week, then this week, it's—"

"That's the situation."

Instead of praising him for his sensible acceptance of reality – the same sensible position she loved to wave in his face when they talked about Zakai's envelopes of money – she now chose to hurt him.

"You know, you're taking this so calmly that I'm starting to think it isn't such a big deal for you to see us only on Saturdays."

"Don't be an idiot."

"Don't call me an idiot around the kids," she said in English. "You know what, don't ever call me that."

Her brown eyes flashed. After twelve years of marriage, Eitan still couldn't distinguish between the flash of tears and the flash of anger. He sincerely hoped it was tears. He was much better at coping with her crying than with her anger.

"I'm sorry," he said, "but it kills me that you can't see how much I'm pushing myself for you and the kids, that you really think it doesn't bother me."

As he spoke, he thought about how trite that conversation was. How trite were the spoken words, the cooling cups of coffee, the half-eaten cake on the plate. The only fresh thing here was the lie, pink and virginal. And when Liat repeated, "But why don't you tell him?" he leaned back and let the lie speak for him – "It'll be over soon, honey. It's just a busy time in the department, that's all. In a week or two we'll go back to the usual routine, and then they'll remember who lent a hand and who didn't." As the lie spoke, Liat listened, weighed the words carefully. For a moment, Eitan was afraid she was on to him; her eyes might have been chestnuts, but her brain was as sharp as a knife – no one knew that better than he did. But then she stood up and went to sit in his lap, her nose tickling the lower edge of his cheek. "Sorry... It's just... I miss you."

"Me too, honey, me too." And then he did something highly uncharacteristic: he suddenly kissed her on the mouth in front of the children, in the middle of the yard, surprising himself, as if without his noticing the lie had lured him to a place where guilt and pleasure intermingled.

"Mom, Dad, are you kissing with your tongues?"

"No, sweetie, we're just pretending."

*   *   *

Behind the gas station and restaurant was an unpaved area for unloading trucks. Beyond it, the soil was sandier and the desert took on the shape of a sort of small stream. No water, only the shape. It was hard to imagine that water had once flowed here, though she had already heard people say that water once covered everything. Even if that was true, the desert had forgotten it. The soil of the stream bed was so dry and hot that even thorns couldn't take hold in it. Only plastic bags sometimes came to it from nowhere. Flew out of the restaurant, from the side of the road or more distant places. Who knows, maybe they flew across the whole desert before landing here, got tangled in the sand and the junk in the dry stream bed and stopped. It wasn't a beautiful place, what with all the pieces of junk and plastic bags caught on them, but it was a quiet place. Sometimes, when the noise of the restaurant, the music and shouting made her head ache, she came out here for a few minutes. And of course, she would rather move her bowels here, in the sand, than in the filthy toilet inside. You just had to walk a little further into dry stream, or else you could be seen. Further into it, past the place where the shit was pretty smelly, the stream became wider. There was no more junk there because anyone who wanted to throw something away didn't bother to walk that far. There was only a plastic chair that Asum once stole from the restaurant and used to sit on to smoke. She sat on the chair and thought, you know he can't see you. But a moment later, she got up. Then sat down again.

His cigarette butts lay on the sand beside the chair. She picked one up. Rolled it around in her fingers. Put it in her mouth, even though she knew that the smell of tobacco made her nauseous, but not very. Not as nauseous as she became when Asum talked to her with his face very close and the tobacco grabbed her by the throat and squeezed. And somehow, the nausea passed after a few minutes and she enjoyed sitting on his chair, chewing on his cigarette butt and looking at the dry stream.

She pulled her feet out of her flip-flops and stuck them in the sand, which was dry and hot. Asum's big toes were normal, but the toe next to them was unusually large, longer than the others. There was no particular reason to remember that; it was just one of the things a woman knows about her husband. She might forget it someday. Or not. Maybe she'd remember that especially large toe next to his big toe until the day she died. A person dies, but things remain. A chair. Cigarette butts. The memory of a foot. And maybe the song he used to whistle, which she couldn't remember now. It was unbelievable that she couldn't remember it. But maybe his whistling was like the plastic bags, still roaming over the desert. A person dies, but his whistling still runs on the wind, crossing roads and ravines, getting tangled in the sand and junk.

Three viral infections. Two intestinal infections. One broken bone. A suspected sprain. Nine infected lesions, one serious. He worked quickly. Skipped the "this might hurt a little" and the "it'll be over in a minute". Gave short replies to long questions. The exhaustion was killing him, and killing him even more was the duress. He didn't want to be there, he had to be there. He shouldn't be thinking about that. He should be thinking about the man he killed. About a life cut short because of him. The fact that he wasn't thinking about that merely intensified his guilt. Perhaps people might forgive him if he confessed to them that he had run over the Eritrean and driven away, that he had been consumed by remorse ever since.

But the truth was that he had hit and run, and since then all he could think about was how to get out of it. You couldn't confess to something like that. People would be horrified. And at the same time, he was filled with disgust for those horrified people. They would look at him with moral contempt, their conscience clear, because they happened not to have been there at that moment. As if they weren't killing Eritreans left and right. After all, each one of them could save the life of a starving African if they contributed only a fraction of their monthly earnings. A bank balance of 30,000 shekels would lose nothing if a mere thousand were taken from it. Many people could be saved with 1,000 shekels. Food for babies, purified water. Nevertheless, the money remained in the bank. That was where it belonged, and the moral discussion remained around the living-room coffee table, where it belonged. They were no different from him. He had abandoned an injured Eritrean on the side of Route 40, while they left their Africans in the savannah. It was a clear option: 1,000 shekels for a person's life. Any takers? No. Of course not. The issue wasn't what you were running from, only whether you got caught. And everyone was running from the same thing. Unable to look their role as masters in the eye. Everyone hits and runs. But he'd been seen. He'd been caught.

When he finished up and finally left the garage, several Eritreans who were talking outside hurried over to him. They wanted to thank him again. A thin man reached out for a handshake, and Eitan shook his hand, thinking that somewhere along the way his empathy button had stopped functioning.

He should have felt something. Kindness. Compassion. The responsibility of one human being for another. Not only toward this man standing here and shaking his hand emotionally while he himself was only waiting for him to stop. He hadn't felt anything for the man who had lain on the ground with his head split open either. Or perhaps he had felt something, but not the right something. Not what he should have felt.

He thought about him now: an Eritrean lying on the side of the road. Sometimes he felt it was a bit strange that he still called him the Eritrean, although he knew his name was Asum. It was even stranger that he didn't know whether he had a surname or not. Well, of course he had one, but Eitan didn't know what it was. And when you think about it, perhaps he didn't actually have one, maybe that wasn't how it worked with them. Maybe they had tribal names, or dynastic names. He had no idea and he didn't try to find out. Yes, he could ask Sirkit. She might even answer. And if he were already asking, why stop with the surname. Why not ask about the nicknames his pals had for him, if he had any pals. His favorite color. His hobbies. If he wanted, he could ask many questions about what the dead man was like. Grab him by the hand (soft? calloused?) and pull him out of the sea of identical, faceless people. He could have made an effort and granted him something apart from the cracked skull, the wetness of his blood on the desert rocks. He could have tried to persuade himself that that man had some value while he was alive, not only at the moment of his death. Thin body. Old clothes. Blood trickling from his black head. Less than a month had passed, and he already seemed so distant, as did that stomach pain he'd felt a moment after, the terrible need to move his bowels. Something that had happened to someone else. But he recalled the details precisely: the dull sound of the suv hitting a man. The wonderful, hoarse voice of Janis Joplin in full howl. The horror of the body slamming onto the ground. He remembered the sound of the gravel path under his feet when he'd got out of the suv. The contrast between the warm seat and the cold air outside. Remembered that as he hurried over to him, he still had a fleeting hope that maybe it was okay, maybe in another second that man would get up and shout at him to watch where he was driving. He remembered all that from a distance, as if it had happened to someone else.

But it happened to you. Not to someone else.

To you.

And yet it still did not feel real to him. As if the thing itself, the actual thing, could not truly penetrate his mind. Could not persuade his mind to take it in, internalize it. The run-over Eritrean stood outside the walls of his consciousness and pounded on the door, screaming to be let in. But inside, only a faint noise could be heard. Like the muted sound he'd made when the suv had hit him.

Perhaps that was good. Perhaps that was how it should be. What was so urgent about having the refugee take up residence in his mind? He extricated his hand from his grateful patient's prolonged handshake and headed for the suv. The sight that greeted him hit him like a punch in the stomach.

94

It left him breathless. The body of a black man lay against the right front tire. His arms were stretched to the sides. His legs were spread on the ground. Eitan tried to tell himself that it wasn't real. An optical illusion summoned up by long hours of wakefulness, fabricated by the night. But the man was really lying there beside his SUV, and when Eitan realized that, his legs began to shake.

It made no difference at all that a moment later, someone called the name of the sleeping refugee and the man lying beside the SUV stood up and went somewhere else. It made no difference because when Eitan had first looked at the body sprawled on the ground, it was the Eritrean's body that he saw. But this time he really saw him, suddenly felt the switch that had cut his mind off from his body since the accident flip in the other direction, and an enormous wave of nausea rose inside him. He'd killed someone. He'd killed someone. His split skull lying among the rocks. The blood oozing from his ears. He'd killed someone! Killed! Someone! And to the Eritreans' surprise, he knelt down beside them and vomited up his guts, a burning yellow torrent. Someone ran to the garage and came back with water. Eitan sat on the ground, his legs trembling. The Eritrean's legs had been stiff and shriveled. He hadn't been able to move his hands either. But his eyes had fluttered a bit. His eyes had looked at him.

He bent to vomit again, only this time there was nothing to bring up. His stomach contracted with strong, uncontrollable spasms, and in the midst of all that, he suddenly knew that he wanted his mother. Wanted to curl up in her soft, comforting arms, which would push away the hair stuck to his sweaty forehead, wipe the remains of vomit from his lips, calm his trembling body and everything would be fine.

He'd killed someone.

He'd

killed

someone.

Again, he sat up. Again drank water. And again the face, the eyes, the cracked skull, the blood from the ears. But this time, instead of nausea, something else rose in him. The beginnings of a terrible anger. A thin thread of anger. He didn't understand and didn't want to understand. He waited for his breath to come back, to return to normal, and then he hurried to the suv, barely hearing the cries of his escorts, concerned Eritreans who walked beside him, offering him water, and followed him with their eyes as he drove away from them.

Liat makes the chicken schnitzels in the oven. It's healthier and less of a headache. She puts four chicken breasts in a bowl. Marinates them in a mixture of date syrup, soy sauce and a spoonful of paprika. The alarm on her cell phone rings two hours later, reminding her of what she remembered anyway: beat an egg, add crushed garlic and olive oil. Dip the chicken in the egg mixture and then the breadcrumbs. Pat them well onto the meat. Place in a moderate oven, fifteen minutes on each side. Yaheli wants store-bought chicken nuggets shaped like animals, the kind that Tamir, his friend from nursery school, eats in his house. But they are full of preservatives and food coloring, and she won't hear of it.

When Eitan comes home, he'll set the table and make the mashed potatoes. That's his specialty. Yaheli will ask if he can watch TV with his meal and she'll say no, hoping she can stick to it. Instead, she'll ask him how nursery school was, ask Itamar how school was, ask Eitan how work was. The question is a direct continuation of the mashed potatoes and schnitzel, the smell of the shampoo coming from the children's heads and the cups of chocolate milk standing on the counter. But a family sitting at the table is actually made up of loose crumbs of moments. No one knows what the others were ashamed or proud of today. What they wanted, what they hated. They don't talk about it. They eat schnitzel and mashed potatoes. Only Liat, vaguely restless, insists on getting answers from each one. Not just "it was okay," but what actually happened, so she can pat the crumbs of those experiences into a single whole, the way she patted the breadcrumbs onto the pink, moist meat.

He was calm when he arrived at the garage for his next shift. Removed from the vomit and the trembling, from the run-over Eritrean, from the endless procession of bodies he examined close up for long hours. He thought he recognized the faces of those who had brought him water the day before, the people who had helped him stand up when his legs failed him. But they showed no sign that there had been a previous encounter, and Eitan concluded that he had once again mistaken one for another. Whether he was the one who had checked their temperature or they were the ones who had handed him a rag to wipe his forehead, they all still looked alike to him. (Not all. Sirkit stood in a corner of the garage, as distinct as always, a burning spot he made sure not to look at, making her even more conspicuous. He didn't know if someone had told her what happened outside the garage the previous day. And even if they had, could she connect his gross, humiliating vomiting to the illegal immigrant napping beside the SUV? Probably not – how could she understand that he had confused the anonymous, live Eritrean with her dead husband? None the less, he avoided looking at her, embarrassed by his body, which had betrayed him that way in her territory.)

Six hours later, he sent his last patient on his way and left the garage. Once again, they were waiting outside for him, and this time, in greater numbers. "*Shukran*, Doctor, *shukran*." He shook their hands reluctantly. He had already taken off his gloves and washed his hands in the garage sink, and now, after these handshakes, he'd have to be careful not to touch his face all the way back to Omer. Pull into the driveway and hurry over to the hose in the yard to wash away the potential coronavirus, the hypothetical dysentery, his built-in aversion to those foreign hands. He smiled politely to the crowd of devoted patients and tried to walk toward his SUV. But the Eritreans flanked him. What had begun as shy gratitude turned into an emotional outpouring, almost a competition: who would shake the doctor's hand longer; who would thank him with lengthier, more incomprehensible words. Among the extended hands, he suddenly recognized *his* hands, the ones that had lain on the ground, and remembered: a run-over Eritrean on the side of the road. His black legs resting on the ground in an unnatural position. The hands as well, he recalled, had been in an unnatural position. Damn it, his whole body had been blatantly unnatural. Not only because he was a run-over Eritrean. He wasn't even supposed to be there when Eitan was. Eitan's life did not include Eritreans splattered on the bumper, or shaking his hand, or Eritreans altogether. And without his noticing it, yesterday's nausea and guilt began to subside, replaced by growing anger. Why did that fucking illegal immigrant have to be there in the middle of the night? How did he expect someone to see him in the dark? So skinny, so pathetic. Eitan scanned the faces of the grateful patients and restrained himself from shouting at them. How can you be so pathetic! How can you bear this futile, groveling existence?! Why do you follow me like a pack of puppies? He nodded a goodbye and got into the SUV. But the Eritreans irritated him all the way home, like a grain of sand in his eye.

Near the exit for Omer he thought of David the Homo. David the Homo was David Zonnenshein from one of the fourth-grade classes in his school. David the Homo's father was an important man. Head of the Haifa University Psychology Department. But that didn't help David when the entire class bullied him. It might even have made it worse. Because while other children's parents would have intervened if their child had been called a homo and the epithet had been scrawled on all the doors of the school bathrooms, David's father took no concrete action. He might have thought it was something that children did and would pass. Maybe he was busy with the problems of other people, who paid him a great deal of money to solve them. Or maybe deep inside, like everyone else, he knew his son was a lousy little homo.

Eitan hadn't been one of the kids who'd bullied David the Homo. Not because he was especially virtuous, but because he had other things to do. But when he saw him being beaten by some third-grade kids who were a head shorter than he was, Eitan almost went over to hit him himself. How can you let them do this to you? Why are you such a homo? David the Homo had the kind of face that invited you do anything to him, and so you did. Children like David the Homo turn other children into monsters. Even if you swore to yourself that you wouldn't do anything to him, even if you wanted to feel sorry for him, the moment always came when you couldn't hold back anymore. You began hating him for being such a nothing.

David the Homo didn't move on to the same middle school. Eitan didn't know whether it was his idea or his father's to change schools, but it seemed like a good decision. In high school, he sometimes saw him on the bus and quickly averted his glance. They both knew things about each other that they didn't want to know. For example: that David was a lousy little homo. And that Eitan was a lousy little asshole.

In their senior year, Eitan and his classmates went on the March of Life trip to Poland. He stood with them in the central yard of Auschwitz. The guide told them about life in the camp. This is where the guards were. These are the gates. Those are the showers, the gas chambers, the crematorium. Ohad Sagi raised his hand. "But why didn't they try to run away?" The guide explained that it was impossible. Ohad Sagi persisted. "There were more prisoners than guards, and it wasn't like they had anything to lose." The guide looked a bit less patient. He said that anyone who didn't know what it meant to be so terrified couldn't judge. "Don't start that lambs-to-the-slaughter business with me," he added. In the hotel that night, Ohad Sagi suggested that everyone jerk off to see who would come first. After that, he said, "I don't understand it, why didn't they try to fight back? They were just a bunch of homos." Eitan thought about David the Homo, about how much he had hated him, and thought that deep down he had also hated them, all those emaciated Jews, walking skeletons, who seeped so deeply into your soul that you couldn't even jerk off decently.

He parked the suv and stepped out into the yard. Tried to understand why he couldn't sustain compassion for them for any length of time. Why that anger always crept in behind the sympathy. Just as the smell of blood drove sharks mad, the smell of weakness freaked him out. Or maybe it was the opposite, and it wasn't that he had the power to destroy them that made him angry at them, but the clever way they destroyed him. The way their wretchedness oppressed him, accused him.

He opened the door and went inside. Closed it behind him quickly, like a person fleeing.

*   *   *

He didn't like to admit it, but he was becoming a more pro-
ficient liar. Liat continued to complain about his many night
shifts, and he found himself joining Eckstein's poker group.
A brilliant, detestable arrangement that had repulsed Eitan
the first time he heard about it, but later became a life saver.
Eckstein's poker group had been meeting every Wednesday
for years, except that each of the members met in a different place: Eckstein in the bed of the current female intern;
Berdugo in the car belonging to his ex, who herself had to
join a group to get away from the house; Amos in the speech
therapist's office, on the couch where, in the afternoon, his
son had sat and learned to pronounce "sh". Eitan knew the
arrangement and was repelled by it, but he knew how much
Liat needed to see that he had indeed assimilated into his
new place of work, and he knew that the weekly poker group
played to exactly that need.

And then there were those half-night shifts when there
were complications in a surgery and it went on until dawn.
And there were one-third night shifts filled with crises and
system breakdowns that required the surgeons to stay late.
There were after-hours surgeries it would be a shame not to
take because they needed the money, and medical conferences,
the invitations to which were hung on the refrigerator door
at home some time before they were due to take place. The
conferences were real, as were the invitations, but if in the
past they had ended up in the trash even before they'd been

fully removed from their envelopes, now they were respectfully attached to the refrigerator door with a colored magnet. "THE FUTURE OF NEUROSURGERY." At Ichilov Hospital in Tel Aviv. The program ended at 9:30, which meant that there was no way he could get home before eleven. The department was another story. He'd used up his annual sick days a long time ago. He'd buried two grandmothers. Took the kids for a series of tests that showed nothing. He'd even told them that he was called up for emergency reserve duty in the Medical Corps, and hoped that by the end of the year no one would remember that he hadn't brought any documents to verify it. He counted three small canker sores on the underside of his lips, but was too upset and busy to treat them.

6

THEY ARRESTED THE KID not far from Yeruham. He was driving a black Mercedes GLK-Class, and showed no surprise when three armed detectives jumped out in front of him at a traffic light. The owner of the Mercedes called the police two hours later, when he'd come back from a swim in the Ein Akev spring with his children to discover that someone had stolen his car. He was so surprised to learn that they'd already found the SUV that he repeated the license plate number twice and insisted that the operator confirm it. Esti said, "Sir, what's so hard to believe? The Israeli police found your car for you," then hung up and burst out laughing. Melamed and Samsonov had never been so lucky, not to mention Cheetah. If that kid hadn't driven right into his ambush, this month's paycheck would have been his last. And the thing was that the only person not excited about it was the kid, no, the young man, no, the young Bedouin who was arrested by Beersheba detectives driving a stolen car. The third item on the four o'clock news. It turned out that the kid's name was Ali. Big deal. Every other Bedouin here was called Ali. Only Allah knew how they themselves didn't get confused.

The weariness in the boy's eyes surprised Liat. A sixteen-year-old just isn't supposed to look at you like that. "I think he's some kind of idiot," Cheetah had told her earlier, "but if you can get him to tell you who he takes the cars to, that could help." She studied the boy again. He didn't look like an idiot. People confuse a glazed look with a vacant look. A vacant look belongs to a brain that has no thoughts in it. A glazed look belongs to a brain with thoughts in it that are located behind a dark, glassy surface. The boy's look was glazed when he was alone and became weary when someone spoke to him.

"Our records show that you don't have a driver's license." Was that a sarcastic smile she thought she saw flash on his lips? "You know how to drive?"

All at once, his chest expanded with pride, his eyes lit up. "I'm a great driver."

Liat couldn't hide her smile. "So this isn't the first time you've driven without a license."

He said nothing and looked at her. Man and boy still struggled in the features of his face – the black bristles of a beard on rounded, almost baby-like cheekbones. A determined mustache above a delicate chin with the hint of a cleft.

"Look Ali, you're not sixteen yet. You don't have a criminal record. And if you cooperate with us, you won't have one."

It took more than four hours, but in the end Liat had a list of vehicles that had been stolen over the last several weeks and the address of a chop shop not far from Tel Sheva. As the detectives were getting organized for the raid, she reread the list of places where the vehicles had been stolen. Ein Akev. Maleh Akrabim. Tlalim. Gevey Havah. Mashabei Sadeh.

Tlalim.

She stood up abruptly and hurried over to the interrogation room. The sudden opening of the door surprised the boy slightly, but his face instantly took on the same bored expression he was so careful to maintain.

"Ali, tell me again when you were at Tlalim."

"Once with the Mazda and once it didn't work out."

"Yes, but when?"

"Hell, I don't remember."

"There's no 'I don't remember,' Ali. 'I don't remember' is dead. Tell me when you were there the last time."

"The last time… two weeks ago."

Eureka.

She rushed out to the precinct commander's office, opened the door without bothering to knock.

"I know who killed the Eritrean."

He shouted. Even cried. Strange to see a sixteen-year-old boy cry. One minute he was standing there with his mustache, his bristles and that Arabic accent that always made them seem older and more frightening in your mind – and a minute later, he started to cry. Like a child. And it was so unexpected that for the first second you didn't even realize that it was tears, not just something in his eye. And as he cried, it suddenly became terribly clear who had won the battle of his facial features, because his baby-like cheekbones were so prominent that the bristles looked pasted on, and the trembling of the lips beneath the mustache made it look like a mistake.

"It's not true," he said, wiping his nose with the back of his hand. Yes, he'd been at that Kibbutz Tlalim. And yes, he'd gone there to steal cars. But he hadn't hit anyone, may Allah strike him down if he was lying.

"Your Allah is a kind of problematic witness," Marciano said. "Can you think of anyone besides him who was there with you?"

In an instant, the child vanished and the man appeared. The boy's eyes once again showed nothing. The tears had not yet dried, but his pupils were already as hard as rocks. "No one. There was no one there with me." Liat shifted uneasily in her chair. Several hours earlier, the boy had said that he would answer all her questions, as long as she didn't ask who went with him on his night-time runs. He was willing to report on the vehicles that had been stolen, the scenes of the crime – he even agreed to endanger himself and give them the location of the chop shop. But never, under any circumstances, would he reveal the name of the partner who was with him. At the time, she'd thought the arrangement was reasonable. She was ready to give up on the small car thief in order to find out where the big money-maker was. A chop shop was worth more than a car thief. But now, the anonymous thief had become much more important – he was the only person who could strengthen the boy's claims.

"I swear I didn't run him over, I swear."

Liat leaned forward. "Ali, swearing isn't enough. We have a man who was run over near Kibbutz Tlalim and we know that you were there with the suv when it happened.

If you insist it wasn't you, give me someone to back up your story."

As she spoke, she tried to catch the boy's glance, but he entrenched himself in his silence and his eyes were glazed, dark, unfathomable. After a while, they realized that he wasn't going to say anything else and left him in the interrogation room. When the door closed, Marciano, a blue-uniformed whale with a broad smile, turned to her and said, "I told you it would end up being some Bedouin." And then he added generously, "But congratulations on cracking the case, sweetheart."

She was no prude.

A blonde is crying on the side of the road. A guy stops his car, asks her what happened. She cries – I have a flat! And when I tried to call a tow truck, I saw that my phone was stolen! And I'm all alone here! So the guy unzips his pants and says – this really isn't your day.

You could tell her jokes like that. She could go with the flow. She didn't play the "disadvantaged" card. She laughed even if, deep down, she hated herself for it. She'd rather hate herself than be considered a prude, defensive about her ethnic origin.

So most of the time she preferred to think that she lived in this world without skin color or a surname, without ethnic origin. Not Liat Smooha from the projects in Or Akiva. And not Liat Green from the private homes in Omer. Just plain Liat.

As a child (with an unruly mane of hair that her mother insisted on gathering into a ponytail and her grandmother insisted on releasing), she had never dreamed of becoming a detective. Assuming that her Purim costumes were an indication of anything, she leaned strongly toward air travel professions. She was a butterfly at nine, a fairy at ten, and at eleven a pilot. When she was twelve, the limits of the atmosphere became too unimaginative and she made a failed attempt to be the first Or Akiva astronaut. Failed because the motorcycle helmet Uncle Nissim lent her was remarkably heavy, and the aluminum foil she was wrapped in tore almost completely even before the first break. She left the helmet in class and went out. When she went back to the classroom, the helmet was gone and she spent the rest of day searching for it. Consumed with guilt, she brought Uncle Nissim her Purim gift basket of sweets as compensation, and he ate a chocolate bar and said, never mind, angel, what's gone is gone.

But she wouldn't settle for that and began her own private operation. In a week, she returned Uncle Nissim's helmet to him, holding it reverently in two scratched hands. Her mother began whining that those scratches were tetanus for sure and wanted to take her right to the clinic, but her grandmother said, wait a minute Aviva, the child has a story to tell us, and she won't die of tetanus in the next half an hour. Liat told them that when she went back to school after the Purim vacation she had looked really hard into the eyes of all the kids in her class and noticed that Aviram was the only one who didn't look back at her. So today she'd gone over to him and said, I know you took it, and he said get out of my face you bitch, and when he saw that she wasn't moving, he himself turned around to go, but she grabbed his hand, and then he gave her those scratches, which looked a lot worse than they felt. Finally he said okay, you nutcase, and together they walked to his grandfather's house, where he'd been living since the court had decided that his parents were not fit. And there, under the couch, was the helmet and lots of other things that Liat recalled had disappeared from class since the beginning of the year. He scratched her hand again, saying take your fucking helmet and get out of my face, you nutcase.

Her mother said, we have to call the police. Uncle Nissim said, we don't need any police, I'll talk to him myself. And her grandmother said, Liati, take really good care of your eyes because that's your gift. Later, after Uncle Nissim left and her mother was washing dishes in the sink, she sneaked two chocolate bars and whispered, "One for Aviram."

They never spoke again, she and Aviram. When she gave him the chocolate bar, he threw it at her and walked off, and a year later she moved to a different school. Her home room teacher called her mother in and told her that because of her good grades and all sorts of other things, she'd be better off in the Kibbutz Ma'agan Michael school.

On the first day of the seventh grade she wore a blouse with gold sequins and agreed, for the first time, to restrain her hair with a rubber band. Her grandmother walked her to the bus stop and said, you're so beautiful, my angel, and your blouse is beautiful, and Liat believed her, even though she knew that she was complimenting her partly because she was her grandmother and partly because she herself had bought Liat the blouse. The bus arrived at Ma'agan Michael and Liat saw more grass than she had seen in her entire life. When she got off, thinking that it would probably be really fun going to school here, one of the kids shouted – take a look at that one with the sequins. When she came home, her grandmother asked her how it was, and she said okay. Then she asked her mother to go to the shopping center with her to buy a black blouse without sequins and without anything printed on it.

Why black, my angel? Black is for funerals. It's boring.

I want black.

In the end she was happy there, in Ma'agan Michael. She was pretty enough, smart enough and funny enough to be forgiven for coming from Or Akiva. Perhaps what helped her most was the fact that she was willing to forget that she came from there, and when she herself agreed to forget, they agreed as well.

The boundaries were thin, hidden, but none the less carefully observed. Consider the surprised expressions of the people interviewing her for entrance into a Master's degree program when they learned that behind "Liat Green" on her application forms stood someone who looked like Liat Smooha. The expression vanished instantly, but Liat was experienced enough to recognize it. Or the first evening spent with Eitan's army friends, the first time they saw her skin color. Or at his parents' house. Or the picnic with the department medical staff and their families. She ignored those surprised looks, just as she had ignored the shocked look of her advisor when she told her that she had decided not to go ahead with her doctorate in criminology and join the police instead.

The advisor had asked why. Eitan had asked why. Her mother and Uncle Nissim had asked why. But her grandmother had made some really strong coffee, looked at the grounds and said, very good, my angel, your eyes are finally going to do what they know how to do: look at people.

Different sorts of surprised expressions awaited her at her new job with the police force. For the first time in her life, her skin color was the right one, but that didn't change the fact that she was a mega-pussy. Hot like you wouldn't believe. And, come here honey, let's introduce you to a few people. And a bitch. "A bunch of baboons," Eitan had said when she came home crying after her first week, "nothing but a bunch of baboons." She was happy for his sympathy, but she also knew that the expression, bunch of baboons, was reserved in his mind for the morons in the police cruiser, never for his army buddies from the elite rescue unit, who laughed their heads off when they talked about harassing the new girl in the reserve unit. He was on her side, of course. Listened at length to all the cases she solved. Opened a bottle of wine for every promotion she was given. But since they'd moved to the south, the color in his eyes had been fading. He no longer liked to hear about developments in her investigations. The only case he had the patience to listen to was the one about the Eritrean, but he listened even to that with a surprising restlessness, as if he weren't really listening to the words she spoke, but searching for something she couldn't name behind them.

7

IT'S DIFFICULT TO HATE for such a long, continuous period of time. Two people work in the same place for hours. Around them, people come and go. But it's always the two of them. Always that place. The night outside is sometimes cloudy and sometimes clear, sometimes freezing and sometimes pleasant. The hours pass. The injuries pass. But it's always the same two people in the same place. And since both of them arrive at the garage after a day of hard work, exhausted from their shifts, they begin to be too tired even to hate. They don't have the strength for burning looks. For flagrant displays of disregard. The first few nights, the hate warmed them. Kept them awake. But gradually, the muscles of hatred grew tired. How long could you keep straining them without a break? Suddenly it seemed quite reasonable to stop, if only for a short time, let's say an hour after the shift began until an hour before it ended. They came to the garage wrapped in their hatred, removed it for a few hours, and then re-wrapped themselves in it before they went out into the night air. The hours in between were silent, strange. Not thundering silence, but a silence of activity. Sometimes, for a few moments, even of tranquility. She sterilized and he bandaged; he palpated and she translated. And the entire time, outside, the night ripened. The dark became darker and darker, until it gave birth to a different, lighter blue, which gave birth to the sun. Sometimes they looked outside, each in turn. Sometimes their looks intersected, and they immediately averted their eyes so that the hatred would not awaken. You ran over my husband and drove away; you stole my nights from me. When the night changed from black to blue, those words had no purpose.

Take, for example, the whistle. Sirkit whistled while she worked and Eitan listened. At first, he listened and hated. There is nothing more loathsome than the whistle of a person you hate. He hated the repetitive melody, the unfamiliarity of it, the way she pursed her lips. The whistle seemed to be nothing but a cry of contempt that had only one purpose: to rile him. But time passed. Two people in the same place, and gradually the whistle began to sound different. Or perhaps it fell on different ears. He began to understand that she wasn't whistling against him, or for him, or even for herself. She was whistling the way people sometimes whistle while they work – distractedly. Unconsciously.

And without his being aware of it, he began to wait for that whistle. One night, when the darkness had changed from black to blue and they were still working in silence, he was surprised to discover that he was waiting for something. A foreign, unfamiliar melody that added spice to the night silence. And if at first he hated the melody, the moment came when he whistled it to himself, waiting for a traffic light to change at the entrance to Beersheba. The melody was so much a part of him now that it required no effort to produce it. Not an iota of awareness. The light changed from red to green and he kept driving and kept whistling, until he reached another traffic light, where he stopped abruptly the moment he realized what he was whistling. He turned on the radio, filled the SUV with news and pop songs, and raised the volume. (To clean that melody out of the SUV. To drive it out. How had that whistling of hers entered his throat and infected him without his noticing?) He thought he'd succeeded, but several nights later he found himself whistling again. This time in the garage. He didn't know how long he'd been whistling before he realized it. He promptly stopped and prayed that no one had noticed.

Of course she'd noticed. He saw it in her eyes, which looked at him with great surprise, almost shock. He saw her eyes but not her heart fluttering inside her body (where had he found Asum's whistle, how could this man be whistling her husband's song to her?). One minute her entire body quivered, and the next it was completely still. Because if it were true, then maybe the whistle didn't belong to Asum at all. Maybe every whistle belongs to the lips that whistle it. That thought was so liberating that for a moment she almost smiled at him, but controlled herself. And yet, stealing other people's whistles is nothing to be proud of, even if it turns out to be something good.

That night, Eitan continued doing his work and Sirkit continued doing hers. The awkwardness of the moment stole the whistle from both of them. But three nights later, the melody returned. Quietly, without announcing itself. Sometimes he whistled it, sometimes she did. It returned and flowed between them without their speaking of it, without their paying it the attention that would destroy it. Not by smiling, not by moving closer. Simply because it was difficult to hate for such a long, continuous period of time.

"It was the sea in Eilat. Or in Greece. The sand was like the Red Sea sand, but I knew from the color that it was Greece. We wanted to get to the water, but it was a long way to walk, and in the middle we had to pass a kind of orange Japanese monastery. Then we walked on a lawn and I thought it was very strange that there was such soft grass near the sea, just like clover. And then you woke me up before we got there."

They were lying in bed. Their bodies were still heavy with sleep, and Liat was vaguely annoyed at him for waking her up. "There was a monk in the monastery, dark-skinned, a little like a caregiver from Thailand. I thought he wouldn't let us pass, but he actually smiled and said okay." She didn't know why she was so determined to tell him that dream. Or what the dream meant. But she needed to tell it. As if there were something extraordinarily urgent about that beach, something vital. That was why it was very important to say everything as soon as you woke up, word for word, like pouring an expensive liquid from one container to another, careful not to spill a drop – that was how she was pouring what had filled her sleep into his ears. None the less something spilled, it wasn't clear how. Somewhere on the way from her to him, it was lost. She saw it in his eyes, which were focused on her, but without true comprehension. And perhaps worse than that, she realized that it was happening to her as well. Right after she woke up, the dream was still part of her, an utter certainty. But from moment to moment, they were separating: part of what had seemed as clear as the sun became as partial as the moon, because what did it mean that the sea was in both Eilat and Greece, and how can you know from the color that it's in Greece? What was so strange about soft grass along the beach, and why was it so urgent to reach the water?

Five minutes after waking, the dream and Liat were already strangers. But she didn't give up, because the feeling that had been so certain in her sleep still surged inside her: a blue sea she urgently had to reach. And they were so very close.

Eitan ran his fingers through her hair. "Maybe it means you need a vacation." He smiled. She did too, knowing how the conversation would continue: first they'd reminisce a bit about vacations at other beaches, and then they'd begin planning the next one. Maybe during the holidays. Thailand, perhaps. The words would carry them forward and the dream would remain behind. A person gets off a boat and begins to walk, and a few meters later he forgets the sea, forgets that the sea joins the ocean, forgets that the ocean surrounds everything. On land, there are paths and mountains and sometimes rivers, and the person drinks from the rivers and doesn't remember the sea, doesn't remember the salt, doesn't remember the very real possibility of drowning. Liat and Eitan continued talking and every word was a step on solid ground, every word drove the water further from their minds.

Perhaps that was how it should be. Because when, ten minutes later, Liat placed cups of coffee from the machine in front of them, the distance between her and her man was already quite small. That was why she told him her dreams every morning. Not so he would interpret them. But so he would know. And she also asked him: did you dream? What about? As if sleep were a common enemy that had to be defeated. An attempt to separate them from each other. For even if they lay in each other's arms on the mattress, holding hands, legs intertwined – each of them still slept alone.

As they drank their coffee, her eyes scanned his face. Stocktaking that he wasn't aware of, but that none the less took place every morning. To anyone used to waking up every day in the same house, it sounds ridiculous. But someone who wakes up once in a house that has been broken into (and it doesn't matter whether it's the jewelry or the father that has disappeared in the middle of the night), knows she must look for every sign of change. Wake up tensed and ready – what happened here while I was gone? Liat knew: sleep was dangerous. There was something almost offensive about the idea that for seven hours a day, you are forced to be apart from your loved ones. Each one goes his own way. No one knows anything. She had already understood that when she was a child. Even before her father moved in with Ronit, she had hated going to bed. None of the lullabies, the hair-stroking, the dolls lying beside her under the covers could lessen the humiliation of sleep. These days she fell asleep more easily, but still with a vague sense of defeat.

And then – the waking up. Her man is lying beside her in bed. They immediately bring each other up to date – where they've been and what they've done. And even if she feels like lingering a while longer with the dream, she nevertheless gives herself over to the conversation. Eagerly, she tells him where she's been so that they can get out of bed as they got into it: close to one another. Knowing one another. (Of course, she didn't tell him everything. Not all the dreams and not all the details. But even when she cleaned the house, she didn't always have the strength to clean the spare room. And that was fine. She knew what was inside it and it didn't frighten her.) She wasn't afraid of sex dreams. Neither hers nor Eitan's. It was like dropping your stools into the toilet behind the closed door. Everyone knew what you were doing, even if they didn't talk about it.

With Eitan, she hadn't locked the bathroom door for years. She peed with abandon in front of him. She hid parts of herself from him and knew that he too hid parts of himself from her, but that didn't worry her. It was clear to her that he had things he didn't tell her. She had a vague suspicion about why he sometimes locked himself in the shower. Sometimes she even asked herself if it was one of her girlfriends he was fantasizing about, or a woman from the department. Those thoughts stung her slightly, but there was also something calming about them. Because she could look directly at the inner sanctum of coupledom, clean the dust off the darkest shelves without fear. But she never went beyond that. Just as you label a carton FRAGILE because of the rattling sound coming from inside, but you don't open it, don't try to find out what it contains.

Sometimes the whistling stopped abruptly. For instance, when an embarrassed man showed him a sheet full of bloody, stinking faeces and he could barely keep himself from throwing up at the sight. Entamoeba histolytica. Sometimes trekkers come home from abroad with it. The wrong choice of drinking water and your intestines turn into a breeding ground for protozoa. Doctors in internal medicine departments were already used to seeing it, especially during the holidays when long-haired youngsters decide to take off from Nepal and spend Rosh Hashanah at home, and two days later end up in the emergency room accompanied by a concerned parent. But even then, the number of cases never approached even a tenth of what he saw here. It seemed as if every other patient was a carrier. They had drunk the water back in Africa, but the protozoa traveled all the way here with them, tiny cysts that adhere to the large intestine and slowly destroy it.

He looked at those people in astonishment. It wasn't the faeces that bothered him. It was the very existence, the very essence of the patients. He arrived at the garage in the evening after a full day spent in the light, looked at them and did not understand. Just as once, on a school trip, the guide had picked up an innocent-looking stone and from under it black, evil soil gaped out at them. A den of worms, dark and hidden life. A muddy, crumbling existence of which he'd had no inkling. It was beneath them all that time, and he hadn't known. The guide then put the stone back and they continued on their way. But the doubt remained about every stone he saw after that, even more so if it was white and smooth. Now he looked at the snaking line in front of the garage. He looked and did not believe that it had been beneath them all this time and he hadn't known. And why should he ever have known?

When he finished work, he washed his hands well, almost rubbing the skin off. She waited behind him until he finished, and when he left the sink, she washed her hands. He thought about giving her the towel, but decided not to.

*   *   *

She walked back quietly. The night was so cold that even the dogs had stopped barking. For a long while, there was only the sound of her steps, and then the roar of a truck pulling into the gas station. Soon after the truck had entered the gas station, the smell of it entered as well. The overwhelming stench of one and a half tons of garbage. Instead of quickening her steps, she stopped to inhale. She remembered that smell very well. When they had burned garbage at night to keep themselves warm, it had smelled exactly like that. Heavy, all-encompassing, enshrouding the village like a blanket. And as much as she had hated that smell then, she was unable to move away from it now. She stood behind the gas station and inhaled more and more of it, inhaled it hungrily, squeezing as much of it as she could into her lungs. Stupid cow, don't tell me that you miss it.

But what could she do? She did miss it. Missed it without knowing she missed it, because she had hoped never to smell the stench of burning garbage again. And yet, when she encountered it again, she clung to it with all her strength, refusing to let it go. As terrible as it was, it was still the smell of her nights. When you smelled it, you knew that night was falling, that you'd finished work. That you could finally sit down and look at the sky. She and Asum would go outside and sit with the others. Sometimes someone would sing and sometimes they would talk. But quietly. The sounds of the night were different from the sounds of the day.

She looked around. Apart from the smell, everything was different. The air here had a different feel. It was hard to explain. The sunsets looked different. Something in the angle of the sun in relation to the sky. It affected everything, also the colors. And that was okay, because that was why she had come here, for things to be different. But it was also terrible. Faces, flavors, smells, songs she would never meet again. And if she came across an echo (like now, a truck stopping at the gas station and suddenly, if you close your eyes, you're there), even then it wouldn't be the same. It couldn't be.

You can't miss the smell of garbage. You can't. But it's out of your control. Like the dreams. Though she was here, her dreams were still there, and sometimes they were both there and here, and sometimes in a completely different place. Every night many people squeezed onto the mattress next to the wall.

They did and said strange things, but the strangest thing was that they were present here, with her, a presence that, in her dreams, seemed understandable, but right after them became truly amazing. How did they get here when they didn't really get here? Hadn't managed to make their way here? Hadn't managed to survive the deserts, the countries, the people? Mainly the people. She had, she was here, but those night-time journeys exhausted her. Because though they were the ones who came to her, she went to them no less. Went to them and didn't always know whether she would be able to return. She woke up tired in the morning, and in the afternoon she went to the dry stream bed and sat on Asum's chair, which was her chair now. A man dies and seems to have left nothing behind, but he has in fact left his wife a chair and a river view, and when you think about it, that was no small thing at all. Her feet dug into the sand, and the sand was warm and smooth. The wind brought it here and the wind would take it away from here, and that was fine because the sand did not remember. The sand didn't know where it had been yesterday and didn't know where it would be tomorrow. If that weren't so, if the sand remembered all the places it had been, it would become so heavy that no wind would be able to carry it off anywhere.

When the truck drove off, she took a last breath, sniffing frantically, chastising herself for clinging to it so foolishly. How dare you miss that garbage, that village. You can't possibly miss the smell of that garbage. But if we don't miss something, what do we actually have? If we are defined by what we have, then your situation is very bad, but if we are defined by what we've lost, then congratulations, you're at the top of the list. And if missing something is like a bite, like skin infected by a parasite that has penetrated it, why does she scratch it so passionately, the smell of garbage and the smell of food, the smell of the earth and the smell of Asum? She walked more quickly. Went into the caravan and lay down on the mattress. Stop it. Stop it. But they kept coming, the smells. And so did the tastes, the colors, the faces. But worst of all was when they stopped coming. When she suddenly realized that she no longer remembered the name of the boy who had lived three shacks away who used to cough all the time. That she could not recall the song men used to sing after all the other songs had ended. She lay in bed and remembered, then lay in bed and didn't remember, and gradually felt the tastes, the colors, the faces leave her body, felt how every moment she was here, something from there faded, was wiped away. Then she heard the women on the mattresses next to her whisper: listen, Sirkit is finally crying.

It's difficult to hate so much for a continuous period of time, but it's also difficult not to. Because he had already sneaked into the drug storeroom of the internal medicine department three times, and it was starting to become dangerous. As he quickly shoved the drugs into his backpack, Eitan recalled the stealing-sweets-from-the-grocery-store ritual, the test of manhood at the end of the fourth grade. Distraction. Rapid infiltration. Escape. But now he wasn't clutching some toffee in his hands, but many packets of antibiotics, and the price of a mistake wasn't a thorough cleaning of the store owner's Subaru. In his attempt to manipulate his way to the drugs he wanted, he had renewed his relationship with a guy he'd known in medical school, now an internist in the hospital, a thin, balding man who looked surprised that Eitan remembered his name. Eitan didn't remember his name. He found him on the doctors' list, looked at his date of birth and where he went to school, and hoped that they had indeed bumped into each other at Tel Aviv University. When he found him beside a patient's bed, he discovered that they really had known each other in the past – the internist immediately said, "You were Zakai's boy" – and the path from there to lunch was short. Over the next few days, he dropped by to see his new friend at every opportunity, until his face became familiar in the department. The nurses no longer wondered what the neurosurgeon was doing in the internal medicine department. But he still had to figure out how the locked door to the drug storeroom could be opened. Finally, he began to tell his new friend about the overflowing drug storerooms in the hospitals further north. The internist's balding head reddened with anger. "You're drowning in drugs and we have a constant shortage," he said. "Come on, I'll show you so you can see what an internist's drug storeroom in Soroka Hospital looks like."

Eitan followed him, making his way between the patients' beds, which blocked the corridor, an obstacle course of moans and groans. The internist finally stopped in front of a locked door, took out his magnetic card and passed it quickly in front of the lock. Open sesame. "Take a look at what we have here. Nothing, absolutely nothing." Eitan scanned the shelves and thought, you have no idea what nothing is. Nothing is what there is in a garage near Tlalim, a twenty-minute ride from here. He immediately pushed the thought of the dark garage out of his mind. He didn't want to think about them, about those people who stole his nights. Most of all, he didn't want to think about *her*. So he turned to the internist and listened to his complaints with interest and took advantage of the moment he turned his back to grab whatever he could get his hands on.

But it wasn't enough. Several nights later, the supply was gone. As he drove the SUV on the dark dirt road, he had to be careful not to hit the dark figures making their way to the garage. Eritreans. Sudanese. Thin, almost skeletal bodies. Bodies crumbling from so much erosion. Stress fractures from hundreds of kilometers of walking. Exhaustion. Dehydration. Heat stroke. He didn't say a word about it. What could he say? He merely asked Sirkit to keep the waiting patients apart. "The last thing I need here is a tuberculosis epidemic."

It was only a matter of time before it arrived, and when an embarrassed Eritrean woman removed her shirt and exposed a back covered with Kaposi's sarcoma, he felt as if he had received a letter he'd been expecting for quite a long time. There was no reason to open the envelope; he knew what was inside: the ugly growths on the young woman's back left no room for doubt. Of all the vicious diseases, AIDS was at least polite enough to announce its presence. The lesions on her back were a clear statement, with dozens of copies: I'm here. None the less, Eitan asked her to open her mouth, and inside it, he saw – as he knew he would – lesions covering her tongue and throat, continuing downward as far as the eye could see. He couldn't know yet whether the metastasis had reached the digestive system and lungs, but at this stage that didn't really change anything. He gestured for the young woman to get dressed and told her that she had to go to the hospital right away.

But the young woman remained standing there. As did the man who had come with her. Eitan didn't have to examine him to know. The lesions covered his face. The couple continued to stand there even after he repeated "hospital" over and over again. The expressions of refusal on their faces required no translation. Their skin was covered with lesions. They had difficulty breathing. Their legs could barely carry them. But their freedom was undisputed: they could still stand under the moon and the stars; they sat when they wanted to and stood up when they wanted to. If they went to the hospital now, that freedom might be taken from them. But not necessarily, Eitan told them, not necessarily. True, there were cases where patients were put in detention camps, but most of the time treatment was given without any problem. After all, it was in the national interest.

The man and the woman stood in silence. Perhaps they understood what Sirkit had translated for them. Perhaps not. Either way, they remained where they were. As they stood there, Sirkit spoke in an expressionless tone. Eitan didn't understand what she said, but he saw the arrival of two men who, until then, had been waiting outside the garage. Despite the severe intestinal infection they both suffered from, they were still more muscular and robust than all the others. Now they stood in front of the man and woman, studying them with veiled eyes.

Sirkit spoke to the man and woman, and there was suddenly a softness in her voice that Eitan did not recognize. (He had heard her giving orders. He had heard her keeping the patients firmly in line. But he had never heard her speak this way before. And for a moment, he wondered what other tones existed in her throat that he hadn't even guessed at. When she sang, for example, if she did sing. Then he quickly cut off that thought in disgust, because what did it matter whether she sang or not?) The man replied to what she said. Sirkit paused, then went on speaking. The sounds emerged from her mouth so gently that Eitan could barely hear the words spoken, although he knew their meaning very well.

But the man and the woman remained where they were. The woman's lashes fluttered so quickly that if eyelashes were wings, she would have flown off into the air a long time ago, fluttering her way to the moon. But then he noticed the tears that fell from the black woman's eyes, the lashes pulling them down, large and heavy. She could never fly like that. Sirkit did not look into the woman's eyes. Nor into the man's eyes. Her gaze was fixed on the tin wall of the garage.

Go.

The man and the woman remained standing where they were. The two Eritrean men took another step inside. There was not a bit of aggressiveness in their eyes. Certain things would be done if they needed to be done. That was an established fact. There was no need for more than that step. The man and woman turned to go.

There were others. There were always others. The supply of drugs ran out, and once again Eitan found himself plotting another way back into the drug storeroom of the internal medicine department. At lunch, he took advantage of the wonderful chaos of cups and napkins and plastic trays and switched his magnetic card with the internist's. When they parted, Eitan said he was going back to work, but in fact he waited until he saw his friend leave the internal medicine department heading for the neurosurgery department, holding the magnetic card he needed to exchange with Eitan. Then he hurried toward internal medicine, calculating how much time it would take the internist to reach neurosurgery, learn that Dr Green had not yet returned from lunch, and go back to the internal medicine department. It would arouse no suspicion if he bumped into him in the department corridor, just a small mix-up. But if the internist saw him use the switched card to get into the drug storeroom, things would get a lot more complicated.

He acted with a speed that surprised him. In only a few minutes, the backpack was filled with treasures of Western medicine. Ciprofloxacin for intestinal infections. Mebendazol for intestinal worms. Ventolin for patients who had breathing problems after weeks of cutting metal and painting walls. Synthomycine for infected, pus-filled wounds. Cephoral for bladder infections. Atophan for joint pain and stress fractures. Isoniazid, Rifampicin, Pyrazinamide and Ethambutol for the inevitable war against the growing number of TB cases. The illnesses that bored him. They were the reason he had chosen to become a neurosurgeon. Why be satisfied with the dreary system when you can get into the control room itself, the command center. How much he missed the beauty of brain cells, the axons as white as a ballerina's dress. So precise. So clean. So different from the infections, the pus and the ulcers he saw every night in the garage. He quickly straightened up the place so it would look as if nothing was missing, and cracked open the door. When he saw that there was no one in the corridor but bleary-eyed patients in their beds, he slipped out. Near the entrance he met the internist, switched cards with him and apologized for the mix-up.

The third time, he swore to himself, would be the last. On the way out he ran into the head nurse, and he didn't like the way she looked at him. Two hours earlier, during a shared coffee break, the internist had told him about a suspicion of stolen drugs in the department. A mistake in the records, or one of the nurses who wanted to make some money on the side. Eitan listened attentively and said, "A mistake in the records. It happens all the time. Why would anyone put his job at risk like that?" The internist shrugged and said that people do all sorts of strange things.

When he reached the garage that evening, he was upset and angry, and mostly late. Yaheli's long bath, a lengthy and stormy discussion of pirates at Itamar's bedside, a leisurely cup of coffee on the living-room couch. He hadn't decided in advance to be late that night, but something inside him clearly rebelled against the need to arrive on time. It was almost eleven when Liat turned her gaze from the TV and asked, "You're not on call tonight?" And he, instead of hurrying to stand up, ruffled her hair and said in a calm tone, "Nothing will happen if they wait a while."

But that calm faded as he drew closer to the garage. He could already picture Sirkit's icy, penetrating glance. He tried to calculate the number of patients already gathered there, outside the tin door, waiting for him to arrive. When he turned off the main road onto the dirt road, he suddenly realized that the thing pressing against his temples was nothing but his guilt for being late, and that realization only made him angrier as he slammed the SUV door behind him and declared, "I'm here." He expected Sirkit and the patients to come out to him, either hopeful or angry. But the garage remained silent. No one hurried out to greet him.

For a moment, the faint hope flickered inside him that they'd all been caught. One raid of the immigration police and there he was, a free man. Every day, he imagined the anonymous phone call to the police. But he knew that with the police came an investigation, and with the investigation would come the revelation. It was complete idiocy to assume that Sirkit would keep his secret. He began walking more quickly now, hurrying toward the garage. That silence worried him.

First he saw Sirkit, her black hair pulled onto the top of her head in a thick bun, a coiled, sleeping snake. After spending the entire drive thinking about the admonishing look he would get from her, Eitan was surprised to discover that she wasn't even looking at him. A moment later, when his eyes had grown accustomed to the lighting in the garage, he understood why – lying on the rusty iron table was a young man staring vacantly into space. Sirkit was focused entirely on his left hand. She was stitching it up with quick, sure movements.

"What are you doing?" Eitan's voice shook with astonishment.

She said he'd come at exactly the right time, because she wasn't sure she knew how to finish it up.

"You're completely mad. Only a doctor can do that sort of work."

There was no doctor here.

She watched him calmly as he went over to the faucet and washed his hands. When he approached the table, he had to admit that she'd done a good job. Amazingly good, in fact.

"Where did you learn to do that?"

She told him that in Eritrea, she'd started sewing the minute she could hold a needle. In the end, a linen blouse isn't so different from human skin. She told him about the medical delegation that came to the village, how she ran after them everywhere they went and watched, and one of the women doctors saw and explained to her. She told him that for three weeks she'd been carefully watching everything he did here and tried to remember. And Eitan, instead of noticing that for the first time she wasn't speaking to him in sentences of one syllable, stared mesmerized at the light coming from her face. The woman before him was radiant.

He knew that radiance. The first time he had stitched a patient, his heart pounding and his fingers trembling. The first time he had cut through a patient's dura mater. Sirkit's eyes remained calm, but there was no mistaking the exhilaration on her face. She's like me, he thought, she's the way I was when I was just starting out.

Sirkit moved aside, giving him room. "No," he said, "finish what you started." A small smile came to her lips, lingered a moment and vanished. Eitan directed her movements in a quiet voice. After endless hours of working together, this revelation of her abilities was enormously exciting to him, almost embarrassingly so. Because he had never thought for a moment that she could. It had never occurred to him that, with the proper training, this woman was capable of doing exactly what he himself did. Damn it, this woman had learned to suture by watching others, from oral instructions in a field clinic. She went over to the shelf of drugs to get some more antiseptic liquid and Eitan watched her with new eyes. (And perhaps it wasn't her ability that suddenly drew him closer to her, but the discovery that they shared the same passion. They were both enthralled by the possibility of seeing people from the inside.)

They worked in silence for a long time. Suturing, cleaning, sterilizing, washing their hands, arranging the new drugs on the garage shelves. When Sirkit picked up one of the packets and asked what Ciprofloxacin was, Eitan told her, and when she asked more questions, he explained and expanded, describing the various bacteria that attacked the intestines and how the antibiotic worked, quoting new research and attacking old assumptions. He had never noticed before how much he enjoyed teaching. He recognized in her the same curiosity he himself had, the same demanding, sometimes overbearing desire to know. That night, Eitan spoke with Sirkit for hours. Patients came and went. One pain was exchanged for another. Drugs were distributed. And when he finished setting an injured girl's leg, he turned around and saw a cup of tea being held out to him.

I made some for us.

He took the tea and thanked her. They stood there awkwardly for a moment, and then Sirkit walked over to the tin door. The desert night was coming to an end, and the taste of the tea in Eitan's mouth was hot and sweet. Standing beside him, as silent as a marble statue, the woman sipped her tea. Under cover of darkness, he studied her face. The straight, simple nose. The arched eyebrows. The curve of her lips. He knew that she was beautiful, and he knew that if he were to see her in the street, he would not give her a second glance.

The laundry came out of the dryer warm and fragrant, and Liat put it in the large plastic tub and walked into the living room. It was late, and the radio was playing quiet, uninterrupted jazz, the way she liked it. Every now and then, the music stopped and the announcer read the news. His voice was quiet and clear, and he spoke the words as if he were reading poetry. She hummed the previous song to herself and sat down on the couch. She divided the laundry into four piles – this is Eitan's, this is hers, here is Yaheli's, these are Itamar's. She folded them quickly, surely. She knew every pair of pants, every piece of underwear, every sock. The smell of the laundry was hot and sweet, and there was certainty in every shirt. Their lives were spread out in front of her so she could fold them, and she was deeply involved in every single item. The stain on Yaheli's pants from the birthday cake he ate in nursery school. The torn shirt that Itamar refused to throw away because it had an elephant printed on it. She could identify their socks – black, simple – in any lineup. She had divided up her life like this so many times, in the middle of the night, stacking four folded towers of clothes on the couch. Eitan's, Yaheli's, Itamar's, and hers. Though she was separating the clothes, sorting them, it was clear to her that she was actually joining them together. The towers of clothes piled on the couch were the absolute opposite of the Tower of Babel. One language, down-to-earth, no aspirations to reach the sky. One living room, one couch, the delicate fragrance of soap was enough. For example, Eitan's shirts. Button-downs. Only she knew how much the labels drove him mad. How he had to remove them the minute they came home from the shop. There was no special meaning in that, but somehow it made Eitan's shirts her shirts. Quiet ownership, unspoken, between the man who wore the shirt and the woman who folded it. Even when they were in a public place like the mall. Visible to one and all. Speaking about things that had no softness or special purpose, for instance, the shopping list they had split between them – you go to the stationery store and I'll go to the supermarket because it's more efficient that way – even then, she was the only one in the crowd who knew that this man, the impressive doctor, was wearing a button-down shirt that had no label. Because it caused a rash on the back of his neck. In the precipices of everyday life there was much comfort in that knowledge, even if it wasn't always discernible.

She wasn't a religious person in any way. But she had sacred rituals of her own. The precise rituals of the house. Schnitzels had to soak in marinade or they had no taste. Laundry needed to be folded right after the dryer finished working so that the fabric didn't have time to wrinkle. Cocoa powder had to be mixed well so it didn't have lumps. They whispered their dreams to each other. Asked how it was in nursery school, at work, at school. Watered the garden. Dusted where the cleaner had been careless. Worked hard. Went on trips abroad. Kept a balanced account of guilt and desire, emotional economics that had no flare-ups and no overdrafts. Outside the front door was a crazy country. Not only Arabs and settlers and soldiers. Also the Russian boy who stabbed his friend at the high-school entrance. And the girls she heard in the mall bathroom, betting on who would be the first to vomit up her lunch. Or an Ethiopian security guard who shot at customers and then said he heard voices. And a foreign worker who raped the old lady he was here to look after. She drove 110 kilometers an hour on the toll highway, looking at passing cars, unsure of what she actually shared with those people beyond the road they were driving on. During wartime, it felt different. When sirens sounded announcing that rockets were on their way, everyone got out of their cars and ran toward a shelter, and for a moment it really did make a difference to you what the people around you were feeling, and when it was over you said *we're* fine, not *I'm* fine. But the rest of the time, it was only the house. White walls and walnut parquet. She gave her full attention and constant devotion to running her life in this house. Even if not everything was clean, even if not everything was tidy – everything was in its place. The announcer finished speaking and a clarinet began to play. Liat straightened the hem of Yaheli's tracksuit and tried to remember what the weather forecast was but couldn't, and consoled herself with the knowledge that it didn't matter. The house was heated in any event.

*   *   *

Long after he left the garage, she still felt his gaze on her. Men can fasten their eyes on you the way people put a collar on a dog. They didn't have to tug it; just knowing that the collar was there was enough to make the dog behave. Men could also not look at you at all. Like you're a beetle in the corner of the room they don't even notice, or if they do, there's no reason to talk to it. At most, they flip it on its back to see whether it can turn itself over again. Until she was fourteen, she was that beetle. People saw her without seeing her. Forgot her as soon as they walked past her. Sometimes while they were still walking past her. When she grew up, they looked at her differently. They no longer forgot her. Now they followed her with their eyes as she moved away, watched the intimations of her full, round ass through the folds of her dress. They stared at her when she walked and imagined her when she was gone, but at no point did they ever see her. They merely piled their desire on her, the way jugs of water are tied on a donkey's back.

She came out of the garage and headed toward the caravan, thinking about Asum and the way he used to look at her. The way he looked at her the first time, when she carried the boxes into that shack. At first, she thought it was the heat of the fire that burned her face and stung her eyes. But it wasn't the fire. She knew that because that night, she stayed in the shack for a much longer time waiting for her mother to finally finish talking to the owners, and meanwhile the fire went out, but the heat on her face remained. Asum sat there, frying her with his glance, roasting her well on both sides. Even now, as she walked alone, completely alone but for the distant barking of dogs, she suddenly could feel his glance. As if someone had lit a match under her shirt. It was funny how she felt his glance on her even though he wasn't here to glance at anything anymore, as if a person's glance, like his whistle, could continue even when the person was no longer here.

When she was cleaning off the tables in Davidson's restaurant, she was a beetle again. Sometimes the patrons kept on speaking as she leaned over and picked up the plates, and sometimes they were silent. But they never looked at her, neither with a smile nor a scowl. Only the children, the youngest among them, occasionally made eye contact. Eyes that were curious or frightened, laughing or crying. And she actually wanted to look at them, but averted her gaze immediately. Because she didn't know whether it was allowed.

The first time she arrived at Eitan's house the street was bustling with parents and children. It was morning. The doors opened one after the other. People got into their cars and drove the children to school and themselves to work. Sirkit looked at them, afraid that her presence here would be too conspicuous. She quickly realized that she was wrong. No one was aware of her. Just like when she worked as a cleaner in the Tel Aviv central bus station and her glance met that of the man handing out newspapers. He was a gray-haired Israeli wearing red overalls that had a logo printed on them. She swept the stairs and he handed out newspapers to the people going up and down the stairs. They were surrounded by a great many hurrying feet. Skirts, sandals, soldiers' uniforms and high heels. She swept and he handed out, and for one moment their activities intersected. You might think that they smiled at each other, but that man's eyes had no pupils. They were two dark stains that reflected stairs. And the feet going up and down and up and down. She looked away. Horrified. She didn't need a mirror to know that her eyes were like his. Without pupils. Two dark stains, and stairs.

And that was why the doctor's glance threw her into such turmoil, remained with her long after he'd gone, when she left the garage alone and walked to the caravan. When he looked at her, she wasn't a beetle, or a dog or a donkey. Not an Eritrean woman who cleaned the central bus station and washed dishes at the Tlalim junction. Something else. Not because he wanted to see her differently, but because she had the power to force him to.

(But did he see her? At first, she had been the thing he was running away from. That he was guilty of. Now, when he looked at her, for a brief moment she was the thing he wanted. Always the thing. Never Sirkit.) And somehow, she was sure that even if he thought about her when he was there, in his private home in Omer, even if he carried her with him after he left the garage, he thought about her from the outside. Imagining her cleaning, suffering. It never occurred to him that behind the gas station there was a plastic chair facing a dry stream, and that she sat on it, dug her feet into the warm, pleasant sand and whistled Asum's whistle. The whistle that came back to her one night after she had given up trying to remember it.

She opened the caravan door and collapsed onto the mattress, dead tired. In the twilight of sleep, the doctor came to her. Had she been more awake, she would immediately have driven away that fantasy, so pointless and hopeless. But she was too tired to drive away the fantasy and too tired to tame the desire, and maybe that was good. Because when she allowed herself to want him that way, lying on the mattress in the caravan behind the gas station, she was actually saying – to him and to herself – yes. She was allowed to want.

The guilt did not come until dawn. Why him, of all people? Why such a perverse choice? She didn't understand that she had chosen him precisely because he was such a perverse choice. That her first desire would be defiant. Shameless. Because if she felt guilty, it wasn't because of that desire, but because of all the things she hadn't desired before. Guilty because of all the things she dared not do. And it was true, there was no reason to dare, and she had to be in the restaurant in another ten minutes. But she was allowed to want. At least to want.

(But if they knew, those people on the mattresses beside her. If they only guessed what was under her blanket. What was there while she slept. They would tell her to be ashamed of herself. Or they would shun her completely. And they wouldn't know that she shunned herself for the opposite reason. They would shun her because of her desire and she would shun herself because of its absence. She would shun the previous Sirkit, who let the world treat her that way for so long. She knew she was guilty, endlessly guilty, because she would have stayed. For her entire life, she would have stayed.)

8

T HE NEXT DAY she suddenly came to him in the shower. One minute he was shampooing his hair and the next he had a huge erection, a high-school kid's erection, thinking about her. Perhaps that should have made him happy. Caused him to feel strong and masculine, the kind of person who, after going a month without sleeping, is still able to think about sex. But somehow it upset him, even embarrassed him, because the soundtrack of *March of the Penguins* was coming from the living room and Liat was washing dishes and shouting at Yaheli to turn it down. He stood there, listening to the sounds coming from outside, shampoo running into his eyes, and his prick screamed Sirkit. It embarrassed him, even rattled him. Why was his desire for her sneaking in here like this? Sneaking through the bathroom window ever so quietly, attracting no notice? Emptying the house while Liat was in the kitchen and the children in front of the TV? He told himself it was only a fantasy, and where else but in his fantasies could he still do whatever he felt like. But that didn't placate him. Just the opposite. The thought that he could fantasize about her – more than could, was *compelled* to fantasize about her almost against his will – that thought drove him mad.

And she wasn't even that beautiful. True, she had that imposing height. Those gigantic eyes. A perfect body he could only barely ignore. But damn it, he'd already seen more gorgeous breasts in his life. He knew more beautiful women. He was married to one. (And yet, something in those sphinx eyes. The feeling that if he simply reached out and touched her shoulder, he would drown in the velvet of her skin.)

He rinsed the shampoo out of his hair and reminded himself that the world was full of women with velvety skin and enigmatic eyes. Such qualities definitely deserved to be admired, but there was no reason to get carried away about it. His prick, however, was not persuaded. It maintained its commanding pose. Eitan refused to submit. He usually felt comfortable enough about jerking off in the shower. It happened at least once a week, and except for a vague sense of guilt, a vestige of adolescence, he saw nothing wrong with it. But today there was something humiliating about the demand of his body. It angered him. As if he weren't submitting to his body, but to her. And he had already submitted to her enough.

But he didn't think it was the submission that was so seductive to him. Because her velvety skin was nothing compared to the intoxicating feeling of being controlled by someone else. She was the only, secret witness to all the things that were never spoken: what a coward he was, how pathetic. He hated her because of that, and he did everything he could to get rid of her because of that, while at the same time, and against his will, she was the only one who knew him for what he was.

The water streamed down his body and he stood in the shower and thought about her. Then he turned off the faucet and reached for a towel.

Eitan went out of the bathroom and Liat went in. Wiped the steam of his shower off the mirror. Reminded herself to buy anti-dandruff shampoo because the bottle here was almost empty. She brushed her teeth with the toothpaste dentists recommended. Spit water, saliva and toothpaste foam into the sink, noticing some drops of blood that clouded the mixture. Her gums were giving her trouble again. She should see a hygienist. She opened her mouth wide and looked inside through the mirror, but not for too long. Liat knew: if you stare long enough, everything begins to look strange. Even your face in the mirror. When she was a child, she'd spent hours in the bathroom examining her features. Trying to determine what came from Mom and what came from Dad, not always succeeding. She preferred to take as little as possible from him, but had to admit that the jaw was his. And the dimples. A man wakes up one morning and goes to live with his Ronit, leaving you with two dimples and a pointy chin. Every time you smile, you see your mother's eyes moving to the dimples and wonder if she's thinking about him.

In the long hours spent in front of the mirror, she tried to remove the dimples from her cheeks, without much success. She also tried to make a final decision about the eyebrows – his or hers. And always, when she'd looked at herself for a really long, continuous period of time, the moment came when the face in front of her turned into a different face. Not a reflection, but a deflection. The same eyes, nose chin, forehead. But even so, a different girl. And the eyes – she wasn't all that sure anymore that they were eyes. And the nose and chin began to unravel. Meaningless shapes. One moment of concentration was enough for the feeling to disappear, and she would once again be Liat in front of the mirror, nothing more. But sometimes she deliberately delayed that moment, staring in amazement at the accumulation of unfamiliar shapes that were, in fact, her face. Like that game when you keep repeating the same word until it dissolves on your tongue. The end touches the beginning touches the end. For example: bananabananabananabanana, until you can't tell where it begins and where it ends, and even the familiar sound is suddenly different, alien. The words unravel into syllables and the syllables unravel into sounds, and where the sounds unravel, there is only deep water, a thousand streams of blue through which the light cannot pass. If you look long enough, everything begins to be strange. Your words. Your face. Your man. So it's very important to know when to stop. To walk away from the bathroom mirror a moment before it gets really frightening. To brush your teeth and go to sleep in a room where you don't have to turn on the light to find your way. Because everything is in its place.

9

THE TASTE OF THE TEA she'd given him was still in his mouth as he drove toward the garage, three days later. Hot, sweet, soothing. When he emerged from the SUV, she came out to greet him and he said the same "good evening" to her that he said to the nurses at the beginning of his shift. A slightly reserved greeting – no doctor was happy about starting an exhausting night shift, but they still greeted the nurses because they clearly weren't to blame for the shifts, which were just something that had to be done. He thought he might be able to see his visits to the garage that way – a tiring obligation that was no one's fault, a chore he had to complete with a minimum of thought. But she, instead of returning a "good evening" with the submissive smile of a nurse, gestured for him to follow her. And once again, the controller became the controlled, the authoritative doctor doling out generous greetings became the extorted doctor stumbling into another unpredictable encounter. Once again, he hated her.

Lying on the table was a large muscular man with a battered face. His loud, labored breathing split the air of the garage in two. He shook. Eitan looked at the muscles of the large man's hands, which tensed under the skin with every wheeze and cough. Bedouin smugglers or Egyptian soldiers – someone had beaten the living daylights out of this man. He was lucky to have reached the border. Grudgingly, he admired this black giant who had traveled such an arduous path to get here. Until now, he had never asked the patients' names. He saw them one after another: a scratched hand followed by a broken leg followed by stress fractures followed by a snakebite followed by gunshot wounds. A long chain of bodies and injuries, foot after foot, hand after hand, an endless black centipede. Until now, he had never tried to differentiate between them. Seeing them as one lump made it easier for him to forget them when he got into the suv and finally drove home, close to dawn. But now he was curious to know the name of this man who should have fallen down dead, yet was still here. The nobility of his face attracted him, the tired smile on his lips even when they were distorted by yet another cough.

He took the money of the people who were with him in the camp in Egypt. He grabbed them one at a time and because he's big, they had no choice. He arrived here last night. This time, when they met him, they were in a large group.

Eitan looked again at the man on the table. The only one whose name he wanted to know was nothing more than a thief. Yet it was his face that looked so aristocratic, a face that held a secret.

"So they beat him up and then called a doctor?"

Sirkit shrugged. *They wanted to punish him, they didn't want him to die.*

He went over to the man. Clammy skin. Rapid pulse. Increased abdominal sensitivity.

"Did they hit him in the stomach?"

She didn't reply. Perhaps she didn't know the answer. Perhaps she thought it was obvious. He checked the stomach again. When he touched the upper left quadrant, the man cried out.

"If you don't want him to die, I have to take him to Soroka."

She smiled at him as if he were a child. She didn't even try to argue.

"The man needs surgery," he said, "this much internal bleeding is not something to play around with."

He won't go to Soroka, she said, *he's from southern Sudan. Everyone from his area has already been deported. If they catch him, it won't be a detention center, it'll be a quick exit out of here.*

"But first they'll operate on him."

And then deport him.

"Sirkit, if this man doesn't go to the hospital, he'll die."

Not if you operate on him here.

"I can't operate on someone in a garage. It's irresponsible. And extremely dangerous."

She looked at him, her smile even broader than before (how much she reminded him now of the wolf from "Little Red Riding Hood". Who knew what lay in this woman's stomach).

We'll see.

*   *   *

She watched him as he left in a rage. Even when he was angry, there was something relaxed about the way he walked. As if deep inside his body knew that nothing bad would happen to it. If she asked him about it, he wouldn't know what she was talking about, but anyone who saw truly frightened people could spot someone who was not ruled by fear. Of course, her doctor knew fear. Maybe a stray dog had attacked him once, or something had happened to him in that army of theirs. But for him, fear was an uninvited guest, definitely not a permanent resident. His eyes told her that. The direct way he looked at people. Frightened people do not look directly at others to keep from arousing disapproval or rebuke. Frightened people lower their eyes, blink, do not dare to demand a bit of someone else's face with their glance. That's how they are when they work in Davidson's restaurant. That's how they are in Bedouin camps. Eyes staring at the ground of the Sinai Desert, eyes staring at the ceramic tile floor at the Tlalim junction. Never raised, defiant eyes: I am here.

Eitan didn't know that a glance was freedom. But Sirkit did. And whenever she saw him get out of the suv and survey the patients as he walked to the garage, anger rose in her. His smug, unhurried gait, his indifferent glance. Of all the Eritreans standing at the garage door, she was the only one who looked the doctor in the eye. If anyone else dared to raise his glance, it would be accompanied by an obsequious: *I am here – do what you want with me.* Hers were the only eyes that persisted in asserting: *I am here – do what I want.* For the first few days, that was the only thing in her glance – *do what I want.* Then, when she saw that he was indeed doing what she wanted, she was tempted into examining the other possibilities held in a glance. Beyond the freedom lay the pleasure. She could look at him for hours. Study the curves of his lips. The line of his chin. The shape of his nose. Wonder about every single part of his body – beautiful or not. It was hard to know what gave her more pleasure – looking at Eitan or the knowledge that she could look as much as she wanted.

She knew – at some point during one of those nights, he began looking at her as well. She asked herself what he saw. And after a while, she also wondered what she saw. At first, she thought she saw Eitan, but as time passed she grew unsure. If fate had delivered a different doctor to her that night, would she still look at him this way? Did it even matter whether his eyes were gray or brown, if his nose was bulbous or long? Maybe not. Maybe the only thing that mattered was: a white man. And when he looked at her, did it matter if she was tall or short, fat or thin? Did the sound of her laughter matter? Her smell? Or simply: a black woman.

But no, that way there could be no desire. Desire needed one clear thing – *his* lips. Only them. Otherwise, it was impossible. If it made no difference whether his eyes were brown or gray, if it didn't matter whether his name was Eitan or Yoel, then there was no urgency. No pressing, burning need for *it*. For it and only it. And that was a good thing. Anything else would be a disaster. She had to guard carefully everything she had and not want too much. But sometimes, at night, as she lay on her mattress, her hand between her thighs, she wondered: Maybe. Maybe, after all, those specific eyes. That frightened her so much that she quickly turned onto her side and went to sleep. She only hoped that Asum heard her thoughts in his kingdom of demons, and was going mad.

Now she followed him with her eyes as he left the garage, angry. She saw him get into the SUV, slam the door and start driving back to his life, to forget this place for a few hours. Forget her. And she pictured, not for the first time, flames consuming the private house in Omer.

When he reached home, his heart was still pounding rapidly. He had to stop himself from slamming the SUV door angrily. The last thing he wanted to do now was wake somebody. But when he went into the house, he found Liat sitting on the couch, awake. For a moment, he thought she knew. Everything. And was surprised to discover how much of a relief that thought was. She knew he'd lied to her, she knew he'd run over a man and driven away. Yet she was sitting there in the living room wearing his T-shirt, which was too big for her. She was angry, disgusted, judgmental – but she was here.

"How was your shift?"

"Okay." And a moment later, "Why aren't you sleeping?"

She said there was no real reason, work stuff, and he should go to sleep. He said there had to be a reason, something was bothering her, and he wouldn't be able to fall asleep now anyway. So she told him about the Bedouin kid they'd arrested two days before, that at first she'd questioned him about a stolen car and then, almost by chance, she'd solved the case of the Eritrean's hit and run. It took time. The kid confessed that he was driving an SUV near Tlalim on the night of the accident, but he insisted, he actually swore that he didn't hit anyone. They didn't know what to do. It was clear that someone else was with him in the car – a potential witness – but the kid refused to say a word about him no matter how much they threatened him. Marciano finally agreed to send a forensics team to the site, but since almost four weeks had passed, they didn't find anything. She gave up – without a confession, and with only some featherweight circumstantial evidence, there was no way anything would come of it. But then Cheetah asked for ten minutes with the kid, and when he came out the Bedouin immediately signed a confession, no arguments. And yes, she was supposed to be happy now but...

"But what?"

Liat sat in the dark living room and replied to the question without noticing the paleness of the face that uttered it, the strange quaver of his vocal cords, the hands of the man clutching the couch backrest like a drowning man clutching a rope.

"That Cheetah, I don't really know him yet, but I don't trust him. Esti told me today that they almost fired him this year for insubordination. And after the kid signed the confession, I went into his cell and saw that his left thumb was completely broken. He said it was from before the arrest, but I'm not sure. Maybe Cheetah scared him, who knows."

Liat leaned her head on the couch backrest and closed her eyes. When she opened them, her husband was still sitting on the couch, speaking in a voice that wasn't his. "He didn't do it."

In the darkness of the living room, she looked at Eitan. It wasn't only the voice that wasn't his. It was also the color of his face. The glitter in his eyes. Suddenly, it was clear to her that the man sitting in the living room now was different from the man who had come in. She saw it, but didn't know why. Maybe she bored him with her investigation stories. He'd come home from work dead tired and had felt obligated to ask her to tell him. But he didn't look bored. More like a wax figure of himself. Like that museum in London when you stand as close as you can to John Lennon but know that there's not even a single internal organ behind the shiny skin, and if you peer inside that mouth, it will be hollow all the way down to the feet.

She sat up on the couch, tried to make eye contact. Eitan didn't look at her, stared into space, and Liat thought that if he wasn't bored, then maybe he was sick. Or more tired than usual. Maybe he'd fought with someone at work, or had gotten into another hypothetical argument with Zakai on the drive home. But then he looked at her again and repeated, "He didn't do it," in a voice that shook so much that she went and got him a glass of water, saying, "Don't tell me you caught a virus in the department again. Last time the whole house was sick for a month." He drank some water. She put her hand on his forehead and was glad to discover that it wasn't hot. Maybe just a tiny bit.

"I don't think he did it either. At first, when I found out he was at Tlalim that night, I was sure the case was solved. But the more I think about that kid, the more sure I am that he isn't capable of doing something like that."

A pale moon illuminated the living room through the window. Outside, the rosemary bushes trembled in a light gust of wind. Liat looked at them for a long time. "I'm thinking of going to his village. I want to find the person who was with him in the car and question him without Cheetah getting in my hair. I want to understand what happened there."

Eitan was silent. Liat was silent. She wanted him to say something. She'd waited hours for him to finally come home tonight, to come home and calm her down. And although in her heart she had granted him full permission to go to sleep when he came home from his shift, she was happy that he had insisted on asking what was bothering her. She'd wanted to tell him. And now he was sitting on the couch beside her, removed and silent, and though she reminded herself that he was wiped out and maybe sick as well, she realized that she felt hurt. It wasn't fair to be angry at him, she told herself, distancing herself from the hurt, not happy that in doing so she was also distancing herself from Eitan. Because when she stood up, the longing that had turned into hurt now turned into the sort of coldness that lasts through the night. Only four hours later, when she woke the kids for nursery school, he said to her, "Investigate some more. I'm sure he didn't do it," but she was already too distant from him, nodded distractedly and said, "See you in the afternoon," and then became even colder when he said, "Not today. After-hour surgeries."

10

WHAT CHOICE DID HE HAVE? He waited until seven in the morning and called Visotski. Before leaving the garage, he had bombarded the Sudanese with fluids and managed to get him stabilized, but it was only a matter of time before his condition began deteriorating again, and he knew that he had to hurry. It took twenty rings for the anaesthetist to finally answer, and even then he didn't sound as if he were really awake. Eitan told him what he wanted and Visotski said nothing for a long time. Eitan was beginning to think that he'd fallen asleep again, but then Visotski spoke. He said that he was really sorry, but Eitan would have to manage on his own. There were a lot of things he was ready to do for a friend, but he wouldn't steal an anaesthesia machine in a van, and he definitely wouldn't perform any operations in a garage. Visotski was no Physician for Human Rights, and if Eitan had any sense he would get himself as far away as he could from that business; he couldn't understand why he'd got involved in it in the first place.

Eitan said, "Visotski, I need you," and Visotski was silent. This time it clearly wasn't because he'd fallen asleep. Eitan took a long breath and reminded Visotski about something he didn't want to remind him about. The narcotics that sometimes disappeared during long surgeries. The department investigation, which found nothing because Eitan told no one about the time he saw Visotski take home five grams of morphine. Visotski remained silent, but now his silence was different. Finally, he spoke about his son. A year ago, a kid from school had hit him on the head with a rock and he hadn't opened his eyes since. Eitan said he knew. And that was the only reason he hadn't told anyone.

"I've stopped all that," Visotski said. "It was only for a few months, just so I could keep going. I haven't touched the stuff for two months."

Eitan knew that as well. He'd sworn to himself that if Visotski filched any more narcotics, he'd report him. He'd been checking the storeroom carefully since that time, and it was true that nothing had been taken.

"So what do you want from me now?" Visotski asked.

"I want you to help me. The way I helped you."

"And if I don't?"

This time, Eitan was the one who said nothing.

It was almost ten when they reached the garage. Visotski had a key to the hospital's large supply room, and taking an old anaesthesia machine out of there was almost unbearably easy. It was much more difficult explaining to Prof. Shakedi why he wouldn't be in that day. The head of the department did not exactly look at him with affection, what with all the changes in his shifts he'd been asking for recently. It would have been different if he had sucked up to them during his first months here, as a new doctor was expected to do. But he was busy licking his wounds – Prof. Zakai's slap in the face still stung and he forgot to worry about politics. How could he have known that, a few months later, he'd have to switch shifts constantly. In the end, Shakedi let him go, but he didn't look at all pleased, and Eitan knew that he hadn't heard the end of it.

Sirkit was waiting for them at the entrance. She'd washed everything twice, and had also sterilized all of it with the antiseptic Eitan had brought last time. He told her to clean everything again. It wasn't good enough. He looked at her as she scrubbed the floor, kneeling on the ground. It felt good, seeing her like that. It diverted his attention from the fact that the last time he'd opened someone's stomach was during his rotation in general surgery. And more than twenty years had passed since then. He'd been watching abdominal operations on his iPhone since morning, but that didn't really calm him down. You don't learn how to swim through a correspond-ence course, and you don't learn how to operate by watching YouTube. He shifted his glance from Sirkit to the Sudanese lying on the table. The patient was undoubtedly more stressed than he was, but considering the situation, that was understandable. The only one who looked calm was Visotski, who plugged the respirator into a socket and placed a generator next to it, just in case. They hadn't exchanged a word since Eitan had picked him up. He barely looked at Sirkit or the Sudanese they were about to operate on in a garage. Eitan knew that he'd served in the Russian army before emigrating to Israel, and asked himself if that was how you spend three years in a tank in the middle of Siberia – press OFF and disconnect.

Should we start?

And suddenly, he realized that she was also keyed up. Her voice was steady and her eyes had their same usual coldness, but something in the way she stood was different. When Visotski placed the mask on the Sudanese's face, Eitan turned to her, intending to suggest that she leave. In another minute there would be some unpleasant sights here. But when he looked over at her, he saw that she was far from being frightened. She looked at the Sudanese with fascination, her lips slightly open with childlike wonder. When the surgical scissors pierced the Sudanese's skin, he looked up and studied Sirkit again. If she was planning to faint, she should do it now. But Sirkit showed no intention of fainting. She observed the incision with such interest that it was doubtful she had seen Eitan look at her.

"Scalpel."

At first, she didn't react. Perhaps she thought he was talking to Visotski. But a few seconds later, she looked up and her glance met the doctor's. Gray eyes and black eyes. She handed him the scalpel. He didn't say thank you, didn't even nod, but from that moment on, through all the hours that followed, he treated her the way he treated every operating-room nurse.

*   *   *

And in the midst of all that, the humiliation of the desire.

(But him, of all people? Him? Didn't she understand how much that desire humiliated her? How could she even think that she would want him, and how could she still be the dishrag she had been. Still pathetic. Even though she had freedom, she still chose the ridiculous, humiliating thing. Humiliating humiliating humiliating. She didn't pay attention for one minute, and a new weakness snuck inside her, as if the ones she had were not enough. And much more than the humiliation of the attraction itself, the reason for it was humiliating, the truth of that desire. And the truth was that she owed everything she had to this man and his suv. Owed everything to someone else's bad luck. She had received her life as a gift from someone who had never intended to give it to her. How could she not want him for that. How could she not hate him for that.)

He didn't think about her on the way home. The suv raced along the asphalt and he didn't think about her. He thought about the patient, about the operation, about how easily it could have ended differently. A wave of adrenaline surged through his body, and he didn't think about her. He thought about death and how he had managed to beat the crap out of it today. He thought about Prof. Zakai and the expression he would certainly have had on his face if he had seen that operation. At first, everything looked simple, they removed the spleen without difficulty, but then… what a mess. Visotski thought the Sudanese was a goner. He saw it with his own eyes. Eitan also thought that the Sudanese was a goner. No makeshift hospital could handle that amount of abdominal bleeding, and certainly not if the chief surgeon was a neurosurgeon, an expert in opening brains who hadn't touched a person's abdomen in more than a decade. When the bleeding continued after the splenectomy, it was already clear that it was over, that man was going to die and all the IV fluids in the world couldn't help. Then suddenly he had the idea to dissect, to look for the source of the bleeding in the lower branches of the splenic artery. It took half an hour but he found that bleeding branch and tied it off. Even Zakai himself might have failed here. For a moment, he was sorry he couldn't tell him. In fact, he couldn't tell anyone. The most glorious moment in his career, the moment that made studying medicine worthwhile. An operation that didn't happen on a patient who didn't exist. And maybe it was better that way. Because even the secret had a taste of its own: a pleasurable sweet bitterness that was still on his tongue when he went into the house. He wouldn't tell anyone what had happened in the garage that night. An adult's pride and a child's joy, both would remain inside him, behind sealed lips. But even if his lips could not speak, they could still find other ways to express that bitter sweetness. He leaned over Liat and kissed her as she slept, moving his tongue along her soft neck. She opened her sleepy, surprised eyes. It had been years since he'd woken her up to fuck. And he surprised himself as well, but only momentarily, because the next moment he shook off the surprise and attacked her soft, round breasts, her nipples hardening under his hand. At first, she drew back. The hurt feelings and the anger, and more than a little bitterness were still there, in bed with them. But his passion was so great and so infectious that cold remoteness seemed like a total waste. Liat and Eitan held each other, their fingers spread, their legs intertwined, in their peaceful bedroom in Omer, behind shuttered eyes.

(He didn't think about her smell wafting toward him when she bent over the patient. Didn't think about the sigh she would utter at the moment of penetration, when he would finally know her from the inside, and even then, wouldn't know her enough.)

Sadness always waited for her at the far edge of her orgasm. One minute all was sweetness, and the next everything was spoiled. Her husband was between her thighs, heavy and sticky, and suddenly she was acutely aware of the uncomfortable angle of his head on her shoulder. She was still breathing heavily, erratically, but the heat that had been flowing through her body a moment ago vanished and the coldness of the air began to be palpable. Once again it wasn't clear who had been moaning a moment ago, bent under the weight of enormous, inconceivable fullness. And the words she had whispered to him hoarsely were now embarrassing, hanging in the air. She got up, turned on the light and went into the bathroom. He stayed in bed, eyes closed, a self-satisfied half-smile on his lips. How much gentleness there was in the way he lay there. How much confidence. A few minutes later he joined her, still fuzzy, and kissed her on the lips with a mouth that was all body. All the kisses and licking and tasting of her were returned to her in that kiss, from his mouth to hers. Meanwhile, she washed between her legs where it was sometimes sticky and sometimes slightly painful. She said it was great, because it truly had been. But she didn't say that it had made her sad as well because what could he actually do with that information. He washed himself quickly and told her that her body was one immense amusement park. He'd been telling her that for years, and for years she'd smiled. Then he took a towel and went out, leaving her to wash his semen from between her thighs and her sadness from her chest.

*   *   *

Sirkit knew that it was all because the sun rose on the wrong side here, came from the desert and fell into the water. Sun should come from the water, clean. When the sun comes to you from the sand, your days are never really clean. There, in the village, the men used to get up before dawn to go fishing, and the women went with them because a person can't enter something big like the sea in something small like a boat without a pair of eyes watching him from the land. The men and the women would go down to the shore together, not talking much, because at that time of day every word that hits the air is like the beat of a drum. Not long after that, the sun would come from where it was supposed to come from: the sea, red and beautiful, like a baby coming from the womb. When they saw it come out like that, the men and women felt clean and new, as if they themselves were born from the sea. And they began the day like that, clean and new. But here, in this country, the sun comes out of the land, dirty and dusty. On their knees, bent over the cartons in Davidson's storeroom, the workers lifted their heads when it rose, looked at it for a moment and saw that it was dirty like them, filthy with dust and mud and tired even before seven in the morning.

At 5:30 in the morning, on her knees in the storeroom, she thought about her captive doctor, trying to guess how he slept. On which side of the bed, for example. And what he wore, if anything. Hugging his wife or not hugging her, and if he did hug her – did he do it because he wanted to or out of force of habit? She thought about the sheets, amusing herself with thoughts of red satin versus white cotton, in the end going with the cotton, because satin was definitely too sensuous for him, too erotic. And she was already drawing a small circle of saliva on the pillow, a masculine arm flung across the mattress, quiet, calm breathing. Did he dream or not? And if so – what about?

That's enough, she said to herself as she straightened up, moving on to the next carton. She had neither the intention nor the ability to guess the dreams of the white man lying on the white cotton sheets in his whitewashed home in Omer.

And suddenly she wanted him to wake up, wanted to throw him out of bed. Yank the pillow with the small, innocent circle of saliva on it from under his head. Grab the limp hand and give it a good shaking. Bend over his head, the hair dotted with its first flowering of gray, and scream her lungs out. Or maybe she'd do the opposite, slip as quietly as the sunset into the narrow space between him and his wife. Smell the cotton sheets. Her. Him. Wallow in the mud of their dreams. The sun rose out of the dust and Sirkit bent over the cartons, all the while screaming, raging, hugging and moaning in the peaceful bedroom in Omer.

PART TWO

1

ONLY AFTER SHE STEPPED OUT of the cruiser did she think that maybe it hadn't been such a good idea to come here alone. In less than five minutes, fifteen people had gathered around her, most of them young men. Other eyes, female eyes, peered at her from the tin shacks. A dog barked loudly. She couldn't tell if the barking was directed at her or simply a general statement to the world. Either way it stopped when one of the young men picked up a stone and threw it at the dog's head. That calmed her down, because the barking had begun to be really frightening. But it also worried her to see the dark-skinned fist close around the stone, throw it and hit its target.

She was dying to put her hand on the butt of her gun, but forced herself to walk with her hands hanging loosely at her sides. What was she actually doing here? She was completely blinded, but didn't want to rummage around in her bag for her sunglasses. Maybe she could turn around. Drive to the precinct. Turn her head away when she passed the kid's cell. He didn't look when she walked by anyway. Kept his brown eyes glued to the floor as if he found the dead roaches lying on it the most interesting things in the world. Yesterday, she'd tried to ask him about his confession and he hadn't said a word, but his hand had moved instinctively to his broken thumb. He pulled it away a second later, but she had managed to see it, and he knew she had. Her grandmother always used to tell her not to get it wrong – you should never pay too much attention to what people tell you with their mouths. It's their bodies that tell you everything you need to know. But what would her grandmother say about a Bedouin kid who hadn't said a word for a day and a half already, and his body was, on the one hand, as slight as a bird's, and on the other, hard, really hard, with those bristles, that veiled look.

She looked at the faces of young men around her and said to herself that they looked like him. Brothers, or cousins. Or maybe it was just that they all looked alike with their faded clothes, bristles, hooded eyes. Maybe the similarity she saw among them said more about her than it did about them. Because now, glancing at them again, she realized that they were looking at her more with curiosity than with animosity. And when she maintained eye contact long enough, one of them even smiled at her, and the kid next to him broke the silence, saying, "*Ahalan*," and suddenly she heard "*Ahalan*" and "*Salam alaikum*" coming from every direction, and although she also felt a slight wave of "what-do-you-want-here" hostility, she was ashamed of herself for having been so anxious to touch her gun.

"I came to talk to the family of Ali abu Ayad." One of the boys walked away from the group toward one of the tin shacks. Even before he reached the door, a bearded man came out and Liat understood that he had been watching from inside since the moment she'd arrived. A woman wearing a burka walked out behind him. The burka did not hide how large she was. At least 100 kilos. The man reached out to shake Liat's hand. His was a rough hand with a Rolex on the wrist that Liat avoided looking at so she wouldn't have to wonder how he had come by it. "Shalom, we are Ali's parents." The Hebrew came easily to him, unlike his son.

"Do you know that he has been arrested for stealing a car?"

Once again she thought she shouldn't have come here alone, and this time the hostile noises coming from the young men around her only reinforced that thought. But the bearded man continued to smile as he replied, "We know, but it wasn't Ali. Our boy is as good as gold, thank God." The "thank God" was spoken a bit more loudly. The words gleamed above the dusty ground. Defiant, incongruous, like the Rolex on his calloused hand.

"I'm less concerned about the car at the moment," she said, and explained that she was more worried about the fact that the boy had confessed to running over and killing a man two weeks earlier, near Tlalim.

The bearded man stopped smiling. The woman behind him froze. When she spoke behind her burka, Liat was surprised by the contrast between the black sack of coal standing in front of her and the delicate voice that emerged from it. "Ali did not do that."

Liat looked into the woman's eyes. "I'm looking for some-one who was in the car that night to give evidence." The air filled with muttering in Arabic. The young men whispered to each other. Those who understood translated for those who didn't, and those who thought they didn't understand asked in order to confirm that they actually did, and the commotion grew louder from moment to moment – until it stopped all at once. One minute they were all talking, and suddenly they were silent. There was no mistaking that silence. Once again, she wanted to place her hand on the butt of her gun, and once again she forced herself not to. The woman in the burka spoke again, her delicate voice resonating among the tin shacks. "We don't know who was with him, and it doesn't matter. What matters is that he didn't do it."

"He himself said he did it. Maybe he said it so we wouldn't try to find the other thief. I don't know. But it would help him a lot if the person who was there came to the station with me."

There was another flood of murmuring in Arabic, this time even stronger. More and more young men were gathering around in a circle. Behind them, women were coming out of the shacks, faces covered, wrapped in burkas, and beside them young girls in faded skirts and long-sleeved blouses despite the heat. A barefoot toddler of about three ran to the center of the circle with a cry of joy, delighted with the attention. He held a bag of peanut-flavor snacks in his hand and continued to clutch it when his mother swooped him up and scolded him. The voices died down slowly until all was silent again. Liat scanned the young men's faces, searching for a trembling lip, frightened eyes, an attempt to flee. Instead, she found quiet, blazing anger.

Finally, the bearded man spoke again. Not to Liat, but to the young men. He spoke and looked at their faces, his glance moving from one to the other, lingering on each of them. When he finished, his wife spoke again, her delicate voice rising and falling in what Liat suddenly realized was actually weeping. The woman was crying behind her veil. You couldn't see the tears, but tremors shook her entire body and her voice broke in the middle of a sentence. The boys looked at the bearded man and his sobbing wife, some surprised, some sad. But none of them uttered a sound. None of them stepped forward and said "It was me."

And then a young girl did. At first, no one realized that she had done it, that she had stepped forward. It seemed as if she might be looking for her little brother, to admonish him to come home. But she stood in front of Liat and said, "It was me." Then everything happened very quickly. The bearded man opened a pair of bewildered eyes, not understanding. His wife, however, understood immediately; it was her wails of sorrow that made it clear to Liat that she had to get the hell out of there. The young men were still standing there watching the goings-on, but some of the older ones had already taken out cell phones and were punching in numbers, maybe trying to reach their fathers. Liat told the girl to come with her and headed for the car. Her biggest fear was that the girl would begin to run. When you run, people understand that they're supposed to chase you. But the girl walked slowly, almost too slowly. As if now that she had revealed her secret, she no longer had the strength for anything else. Liat opened the door for her and started the car. In a few seconds, the cluster of tin shacks had disappeared. She breathed a sigh of relief when they turned off the dusty dirt road onto the asphalt road leading to Beersheba.

"He won't look at me, that kid. I'm telling you Tani, he won't talk to me. If I hadn't gone to his village, he'd be spending the rest of his life in prison, but he still doesn't get that. He's angry at me for exposing their romance. Would he rather be convicted of manslaughter? And his girlfriend, Mona, she's really kind of sweet. I asked them to let her sit in his cell with him for a little while, and they kissed when they thought I couldn't see. Then Cheetah threw her out – he's still pissed off at me. He should thank me for not digging into that business of the broken finger. It's very convenient for everyone to think that the kid confessed in order to protect her, but if all he wanted was to hide his relationship with Mona from his family, it was enough just to keep quiet about who was with him. He didn't confess because of her, he confessed because Cheetah hit him. Probably threatened him, too. But the minute she showed up, it was clear that the confession was a load of crap. He didn't even go there that night to steal a car, he just wanted to fool around with his girlfriend in peace. And the alibi she gave him was foolproof, a good story the way only a true story can be. It seems they weren't even near Tlalim when the Eritrean was run over – he took her home at two, which is when her shift at the gas station ends. And that Eritrean, he wasn't run

172

over until almost dawn. Can you believe how close we were to throwing someone in prison for no reason?"

Yes, he believed it. He slowly sipped the tea with the lemongrass Liat had picked from the garden, and he believed it. And as he sipped, he asked himself – what if that Mona hadn't stepped forward. If she hadn't said that he didn't run over anyone, she was with him. At what point would he himself have stepped forward? When would he have gone to the lead detective, who just happened to be his wife, and told her that they had to talk? No, not about the mortgage. And not about the kid Yaheli bit in nursery school. Something else.

"You're not listening to me," she said. He looked up from his cup of tea, expecting to see her face blazing with anger. But instead he saw tired, sad eyes.

"I'm sorry," he said, "I'm just tired."

She was quiet for a moment, then said, "But it's not just today, Tani. You haven't been listening to me for a long time now. Weeks." He wanted to tell her that it was exactly thirty-four days that he hadn't been listening to her, and not only her – he didn't hear the words Yaheli made up when he sang in the bath, a mishmash of gibberish and real words that used to make them roar with laughter once. He didn't hear Itamar's questions about dragons and dinosaurs – if there are dinosaurs, why can't there be dragons too? He didn't hear what people said to him at work either, which was a problem because even if he didn't screw up during surgery, they noticed that he wasn't really there. He wanted to say all that, and instead he said, "I'm sorry, Tul, it's just a bad time."

Liat looked at him for another moment, opened her mouth to say something, then stopped. She, of all people, who made him laugh so hard when she quoted her grandmother, who said she should always say what she thought "because words you don't say give you constipation". At the time, he told her that in his family it was just the opposite – when he was a kid, his father explained to him that if you talk too much, you use up all your words and have to be silent for the rest of your life.

"And that scared you so much that you turned into a miser with your words?"

"Me? A miser?"

"Really, Eitan," (she hadn't started calling him Tani yet), "senior members of the Mossad give out more information than you." She'd been right. He really didn't talk very much. He preferred to keep himself to himself. But with her, it was different. Only with her did he really say what he thought (how much he hated Yuval because their parents loved him more. And how much he hated himself for hating him. How scared he was that he might not be able to make his dream of becoming a neurosurgeon come true. How much he loved her pussy). During their first year together, he said things he had never dared to say even to himself. And even if he had begun to censor himself more in the years that came after that, he was still always proud that he and Liat were almost completely open with each other (except for that conversation about fantasies of other people, which had really been unnecessary). Now he was silent, had been silent for an entire month, and from day to day that silence was becoming heavier, hungrier, devouring larger and larger pieces of what had once been his life.

That morning, after a tense twenty-minute silence, Eitan was horrified to discover how relieved he was when his wife said, "Okay, I have to get to work." And he was even more alarmed to realize, in the midst of their equally strained dinner, that he was anxiously awaiting the moment that the hands of the clock would send him to the garage.

The truth was that he was always angry these days. Embraced Liat in the bedroom in Omer and was angry that her body wasn't *her* body. Worked in the garage, centimeters away from Sirkit and was angry about her presence, which was insinuating itself inside him. Why? Who was she that he wanted her so much? In the middle of the night, he got into the suv, left a woman staring and silent and returned to a woman sleeping and silent. The hands on the steering wheel belonged to someone else. Clipped nails. Marriage band. The hands of a stranger. But the desire that drove in the suv with him, the attraction that wove its web inside him all night as he worked beside her in the garage – they too were alien to him. Something external that wrapped itself around him, something that happened to him without his having chosen it. And so he lived, cut off from himself by his own desire, like patients who came in with a urine sample they held as far away from their bodies as they could – this has nothing to do with me!

Once again, she didn't speak a word to him all night. She looked at him as she sterilized and cleaned and tended to patients. Handed him the instruments he asked for and was silent. Between patients, he glanced at her briefly. If she noticed, she showed no sign. Most of the time she stood with her back to him, gazing through the garage door at a night as dark and opaque as her eyes.

What did she see there? What was she thinking about? He peered outside as well, as if that were enough for him to see through his eyes what she saw through hers. But outside the garage there was only darkness, and everyone placed their own treasures in that darkness. He was barred from her night.

When the last patient had gone, he took off his gloves and went out to the SUV. She was sterilizing the rusty iron table and nodded goodbye to him. He'd been there six hours and they had not exchanged a single word. He couldn't explain what was bothering him. Most of the time, he liked working in silence. Other doctors listened to music while they operated. Prof. Zakai was a big Stravinsky fan. Prof. Shakedi didn't start cutting through a patient's dura mater without the accompaniment of a Matti Caspi pop song. Anaesthetists preferred listening to the army radio station, or arguing politics. It took him a long time to get used to that noise, and as soon as he became a senior surgeon he informed his team that in his operating room, they worked in silence. Yet here, in the garage, the silence drove him mad. Perhaps because he had no idea what words were inside her. He knew quite well what the head nurse or the anaesthetist would talk about, given the chance. But he had no idea what Sirkit would talk about. So he filled the void, her silence, with images of what she might say. Every night he carried on a long conversation with her, all of it in his mind. Every night he filled the space with something else, put words and sentences in her mouth, and there was always room for more, so she expanded, grew larger in his mind.

While he was being driven mad by the enigma of her silences, she looked at him without the slightest bit of surprise. There was nothing mysterious about him. When they lay down to sleep, he in his private house in Omer, she on her mattress in the caravan, they had fantasies about each other, alternately and together. And after he had explored every part of her, he finally came in a wild explosion (in his imagination, that is. In reality, he came in total humiliation, masturbating in the shower, quietly, guiltily in the shower, less than ten meters from his sleeping wife.) And after he came – calm. His body relaxed into its usual languor. But even then, a moment later, the feeling that he was once again absent began to grow.

In her bedroom in Omer, Liat lay with her eyes open. She looked at the face of the man beside her for a long time. He'd come home long after she had fallen asleep. Now she was awake and his eyes were closed. Behind the screen of his closed lids, his eyes darted back and forth. Her man was dreaming. Had his dreams, like hers, become boring? Once her dreams had been an untiring source of fear and pleasure, desire and guilt. Appearing one after the other were people from work, past lovers awash in lust and vitality, enormous waves, fires, bodies, an embarrassing understanding of what stripping in public meant, attempts to fly that succeeded sometimes briefly, sometimes longer. But for the last few weeks, her dreams had become as arid as the hills outside Omer. Tonight, for example, she'd dreamed that she was standing in a line. That's all. She woke up bored by herself. Really wanted to go to work, to fill that emptiness with reports and investigations and record-keeping. But a moment before she got out of bed, she saw him and was startled. She knew, of course, that he was there, beside her, but that knowledge was totally taken for granted, like the fact that her pillow was there, or the blanket. She certainly would have noticed if he hadn't been there, but was that enough, knowing that something exists only by becoming aware of its absence? So she lay down again, facing him.

He was handsome, her man. Still handsome. With that Roman nose and those thin lips, and that aggressive chin. But why even now, when he should have seemed as helpless as a child, did he still look proud, almost arrogant? How could a person look so arrogant in his sleep? Suddenly, as if by invitation, all the rats of doubt emerged from their holes and began to gnaw at the sleeping man – that hair sprouting from his nose repelled her. The small shaving cut on his cheek that had become infected and filled with pus. The anger line on his forehead. The mild whiff of morning mouth coming from his slightly open lips. The criticism she thought she saw in the corner of his eyes.

The sun danced on the wall in splashes of color, and Liat lay on the cotton sheets, looking at her husband with merciless eyes. It was as if an evil hand had pushed aside the garment of light and tenderness with which people cloak their loved ones, revealing the beloved body as it was, naked and exposed, flesh and blood and bone. That moment was so cruel, so horrifying, that a few seconds later Liat looked away. Now she was frightened to the depths of her soul, and felt very, very guilty. There was nothing like fear and guilt to drive away the rats of doubt: Liat was so upset by what she had seen when she looked at Eitan with open eyes that she quickly closed them and curled into his arms. His large hands wrapped around her as he slept, no questions, no doubts. When Eitan Green woke up that morning, he and his wife were embracing each other as they hadn't done for a long time.

The next day, at four in the afternoon, he found himself in the mall with Itamar and Yaheli. Liat had remembered that they needed presents for a series of birthdays in Itamar's preschool, and said that because she was so loaded with work, there was no way she could buy them herself. The three of them wandered through the shops and stopped at the stands. At first they talked to each other, but slowly grew silent. The mall rocked them in a giant cradle of music and loudspeaker announcements as they moved from shop to shop. Yaheli had stopped shouting, "I want that!" and only stared with glazed eyes at the amazing number of toys, clothes, electric appliances. Itamar stopped in front of a TV store, his astonished eyes following the dozens of identical images of Barack Obama delivering the same speech behind dozens of identical lecterns. There was a 50-inch Obama and a 30-inch Obama, a Toshiba Obama and a Samsung Obama. Each of them gave the same muted speech. The President of the United States reproduced in massive numbers, but not even a single word of his speech could be heard. The TV store preferred playing the latest Shlomo Artzi disk. Obama gave a speech and Shlomo Artzi sang, and Itamar pulled Eitan's hand and said, "Can we go?"

Wait a minute. On the left corner of the display window, one of the TV sets suddenly went out of synch. The American president and his lectern weren't there anymore, replaced by a cascade of black-and-white particles. Neat rows of Barack Obama that suddenly had a hole dug in them. And although it was just one TV set among dozens, some of that black-and-white dripped onto the entire display window. The malfunction was there, in the left corner, mocking Obama's purposeful speech and Shlomo Artzi's caressing voice. And it was to that corner that Eitan's eyes were drawn, to that non-picture. As in museums, your glance goes immediately to the one rotten fruit that every still life painter puts into his lush bowl of fruit. Amid all that abundance, something embarrassing. The roundness of the pears. The roundness of Barack Obama's cheeks. It could easily deceive you. How rapidly it could turn into meaningless flickering.

It didn't go on for long. Several seconds later the cascade of black-and-white particles vanished and the screen went completely dark. Eitan looked at the black screen through the display window. A man with two children standing in front of a TV store. A father. A married man. In the mall looking for birthday presents for seven-year-olds. If he simply turned his head around to the passers-by, he would see dozens of images of himself, replications. A father with a son and daughter. A mother with two daughters. A father and mother with twins. But *this* father, *this* married man, had something else. Not only two kids clutching his hands at either side. Also a dead black man whose blood had stained the running shoes he'd bought at the duty-free shop. And a living woman who stroked his neck with her tongue, her black snaky hair on his chest. Obama spoke and Shlomo Artzi sang, and Eitan was once again engulfed in a wave of desire and guilt. How he wanted to shake them off. To toss that horrible guilt away once and for all. That appalling desire. But, a small voice in his mind said, you were the one who brought them here with you. You buckled Itamar and Yaheli in the back seat, put Sirkit and Asum in the trunk and drove to the mall.

Yaheli tugged his arm and demanded ice cream. Eitan picked him up and gave him a hug that surprised both of them. He devoured the soft curls, bit the sweet button nose. And in the midst of all that sweetness, he felt his heart clench, knowing what Yaheli, Itamar and Liat did not know. And that made his hug stronger, and Yaheli's curls softer.

*

In a dreary Beersheba police department office, Liat Green leaned on her detective's desk. She was tired, and the yellow cloud enshrouding the city, visible from the window, didn't help. On her desk was a photo of the split skull of the Eritrean illegal immigrant. Not far from it, in a lovely wooden frame, was the photo of a man who had hit and run. Less than twenty centimeters between the picture of the victim and the picture of the driver who had hit him, and she didn't see it.

How could she miss it like that? She, of all people, who should have seen it. Liat Green, senior detective. Formerly Liat Smooha, chief observer. She, who sometimes worried that she looked at life so much she had forgotten how to actually live it – she didn't see it.

But it was really so simple. She didn't see what was right in front of her because she wasn't truly looking. She was searching for someone else. Always sure that she was missing something. But it wasn't someone that was missing. Not "the hit and run driver" or "the car that hit the man". She was so preoccupied by the mystery that she never saw the estrangement. And perhaps the estrangement was the true mystery, because how was it possible that such a gap had been created between a man and a woman who loved each other, so close they were almost a single body, and it was never mentioned. After fifteen years together, they listened in amazement when a story they hadn't heard before suddenly surfaced, thinking that maybe that was it, the final story. Now everything had been spoken, everything had been told. She already knew about the black-tailed cat that lived under his building, and he knew about her purple bike and its tragic demise.

And so Liat searched for the criminal who was hiding from her, never realizing that she was the one hiding him from herself. Unwilling to see that her man, so close to her, so known to her, had become distant. Especially because they weren't the sort of couple who were distant from each other. They still had amazing conversations, the ones that began as they left Omer and didn't end until they reached his parents' house in Haifa, more than 150 kilometers away. They still made each other laugh and enjoyed fucking. She could say in total honesty that she still loved her man. And he loved her. All that was definitely true, but it didn't cancel out the bit of estrangement that existed now in even the most familiar place. Estrangement that, by the very fact of its possibility, offended her, as if she had discovered that she'd gone an entire day with something stuck in her front teeth. Or something was hanging from her nostril. Embarrassing incidents might happen to other couples, but not to her and Eitan. She firmly believed that, and that was her mistake. No one ever knows another person completely. Not even herself. There is always a blind spot. An invisible line that crosses her desk. On the right – the photo of a cracked skull. An open case. A mystery. On the left – the photo of a beloved, familiar man, Eitan, hugging the boys. The lawn was in the background, and although the photo was cropped, she knew very well what was behind the image. She could recite the order of the trees in the garden in her sleep. She knew her yard by heart, and she knew her man by heart, and that was why she didn't know the hit and run driver. She barely glanced at the familiar, framed picture of her husband. She stared only at the cracked skull on the right-hand side and wondered: who did that to you? And where is he now?

2

I T DIDN'T EVEN LOOK like a place people lived in.
Nevertheless, it was a place people lived in.

And for the people who lived in it, it was a supremely logical place for people to live in.

So when, one day, other people came to that place and told the people who lived there that they weren't supposed to live there and had to go and live somewhere else, the people who lived there were very surprised.

And then they were angry.

And then they waited.

To see whether the people who told them to go and live somewhere else really meant it. And how much.

The flame ignited all at once in the tin shack, as flames are wont to do. The man holding the lighter moved it closer to the sleeping boy, touched his shoulder lightly. The boy stayed asleep, as boys are wont to do. The man closed the lighter and left the boy. Stepped outside. Darkness returned to the shack, but a bluish light, first light, seeped in through the narrow space between the walls and the roof. The man went back into the tin shack. He was holding a glass in his right hand, and a smile had begun at the edge of his mustache. He moved the glass close to the boy's nose. The aroma of the coffee filled the room, entering the boy's nostrils. The boy inhaled in his sleep, and in a moment, was no longer sleeping. You could tell – not from his eyes, which were still closed, but from the smile at the corners of his lips. Now both father and son were smiling. A few moments later, they were already in the unpaved area outside the tin shack, drinking their first morning coffee in silence, looking at the village. The village was stuck in the middle of the desert. Not near anything. Equally distant from everything. Distant even from itself. There were ten tin shacks and two goat pens. A large container that held water, a generator for electricity, and shady, quiet corners like the one where the father and son were sitting now and drinking their coffee. The coffee was bitter and the air was cold, and at that particular moment both father and son were quiet and peaceful.

So it was every morning. The father moved the glass close to his son's nose and the son was awakened by the smell of the hot coffee and cardamom. They both loved this wake-up ritual so much that even if the boy happened to wake up before his father, he continued to lie there in his bed, waiting with closed eyes for him, even if he needed desperately to pee.

On the way to school, he saw that the birds had already destroyed the body of the snake he'd killed the day before. He'd seen it on the way home from school, and had crushed its head with a stone. He'd wanted to call his father to come and see, but the snake had crossed his path three kilometers from the village, one and a half kilometers from the school, and there was no one he could impress with it. Walking past that rock now, he saw that nothing was left but the snake's head, a dark mass with a barely recognizable forked tongue.

Twenty minutes later, he reached the road. A tour bus passed him with a roar. Looking at him through the windows were boys his age. The bus drove away and he was about to cross the road when beyond the curve another bus appeared, this time a public bus, and the driver deafened him with a long, admonishing blast of his horn. This time he waited before trying to cross, letting two cars pass before he broke into a run, his head filled with a picture of the crushed snake, the forked tongue.

He arrived at school late, and when Tamam, his still unmarried teacher, asked him why, he shrugged and said nothing, his eyes fixed on the flag hanging behind her desk, avoiding the disappointment in her eyes. If she had known how he thought about her at night, she wouldn't have spoken to him about his lateness. She wouldn't have spoken to him at all.

When the school day ended he was the first to leave, bursting out in a run and not stopping. He'd turned sixteen four days earlier, and today he'd go to work with his father for the first time. His mother claimed he could have done that a long time ago, but his father had refused. "First, let him go to school, then we'll see." So he went to school, memorized letters and the multiplication table, wrote sentences neither of his parents could read with a pencil that shook from the effort. And the entire time he waited for this day, when he could follow his father into the van and drive *there*.

He didn't know what *there* was. His father never spoke about it, and he had already learned not to ask. At night, his father returned from there tired and pleased, the notes rolled up in his hand, warm like bread right out of the oven. Today he was going with him, and though his lungs burned from the running and he had a stitch in his side, he still ran without stopping.

Near the tin shack he met Sayyid, his father's cousin. Sayyid's car was clean and new, and his clothes were clean and new, but Sharaf didn't speak to him. He knew that his father didn't like him to. But Sayyid wanted to talk to him. He patted him on the shoulder and said, how are you man, and Sharaf smiled, but knew that Sayyid spoke to him as if he were a grown-up, not a boy, so that he would *feel* like a grown-up. Then Sayyid asked him when he was coming to work for him, and Sharaf shrugged and stared into space, which was the best answer he could find to questions he didn't know how to answer. Sayyid asked again and Sharaf understood that this time he'd have to come up with a different answer, when his father walked out of the shack and told Sayyid that it was fine, the boy already had a job. Sharaf's heart almost jumped out of his chest and began to pound because if that's how it was, then today's drive wasn't just a visit. It was a beginning. He and his father would work *there* together all day after school and maybe, if he was lucky and a good worker, he might even go *there* with his father instead of going to school, because he was really getting sick and tired of the multiplication table.

His father told him to get the van, and he went quickly around to the back of the shack, turned on the engine with a practiced hand, shifted into third gear in front of the dirt hill and smiled at the goats darting out of his way in alarm. His father got in and they drove off. He hoped that this time his father wouldn't tell him to switch places with him when they reached the road – after all, he was sixteen, and they'd once let Mohannad drive all the way to the Beersheba market. But as they were about to drive onto the road, his father told him to stop and switched places with him, and he didn't argue.

The gate at the entrance to the kibbutz was locked, and until the guard came and pressed the button that opened it he had time to read the sign. "ENJOY THE HOSPITALITY OF THE PEOPLE OF THE DES—" The gate opened and his father drove, and he figured out himself that the HOSPITALITY was of the PEOPLE OF THE DESERT. A few dozen meters later they passed another sign like that, and now he had enough time to look at only the last word and see that he'd been right, it really was DESERT. They continued and passed the kibbutz houses. Because of the traffic bumps, the van moved slowly and he could look at the houses and the windows of the houses, and at the people who sometimes appeared at them. The van kept moving, faster now because there were no more traffic bumps, and suddenly he saw, sticking out like a sore thumb at the far edge of the kibbutz, a large black tent.

At first he was so shocked that he asked his father whether Bedouins lived there, and when his father laughed, he understood that he had spoken like a child again, because what were the chances that anyone would let a group of Bedouins live in the middle of a Jewish kibbutz. His father stopped the van near the tent, in front of another ENJOY THE HOSPITALITY OF THE PEOPLE OF THE DESERT, right next to a large poster showing a drawing of a Bedouin riding a camel. The camel in the drawing was smiling and the Bedouin in the drawing was smiling, and the man who came out of the tent and walked over to them was also smiling as he said, "*Ahalan* Mussa, you finally brought the boy."

Sharaf knew that he was the boy and he didn't like that. But when the man, whose name was Matti, reached out for a handshake, he shook his hand and even smiled. The man called Matti said, "Wow, what a handshake," and Sharaf's smile changed from a have-to smile to a genuine one. He'd worked a long time on that handshake, ever since Mohannad told him about that movie where the hero knew who was a man and who wasn't by the way he shook hands. The man let go of Sharaf's hand and pointed to the tent, saying, "*Tfadalu*" with a Hebrew accent. Sharaf went inside. It was definitely the weirdest thing he'd ever seen in his life. One side was like a regular tent, with cushions and mattresses and everything. The other side was nothing like a regular tent. It was like a kibbutz house dressed up like a tent. Dressed up really, really well.

Matti answered his phone, which rang, and said, "Great, turn right at the roundabout, then straight all the way," and then ended the call and said, "Ya'allah, Mussa, let's get to work." Sharaf followed his father to a corner of the tent and watched him as he took off his jeans and shirt and put on a white *galabiya* and tied a white keffiyeh on his head. Then he took out another *galabiya* and told Sharaf to put it on. They began to hear voices outside. Lots of people. The bear-like laughter of men, the sharp, arrogant speech of teenage boys, the cat-like screeches of teenage girls, the twittering rebukes of women, and in the midst of all that, the rise and fall of a baby's crying, and though there was no way of telling how many throats it was coming from, it was clearly more than one. Sharaf looked at his father, who was calm and quiet, and tried to look calm and quiet himself, because even if there was no way he could look like his father, kind of aristocratic and strong, at least he wouldn't look like a scared baby on his first day of work.

He finished getting dressed at the precise moment the first man came in. His father put a hand on his shoulder and said, "Today you just watch, understand what the job is, and then walk around and say *ahalan ve'sahalan*" to everyone who comes in." From a corner of the tent, Sharaf watched his father, who talked to the people gently and confidently, and he could see how much they respected him and even took pictures of him with their phones when he picked up the *darbuka* and began to play. He played really well. Better than anyone Sharaf knew. When he banged the *darbuka*, it let him in, and when he was in, he did whatever he wanted to it. And it was so clear, and so beautiful, that at first he just didn't believe his ears when one of the boys shouted at his father, "Hey bro, why are you wearing a dress?"

He expected silence. The rude, insulting words would be met by a fortified wall of closed, grim mouths. His father would stop playing and tell the boy to get out in his quiet voice, the one they always obeyed because if they didn't, a beating would follow. But his father kept playing as if he hadn't heard, and the guests, instead of telling off the boy with the big mouth and teaching him a lesson, responded with happy cheers and laughing. "Wow, get a load of that embroidery," the big mouth said, "just like a girl's." He'd already stood up and started walking toward his father, pointing to the embroidered sleeves of the *galabiya*, staggering slightly, drunk with the cheers of the crowd and the laughter he'd managed to squeeze out of them.

Then it happened: the boy's hand took hold of the edge of Sharaf's father's sleeve and displayed it to everyone. And Sharaf's father's hand, instead of dropping the *darbuka* and grabbing the boy by the throat, instead of punching him in the diaphragm or slapping his pimply cheek, Sharaf's father's hand continued playing without missing a beat.

3

THREE DAYS AFTER the visit to the TV store, Eitan instructed Sirkit on how to remove the bandages from the stomach of the Sudanese they had operated on. The wound looked great. The redness and the swelling had gone down faster than he'd expected, and that made him proud. He knew that it was ridiculous to take credit for the rapid recovery of another organism – after all, it was the Sudanese's immune system, not his, that was doing the work – but none the less, he was proud. As if that rapid recovery proved something about his abilities. He had never felt such pride about how patients healed in the neurosurgery department, although the excision of a growth from the corpus callosum was an infinitely more complex surgery than the one he had performed in the garage. But even Itamar, when he took him camping, had said that the pasta they cooked on the campfire was the best he'd ever eaten. Because they expected the pasta they cooked on the stainless-steel counter at home to be good, but the pasta they cooked that night at the campsite was a kind of miracle. When Eitan thought about Itamar, the miracle of his patient faded slightly. How long it had been since he'd spent an entire evening with that quiet child of his. Yaheli screamed and cried when he left the house for his shift, but Itamar merely looked at him with that quietness of his and said, "Call if you have time." He was like that at school as well. He didn't take back a pencil case that had been snatched from him, didn't demand that he be allowed to participate in football, didn't say that now it was his turn to use the computer. And Eitan wanted to say, "Shout, kid, slam your hands down on the desk and shout, because otherwise, the world will simply go on turning." But Liat said, "That's his way, Tani, and he's okay with it. Just be careful that you don't feel so bad for him that he starts to feel bad too."

When he was born, they'd called him E.T. until they decided on a name. The first several days after his birth, with those huge eyes and wrinkled skin, he really did look like some creature from another planet. Even when he grew into a beautiful baby, they kept calling him that. It seemed to them like an abbreviation of Itamar, and also it had been Liat's favorite movie, because there was always the possibility that if you pedaled your bike fast enough, it would take off from the ground and soar to the moon. But for the last several years, when Itamar wrapped himself in his quietness like an astronaut in his spacesuit and helmet, Eitan had stopped calling him that. He wanted to ask Liat to stop, but didn't know how to explain why. When he saw Itamar remain standing where he was during the Lag B'Omer party in Omer while his classmates shoved each other to get at the ice-cream pops that were being handed out, he thought he was from another planet, that child of his. But he didn't know how to bring him to this planet, and he didn't know how to remain on the other planet long enough to keep that undertone of rebuke (but why, kid, why don't you tell them) from his voice.

Eitan straightened up from the Sudanese's wound. Sirkit stood beside him, waiting for him to speak. "It looks very good," he said. "If it continues this way, he'll be back on his feet in a couple of days." She translated for the patient and his face lit up.

"Do you want to bandage him yourself?"

You bandage him, I'll go get him some food.

When she turned to leave, he hesitated for a moment, and finally said that he'd go to the restaurant at the adjacent gas station himself and buy something to eat. The darkness of the garage suddenly seemed depressing. He wanted to call home; maybe the kids hadn't gone to bed yet. "You know, Itamar, that's an excellent question about dinosaurs and dragons. Maybe next Saturday we'll drive to the Ramon Crater and sleep there, look for dinosaur footprints, or dragon tracks." He was already planning how he'd slip out of the tent in the middle of the night to draw huge footprints in the sand for the boy when Sirkit said, *Okay. You go. But not to the gas station, to the caravan behind it.*

He was so glad to get out that it wasn't until he'd taken a few steps that the realized he was walking to what was actually her home. He stopped thinking about dinosaurs and dragons and tried to guess what he'd see there, behind the door. A pot of rice on a portable burner, that's what she told him when he left, but what would he find apart from the pot? And what, in fact, was that curiosity all about?

As a child, he had stared unashamedly at people's houses. As soon as the door opened he was already surveying the interior, the owner's possessions. Shoes tossed here, an unread book left there, and what was in the fridge and in the closets. Most of the time there were no particularly interesting items, because what could you keep in a fridge? And yet, when all the details joined together into a whole, he felt an odd sense of gratification, the same feeling of satisfaction he had when he succeeded in assembling a complicated puzzle, and it had nothing to do with the complete picture it showed when it was finished. A fridge filled with low-calorie cheeses, and deep inside it, hidden behind organic Quaker Oats, a half-eaten cake. A book abandoned on the cabinet, opened, of all the possible places, to the page where the heroine confessed to a despicable betrayal. And the other books – titles displayed on the shelf in all their majesty, with only the stiffness of the covers to indicate that they had never been opened. He loved to see the closets full to bursting with clothes, their doors hastily closed by the embarrassed owners. A sensual heap of shirts and dresses, underwear and socks, a chaos of wrinkled fabrics with the fragrance of laundry detergent and the musty smell of the closet fighting over them as if on a battlefield.

He tried to tell himself that Sirkit's house was like those houses, that the excitement that gripped him when he opened the door was nothing but a distant echo of the excitement he had felt then. But there was something else. At his cousin's house in Haifa, on the balcony overlooking the wadi, he had once seen a woman sleeping in an armchair on the balcony below. She was about thirty and he was only a teenager; she was wearing a housedress with an awful floral design, and lying at her feet was a mystery novel that looked idiotic. But her housedress blew gently in the wind that rose from the wadi and he was shocked to see that she wasn't wearing panties. Far below, the tops of the pines and oaks swayed from side to side, from side to side, and so did his glance, from side to side, from side to side, because the woman's thighs spread slightly in her sleep and from the balcony above he saw all that he had never dared to hope he would see (at least for as long as he had pimples on his face and his voice hadn't changed). The whole world spread out beneath him that afternoon, naked and exposed to his glance. The green wadi flowed into an endless sea of possibilities, and that pinkness broke through that green and blue, throwing him into turmoil and hurting his eyes so much that several moments later he turned and went back into the living room, almost at a run.

When Eitan opened the door to Sirkit's caravan, the heat of that glance above the wadi flowed through his veins. And though this time he had been asked to go inside – it was Sirkit herself who had sent him – he still felt chills along his back when he opened the creaking door, and for a fraction of a second the smell of desert dust was replaced by the light scent of pine that rose from the wadi in Haifa on hot summer days.

When he turned on the light, the room spread out before him in all its defiant meagerness. (What did you think you'd find here, lace panties? A vast library? Children's drawings on the fridge?) Eight mattresses and pillows made of rolled-up

197

shirts and pants. On one side of the door was a portable burner with a pot of rice on it. Several tablespoons, a few plates, and a strong feeling that he had been here before. If not in body, then in thought, the same thought he'd had when he first heard "Goldilocks and the Three Bears". A little girl walks through a forest and reaches a house that isn't hers. The chairs aren't hers. Neither are the bowls of porridge or the beds. But she treats them as if they were: she sits, eats, lies down. The magic of an empty house is that you can walk around in it and ask if it could be yours. He was already asking himself, if he had to sleep here, which of the mattresses on the floor he would choose? And he knew immediately, the one near the door. Even if at night the cold air seeped in through the opening and froze him in his sleep, he'd still prefer it over the others. And if he had to eat here, then it would be from the tin bowl. The glass ones didn't look clean enough. For a moment, he considered picking up the bowls one by one, and thought about lying on each of the mattresses. To close his eyes and see how it felt to sleep here in the symphony of inhaling and exhaling, what it would be like to wake up. Goldilocks hadn't stayed long enough to know. The bears came home, large and black, and she escaped through the window before they managed to make up a bed for her.

He looked at the mattress near the door again, and knew for certain: that was the one she slept on. It wasn't a guess, but a firm conclusion: that was her place. Because she, like him, needed to be sure that she had air close by whenever she was with other people. A gentle breeze from outside blew through the room, and Eitan thought that perhaps this was what it felt like when she closed her eyes here, and why he was so sure that even when the wind was cold, she still lay with her face to the outside, to the desert, turning her back to the other people who lay inside, snoring, or tossing and turning, or talking in their sleep. Scratching as they dreamed, farting unknowingly, drooling threads of saliva on their pillow. Things that people should do when they're alone are done here in the company of others, turning private shames into public ones. Or worse – into the absence of shame. But she maintained her boundaries, lying with her face to the outside and her back to the collection of thrashing, secreting bodies. He looked at the mattress near the door and saw her refusal to be absorbed into the human mass squeezed into the caravan. He saw and admired it.

(Nevertheless, he was wrong. Her mattress wasn't the one near the door; it was in fact the mattress furthest from the door, next to the wall. She had hurried to put her belongings on it the day they had arrived there and hoped she wouldn't have to move them again. Being close to the wall calmed her. She liked to fall asleep with her face right up against it, her nose almost rubbing it. She felt good lying like that. Curled up in the corner and not moving. She slept more soundly that way, was less exposed to the noise of the others.)

Sirkit's things lay in a jumble on the bed. They might have held a great truth, a supremely important message for the man looking at them. But he wasn't looking at them. His gaze was focused on a different mattress, the one near the door. What a shame. Because the pile of clothes on the mattress near the wall

199

had been left there for him. A Rosetta Stone that he skipped over casually. After all, she had not sent him to the caravan for nothing. This is where I am when you're not looking at me. Here I am when I haven't prepared in advance for your glance. She had left her belongings in a jumble that morning because she could not have known he would come, although she might have contemplated the possibility. Imagined, even for a moment, that he was standing over her mattress and looking at her things. Much stranger thoughts than that can pass through the mind of a person when she is washing a floor. Water from the rag washing the floor, and washing other things along with it. For example, what would happen if. If he were to come into the caravan and look at her things. Without her actually paying attention to it, that possibility was washed away with all the others in the rhythmic sweeps of the squeegee. But something of that possibility must have stayed with her, because in the garage the circumstances suddenly changed, one thing led to another, and she sent him *there*. Not in her thoughts, but really. And now she was standing in the garage, realizing all at once that he was in her home, if it could be called a home. He was inside.

It was strange that she felt so defiled when it was she herself who had sent him there. And strange that the first time she called that place "home" in her thoughts was when someone else had entered it. She stood in the garage and pictured him there. Would he be able to pick out her mattress from all the others. What was he looking at now. What was he touching. But she knew it didn't matter whether he touched anything or not, because for her, that place was defiled anyway. When she went back there tonight, the entire caravan would be covered with the imprints of his glance. Even if he'd only taken the pot of rice and left, she'd know he'd been there, his eyes scanning her most secret place, her bed.

It made no difference that she had also scanned. That the first time she went to his house, she had stood outside for a long time, looking. She'd seen the tangled topography of toys left on the lawn. She'd seen the umbrella that shaded the wooden table in the yard, and around it one, two, three, four chairs, one for each member of the family. And now her caravan had been broken into and spread out before him, and he was free to walk around in it to his heart's content.

She knew: her sleep would be strange tonight. But even so, she would lie on her mattress. Wrap herself in her sheet. Press her nose up against the wall. That was the only way she knew how to sleep. But now she was in the garage and he was in the caravan, looking at the mattress next to the open door. And that entire time, on the mattress next to the wall, was a letter written in the ink of the careless way her shirt lay on her pillow, the unbearable sorrow of her hairbrush on the sheet. Because even if she hadn't intended to leave him a message, it was hidden in the pile of things tossed on her bed. The hope of the new shirt she had bought herself. The shame of the old, torn one she hadn't dared to throw away. All of that lay on the mattress right in front of him, but he didn't look at them. He didn't know. She didn't know. A stranger to the letter she herself had written. Not understanding that from the moment she had first thought, while washing the floor, about the possibility of his glance on her bed – from that moment, the bed would never be free of his glance. There would always be the possibility of eyes. That morning, she had left her things there for those imagined eyes. But seen by his real eyes, the meaning of these things was lost, as if it didn't exist.

Finally Eitan turned away from the mattress next to the door and looked again at the door itself. What unphotogenic poverty. Starring in a picture he'd taken on safari in Africa was a rickety mud hut about to fall and yellow savannahs covered with wave after wave of undulating thorns, like a lion's mane. Naked children stared at the camera beneath an astonishingly blue sky. Bare-breasted mothers wore gorgeous jewelry made of lions' teeth. The poverty in the pictures he took in Africa pierced the heart like a well-sharpened arrow. There was a splendid meagerness in the pictures he took in Africa. And here: eight mattresses. A portable burner. Several tablespoons. A few plates.

But there were roses here as well. Between the mattresses on the floor and the burner near the door stood an empty can of corn with roses in it. Three roses, as fresh as if they had been picked today. Suddenly, Eitan remembered a bush he had passed in the dark on the way here, and looked through the caravan door again. In the faint light of the lamp, he saw the outlines of more flowers. The Eritrean woman grew roses. For the first time since he'd met her, he imagined her at her job, cleaning the restaurant at the gas station. Scraping from plates the remains of desserts she had never tasted. Peeling vegetables. Sweeping. Hands covered in grease. Feet covered in dust. A dusty woman returning to a dusty caravan every day, but her roses were as clean as only roses can be.

They moved him, the roses. Truly moved him. He decided he'd say something about it to her. He took the pot of rice, closed the door and walked toward the garage, thinking the entire time of what he would say to her. But when he went inside, the nice words on the tip of his tongue, he found total chaos. Sirkit and the man he'd operated on were still there, but also present were two large Eritreans and a young Bedouin with a furious expression on his face. The Eritreans stood in front of the Bedouin, blocking his way. There was no mistaking their stance: arms folded, feet slightly spread. They wanted him to go and he didn't want to go. But Eitan was sure he was missing something because the man in front of him didn't look sick. Desperate, aggressive, but not sick.

Did you bring the rice?

Sirkit's voice was as serene as always. She was standing beside the mattress on which the man he had recently operated on lay, speaking to Eitan as if they were the only ones in the room.

"What's going on here?"

Sirkit pointed to the Bedouin without looking at him, as if she were pointing at a bit of dirt the wind had blown in. *He wants to bring someone here. And I said no.*

The Bedouin gave Eitan a quick glance, then turned around and left. The bodies of the Eritrean men relaxed abruptly, once again quiet, harmless people. Sirkit left the patient's bedside and went to take the pot of rice. (And she swore to herself that she'd find out how that Bedouin had learned of the illegal hospital, which of the stupid people around her had opened his mouth and what she would do to that tongue when she knew.) As she took the pot, Eitan thought about how far ahead of him she was, because he was still trying to formulate the question about that Bedouin who'd just been there and she, as usual, was already somewhere else. But a moment later, the garage door opened and the Bedouin hurried inside again. This time he had a young girl in his arms. Four large red roses bloomed on her blue *galabiya*, one in each place where a knife had stabbed her in the stomach. "You take care of her," the Bedouin said. "My sister, you take care of her."

As if to explain that he had no intention of backing down, the Bedouin went over to Eitan and handed the girl to him, almost threw her into his arms so that when the Eritreans grabbed him, his arms were already empty and Eitan's very full. Eitan put the girl down on the rusty table and leaned over her. She was breathing, and that was great, but her pulse was very faint. Whoever had stabbed her had done a thorough job. Above his head, Eitan heard the whiplash of Sirkit and the Bedouin's words. Short sentences in Arabic hurled in a clearly threatening tone. Sirkit repeated the word Soroka. The Bedouin shook his head wildly.

He wouldn't go. Eitan would bet on it. Roses blooming that way on a *galabiya* meant either blood revenge or honor killing, two things that the clans would rather settle among themselves. He looked at the Bedouin. Who knew whether the fire in his eyes came from concern for his sister or guilt? He himself might have stabbed her four times, then regretted it. And the Bedouin, as if sensing the question in the doctor's eyes, said to him, "My brothers did it. She was with a man."

"And you?"

"Not me."

He couldn't really have expected a different answer. He cut the girl's dress with a scissors and told Sirkit to get him an IV.

They are our IVs.

He promised he'd bring a new one tomorrow, he'd bring new everything, if only she'd get moving already, damn it. But she stayed where she was.

They don't help us and we don't help them.

Eitan looked at her. She was totally calm as she said it, despite the murderous look she gave the Bedouin. The Eritreans went and stood silently at the door, awaiting her instructions, but Eitan thought she would have been equally calm if she were facing the Bedouin alone. It drove him mad, that composure of hers, it made him so angry that his voice shook when he told her that if she threw that girl out of there, he'd go with her.

She didn't say a word. He went back to the girl. The Eritreans left a few minutes later, but he didn't notice. When the fight begins, the fighter in the ring doesn't really pay attention to the spectators. (In the end, Zakai had said, death always wins by a knockout. The question is, how many rounds can you go?) He wanted to win this round. He wanted to see that girl behind a supermarket cash register in Beersheba, or pouring coffee in

205

the Soroka cafeteria. Nodding hello to him on the street. But her body wasn't really cooperating with his wishes. She hardly responded to the IV, and when he looked at the depth of the stab wounds again, he knew why. It was like pouring a glass of water into a bathtub that had no stopper. He still had to check what was happening to her other internal organs, but at the moment the most important thing was to stabilize her pulse, the rapid, hysterical contractions of a pump that couldn't get what it needed. Behind him he could hear the older brother groan, his eyes fixed on the girl's hands. They were already blue, almost purple, and the purpleness was spreading upward. She wasn't dead, Eitan hurried to say, it was one of the symptoms of blood loss. Like the cold sweat on her forehead. Like the shallow breathing. Like the fact that, for a long moment, she hadn't responded to the voices in the room with even a slight flicker of her eyelashes. Her feet also began to turn blue. He inserted another IV. And another. Minutes turned into hours turned into a mass of time that had no before or after, only the girl's face, the cold sweat that covered it and the cold sweat that covered his.

He couldn't recall with certainty the exact time the girl died. He only knew that at a certain moment he saw that her face was no longer sweating, was no longer moving at all. The pulse had stopped. The breathing had stopped. He tried to resuscitate her for another few minutes (maybe there was still a chance, damn it, maybe), and then he stopped. "When a doctor continues resuscitation efforts for five minutes after breathing and pulse have stopped, he's not a doctor any longer,"

Zakai had once told him. "Resuscitating the dead is the job of messiahs and prophets, not medical students." He heard the Bedouin burst into tears behind him. He didn't turn around. He was still afraid of that fire he'd had in his eyes earlier, not convinced that those hands, now hugging his sister, weren't the ones that had held the knife. He went over to the sink and washed his hands. Dried them well. He had already turned to leave the garage when he recognized a familiar word in the jumble of the Bedouin's words and sobs. A name the Bedouin kept repeating over and over again.

Mona.

Mona Mona Mona Mona.

4

A T 3:30 IN THE MORNING, in the bedroom of the private
house in Omer, Liat was asleep in the double bed. Lying
diagonally across it, with the total abandon of someone alone
in bed. Before falling asleep, she had decided not to hug him
tonight, or let him hug her. When he lifted the blanket and got
into bed, she'd curl up on her side. No more stomach pressed
to back, no more leg against leg. She couldn't go on like this,
not speaking during the day and embracing at night. Two
separate kingdoms, the one of strained breakfasts and silent
dinners, the other of intertwined bodies reveling in each other
in the dark, with only the light from Yaheli's room slipping
in under the door as a reminder that it was actually the same
house. Where the distant, daytime Eitan and Liat became the
intimate, night-time Eitan and Liat. Fifteen years together, and
only rarely had she been distant from him in her sleep. After
especially nasty fights, to-the-death arguments. But even then,
they would almost always feel their way back to each other in
the dark so that the sun would not rise and find them apart.

He got into bed shortly after 3:30. Though she was sleeping, she felt him, and remembered the decision she had made.
Normally, sleep would melt her anger, but tonight the hurt was
part of her body. A limb she felt again when she turned over on

the mattress, no different from the hand or foot we don't think about when we're dreaming, but the tiniest bit of awareness is enough to remind us of their existence. The hand, the foot, the hurt. All of them were totally present. Perhaps that was why several minutes passed before she felt the tremors. She'd been busy barricading herself among the pillows and blankets and didn't feel the odd movement of the air on the other side of the bed. She finally noticed it, and didn't understand.

"Eitan?"

He didn't reply, and for a moment she was angry and decided that if that's how he was going to be, then she wouldn't say anything else. She could do silence as well as he could. But the tremors continued there, on the other side of the bed, and she slowly stopped being angry and began to worry.

"Tani, are you sick?" She put her hand on his forehead, which was fine, and then lowered her hands to his cheeks, which weren't fine at all. Wet and hot. "Are you crying?"

Even before he replied, she said to herself, no, it can't be, her man didn't cry. He simply didn't have those ducts in the corners of his eyes, it was something physiological. But when her fingers moved higher up on his cheeks, they touched moist, salty eyes, and when she hugged him, he uttered a sound that was undoubtedly a sob. So she hugged him, and hoped he couldn't feel the slight suspicion in her hands, the slight awkwardness in the way she held his body, which had suddenly changed. A few moments later, when the tremors had died down a bit, she asked him what had happened. She asked tenderly, quietly, but when several moments passed without a response from him, she once again felt that familiar anger she had gone to sleep with, along with a new, darker question about another woman. Then finally, his voice. Weak, broken, but still – his voice. The stranger of the last several weeks had vanished, and now she heard Eitan, really Eitan, tell her in a jumble of words about a young girl who had died that night on the operating table. "It's my fault," he said over and over, "it's my fault." Tears welled in his eyes again. "It's my fault." Just when she thought he was calming down, when he stopped mumbling and began breathing regularly, he looked at her with urgency, "I have to tell you what happened, Tul, tell you why she died." He was about to continue speaking, she saw his lips shaping the next sentence, when she reached out and stopped him.

"Enough," she said. "You're making yourself miserable, and it's not right." He listened to her silently as she reminded him that he was a doctor, and doctors sometimes made mistakes, but their goal was the noblest one there is. "Patients die sometimes, Tani, that doesn't mean it's your fault. Think about all the night shifts you've had this last month. How can you lie here and tell me that you're a bad person, or not a professional?!" She kissed his eyes, which were wet with tears again, kissed his cheeks and even his chin, kissed them and said, "You're a good man, Tani, you're the best man I know."

Gradually, she felt him relax in her arms. He didn't object anymore when she stroked his head. Didn't try to speak again. She ran her fingers through his hair until his heavy breathing told her he had fallen asleep. Like Yaheli, she thought, like Yaheli who cries himself to sleep, the system closing itself down so it can start up again tomorrow. WINDOWS IS SHUTTING DOWN. But she continued to stroke his hair in a movement that grew slower as the minutes passed, until she too fell asleep.

At seven in the morning, she received the call from the precinct.

He clung to sleep as tightly as he could when Liat's phone rang, clung to it when she cried loudly, "What?!" He kept his eyes closed when she got out of bed and dressed quickly and hurried Itamar and Yaheli in a clearly urgent voice. When he heard the door shut, he straightened the blanket around his body and even then he was careful to keep his eyes closed so that not a ray of sun could penetrate. But he knew that he was awake and that all the ruses in the world could not change that.

A few minutes later, he opened his eyes. There he was, lying in his bed in Dr Eitan Green's bedroom. Yet he wouldn't be surprised if the door opened suddenly and Dr Eitan Green entered and commanded him to leave. The man lying in bed who, not directly but indisputably, had caused the death of a young girl last night, would be tossed out of bed by Dr Green, a man of principle who refused to tolerate bribery. The man who had run over someone and left him on the side of the road, and almost let someone else take the blame for it, would be thrown out the front door by Dr Green. And that man, tossed out of bed and thrown out the door, would stand in the front yard among the rosemary bushes and still wonder. Could he actually be the real Eitan Green?

What defined him more – a full life of careful driving, of medical studies, of carrying an old lady's groceries from the supermarket – or that single moment? Forty-one years of life versus a single moment, and nevertheless he felt as if that moment contained a great deal more than its sixty seconds, just as a bit of DNA embodied the entire human species. And yes, it mattered that he'd been an Eritrean. Because they all looked alike to him. Because he didn't know them. Because people from another planet are not really people. And yes, that sounded terrible, but he wasn't the only one who felt that way. He was only the one who had happened to run one of them over.

He lay in bed and thought about the blood roses on the girl's dress. It was Liat's fault just as much as his. She could tell herself as many times as she wanted that she had exposed the romance to save the boy from false arrest, but the truth was that she'd done it because she couldn't stand the idea that it was Cheetah, not she, who had cracked the case. The boy had told her to stop investigating, but she didn't listen to him, and when she solved the case, she'd been so proud that she never stopped to consider that she was endangering the girl. That's how it was. There were no good or bad people, only strong and weak ones. Perhaps that's what Zakai had been trying to tell him when he gave him that bottle of whiskey.

He shaved carefully in front of the mirror. Yesterday, Prof. Tal had told him that he looked neglected. He'd said it with a smile, with a slap on his back, but he'd said it all the same. Prof. Shakedi hadn't said a word to him for two days. The head of the department's usual admonishing glances had been replaced by open displays of avoidance, which worried Eitan much more. The other doctors barely spoke to him, and he was too tired and upset to carry on a real conversation anyway. Even the young nurse had stopped smiling, deciding to invest her energy in the new intern. Perhaps she might have behaved differently if she'd known that the tired, unshaven doctor was actually the chief director of another hospital. Less well known, less legal, but nevertheless, a hospital. With medical equipment and a variety of injuries and illnesses, and since yesterday with patient fatalities as well – it wouldn't have been a hospital without them.

You need to calm down, he told himself as he buttoned his shirt, you need to calm down or you'll lose your job. He finished buttoning his shirt and moved on to polishing his shoes. Finally, he stood in front of the mirror and examined his image. No, Prof. Tal definitely could not say he looked neglected.

But he sprayed either side of his neck with his expensive only-for-weddings aftershave, just to be on the safe side.

Hours later, when the aftershave had been replaced by the sour smell of sweat, one of the nurses came over to him and said, "Your wife's on the phone." He apologized to his patient and hurried out to answer. He'd been expecting that call since morning. Liat would tell him that the Bedouin girl was dead, and then she'd start to cry. Or first she'd start to cry and then tell him that the Bedouin girl was dead. He'd be no less shocked than she was. He'd calm her down. He'd say, "Tuli, it's not your fault. You were only trying to help." And he'd really believe himself when he said it. He wouldn't think that, in fact, she was to blame for the never-ending investigation and the promotion that might come at the end of it. When he'd hear her crying, he'd know the promotion was just an excuse for something else, that desire of Liat's to be one of the good guys. The ones who do things well, because that's how they should be done. Like doctors. Surely no one did it for the money. Or the prestige. Seven years of school in order to find out that if there were both good and evil forces in the world, you were undoubtedly on the side of the good.

He intended to say all that when he picked up the receiver, which is why he was very surprised to hear not Liat's tormented voice on the other end, but a different voice, a calm and collected one.

I need you to come today.

"Why do you think you can call here?"

You're not answering your phone.

He told her something she already knew, that his phone was turned off during shifts, and she told him that he hadn't answered last night either, or this morning. She said they had patients. Many. Yesterday she'd told them all to go because he decided he'd rather treat that Bedouin girl, but today he had to come. He said, "I can't come today, Sirkit, I'm on duty until late," and she said, *So I'll tell them to come tomorrow,* and hung up.

*

When he got out of the SUV, the first thing he noticed was the moon. A gaping white eye with its pupil ripped out. (And if the moon was full, then two months must have passed; Janis Joplin had wailed inside the car then, and there was a person named Asum outside and you ran him over.) He locked the SUV and walked toward the garage. Ten Eritreans were gathered at the door, peering inside. He thought they were waiting for him, so he was surprised that they didn't even glance at him as he walked past. When he reached the garage door, he understood why. A heavyset Sudanese woman was on her knees, her back to the group, kissing Sirkit's feet. "*Minfadlik*," she said, and then again, "*Minfadlik, Minfadlik*." Eitan knew that word. The Sudanese who came to the garage said it often. Please.

Sirkit replied in soft, melodious Arabic. The sound was so pleasant that it took a moment for Eitan to realize that she was rejecting the woman's request. He realized it when the woman stood up and spit in Sirkit's face.

Sounds of shock passed through the group. The saliva, white and foamy, had struck the arch of Sirkit's nose and was now dripping onto her cheek. How pathetic and ludicrous her proud face looked now with threads of saliva trickling down its entire length. But as the seconds passed and Sirkit remained standing there, Eitan had to admit that she looked more noble than ludicrous. Because apparently the spitting had not changed her in the slightest. She simply continued to stand there without saying a word. When the woman spit again straight into the thick darkness of her eyes, she went over to the sink and washed her face. The Sudanese woman turned around and saw Eitan. Her expression changed abruptly. "*Minfadlak*, Doctor. Sirkit wants money. I have no money." She was about to kneel again, this time at his feet, when the Eritreans Sirkit had appointed to keep order approached the woman. They didn't have to touch her. She stood up immediately. Looked coldly at Sirkit, at the men who were ready to spring into action, at the people watching from the door. Shaking with anger and humiliation, she said to Eitan, "For every blow that Asum gave her, Allah will give her ten."

The last patient walked out of there at two. More accurately, he limped out. Eitan watched him as he hopped out on his bandaged leg. He had told him about the antibiotics three times, but still wasn't sure the man had understood. He'd arrived yesterday, spoke slowly, his eyes dull. Maybe because of the heat, maybe he'd been dimwitted from the outset. But a dimwitted person could not have evaded the Bedouin smugglers as he had, could not have crossed the border without paying anyone. Sirkit said he'd gotten the leg injury from crawling under one of the Egyptian fences. He didn't know if that was true. Nothing she told him sounded true. The only thing he knew for certain was that the leg looked terrible. He'd blitzed the man with half a ton of antibiotics; the last thing he needed now was another emergency operation in the garage.

"Tell him that if he doesn't treat the infection, he'll probably lose the leg."

Sirkit translated and the fellow burst out laughing.

He said the leg will be fine, that you obviously do not know that Eritreans are the world champions in the 500-meter race.

Eitan saw the rare, secret smile Sirkit gave the man. As if they were sharing a joke that had slipped out from behind the bars of the translation.

"World champions in the 500-meter race?"

That is the range of the Egyptian rifles. Anyone who does not run it fast enough does not get here.

She stood up and walked out with the man. The lunar eye illuminated them as the man took some notes out of his pocket and handed them to Sirkit. Eitan watched them, fascinated. Sirkit came back into the garage. She took a squeegee and began scrubbing the concrete floor, her only words to Eitan a request for him to move a bit; she wanted to wash there. He watched her as she cleaned. Practiced, rapid movements.

"That woman who was here earlier."

Yes?

"She said you take money. That anyone who doesn't pay doesn't get treated."

So?

She continued scrubbing with the same movement of the squeegee. Not faster, not slower. And Eitan was suddenly very much aware of the bright circles around her wrist and the cigarette that had burned them into her skin.

"She also said that your husband beat you."

She swept the water out, her hands fisted around the squeegee. She wiped the clean floor with a rag until not a drop of water was left. She folded the rag into four precise, equal quarters.

So?

*   *   *

After he left, she cleaned the garage again. The movements were rhythmic and measured, like the rowing of a boat in calm waters. The place was clean, of that she had no doubt. But she cleaned the concrete floor again anyway, scrubbed the rusty iron table with a cloth. The body worked and the mind was serene or at least tried to be, because as soon as she stopped moving for a few seconds she was gripped by such a strong sense of unease that she immediately began moving again, cutting across the floor back and forth, back and forth.

She'd never know what might have happened if the suv hadn't appeared out of nowhere that night and hit him. How many more times he would have punched her, and whether she would ever have hit him back. And that's how it would always be. She had been given her life by someone else, by that doctor who had certainly not meant to give it to her.

There were five bright circles on her wrist, and she remembered her skin burning and the smell of his tobacco the night he burned them into her flesh. As she dipped the rag into the water again, she thought she hated that woman as much as she hated him, the woman who had knelt on the ground in their shack that night and waited for it to be over. She wanted to grab her by the hair, the stupid cow, to jerk her to her feet so she could hit her again. How could you let him? You didn't even scream. The doctor is guilty of running him over, but you, you are guilty of not running him over. You did nothing.

She put the squeegee in the corner and went outside to hang up the rag. There was no doubt, she was an expert in hiding from life. She had done it for thirty-one years. Mainly from her husband, who had filled the entire shack, bursting out through the roof. Her husband was as large as God, but not as evil. Sometimes he'd sit on the mattress and she would let her hair down, and he would untangle all the knots with his fingers. Gently. So it wouldn't hurt her. She would sit with her back to him, her eyes closed, and he would untangle all the knots with his fingers, the way he straightened a tangled fishing net. He knew how to untangle the strands of the net without tearing even a single one, so gentle were his fingers. She would close her eyes and breathe. Outside the shack, people were burning garbage. Asum's fingers smelled of tobacco and fish. He ran them back and forth through her hair, until there wasn't a single knot left. And then her hair also smelled of tobacco and fish. Sometimes he kept running his fingers through her hair even when there were no more knots to untangle. They would meander up and down, up and down, twisting, winding movements, like a line of ants, like the flow of a river, like a tenderness she couldn't describe now, but remembered suddenly at the base of her skull. And the entire time his fingers wandered through her hair, the whistle wandered through his lips. Stopping only when he stopped for a moment to spit on the floor, then beginning once again.

He had brought the whistle with him one day from the sea. Said he'd gotten it from the fish. That didn't sound logical, but Asum wasn't one of those people you contradicted. And the whistle was really nice. So was the melody, which was different from anything she'd known before, and the way his lips pursed when he whistled it, the way he looked momentarily like the little boy he might have been once, sort of sweet and not at all frightening.

When they left the village, he took the whistle with him, but he no longer looked like a little boy when he pursed his lips. He looked like a tired, angry man. In a few weeks, the smell of the fish left his fingers. They both felt it, but no one mentioned it. Without the smell of the fish, his fingers were like a person whose shadow had been cut away. Everything was there, but something important was missing. Far from the sea, his hands choked in the sun like the fish on the floor of the shack. He kept smoking tobacco, but stopped untangling her knots with his fingers, and he spoke to her as little as possible. There were days when the whistle was the only thing that came out of his mouth. The same melody, but different. Slower, and dusty.

Until the night that Bedouin told her to come to his tent. He walked past the group of seated women, examining them slowly, one by one, and then motioned for her to stand up. She was about to do it when she heard Asum's whistle. This time the melody was fast, strong, almost cheerful. Surprised, the Bedouin turned around to the group of men. Standing among all the downcast faces was her husband, whistling.

The Bedouin cocked his rifle and told him not to be a wise guy. Asum stopped whistling and said, "Let's see what kind of man you are without the rifle." The Bedouin handed his rifle to one of his pals and said, "No problem," but you could see in his eyes that he was a bit worried. Asum was a head and a half taller, and despite everything that had happened since they left the village, his shoulders were still broad. But the Bedouin need not have been concerned. Days had passed since any of them had eaten normally, and since the smell of fish had gone, Asum's hands had grown weaker. He was on the ground in less than a minute. The Bedouin shoved his head deep into the sand and said, "Now let's see if you can whistle." Then he kicked him a few more times and left him, and she would never know if the Bedouin remembered her at that point, whether he intended to drag her to the tent or he'd already had enough amusement for one night, because right after that, Asum whistled again. His face was full of sand and blood was running from his lips. He could barely purse them. The sound that emerged was fragmented, damaged. It wasn't a whistle at all. And yet, she recognized the melody immediately, and so did the Bedouin, because this time he didn't settle for kicking him. He let Asum get up and try to hit him, then started battering him as soon as his fist missed its target. It took a few minutes, but it felt like more, and the Bedouin seemed to feel that way too because when he finally finished (Asum's face looked like a doughy mass), he wiped his hands on his *galabiya*, took his rifle from his friend and walked away.

Sirkit hurried over to the man lying on the ground who was her husband. She wiped the blood from his lips. She cleaned the sand from his face. She wanted to kiss his fingers, which smelled neither of tobacco nor of fish, when he clenched those fingers in a fist and punched her harder than she had ever been punched before. It caught her right in the stomach. He had already hit her before, but never like that. Maybe because this time he'd hit her especially hard. And maybe he'd always hit her like that, but her muscles weren't ready this time. Relaxed, loose, not tensed with fear. When she'd seen him lying there covered in blood and sand, she hadn't felt the slightest bit of fear. She hurried over to him not because she was afraid of him, but because she was concerned about him. He had seen that there was no fear in her eyes and was alarmed, because it was one thing to lose the smell of the sea on your fingers, and something else to lose the fear in your wife's eyes. It didn't matter that the fear in her eyes had been replaced by tenderness. He didn't know what to do with tenderness. He didn't know what tenderness said about him. The fear in her eyes told him he was as he had been before, that nothing had changed. The tenderness said something else that he could not understand. Nor did he want to. Too many things had changed or had been lost. And he needed her fear. He had to have it in order to know who he was.

Now she was the one lying on the ground with her face in the sand. Asum was standing and spitting blood to the side. She looked at him and said to herself, stupid cow, did you really think he did it for you. It was not for you. When a man forces himself inside you and tears your flesh, he has no idea what "for you" is. It is for him. He would not let anyone else do it to *his* wife. No one but him.

Outside the garage, the night was round and quiet. The rocks lay in their place, and so did the sky, and they did not touch each other. On the night of the whistling, Asum was on the ground and she was standing, and then she was on the ground and Asum was standing, and in the middle of the night the Bedouin came and stood over her, and said come. Tonight she stood outside the garage and knew that if she wanted, she could tell her doctor to come, and he would do so immediately. And if she told him to treat a patient, he would. And if she told him to hop (like that boy at the far end of the camp who had pointed his rifle at them and said they were not allowed to be there now, so they should hop all the way back), her doctor would hop. She knew all that. But, she said to herself, you will never know what would have happened if he had not run over Asum that night. If, one day, you would have managed to get up and go, or if you would have stayed with him for ever, living from one punch to another. The silence of the heart between one beat and the next, that was what her life had seemed like to her. And the fact that it did not seem like that now was really very nice. But you will never know, she thought, you will never know how much of that power is yours, and how much is just chance.

They called him twice from the department, but there wasn't a single call from Liat, and that seemed strange to him. He was already beginning to wonder whether the girl who died on the table in the garage yesterday really was the same Mona his wife had talked about. The possibility that she was a different girl filled him with hope. The call from the precinct which had come at dawn could have been connected to some other case. Liat hadn't said anything when she left and he was trying as hard as he could to stay asleep. All the way home, he played with the new possibility that had opened up. Mona and the boy were alive and well. He almost dared to picture their faces, amusing himself with thoughts of those two children's forbidden love. It wasn't the same Mona. Any doubts he had about it diminished from moment to moment. Liat would have called to tell him if that girl were dead. After all, she felt especially close to the case of the Eritrean and the Bedouin boy and girl who had recently become part of it.

But when he went into the house he found her on the couch, her eyes red. He knew right away, and he was angry that he had allowed himself not to know. He had spent the drive home deceiving himself with illusions, telling himself lovely stories about a young boy and girl riding a camel into the sunset. He sat down beside Liat, waiting for the moment she would tell him what he already knew, preparing comforting words in advance, a hug, points in her favor in the argument that was most certainly taking place in her mind. It's not your fault, that girl, it's not your fault. So he didn't understand at first when instead of telling him about the death of the girl, she looked at him with veiled eyes and asked, "Where were you?"

"On duty."

"That's not what they told me when I called the hospital today to tell you that the Bedouin girl died." And before he could think of what to say, she was standing up and looking at him furiously. "They asked me how Yaheli's asthma attacks were, the ones that were the reason you left the hospital early."

5

EITAN AND LIAT HAD NOT been speaking for more than a week. Words were spoken. Words were spoken in response. There's no more milk and where's Yaheli's backpack and I'll take him to nursery school today. Sometimes their shoulders touched when they put the children to bed together or when they were drying them off in the bathroom. Liat set the table for dinner, Eitan put the dirty plates in the sink. Liat loaded the dishwasher, Eitan put the dishes back in the cabinet. Days came, days went, and Eitan and Liat did not speak. And during that time, their kitchen sink filled and waned, like the moon.

Dishes were loaded. Dishes were taken out. Plastic bags filled up with garbage and were thrown into the bin in the yard. The bin in the yard filled up with plastic bags of garbage and was emptied into a garbage truck. The garbage in the truck was dumped at the landfill in the Negev, where it was buried in the depths of the earth. The earth filled up with garbage. Filled and filled and could not be emptied, and the dust rose from it like an affront, rose and enshrouded the city of Beersheba, rose and enshrouded it all the way to Omer. But Eitan and Liat's kitchen sink gleamed in the cleanliness of its dazzling marble whiteness. Glittered in the darkness. Its light bursting through the dust. A marble moon filled and waned in the stainless steel sky.

In the end, she forgave him. He swore to her again and again that the time he spent outside the hospital was spent alone. Air, he told her, he had needed air. He described his drives on the SUV tracks, back and forth on the dirt roads, night after night. But why lie, she asked, why not just say it. His answers were stammering, incomplete, but the scent of perfume did not rise from them. And in his eyes she saw loneliness, not unfaithfulness. As angry as she was at him, she began to be angry at herself as well. What did he have in this place? She had dragged him here almost by force. She could have let him pursue his case against Zakai, could have let him go to the media. He might have lost his job, but his pride, that invisible internal organ men need in order to exist, would have remained intact. So he got into his SUV and drove. For hours. Entire nights. And perhaps it was better that way, because in fact, what would she have done if he had come home with all the frustration, with his anger at the transfer, the missed opportunity? She didn't even know how to handle Yaheli's fits of anger, needed Eitan to calm him down, so how would she have handled the humiliation of a forty-one-year-old man who, for the first time in his life, found himself ousted, outranked, no longer Number One?

She knew that any other woman would have started checking up on him long ago. And she knew that she, who checked up on and investigated others on a daily basis, she, of all people, would never do that. She wasn't willing to look at him with those eyes of doubt. To look for signs, traces. She wasn't willing because if she began doing that now, she wasn't sure she would be able to stop later. On safari in Kenya, after their wedding, the guide had told them that once a lion tastes human flesh, it won't ever want to hunt anything else. Perhaps it wasn't true, just a story for tourists, but her lioness's instincts knew there was no greater temptation, no hunt more tantalizing, than the ambush of your loved ones.

That was why you should not do it. So that they wouldn't lie there in front of you, split open, their secrets spilling out of their intestines. You had to remember – not everything should be examined. And stop. Before.

As it was, she saw too much. Knew that when Itamar said the class trip was fine, he was actually saying he'd had no one to sit next to. Saw it in the corners of his eyes, the slight tilt of his head. But she didn't say anything to him, to avoid embarrassing him, and she didn't tell Eitan, to keep him from worrying. Perhaps she also hoped that one day she would manage not to tell even herself, manage to turn off the x-ray machine in her head that showed her what people had in their suitcases and in their hearts.

It was a complicated business, seeing. Because she felt so big and strong when she rummaged around inside people without their noticing, without a search warrant. Because, when she was doing her bachelor's degree, one look was enough for her to know who was pregnant, not from the girl's body, which was still flat, but from the hand resting protectively on her stomach. And later, when she was doing her master's degree, she had dinner with those same students and their husbands, determining what sort of marriage they had based on whether they held hands only when they walked in, a temporary display, or continued to hold hands later. She could recognize the difference between remoteness that grew out of a lack of confidence and remoteness that stemmed from condescension, between artificial restraint and true calm, healthy flirtatiousness and seductiveness. She knew and held back, always remembering her grandmother's warning: be careful you don't get mixed up with the looks. Don't be too sure that you're looking outside when all you're actually seeing is what's inside you.

How could she really know about Itamar's trip? The empty seat next to him on the bus might not have been empty at all. Maybe she'd confused it with a different seat, a different bus, years ago. An empty seat on the way to a getting-to-know-each-other day during her first week at Ma'agan Michael. She'd looked out of the window then, trying to be interested in the countryside, as if she couldn't have cared less that no one was sitting next to her. But you could see it. In the angle of her eyes. In the slight tilt of her head. On the way back, she was already sitting next to Sharon. Seven hours of class activities had been enough for her to become part of the group. But she remembered the earlier ride very well, always remembered it. Trees and buildings passing by outside. She had looked at them to avoid looking at the gang of happy girls inside. She looked and said, there's a tree. There's a building. There's an interchange. But she was actually saying: I'm alone, alone, alone.

You could never really know what was happening inside someone else's head. But you could try. Watch the windows of the house patiently until a momentary gust of wind pushed the curtain aside. Then peer inside. And fill in the missing pieces in your mind. The only thing you have to remember is that the missing pieces you've added have come from you, not from there.

She wouldn't follow Eitan because she didn't want to look through the window into her own house. There was no better way to desecrate a house. But she didn't want to see Eitan like that, to catch him unawares. As if she were stealing something from him, and he had no idea. So she made a thorough check of his lies when he lied to her, and asked again about where he'd been. But she didn't check up on him, didn't track him. She scrupulously protected him from her hunter's eyes. Protected herself as well.

She started sleeping with him again. One night she removed the imaginary line that divided the bed in the middle and reached out to him, and they slept in each other's arms again. But her sleep was sad and scanty, and the days were enveloped in a sort of yellow haze. There was something he wasn't telling her. The investigator in her knew that even if the woman in her chose to ignore it. She lost it only once. Three days after they made up, he told her he had a half-shift. At 8:15, he called to say goodnight to Yaheli and Itamar. The kids talked to him briefly and went back to watching *March of the Penguins*. She sat on the couch in front of the sea lions and albatrosses and thought that she actually had no idea where he was now. The clear certainty she had felt throughout their twelve years of marriage – certainty that Eitan was where he said he was – collapsed now like a gigantic iceberg crumbling all at once. She sat in the living room and heard nothing but the roar of doubt. Endless possibilities swirled in her mind. He could have been calling from a hotel. A car. Another woman's bedroom. He could have been calling from Tel Aviv. Jerusalem. A nearby apartment. Only one line can be drawn between two points, but an endless number of lies and deceptions can be drawn between two people. From moment to moment, the possibility that he was where he'd told her he was – doing a half-shift in the department – grew dimmer. She thought about calling there, but knew it wouldn't be enough for her. A voice was too abstract. She needed a body. Needed to see Eitan in his white coat, with the stubble of his beard, in the place where he'd told her he was.

The high-school girl who lived across the street said she'd be happy to watch the kids for an hour. Liat explained to her how Yaheli liked his cocoa, left her phone number and hurried to the car. The first call came even before she was out of Omer.

"Mom?"

"Yes, E.T."

"Where are you?"

"Driving. I had to go out for an hour."

"You're coming back?"

"Of course, sweetie."

Silence. He had nothing to say, but he still wasn't ready to hang up. And perhaps she didn't want him to hang up and leave her alone in the car, black thoughts hanging over her like bats.

"Are you going to see Dad?"

She almost slammed on the brakes in the middle of the road, suddenly realizing that Itamar could read her as well as she could read him. That thought upset her, but she quickly reassured herself, kids are like that, they don't understand that Mom and Dad can exist apart from one another; for them, if Mom is driving somewhere, it's to see Dad, and if Dad dials the phone, it's always to Mom.

"E.T., we'll talk later. I'm driving."

She knew she hadn't answered his question, but preferred not answering to lying. She'd rather raise him with questions that remained open than in a world filled with false answers. Or maybe she was using a well-reasoned educational argument to disguise what was in fact nothing but negligence. She didn't have much time to think about it, because five minutes later, Yaheli's call came.

"Mommy, are you there?"

Mommy was there; the question was, where was Liat? Once she thought that motherhood was another thing you added to yourself. Something large, binding, but none the less something that was added to *you*, to who you were. That was how she introduced herself to people: Hello. I'm Liat. Mother of two. But she apparently should have said it the other way round: Hello. I'm a mother of two. Liat. That mother of two had swallowed her up a long time ago. Liat was a leftover, what was spit up when the mother of two burped. But now, tonight, she had to be slightly less mother and much more Liat. Decisive. Impulsive. Listening intently to the voices inside her and not the ones outside.

"Mommy's here, Yaheli, but Mommy can't talk now. Tell Netta to make you some cocoa."

She continued driving. Five minutes later, the call from Netta. Liat was already at the hospital, trying to find a parking spot, trying to explain to a frustrated sixteen-year-old girl how Yaheli wanted his cocoa.

"Did you mix it well enough so there are no lumps?"

"Yes, but he won't drink it. Says it doesn't taste good."

Liat was about to shout at her that there was no reason it shouldn't taste good, it was the same cocoa powder, the same milk, but she knew Yaheli wouldn't drink it until the last necessary ingredient, the secret spice, had been added – total maternal dedication to his every need and desire. He wouldn't drink it until she was there with him, at home. But she wouldn't get home until after she'd been in the hospital.

So she ended the call. Took a deep breath. Put her lipstick on in front of the rearview mirror. It might be ludicrous to put on makeup before an appearance like this one, but she thought it was important to come prepared, not to discover his unfaithfulness without lipstick. Like her grandmother, who plucked her eyebrows carefully before every visit to the tax department. At one time, Liat had found that funny. Even a bit annoying. As if the clerk cared whether or not you were wearing blusher. But her grandmother had continued to cover herself in the armor of her makeup right before taking to the battlefield. Spread her blue powder over her eyelids, knowing that as a small woman facing something large, she had to stand as proudly as she could. Even the day before her last operation, she had asked Liat to dye her hair. Liat hadn't understood why. She thought her grandmother's white hair was the most beautiful thing there was. But her grandmother insisted. "So the doctors won't think I'm old. They'll see red hair and they'll fight harder." Even death was frightened away by red hair, but when it saw white hair, it snatched up what it came for. In the department's disgusting bathroom, under the nurses' noses, Liat had died her grandmother's hair. Her hands shook slightly. Red drops of dye dripped onto the floor. Her grandmother said, "They'll think somebody was slaughtered in here." And they had laughed and laughed, almost until they cried, even though it wasn't all that funny.

Now she finished applying her lipstick and examined herself in the mirror. When all was said and done, she was a beautiful woman. She took out a tube of mascara and applied a heavy layer, blocking any possibility of tears. She wasn't the sort of woman who sobbed, leaving her mascara to run down her face in blue-black streams. She'd get out of the car beautiful and carefully made up, and she'd get back inside it beautiful and carefully made up no matter what she discovered.

The guard at the entrance gave her bag a cursory look. She walked to the elevators and knew she had no idea what she'd do when she got to the department. Look for him? That would be easy if he was there, but so humiliating if he wasn't.

On the other hand, there was a good chance she'd have to talk to someone. For example, if Eitan was in surgery.

But how would she know if he really was in surgery? Maybe they'd just back him up. All of them. Maybe it was a woman from his department he had disappeared with, and the brotherhood of doctors and nurses would close ranks around them. Just as cars moved aside to make way for an ambulance with its siren blaring, other thoughts moved aside in her mind until there was nothing left to block the suspicions from racing forward.

Then they stopped abruptly when, through the glass window of the department door, she saw the face of her man. He didn't see her. Another doctor was standing in front of him, and both were reading through a pile of papers Eitan was holding. Observing him from a distance, she saw clearly how tired he was, how drained and tense. His left hand was on his waist, supporting his lower back after God knows how many hours of standing. His shoulders were slightly stooped. His smile stopped a long way before it reached his eyes. There was something heartbreaking about the man standing on the other side of the door. His innocence, the knowledge that he didn't have the slightest idea that she was watching him at that moment, a witness to his mid-shift fatigue. He was sure she was at home with the children, when in fact she was here, ten meters and one half-glass door away from him. It made him so vulnerable it was almost unbearable.

She turned around and left. On the way back to the car, she found herself crying. The mascara ran. The lipstick remained bleeding in the middle of her face. When she reached the house, she wiped away her tears in the driveway. Rubbed out the black stripes of makeup with drops of saliva. In another moment she'd walk into the living room, smiling. She'd send the apathetic babysitter home, give Yaheli his cocoa and remind Itamar to go to sleep early. She'd act as if she had never gone to check up on her husband. And everything would be fine, excellent even, because although Liat was dying to crawl under the blanket and cry her heart out for the pain of his lie and the shame of her drive to the hospital, for a mother of two there was no such thing as crying your heart out. For a mother of two, everything is fine. So she waited another minute. Even two. And promised herself she would never, ever again in her life check up on her man.

Instead, she did what she always did when the house became an unsolvable puzzle, and focused totally on the puzzle outside. Since the Bedouin girl had been killed, two guys had managed to stab another guy to death at the entrance to the Forum club. Each of them insisted that the other had done the stabbing, which made the whole business complicated. One of them was a soldier on leave, which made the newspapers drool. Punks could stab each other as often as they wanted, but not soldiers. Marciano called her in for a talk and said he was counting on her, and she said, fine, as long as he didn't take her off the case with the Eritrean. It took him a minute to remember what she was talking about. "That case is closed," he said. "Why would you want to go digging up a hit and run that happened more than two months ago?"

The Eritrean's employer, Davidson, kept calling her. He was sure some Bedouin had run him over.

Marciano said he was sick of hearing about that Eritrean, he had enough trouble with the Bedouins. But if that's what she wanted to do in her free time after she found out which of the little shits had stabbed that guy at the entrance to the Forum, then good luck to her.

That made her feel good, his answer. The Eritrean's case hadn't been just a case for a while now; she needed it because of the Bedouin girl. Because she didn't want the whole story to be for nothing. A tremor ran through her when she thought about her visit to the morgue. The girl had been lying there with dry blood covering her stomach and Liat suddenly realized that she had polish on her toenails. She must have bought it at one of the stalls in the Beersheba central bus station. Slipped into the bathroom to apply it, taken off her shoes, waited for it to dry. Then she went back to the village, all covered up. No one but she and Ali knew. Liat looked at her red toenails for another minute, and then knew that if she were to look at them for one more minute she might vomit, so she went out.

Sitting on a bench outside the morgue, she had told herself once again that it wasn't her fault. After all, she'd been the one who'd insisted that they send her to a shelter for at-risk girls, knowing full well what the dangers were. But on the other hand, how difficult would it have been to locate that shelter for anyone who really wanted to? And what were the chances that Mona herself might have missed home, called her mother, given out details?

She decided not to be present at Ali's interrogation. Marciano said that was a shame, maybe her being there would make him say something, but he didn't insist. In the end, they both knew there was no way the boy would tell them who had stabbed his girlfriend. When they walked him to the interrogation room, she saw him through the glass wall of her office. He didn't look at her. In retrospect, it might not have been him. Another Bedouin brought in on drug charges or theft or illegal peddling. A quick look through the glass wasn't enough for a clear identification. And even if the look hadn't been so quick, even if it had been quite long, she still would have felt a tiny bit of uncertainty. Embarrassing as it was, she had to admit that they all looked alike to her. The same. It was difficult to differentiate the boy's face from all the other faces. There was a good chance that if she met him on the street in another two months, she wouldn't recognize him and she'd pass him by without nodding hello. Or maybe she would nod, but at someone else. Someone she had never spent time with in a locked room, who hadn't broken down, hadn't cried in front of her. Someone whose only connection to that boy was the fact that they were both Arabs. Both were Arabs, so they were identical. Both aroused a combination of wariness and shame in her. First wariness, then shame. Their dark faces, which actually resembled the faces of the people she'd grown up with, and yet looked different. The restrained anger she saw in their eyes, whether they were laughing or crying or plastering the building across the street. The Western clothes, which always looked a bit strange on them, didn't suit them. Oddly cut jeans. Arab-style jeans. Shirts that were always too tight or too brightly colored or too shoddy. Shoes that just didn't match their clothes. That hateful signature mustache. The thick black hair. She didn't like feeling that way, but it was how she felt. That they had less intelligence and more hatred. That they were pathetic because they'd lost, but more dangerous because of it, and even though that seemed contradictory, it actually wasn't. Like a dog you've beaten that you now both ridicule and fear. An Arab dog. She would have given hell to any other detective in the precinct if he'd said anything like that, but why? He would only be saying out loud what she shouldn't have been thinking. And that whole struggle with Marciano to let her continue investigating the Eritrean's death was only to prove to herself that she wasn't one of those people who thought all blacks were the same. Or one of those people who thought a good Arab was a dead Arab and a good Bedouin was a Bedouin in prison. She was different. But when it came right down to it, she wouldn't go to a swimming pool full of Arabs even if she ranted and raved when there was a sign at the entrance saying NO ARABS ALLOWED. That was the whole point: to get angry when someone discriminated against Arabs or when there was a racially motivated clash at the Sachne spring, knowing that she herself would never go to the Sachne spring because she spent her vacation at the elegant Mitzpe Yamim spa. There were no Arabs or loud, low-class types there, only people in lovely white robes smelling of lavender.

She promised Marciano the Eritrean investigation wouldn't be at the expense of that business with the soldiers and hurried out of his office. All she needed was for him to dump another case on her now. Back in her office, she closed the door and called Davidson. Asked him to tell her more about the Bedouins. He cooperated happily, said that since the accident, he'd noticed that guys from the Abu Ayad tribe had been driving in the area a lot at night. Maybe she should sniff around there. She said thanks, she'd check it out, and hung up. Two minutes later, she was in the cruiser. She was no longer thinking about small toenails with red polish or about the wasteland of her double bed. She only thanked God for the murders, thefts and investigations that allowed a person to become totally involved in other people's secrets and not ponder her own.

6

A FTER THAT NIGHT in the "ENJOY THE HOSPITALITY
OF THE PEOPLE OF THE DESERT" tent, Sharaf's father
didn't take him to work anymore. It took him time to go back
there himself. Matti offered the boy's family free entrance
for their entire lives, just as long as they didn't post anything
about what had happened on any of those Internet sites. He
also swore to them that it hadn't been a terrorist attack and
there was no reason to call the police. True, the Bedouin's
kid had picked up the pestle generally used to demonstrate
traditional coffee grinding and hit their son in the eye with
it, giving him one hell of a shiner. But it wasn't deliberate.
Just a childish prank. Something meant to be just pretend
that turned out to be for real.

That night, Mussa drove home in silence as Sharaf sat beside
him, still wearing the *galabiya*, because with all the commotion
he hadn't had time to change back into his clothes. Shortly
after they left the kibbutz, Mussa pulled the van over to the
side of the road and said, "Now explain to me what the hell
that was all about." Sharaf said nothing. It was perfectly clear
what it had been about and he didn't see any reason to speak.
Mussa banged the wheel with both hands in a gesture that
was similar, and very different, from the way he'd banged the

241

darbuka earlier. At the end of each night on the kibbutz, he'd return to the village with 150 shekels rolled up in his warm, clenched fist. Now his hands were empty. As was the look on the boy's face.

"Sharaf, those people were our guests. You shamed yourself and hit our guests."

"Our guests? That wasn't even your tent, how can they be our guests?!"

Mussa's hand rose from the wheel and landed on Sharaf's cheek, and however bad that was, it was also good because it meant that his father wasn't a total wimp. He didn't say anything, nor did his father, and his cheek began to grow numb from the slap and heat spread over his entire face. Inside the silence neither of them noticed the cruiser, and so, suddenly hearing a megaphone behind them, both jumped in such a way that on any other day would have been funny.

"Please step out of the vehicle."

Sharaf and Mussa got out of the van and a policeman and policewoman got out of the cruiser. In the dark, Sharaf saw that the policewoman was fat and pretty. The policeman shone his flashlight on them and saw Sharaf's red cheek and the impression of Mussa's hand on it, five fingers right where the slap had landed, and asked, "You have a license and registration?"

Mussa nodded quickly. He went to the van and took out the papers, and all the while the policeman reprimanded him for stopping on the side of the road and not in a proper parking bay, because it was against the law to stop on the side of the road except for an emergency, and Mussa said, "Yes, sir, that's clear, sir, I'm really sorry, sir." A few minutes later the policeman returned Mussa's license to him after checking it on the terminal, and said, "Okay, so who are you waiting for?"

"No one, sir."

"Is that so?" the fat, pretty policewoman said. "No one? A delivery, a stolen car, something?"

Sharaf had already opened his mouth to reply when his father said, "Of course not, ma'am, we're not waiting for anything," and he continued to smile the same smile he'd had on his face when the kid had made fun of him in the tent. "Then *ya'allah*," the policeman said, "get going before I give you a ticket for illegal parking on the side of the road." Mussa hurried into the van and said, "Yes, sir, thank you, sir," and Sharaf followed him inside and said, "Fuck you, sir," but quietly.

7

E RITREA.
A country in north-east Africa on the coast of the Red
Sea. Its sovereignty also includes the Dahlak Islands and several
additional small islands.

Continent: Africa.

Official language: Tigrinya, Arabic.

Capital: Asmara.

Form of government: Presidential republic.

Head of state: Isaias Afwerki.

Independence: May 24, 1993.

Previous rulers: Ethiopia, Italy.

Territory: 117,600 kilometers.

Bodies of water: negligible.

Population: 6,233,682.

GNP per capita: $708.

Currency: Nakfa.

International rating: 170th in the world

International area code: +291.

There were pictures as well, both black-and-white and
color. A detailed map showing climate zones. A historical
summary that began in 2500 BCE. A description of relations
with pharaonic Egypt under the rule of Hephaestus, and of

the occupation of the Ottoman Empire in the sixteenth century. There was an extensive entry on the form of government and less extensive entries on economy, geography and human rights. Eitan read them all. Lingered on the photographs. Looked at each and every one. The ancient site in the south of the country. The Greek Orthodox church in the capital. The insurrectionists' convoy of weapons. Villagers. Men. Women. Children. Some looking at the camera, some looking off to the side. He studied them at length. As if hoping to suddenly recognize her face in that sea of faces.

And if not her, then at least a door. A window. Even a crack. Something through which he could finally enter and understand. He read about the demographic composition. The main exports. He read without knowing exactly what he was searching for, but knew that if he were ever to find it, he'd find it there. Local currency. Average monthly income. Maximum temperatures in August. If a person is a reflection of the landscape of his homeland, then all those details should merge into something. A portrait. The face of a woman burned in 45-degrees-Celcius-in-the-shade and washed in the average precipitation of 11 millimeters per annum.

He had been avoiding her for twenty days. Keeping away from the garage. And now, looking at the enlarged map of the smuggling route pictured on the computer monitor, he tried to find her footprints on it. Eritrea in purple. Sudan and Egypt in orange. Israel in blue. Black lines separating them. And at some point, she had walked along those lines. Had raised a foot and moved from purple to orange. From the orange country to the blue country. The ground, in any case, had remained brown. It had been brown all through the journey. (But how did he actually know? How many kilometers had she walked on white chalkstone, on red loam; when had her feet been defeated by hard gravel and when had she struggled through sand dunes? He didn't know. He couldn't know. He could count the kilometers, but he couldn't describe what she saw on the side of the road.)

Unconsciously, he moved his hand on the desk. The surface was cold, smooth. Not a drop of dust. And yet something in the feel of it bothered him, he didn't know why. As if the pads of his fingers felt how much deception there was in that cleanliness. How much falsehood. He pushed his chair back, looked at the desk again uncomprehendingly. Everything stood in front of him within easy reach. No layer of dirt separated him from the thing itself. (But that wasn't true. A layer always accumulated there, in the center. You couldn't erase the curtain of particles, the veil that separated you from the other. The dust resisted the hand trying to wipe it away. Adding more before you could see it. The dust persisted.)

Finally he stood up. Turned off the computer. He could stare at pictures and maps for hours. Compare the Hebrew Wikipedia to the English entry. Damn it, he knew by heart the GNP for the last ten years – and it wouldn't move him even a centimeter forward. It didn't matter how much he read and studied, even if he caught a plane and toured. He would not understand her. An unknown in an equation he couldn't solve. A reality evading him in an entry on the computer.

He had loved encyclopedias even before he knew how to read. He loved the idea that two shelves in his parents' library could store knowledge on everything there was. Even when he understood that they didn't, he still loved to think it was merely a matter of the number of shelves. If only there were more shelves, everything could be catalogued. Minerals. Butterflies. Capital cities. TV series. Types of irons. Everything. Even if no single human brain was capable of containing all that information, it still existed – sorted, detailed, comprehensible. Just as a person didn't have to actually stand on Pluto in order to appreciate the fact that it was five trillion kilometers from the sun, and that its atmosphere was composed of nitrogen and methane.

But here, with her, he had his first encounter with a fence behind which was knowledge inaccessible to him. Though he had long ago conquered Pluto with the power of his mind, through his knowledge, he was unable to conquer even a small part of her. She put up boundaries against him. Her differentness drove him mad; he was naïve, ignorant in the face of it. She herself was the master of things that existed in the depths of her eyes. He could read as much as he wanted about Eritrea, could wander among countless sites, articles, position papers on Eritreans. But *that* Eritrean he could not understand.

Although occasionally he thought he could. For instance, when he saw her carrying a carton of drugs in the garage one night and accidentally bang into the iron leg of the table. It hurt like hell, her face screamed it. A small but nasty blow, the sort that doesn't do any real damage, but makes you writhe in pain a few minutes later. It happened right in front of the waiting patients, and Eitan suddenly realized that Sirkit wasn't the least bit bothered by the blow, but by the fact that it had happened in the presence of witnesses. It embarrassed her to hurt herself so stupidly in front of everyone, and she was smart enough to recognize the slight undertone of gloating in the others' sympathetic words, ("that's a funny way to get hurt" or "I'm glad it didn't happen to me"). And then, right before his eyes, she did exactly what he himself would have done in that situation – pretended everything was fine. She wiped the expression of pain from her face. Straightened up. Responded with a soothing smile to the words of one of the women awaiting treatment. Then she limped out of there, trying with all her might to hide the fact that she was limping. He watched her leave, his eyes wide, as if he had suddenly met a double of himself on the street. His twin, of whose existence he had known nothing. When he'd fallen from a pine tree during the summer vacation before middle school and received a blow to his testicles that had almost made him faint, he too had pushed away the pain instantly in the face of a larger monster the fear that it would be seen. The terror of mortification was greater than the pain in his groin. The twelve-year-old boy he had been then and the thirty-year-old woman she was now both shrank from a scornful look more than from any physical pain.

There were other moments like that. For example, when he realized that she also stared in fascination through the garage door at the rising of a red moon. Moments when he looked at her and thought: she's like me. (But never, I'm like her.) Such as when he had discovered the roses she grew outside of her caravan, and returned to the garage deeply moved. But then, he reminded himself, when he had returned to the garage, he'd discovered how unlike him she was. She was ready to send away that Bedouin girl. Africa is a cruel continent, and a cruel continent grows cruel people on it. Savage people. She was ready to let that girl bleed to death. Had looked at her with the coldest eyes in the world. And you, he thought in sudden anger, weren't you ready to let someone bleed to death? How do you even know about what unfinished business she might have with the Bedouins? Then that fleeting sense of kinship with her was gone again, and he realized once again how unlike him she was. The distance between a hungry person and a sated one is greater than the distance between here and the moon.

He left his computer on the desk and went over to the fridge. Goat yoghurt, granola, a banana, an apple. He put everything on the counter and went out to the garden. The ground was still damp from the rare, pre-dawn rain. He ignored the manicured lawn, squinted and focused on the moon. She would have loved the smell. There was no one who didn't love that smell. He inhaled the miracle of the night rain and thought that perhaps she wasn't really that distant. Because he knew with absolute certainty that her nostrils would widen with pleasure at the smell of rain-wet earth. And if there was rain-wet earth, then there certainly must be other things. They could understand one another. She was angry at him, and he understood why. And if her anger was comprehensible to him, it meant he could imagine how he himself would feel in her shoes. (In her sandals? In her bare feet?) And when she smiled, an event even rarer than desert rain, he understood why. He could guess her and she could guess him, and since a guess was always based on the guesser's soul, then apparently their souls were not so distant.

In the end, what was there? Spleen, pancreas, liver. When it came right down to it, all bodies resembled each other. But it was a great affront to say such a thing about souls. A person could easily bear the idea that his lungs functioned the same way as another person's. But not the possibility that his love, or his loss, were identical to his neighbor's. On one hand, that was true; one person's affront or jealousy was not identical to another's. This one's jealousy was inflamed and that one's was mild. Here the affront was benign, there malignant. On the other hand, despite changes in shape and size, their internal organs were the same: jealousy, greed, desire, affection, guilt, anger, affront. He could not imagine even one day in the lives of those people in Eritrea, but he could picture clearly how they would respond to trust that had been betrayed.

And it was precisely that duality that he found so alluring. The fact that one moment she looked so familiar, a variation of him. And a moment later she looked so distant, a miraculous force of nature he was encountering for the first time in his life. She worked the same terrifying magic on him that you feel when you're wandering through your house late at night and for a moment it's not clear whether there is or isn't another presence on the other side of the curtain. That deadly triviality of couch-carpet-TV peeled back all at once, and the house under it is revealed in all its unfamiliarity. Suddenly, in the dark, you're no longer certain where the wall ends and the door begins, and whether it's really a dining-room table standing there on four legs, or something else.

But now there was light, and when he left the garden to go back inside, he found it familiar, so very familiar. He sighed without knowing why. Sank into the uncomfortable softness of the couch, put his feet up on the coffee table. On the other side of the table, the other couch. Simple and present. Sickeningly familiar. No glittering eyes peered out from the darkness beneath it. In the hidden corners of the house lay only a lost coin or a forgotten toy. Or a scorpion, which was truly terrifying, but in today's medical reality posed no danger. Eitan leaned his head back and closed his eyes. He was in his home, his private house in Omer, and there was no danger in it. In the hollow of Sirkit's throat, on the other hand, there definitely was. And in the place where her forearm met her upper arm. Where her calf met her thigh, in her underarm.

Concave places where odors rise from the skin. If someone were to look through the window that morning he would think, look, here's a man tired after a night shift, his legs spread on the coffee table; he doesn't even have the strength to turn on the TV. But Eitan knew he had never been more awake. And, appalled, he realized that at that moment, at that specific moment, he was prepared to set the whole house on fire.

8

E ITAN AND LIAT are sitting on the edge of a cliff waiting for a deluge that isn't coming. Winter. The wind blasts mercilessly. Far below, the Dead Sea disappears behind a cloud of dust and sand. It's supposed to be romantic; when they spoke about it at home, it sounded romantic. But it's actually desperate. The weather forecaster says there is a chance of flooding in the Judean Desert. They are sitting in the living room watching the rain smear across the windows. Inside it's dry, too dry. The last time anything washed the place was ten days ago, when the cleaner was there. They keep watching TV even after the news ends and a man in a white lab coat is explaining something about laundry detergent to a beautiful-but-not-too-beautiful woman. A few minutes later, a presenter in a suit promises exciting, hilariously funny auditions. They remain sitting. They feel like being excited or laughing hysterically, or simply ridiculing other people. Ridicule can be a fantastic bonding substance when properly applied.

But when the program ends after forty minutes and three visits by the man in the white lab coat and the beautiful-but-not-too-beautiful woman, everything stays the same. They aren't excited, don't laugh hysterically. They don't even manage to enjoy any satisfactory ridicule. Or feel any of that nausea you get after you eat too much or watch too much TV, the nausea that is your body's way of saying you've ingested something bad. They are exactly as they were before the program; the program seeped through them like water through a strainer in the cooking program now being broadcast, or like blood through the dozens of bullet holes being pumped into a body on another channel. That moment, if they could freeze it, would contain hundreds of simultaneous possibilities. Dozens of channels. An endless kaleidoscope of activities and choices: someone steaming broccoli. Someone burying a body in the depths of a forest. Two women playing tennis. Two men arguing politics. A broadcaster speaking Arabic. German. English. Russian. (Eitan knows it isn't the same guy, but the resemblance is so great, the same suit, the same intonation, that he wonders if all the broadcasters aren't the same man, a language expert, hustled from studio to studio by the zap of a remote.) Liat persists in zapping avidly, refusing to give up. After all, somewhere, with one more zap or another 20,000 zaps, somewhere a program that will salvage the evening is waiting. Someone will make them laugh or excite them. Or at least allow them to connect to each other with the glue of ridicule. Someone will remind them how to speak to one other.

Then it suddenly occurs to her that the person has already appeared. Maybe it's the weatherman. With that arrogant smile of his and that eternal, sterile flirting with the anchorwoman (she'll never fuck you! She's only nice to you because of the cameras!): possible floods in the Judean Desert, he said, we'll be back tomorrow with pictures. Liat knows that there is no way the weatherman himself will go out to film floods. He'll wait for them in the studio, with his suit, his makeup, and his frantic efforts to find something clever to say to the anchorwoman by the next day. He won't go out to see the floods, just as he won't go out for a swim in a calm summer sea or hurry off to the winter snow in the Golan Heights. His job is to report on the weather, not to experience it. But what prevents them from actually going out to hunt for a flood? An hour-and-a-half's drive away, streams are overflowing their banks. A desert is spilling into the sea, the water washing over everything. Maybe if they go there, it will wash the heaviness off them, the silence that has solidified their tongues. Cautiously, she suggests the idea to Eitan. It's still so fragile that one gust of frost from his gray eyes will be enough to bury it for ever. But his eyes actually light up. A brilliant idea, he says, it'll be great.

They turn to each other and begin to plan. Not yet sure enough of the miracle of conversation that's happened to them to dare and turn off the TV, they shift their glance from the stir-fried broccoli, hoping they won't have to return to it. They'll drop the kids off in the morning and leave. Take a picnic blanket and some fruit with them. Maybe they'll stop to buy hummus. They'll dress warmly. Take a map. Bring newspapers. (Liat is already beginning to tense up. Why is he so anxious to bring newspapers? What would happen if, for once, it were only the two of them? Without distractions? Without other people's words to escape to? But she immediately warns herself not to say anything, not to spoil this delicate thing that is finally beginning to grow between them.)

Fifteen hours later, a man and a woman are sitting on the edge of a cliff, waiting for a deluge that doesn't come. They've already read all the newspapers and eaten all the fruit. They've folded the picnic blanket and put it in the trunk because it almost blew away in the wind. Winter. Far below, the Dead Sea disappears behind a cloud of dust and sand. They once swam there in the nude on a hot July night. It burned like hell, but was terribly funny. They're both thinking about that now, but neither one mentions it. When the flood comes, adrenaline and excitement will blast their bodies. The water will flow down from Jerusalem, gathering speed with each meter, a muted sound coming closer and closer until it bursts all at once in a huge rush. In the face of something so large, everything else looks small. You know it could be you there in the flow instead of that empty can bobbing in the current. And that knowledge does something to both exalt and diminish you. When you look at the flood, you are the flood, and then you're the greatest person in the world. But that doesn't last very long, and soon enough, when you look at the flood, you're merely a person looking at a flood, and then you go back to being very small, profoundly aware of such concepts as proportion and humility.

But when you're waiting for a flood and it doesn't come, you don't feel great and you don't feel a sense of proportion. You feel as if someone is laughing at you. The dry stream bed remains dry, as does your soul; it wants water but doesn't say so. Because in order to say what you want, you have to believe that someone is listening. Otherwise there's no point.

Otherwise the humiliation stings. When they finally get into the car to drive back to Omer, that's exactly what they feel. Humiliation. As if someone has been toying with them. Has allowed them to believe, then screwed them. They wanted to be the sort of couple that gets up in the morning and spontaneously jumps into the car to go to see a flood. Instead, they're the sort of couple that drives silently in their car and turns on the radio so that someone else will talk.

Not far from Beersheba, Liat turns off the radio and suggests they stop for some hummus. Eitan agrees quickly. Maybe they can still salvage something of the day. But then Davidson calls and asks if there's any news about the hit and run of the Eritrean, maybe one of the Bedouins said something. Liat promises to check it out, and suddenly thinks that maybe it would be better just to go back to work now so that she loses only half a day of vacation time. Yes, that would be better, she decides, both sad and relieved. Eitan says it was a pity, not entirely sure what he's referring to.

Guy Davidson ended the call after thanking Detective Liat Green who, by the way, in his personal opinion, was a very beautiful woman. He offered his personal opinion to the man standing beside him. "Don't worry, Rachmanov, that hot little pussy from the police will find those shits who stole our shipment."

The man called Rachmanov said, "What good is that? She won't give it back to us."

Davidson said, "What's gone is gone. The important thing is that it doesn't happen again. Whoever killed that Eritrean could kill the next Eritrean too."

"Tell me," Rachmanov said, "how come Sayyid didn't catch the guy who did it? He really doesn't know which one of his cousins wants to fuck him?"

Davidson shrugged and said, "Who knows, maybe it's Sayyid himself. He said they robbed him because he doesn't feel like paying."

Rachmanov's expression grew very serious. "If it's him, and she catches him, he'll fuck us up."

Davidson's face remained calm. "If it's him, and she catches him, he'll keep his mouth shut. I can fuck him up a lot more than he can fuck me up."

Rachmanov still looked grim, so Davidson said, "Come on Rachmanov, you look like you're going to shit." Rachmanov gave a short, nervous laugh and Davidson gave a bear-like laugh that lasted a great deal longer, and the Eritrean woman sweeping the floor near them didn't laugh at all, which didn't seem strange to anyone because she didn't know Hebrew. When she finished sweeping, she went to water her roses, majestic and proud despite the scorching desert sun.

9

THE MAN ACROSS FROM HIM talked non-stop. He was very religious and very fat, two qualities that Eitan did not especially value. But he had a certain zest for life that made doctors linger even after they'd finished examining him. Time and again, they were amazed by the vitality that poured from him; perhaps a bit of it would slip out from under his fur hat. "Original fox," he told Eitan, "I bought it from a *chasid* in Zefat." Under that original fox fur was a completely bald head, like a round stone on which much water had been poured. He would be going in for surgery tomorrow.

Prof. Shakedi observed them from the door. Less than an hour ago, he had threatened to fire Eitan. Threatened with hints, gently. But still. "You're careless," he'd said. "You leave early and arrive late, and when you're here, you're always tired. It can't go on this way." Now, the professor watched him as he spoke with the ultra-Orthodox patient. Sirkit called again and again, vibrating in his pocket, against his thigh. He didn't have to look. He knew it was her. Prof. Shakedi nodded in approval when he left the religious patient's bed and moved on to the next bed. Individual attention to every patient for a total of 300 seconds on the clock.

"Dr Green, your wife's on the department phone." The

nurse's voice was toneless, but Eitan could see the admonishing look even through the mascara. Prof. Shakedi watched him with angry eyes as he left the patient's bed and picked up the receiver. He recognized Sirkit even before she spoke, guessing her presence on the other end of the line.

"I'll talk to you tonight, honey," he said and hung up.

Under Prof. Shakedi's gaze, he walked back to the patient's bed. The head of the department might think he was the reason Eitan had cut the conversation short, to keep his job, but it hadn't been about his job for a long time. It was about his home. About Liat, Yaheli and Itamar, and his clear under-standing that if the whole business didn't stop, he was liable to lose them. He had been avoiding Sirkit for two weeks. At first he told her he was sick, then he texted her that he was doing reserve duty. After that, he simply stopped answering. She called every day, sometimes several times. Every call ter-rified him. (But was there something in him, even the slightest something, that missed her? That was drawn to the intensity of those nights in the garage? No, he replied adamantly, absolutely not. And added an exclamation point to reinforce that categorical no of his – No! To keep that illegal immigrant from crossing his borders and turning his no into a maybe. Or worse, into a yes.)

He knew he was taking a risk by not answering. He knew she could grind him into dust with a single conversation. But he couldn't. It was too much. That shameful moment when Liat hurled his lie back in his face. The fact that the lie had included Yaheli, those imaginary asthma attacks he had inflicted on his son. It was contemptible, and even more contemptible that he had grown used to it. The lie, like a wool sweater that was itchy at first, had become something he was accustomed to wearing. Felt comfortable in. So he sealed his ears to her calls, to the siren songs that came through the phone. He didn't answer. To keep from drowning.

True, it wasn't rational. And yes, she could call the police, but something inside him knew she wouldn't. (In his mind, Zakai was already chuckling: because she grows roses? Because the cigarette burns adorn her hand like a bracelet, and the ornaments of suffering are a guarantee of discretion? If you'd wanted her to keep quiet, you should have given her a hefty bribe, or gotten her into so much trouble that she had something to lose. Right now, you're counting on your luck. And that, as you well know, is the worst thing a doctor can do.)

But Eitan ignored Zakai the way he ignored the calls. The way he ignored the scrutinizing looks of Prof. Shakedi from over his shoulder. He knew. He wasn't counting on his luck. But he didn't understand that the thing he was counting on was much riskier – a pact. A connection between two people.

He continued his examination of the patient and Prof. Shakedi continued on his way. Two hours later they met again, this time at the department candle-lighting ceremony for Hanukkah. Eitan held a jelly doughnut that had seen better days, studying it carefully. The alternative was to study the faces of his colleagues in the department, and he really had no desire to do that. The doughnut, on the other hand, was fascinating.

Workplaces like to celebrate holidays. Not only hospitals. Law firms, city government offices, bank departments. The opportunity to see your boss sing, to eat something, to pretend we're all one big family. And if not, then at least friends. Acquaintances. It can't be that we're just a group of people closed up together between cement walls, under artificial lighting, from morning until night.

He felt his phone vibrate against his upper thigh again, and again ignored it. Half an hour earlier he'd called Liat, and she'd put him on speaker so they could light candles together with Yaheli and Itamar. He thought about them at home, in front of the menorah, and it only made the department candle-lighting even more repugnant. There are things a person should do with the ones truly closest to him. Otherwise they become an empty ritual, as rubbery and sticky as the doughnut he was still holding in his hand. Where the hell could he throw it now? (And the phone – how much longer could he ignore the phone?) He waited until he saw Prof. Shakedi leave. Two minutes later, Dr Hert left. He wondered whether they'd bother to take their own cars or they'd give up on the exhausting games of hide-and-seek and simply drive together to wherever they were going. It would be interesting to know where that was. In Tel Aviv, there were luxurious hotel rooms, apartments of friends who knew how to keep a secret. But here, in the middle of the desert, the most they could find was a Bedouin hospitality tent. (That wasn't true, but it made him smile. Dr Hert riding Prof. Shakedi in a tent made of goat hair. The fleas on the mattress feasting on the naked body of the head of the department.)

He waited another ten minutes, then slipped out quietly. He met Visotski at the elevators. The anaesthetist was holding a huge doughnut that didn't look much better than the one Eitan had been holding until a minute ago.

"In the Russian army, we used to hunt pheasants with rocks like these," he said, pointing to the doughnut. "Smash the bird's head with one of these and bam – you have dinner." Eitan couldn't tell if Visotski was kidding. The anaesthetist's expression was totally serious. The elevator arrived. Visotski looked around, then tossed the doughnut into the garbage pail in a quick movement expressing profound disgust. They rode down in silence.

The hospital parking lot was fairly empty at that time of day. Eitan and Visotski walked side by side toward their cars. Across the street, a group of students was singing holiday songs at the top of their lungs. Eitan couldn't decide whether they were drunk or just happy. Visotski stopped at his car. Eitan stopped at his. "How's your son?" he asked, and Visotski took his keys out of his pocket.

"Breathing on his own, and that's about it. But the grocery store decided to give me a discount on disposable diapers." Visotski got into his car and closed the door. He nodded good-bye to Eitan. It was a small gesture, and Eitan was surprised at how relieved it made him feel.

Before starting the suv, he called Liat. Wanted to ask if she'd put the kids to bed yet, maybe they could still wait up for him. "They're sleeping already, and let me tell you, it wasn't easy. I'm tiptoeing around."

"If that's how it is," he said, "maybe you should undress and get into bed. I'll be right home."

She laughed, but he knew she didn't really take it seriously. Neither did he. They said things like that to each other, but only rarely did anything about it. Most of the time it was simply a way to feel sexy. A sort of game which, to be honest, felt a bit artificial to him now. As if it wasn't Eitan and Liat speaking, but people who were supposed to be Eitan and Liat. The way the furniture you bought in Ikea always looked weird when you got it home, as if it missed its former home, the one in the catalogue.

The sign at the entrance to Omer wished him a happy holiday. The suv passed over one traffic bump after another like a ship crossing waves. He stopped the car in front of the rosemary bushes and was about to get out when he suddenly saw a shadow on the other side of the street. (Later, he thought he'd been waiting for her the entire time. Waiting without knowing he was waiting. Otherwise, why did he see that particular shadow on a street full of shadows? A couple in running clothes. A stray dog. Recycling bins waiting with open covers. But his eye leaped to that place, to that straight neck, that relaxed way she was sitting. The gleaming whites of those eyes.)

"What are you doing here?"

She didn't reply. Didn't hurl in his face all the calls he hadn't answered, the days that had passed without a response from him. She rose slowly from the stone fence she'd been sitting on. Now she was slightly taller than Eitan.

264

Let's go.

When she said that, he knew immediately that he would go with her. The black of her eyes had never been brighter. He'd go, and if he didn't, she'd walk straight across the street to his house and ring the doorbell. Yaheli would wake up immediately. He was a light sleeper. Itamar might stay asleep. Liat would open the door in her pajamas, silently cursing all those neighbors who didn't know when it was too late to ask for a cup of sugar. Then she'd see Sirkit. Who would tell her everything.

They drove to the garage in silence. He thought about stealing a glance at her, but was too proud and too angry. But she looked at him occasionally, considered his forehead, his nose. Reached no decision. Of one thing she was certain: he looked different. Two weeks was more than enough to create a genuine gap between the memory of his face and his actual face. Not a great difference, because it had only been fourteen days. And yet – a gap that had to be closed. Subtle, yet visible differences between that Eitan and this one. The difference between the image in her mind and the one sitting beside her now was almost impalpable. Yet it still bothered her. She remembered him differently. It was difficult to say how. Not exactly more handsome or less impressive. The differences were not in the proportions of his nose or the receding hairline. It was really difficult to say. But it seemed to her that there was something deliberate about the changes. If the image in her mind tended toward any direction, it was toward the famil-iar. Earlier, his face had been more familiar, and now it was unknown. Earlier his features had been joined together into one clear meaning, and now those same features – nose, eyes, mouth, eyebrows – were inscrutable and alien. Unconnected.

There was reproof in the glance Sirkit gave Eitan now. Not only because he had disappeared, but also because he had changed, even though the changes were so small you couldn't really talk about them, only sense them. And along with the reproof she felt curiosity: who was the man driving and why did he look different from the man she remembered? And amidst the reproof and curiosity was a fleeting moment of wondering whether she looked as different to him as he did to her. What had he thought when he saw her? But she actually knew the answer to that question. She had read it on his face, familiar or not: at first he was frightened. Then angry. (And between those emotions, for an instant that might have escaped them both, also happy.)

He kept driving and she looked away from him because she saw that her glance was making him uncomfortable. She looked outside instead. At a traffic light, her eyes met those of a pair of sightseers in the car next to them. That they averted their glance so quickly could only mean they were talking about her. About them. A white man driving an SUV with a black woman sitting beside him. A mixed couple on their way to a vacation. The woman in the other car said how nice it was to see that there were people like that. The man beside her replied: even though society can be very judgmental, and that's not right. The woman nodded. The light changed. The car was fueled by the subject of their conversation and could go on its way now. The woman in the passenger seat smiled encouragement at Sirkit. Sirkit smiled back, thinking: they don't know that he was coerced into driving with me. They think he's chosen to do so.

Inside the suv, Eitan saw Sirkit's smile and didn't know what to make of it. Her smiles were so rare, so unclear, and they always left him with the feeling that he was missing something. He accelerated and moved out of his lane to pass. He had driven to the garage many times at this hour, but the road had never been so busy. The Hanukkah travelers were making their way to one desert B&B or another, or perhaps they were going as far as Eilat. Eitan wondered if any of them had looked into the suv driving beside them. If any of them had seen a white man sitting next to a black woman, and what they thought. When he turned onto the dirt road leading to the garage, he was glad to get away from the sea of potential glances on the main road. But when he heard the first scream, he turned to Sirkit, shocked.

"Don't tell me someone's giving birth in there."

She didn't have to reply. The screams replied in her stead. The sound was unmistakable. Over the years, Eitan had heard many different screams of pain, but women in labor had a scream all their own. Perhaps because, apart from the pain, there was something else. Expectation, let's say. Or hope. He wasn't sentimental. He had spent two months of medical training in the obstetrics department. He knew quite well that, between labor pains, 70 per cent of women scream that it's a living hell. Maternal tenderness comes only after the epidural. Sometimes the pain was so great that they no longer remembered where they were, who they were, and wanted only for it to end. But even that wasn't just a nightmare. It wasn't like the screams of people whose pain comes only from the realm of death. The pain of life sounds different.

The woman was standing in a corner of the garage, sweaty and panting. Her huge stomach jutted out from under her dress. Two worried-looking women stood on either side of her. When they saw Sirkit, they hurried over to speak.

They say that the water from her belly spilled out a long time ago. They say that the baby should have come out by now.

The woman swayed from side to side, gathering strength for the next pain. She hardly looked at Eitan, Sirkit or the other women. Eitan remembered those delirious eyes. He had seen them as a student in the department. The whole body is focused inward, the outside becomes a blur of images and sounds. The problem was that he didn't remember much beyond that. When Itamar and Yaheli were born, he had been an observer. He had watched from the sidelines while Ami gave Liat the most personal treatment a woman giving birth could receive. He and Ami had played basketball together twice a week, and although at some point Eitan grew tired of his idiotic jokes and the never-ending political arguments, he had always known that gynecologists were a long-term investment. But now Ami was at Ichilov Hospital in Tel Aviv, while he was here, in the middle of a garage, with an Eritrean woman about to give birth.

"What's her name?"

Semar.

He went over to the woman and said her name. He said it twice before she looked at him. It was then that he realized he was actually glad to be there. (Because it really wasn't a good thing for someone to give birth this way, alone in a garage, like a work animal on some remote farm. And because there was a tiny person in her womb who wanted to come out and he knew he could help it. Because the pleasant tickle of adrenaline was caressing him inside as he began reminding himself of the procedures for delivering a baby. Because he was sick and tired of feeling small and guilty, and now he could finally feel large and needed. Because Sirkit looked at him with those black eyes of hers and asked him, *What should I do?*)

It took less time than he thought it would. Or perhaps he had just grown accustomed to preparing himself for the worst. But six hours later, he was standing between Semar's spread thighs, shouting at her, "Push, push." Along the way, there had been labor pains and screams and faeces and urine, and genuine danger to the eardrums of everyone present. But he didn't give any of that even a moment's thought, although it was the sort of mess that had led him to choose neurosurgery. He liked meeting his patients when they were anaesthetized. People tended to be much more courteous and cooperative after induction with propofol. And here, instead of the gleaming white of the department sheets, were the rust stains on the table, which refused to go away no matter how much Sirkit scrubbed them. But on that rusty table, in that filthy place, he heard a new scream six hours later. The one that doesn't come from the mother's mouth, but from the mouth of the newborn, which a moment earlier hadn't been there and now inhaled air lustily. Inhaled the cold air of the desert on the outskirts of Beersheba, inhaled the night's breath in the deserted garage, the sweat of the doctor and the women, the smells of neglect from the caravans. Inhaled – and immediately exhaled it all with its first scream, with an enormous huge, infant cry that was all disbelief: this place?

He instructed Sirkit on how to cut the umbilical cord and handed the baby to its mother. Semar reached out with tired, gangly arms. Like a doll that had been handed a smaller, baby doll, Eitan thought, which she held because it had been handed to her. But when she looked at the baby, she was suddenly revitalized. She was still lying there, and the baby was still in her arms, but now there was no doubt that the baby hadn't simply been put into her arms – she was holding it.

Eitan turned to look at Sirkit to see whether she had noticed that change, and was surprised to see that she had disappeared. He gestured for the Eritrean women to watch over the new mother and left the garage. A moonless sky. Anonymous stars (they had names, of course, but Eitan began to wonder why he had ever taken the trouble to learn them. A person gives a name to something that is his. His dog, his car, his child. How much arrogance it took to give names to those points of light). He didn't see her in the unpaved area around the garage, so he kept walking toward the hill.

She was sitting on the sand, her back to him. He considered sitting down beside her, but remained standing.

That was so terrible, she said, *so terrible and beautiful.*

"Yes," he said, "it really was terrible. And beautiful."

She turned around to him and he could see that she had been crying. Her black eyes were red-ringed. He wanted to hug her but had no idea how to even begin to embrace a woman like Sirkit. So he simply stood there and looked at her, thinking again that she was a beautiful woman, knowing again that if he were to pass her on the street, he wouldn't give her a second glance. A few moments later, it began to feel strange, standing beside her like that. "I think I'll go to sleep for a while," he said. "She's still bleeding, so I'll stay here tonight and keep an eye on her." Sirkit smiled and said she'd go to sleep for a while too, and she went and brought two thin mattresses from the caravan to the garage. They placed them on the floor, Sirkit put hers next to the new mother and Eitan put his near the door.

"Goodnight," he said.

Goodnight, she replied.

But he couldn't sleep, and even though there wasn't a sound in the dark garage, he knew that neither could she. Not after she had held that small round head in her hands and pulled it into the world. He thought again about her red eyes. Excitement? Gratitude? Sorrow for the children she had never borne? Sorrow for the children she had left behind? It was no wonder, he thought, that he didn't dare to hug her. That woman who had ruled two months of his nights – what did he actually know about her? That she had been married to a man he had killed. That the man had beaten her. That she grew roses. That she wasn't afraid of blood or people. That one battered Eritrean had called her an angel and one grief-stricken Bedouin had called her a devil, and that both of them were wrong, had to be wrong. Because neither angels nor devils existed. Of that Eitan was convinced. People existed. That woman lying on the mattress only a few meters from him, that woman was a person. She slept. She ate. She urinated. She defecated. And suddenly, before he had time to object, he had a clear image in his mind of that woman fucking, and his body responded to the sight with such a powerful erection that it took his breath away.

Lions roared inside him all night. He turned onto his side. Tried to think about Itamar, about Yaheli. In the darkness of the garage, it was suddenly remarkably clear to him how easily he could lose his family. Not because of a fatal car accident, or two planes colliding on a stormy night, or a terrorist attack. Because of him. Like others, he sometimes had horrible thoughts driving home at night. His brain conjured up endless possible accidents, disasters, funerals. Hinted at the question, how will you go on? and replied, you won't, this is the end. When the anxiety grew too great, unbearable, someone in his mind turned on the lights, stopped the horror movie and said, calm down, it's just a daydream. Wandering thoughts. And it was funny that, with all those scenarios, it had never occurred to him that he could be the cause. That he would live his life without Itamar and Yaheli not because of an evil terrorist or drunk driver, but because Liat would take them from him. That strange phrases like custody rights would become quite familiar to him. It would be his fault. Because he hadn't taken good enough care of his family, and families were fragile things.

He had sworn to himself, long before he got married, that he would never touch another woman. Fantasizing was fine and he could look as much as he wanted, but he would never actually endanger the thing he had built. He saw friends from school, doctors in the department. He could recognize unfaithfulness from a distance, just as he could recognize pneumonia even in its earliest stages. The faces radiant with a secret. The new skin glow. The dreamy walk. The relaxed posture. And several weeks later – the haunted look in the corner of the eyes. The intense stiffness of the upper back. Oral herpes due to tension. No fuck is worth that. No fleeting passion justified that moment when you sat your kids down on the living-room couch and said, "First of all, you have to know that your Mom and I love you."

But if that were true, why was he thinking about her so much, thinking about her – he hated to admit it – more than about them. How could it be that, over the weeks that had passed since the extortion had begun, he often found himself counting the hours until he would see that woman, when he should have been doing everything to see her as little as possible. How had she gained such a hold on him, what had she done to make him want her like this? Less than four meters between his mattress and hers, and her body throbbed at him in the darkness.

Although he knew that nothing was visible in the blackness of the garage, he turned on his mattress to face her and opened his eyes. Total darkness. He saw nothing, and that was precisely why he saw everything. There was her round shoulder gleaming at him every time she bent to lift something and her dress fell slightly to the side. And there were her breasts, finally released from the restraints of her cotton dress, round and proud and full. And there were her lips, her cheeks, her thighs. And the cat-like way she moved and walked, so suggestive of dormant, wild passion. Her remoteness, her strength and the knowledge that he would never be inside her even if he were inside her – all that stirred his blood until it almost hurt.

Calm down, he told himself, calm down. But he didn't calm down. Just the opposite. His brain continued to draw more and more pictures of Sirkit in ever-greater detail. Even when he tried to erase them along with the cerebral processes that were creating them (his pituitary gland was working overtime, there was no doubt about that), they still appeared, clear and seductive. When she finally lifted the blanket and lay down beside him in the long chaos of the night, he drowned in the blue-black of her hair and kissed her silent lips, and he didn't think about angels or devils. Or about people either.

*   *   *

She didn't need to look in order to see that he wasn't sleeping. She could hear his desire for her in every heavy breath, in every loud swallow of saliva. The air in the garage was heavy and

274

quivering, and so was her doctor, heavy and quivering. And there was an unbearable, almost painful sweetness between her legs, and inside, something thick and trembling waited. But she didn't get up and go to him, just as he didn't get up and come to her. Less than four meters between her mattress and his, but a large desert separated them. And that was good. She had crossed enough deserts to know that nothing waited on the other side but another desert.

So she closed her eyes, even though she knew she wouldn't sleep, and when he finally lifted the blanket and lay down beside her in the long chaos of the night, there was no desert, and it was because he didn't come to lie beside her that they were finally able to evade the desert, and she finally found sweet water in it.

10

IT WAS SLIGHTLY AFTER SUNRISE when Semar began
to scream, and for the first moment Eitan was sure the
screams were coming from his commander in the army, about
whom he was dreaming. A moment later he was awake, and
two moments later he was standing over the baby and knew
they were in trouble.

The baby's skin had a repulsive blue tinge. The color itself
wasn't repulsive. People buy sheets that color. And bedspreads.
And dishes. People buy very expensive tickets in order to travel
to countries that have beaches or lakes exactly that color. But
they don't want to see babies that color. Babies are supposed
to be pink. Pink is healthy. Pink means a proper pulse and
good blood circulation and oxygen sailing on the blood like
tourists on a cruise ship.

Blue is the opposite. Even if people don't know why, even
if they have no idea what hemoglobin actually is, they still
know that blue is the opposite. Semar, for example, knew that
something was wrong with her baby the moment she opened
her eyes and saw he was blue. That's when she began to scream.
Simply because that was the only thing she could do. When
the baby's father had sent her to straighten the storeroom and
then came and grabbed her from behind, she could also have

screamed. But she hadn't. She knew screaming would have consequences. She knew that the consequences would take a great deal of time and that what the baby's father wanted to do would take only a few minutes. She hadn't thought of him as the baby's father then. There hadn't yet been a baby that would make him a father. When his semen dribbled onto her thigh a few minutes later, she had hoped that would be the end of it. But that man's semen was exactly like the man himself – it grabbed her by force and didn't let go. At first, it angered her. It angered her even more than what that man had done to her. She thought about a baby with that man's face sitting in her belly and gorging itself all day, gorging on her. A baby with that man's face deciding when she'd go to the bathroom, when she'd eat, when she'd vomit. It angered her so much that she punched herself hard in the stomach, aiming directly at the face of that man who was growing inside her. But no matter how much she punched it, the baby simply grew and grew, and the more it grew, the more she hated it. Like that man's prick, which hadn't even been hard when he first grabbed her, but when he felt her recoiling, swelled suddenly – the baby grew on her hatred the same way.

So one day she took a long iron pipe from the storeroom and cleaned it well. Then she lay down on her back, legs spread, and told herself to be calm, it wouldn't take very long. She had already pushed the pipe inside her when Sirkit opened the storeroom door and saw her. Idiot, she had cried, stupid little cow. Don't you understand that you have money between

277

your legs. Sirkit told her that when the baby came, everyone would know that the father had fucked her in the storeroom, and he would have to give her money. A lot of money, Sirkit said. She helped her remove the iron pipe and smiled when she saw that there wasn't much blood on it. She told her that no one must know about the baby, especially the father. Sirkit told her she had to take very good care of it and feed it, the way people took care of their pigs in the village. They fed them and took care of them even though they were ugly and smelly, because they knew that in the end, they would make money from them. Semar kept the secret of the baby in her belly and took good care of it, thinking all the time about the pig growing in her womb, smooth and pink. When it began to move inside her, she thought about the piglets in the village and how they used to run away from the children when they chased them, trying to scare them, and that made her laugh. She no longer thought about a large, hairy pig. She thought about a cute little piglet and was ashamed when she remembered how she had almost skewered it with that iron pipe.

On the night her water burst, she was suddenly frightened. That cute little piglet and the baby's father became confused in her mind and she didn't know which of them was going to come out of her. Then the pains were so strong that she was convinced it would be the father. The piglet would never hurt her so much. The baby's father would hurt her coming out as much as he had hurt when entering her. In a moment she would see his disgusting face and no one would stop her from shutting his mouth the way he had shut hers in the storeroom, although it hadn't been necessary because she wouldn't have screamed.

But when the baby finally emerged, he didn't look like his father at all. Or like the piglets in the village either. If anything, he looked like a dolphin. She'd seen a dolphin only once, but she remembered it the way a person remembers the one time when things were really okay. Her father had rowed the boat into the sea and she sat with him, mending the holes in the net. The sun had just risen, but it was as hot as it was at noon, and the silence was broken only by the sounds of the oar in the water. Her mind was focused on the net, on the small repairs that wouldn't hold for very long, but would do for now, and then she heard the silence. That is, she heard that the oar was no longer hitting the water, and since her father never stopped rowing so close to the shore, she raised her head. The dolphin was right beside the boat. It was beautiful. It was the most beautiful thing she had ever seen, and even though she was only six, she knew it was the most beautiful thing she would ever see in her life. It swam alongside the boat, and her father gestured for her to put down the net and come to him. Then he did something that made her forget the dolphin. Something truly wonderful. He picked her up in his arms and held her in the air above the water. He did it so she could see the dolphin. So that the dolphin could see her. Her father knew that dolphins and little girls didn't encounter each other very often. But she didn't look at the dolphin at all. She looked at her father as he held her above the water. It didn't last very long and it never happened again. He put her down. She continued mending the net, he continued rowing, and the dolphin continued on its way.

When Sirkit and her doctor brought her the baby, she saw immediately that it looked like the dolphin. That made her happy. That made the pain between her legs less painful. She counted his fingers, thinking how small they were, and then remembered his father's fingers, how he had forced them inside her, and thought they had once been that small too. Sirkit took the baby and told her she needed to rest. She didn't argue. It seemed like a good idea, to rest. When the baby opened its eyes for a moment, they didn't look like his father's eyes at all, and that calmed her down. But then she thought about all the other parts of his body, how you couldn't know now what they would look like later. His nose, let's say. Or his ears. Not to mention his voice. She didn't know what she would do if he had the same voice. But he wouldn't have the same voice, she reassured herself. He wouldn't. Because your voice comes out of your mouth, and her milk would flow into his mouth.

She fell asleep with that thought, and when she woke up, she saw that the baby's skin had a blue tinge. That's when she began to scream.

The baby wasn't dead, but it didn't look good. The garage wasn't equipped to treat respiratory distress. Nor was it equipped to treat Semar's screams. At Soroka, the nurses kept the family away when complications developed. They called security. That might seem harsh, or heartless, but hospitals cannot work with all that screaming. It frightens the other patients. It distracts the doctors. It lowers the morale in the battle against death. Semar screamed and screamed, and Eitan was about to tell Sirkit to take her out when he realized that he himself was the one who had to leave.

He picked up the baby, surprised by the incredible lightness of the small body. Three steps and he was at the door, calculating the quickest way to the hospital –

Stop.

She stood before him barefoot, her hair in tangles. Some part of his mind registered the outline of her nipples under her shirt. The softness that her body projected, the scent of sleep that rose from her – they stood in direct opposition to her cold, metallic voice as she told him he would stay here.

They will want to know where you brought it from. They will come here.

"Then I'll make up something," he roared at her, holding the baby in one hand, searching for the keys to the SUV with the other. "I won't let it die here."

I will not let one baby bring down a whole hospital.

He finally found the right keys. The SUV gave a cheerful chirp when he pressed the remote to unlock it. He raced toward it, Sirkit in pursuit. For the first time since he had met her, he saw her upset. Not because of the baby with the blue skin, but because she realized that he had decided to disobey her. *I will go to the police. If you go to the hospital, I will go to the police.*

He looked at her for a moment. Enough to know that she was serious. He closed the door and drove off.

*

The road to Beersheba was completely empty at that hour. He drove as fast as he could. He talked to the baby. He told him to hold on. He promised him that everything would be fine. He updated him on the number of kilometers they still had to drive. He assured him it was really close. "Another little bit," he said, "just another little bit."

The baby was in the back, in the car seat Eitan had bought and installed for Yaheli, which was, of course, too big for him. There was no real reason to put him there. He could just as easily have put him on his lap. That might even have been more logical, because he could have seen what was happening with him. But his father reflex went into action – babies are put in the back, buckled in. Anything else was irresponsible. And there he was now, a forty-one-year-old man, speaking to a baby in the back seat. And the baby wasn't answering. It was a baby, after all. A blue baby.

Seven kilometers to the city of Beersheba, and Eitan's voice rose to a shout. It'll be fine, he screamed to the back seat, it'll be really fine. We're almost there. And then he realized that he'd been avoiding looking at the baby. He had spoken to him, promised him, sometimes pleaded with him, but he hadn't looked at him. He straightened the rearview mirror and peered at the back seat.

Five kilometers from the city of Beersheba, he stopped the car. He couldn't tell how many minutes he'd been racing like that to no avail, making promises to a dead baby.

*

It was 7:30 in the morning and Eitan still hadn't come home from the hospital. Liat walked around the living room, wiping invisible dust from pillows and sofas, straightening up what was clearly straightened. Her grandmother would have known what to do. Her grandmother would have looked him right in the eye for ten seconds and known. But her grandmother had been gone for three years now. Four, if you count the year after her stroke, before she died. She'd had it right after the operation, and had never opened her eyes again. She simply lay in her bed in the hospital with her eyes closed. Who knows whether she was there at all. So what if she breathed? Her grandmother was the world champion of pretending she was home when she actually wasn't. Because of the thieves, she'd told Liat, so they won't think no one's home and go inside. She left the lights on and the radio playing loudly – and went out. Maybe it was like that during that year in the hospital. All the doctors and nurses checked the signs of life like thieves listening at the door, but she'd left a long time ago.

It was just like her grandmother to trick them like that. After all, for years she'd been hiding the fact that she had a problem. Didn't tell anyone she was sick. Hid it so well. Hid it even from death. It forgot her. Like a cleaning woman who promised to come on Sunday but forgot, and the house was a mess all week. Death, like someone with Alzheimer's, knew it was supposed to meet a woman, but couldn't remember which one, couldn't remember where, roamed the street in confusion. On the way it met other grandmothers, but not hers.

In the end, they met. Almost by accident. The pneumonia she caught lying there in the department with her eyes closed finished her off in less than a week. Liat was left to look at coffee grounds alone, and saw nothing in them. Now she tried again: she made coffee and examined the grounds carefully. Perhaps they'd tell her where the hell her man was. She could call the department. Ask if he was there. Try to spot, through the receiver, the subtle tones of a lie. The giggle of a reception clerk. Or the opposite – a surprised, awkward silence. Or the high-pitched, false voice of a nurse. They knew where he was and wouldn't tell her. The doctors, the interns, the entire hospital was probably laughing at her behind her back.

She put the coffee cup in the sink and called the children. They came immediately, all ready. Itamar had dressed Yaheli and both now stood in front of her, ready to move. She felt awful seeing them dressed like that. She looked at the shoes and knew: they understood that something was wrong. Itamar had tied Yaheli's shoelaces, and Yaheli had let him without crying or carrying on. But children were supposed to cry and carry on and not see anything but themselves. If they came the minute you called them, dressed like photos in a magazine, then the situation had to be really grim.

He looked at them as they left the house. Yaheli with his dog hat. Itamar with his football-shaped backpack, even though he didn't like football at all and the other kids never let him play. Liat, her hair in a ponytail, and around her neck the necklace she hadn't taken off since her grandmother had given it to her as a wedding present. His family left the house and he watched them as they walked down the driveway. Unknowingly regal. Unaware of their true worth. Perfect in their ignorance.

Itamar saw him first and waved. Yaheli, who, as always, watched every movement his brother made, saw him next. He dropped Liat's hand and ran to him.

"Daddy!"

Eitan picked him up in his arms, momentarily surprised at his weight. The kid has gotten heavy, or else I've gotten weak. When he put Yaheli down, Liat was already standing beside her car.

"*Ya'allah*, sweeties, we have to get going."

Her voice was light and playful. A light and playful iceberg. Eitan wondered if the kids noticed it or only he did.

"I want Daddy to take me," Yaheli said, "I want to go in the SUV!"

"Daddy's tired," she said, "he didn't sleep all night." Don't put your money on Oedipus, she thought. This little kid had already forgotten who had bathed and diapered and nursed him, and he ran toward his father's SUV, straight into the arms of the enemy. Eitan was probably thrilled. Another point for him in the unspoken, silent but bloody battle – who did they love more?

But to her surprise, he rejected the tribute. "Not today, Yaheli, go with Mommy." Maybe he really was tired. Or wanted to send her a gesture of conciliation. In any event, it would take much more than that to persuade Yaheli. He ran to the suv and climbed inside through the open door of the driver's seat, crawled over the gear box and landed in his car seat. Liat smiled despite herself. He was such a determined little monkey. But Eitan didn't smile. When Yaheli's body touched the seat, he suddenly paled. His lips trembled.

"Yaheli, get out of there."

She had heard him speak in that voice only once. Years ago, in the Judean Desert, on one of their first hikes together. It was in the middle of the week, and there was no other living creature at Nahal Mishmar, so they allowed themselves to fuck in the dry stream bed near the cistern. A long, slow fuck, not only because they'd met only recently and were very attracted to each other, but also because they wanted to impress each other. She was on top when she felt his entire body tense, and thought he had come. "Don't move," he said. His voice was strange, icy. She didn't move. She was sure that it had something to do with some orgasmic spot in the masculine anatomy. A moment later she saw the snake. It was small and black and very close. Time passed, ten seconds, a minute, five. They didn't move. The snake's tongue moved in and out, in and out, almost as if it were saying, "I saw your in-and-out, now you look at mine." At some point, it stopped. Slithered away. They watched it, naked and tensed. After that, fucking was impossible, and being naked in the middle of the dry stream bed seemed weird. They dressed and continued their trek, trying to laugh about it, but back home they never mentioned that snake again.

When Eitan ordered Yaheli to get out, something inside her recognized that voice. There was something in the SUV. A snake, or a scorpion. Something bad. She hurried over to look inside and saw nothing. The car seats. A few toys. Empty pizza boxes. It couldn't be that Eitan was so stressed because of pizza boxes.

"Yaheli, I told you not to sit there. Out!"

Eitan's voice rose to a shout. She'd already heard him shout, but never like this. His shouts were always brief, decisive. When Itamar ran into the road in front of their apartment in Givatayim. When the nurses in Tel Hashomer Hospital put her grandmother in a bed in the corridor. As if he had first checked all the possibilities carefully, and when he saw that there really was no other choice, he shouted. But this shout was different. Yaheli began to cry. Itamar also had tears in his eyes. A moment later, Eitan kneeled down in front of the sobbing child. "I'm sorry. Daddy's sorry." But Yaheli didn't calm down. Just the opposite. The thought that his father could shout at him that way for no good reason was more frightening than the idea that he'd done something to provoke it.

Liat looked at her watch. She'd be late getting to pre-school, a crying child in tow. The other mothers would ask, "Tough morning?" their sympathetic tone barely covering the gloating, the way the tight swimsuits they wore at the country club couldn't hide their cellulite. She'd smile and say, "It happens," and wouldn't say a word that might give away the fact that for more than a month, her man had been disappearing at night and she didn't know where. Thinking about it upset her so much that she bent down and picked up Yaheli.

"Come on, sweetie pies, we don't want to be late."

Her voice was bright and calm, but her voice was lying. She knew it. Eitan knew it. Even Itamar and Yaheli knew it. Yaheli stopped crying, just sat quietly in her arms and looked at his father. Itamar didn't look at his father. Or at her. He focused his gaze on a nearby ants' nest, which looked disorganized at first glance, but was actually remarkably organized. Ants had rules, and they stuck to them. If you studied their rules well enough, you'd know exactly what ants would do. For some reason, it didn't work that way with grown-ups.

"E.T., get into the car."

Itamar looked away from the ants' nest and walked over to the Toyota. Eitan watched him. He wanted to call to him, but there was no point. He wouldn't put them in his car. His children wouldn't get close to that suv, to that blue baby. He trembled when he remembered the small mound of sand five kilometers from Beersheba. He needed to take the car in to be cleaned. Maybe he'd sell it. The car seat had to go, that was for sure. He couldn't see Yaheli sitting in the same place where that... thing had sat. (Because that's what it was. A thing. Not a person. It hadn't had time to be a person. When he'd stopped the suv, it hadn't even looked like a doll. But it had five fingers on each hand, and that finished him off. The fingers finished him off.)

Liat's Toyota pulled out of the driveway and drove down the street. He waved goodbye to the kids. They waved back from their seats. Seeing that, he allowed himself to think that maybe everything was okay. Children are more resilient than we think. Their bones are more flexible than adults' bones. Evolution did that to protect them from the blows they were going to receive.

The car disappeared around the curve. One minute they were there, Liat holding the wheel, Itamar and Yaheli waving – and the next minute, they weren't. They continued to exist, of course, continued to move in the space outside of his field of vision. Until recently, Itamar used to doubt that. "When we go to sleep," he'd said many times, "how do we know that things in the world don't start to move? The tree in the yard, or the mailbox, how do we know they're still there?"

"Because they're there," Eitan had replied, knowing that wasn't really an answer. At the time, the sink full of dirty dishes waiting for him outside Itamar's room didn't leave much room for philosophical matters.

"But Daddy, if you don't see them you don't know they're there."

Even so, they're there. Liat and Yaheli and Itamar. They don't disappear when you don't see them. They can't disappear. They're on the HMO registry, in the Ministry of Interior files, in the National Insurance computers. People know them. People are seeing them at this very moment. The boss, the preschool teacher, the grocery store clerk. And all of those people are on the lists as well. People know them too, and that's how they validate each other's existence, with a nodded greeting, official letters, certificates and glances. If one of them were to disappear, one of those other people would notice. And if no one did, then the official institutions would. It would take longer, but in the end some computer would send out a warning about unpaid property tax, outstanding bills, a child absent from the first grade. People like that don't disappear. The world doesn't let them disappear.

But there were other people as well. You see them, but you don't know they're there. About those people, Itamar was right: you close your eyes and they disappear. You don't even need to close your eyes. They disappear in any case. A quick flash on your retina, nothing more. The blue baby, for instance. He wasn't on the lists. Nor was his mother. Ordinary people don't know them. Real people, the sort who are registered in institutions and whom other real people know, the sort who don't know anything about the blue baby or his mother. And so the blue baby and his mother can drop out of the world without anyone noticing.

He still had to tell the mother. Eitan's stomach contracted when he thought about that. The blue baby was under that mound of earth, and the Eritrean woman in the garage didn't know anything. Or maybe she did know, with that intuition mothers have, the way his mother had known about Yuval that morning. She had woken that day and shouted at his father to turn off the radio even though, since the military operation had begun, all they did was listen to the radio. Perhaps they'd thought that the endless jabbering of the broadcasters, the journalists, the interviewed people who had suddenly heard a boom – all those words somehow protected them. An invisible wall of situation analyses and predictions through which no bullet could pass. But that morning his mother had turned off the radio, and suddenly there was silence in the living room. After so many days of noise, it was strange. Unpleasant, even. He and his father exchanged a glance that said, be careful, Mom's jumpy, and his father said, sit down Ruti'le, I'll make you a cup of coffee.

She never drank that coffee. When his father handed it to her – in a glass cup, one saccharine – she was already hanging laundry in the yard. Ten years earlier, they'd bought a large German-made dryer, but after using it twice she said it had been a mistake. "It might dry the laundry, but it doesn't stop the buzzing in my head." His mother had an entire theory about the buzzing in your head, about how the only way to stop it was to work with your hands. Yuval had developed a formula that enabled him to predict how many plates she needed to wash in order to calm down after a medium-size argument. "Laugh all you want," she'd tell them, "but it's definitely better than all those sunflower seeds you devour when you're upset." Sunflower seeds were the official tranquilizer for the men in the family. A small bag before a big exam. A large bag after splitting up with your girlfriend. Three kilos during the shiva for Grandpa David, his father's father. They had sunflower seeds and she had the dishes or the laundry, and sometimes, on the really tough days, also the bedclothes in the very large linen closet, which were all neatly folded, from top shelf to bottom, on the days of the shiva, and then refolded, from bottom shelf to top, on the days that followed the shiva. The new dryer remained in the bathroom, white and shiny. His father refused to throw out something that had cost so much money, and perhaps he took some small pleasure in looking at it occasionally and sighing loudly enough for his mother to hear. Gradually, they started leaving things on it. Laundry soap. Fabric softener. A pile of clothespins. Shaving cream. The white elephant became another shelf in the bathroom, and probably would have continued being that if Yuval hadn't come home from his first week of basic training and announced that from then on, he wanted to put his laundry in the dryer (he said they could call him up at any time; he needed his uniforms to be done quickly). His mother objected mildly, but finally agreed. In part because it was logical. But mainly because it was Yuval. She always agreed when it was Yuval. Eitan had to threaten to run away from home to get permission to go to Eilat with friends when he was at the end of his junior year in high school; Yuval they drove to the central bus station. When Eitan wanted to skip the educational field trips in his senior year, he had to forge sick notes; when it was Yuval, his mother simply called his teacher and told her that he didn't feel well. When he saw how readily she offered Yuval the car on Friday nights, he could keep his mouth shut no longer – it had taken six months for him to get the Suzuki at night. She was surprised. She apologized. Tried to say that it was a classic case of big-brothers-little-brothers. It had been the same with her and Aunt Naomi – everything she spilled blood to get was given to Naomi on a silver platter. But Eitan knew that it was more than that. There was something about Yuval that made people say yes to him even before he asked. Sometimes he thought he could see a bit of that trait in Yaheli. Pre-school teachers loved his younger son. Sales people in shops did as well. All he had to do was look at something – candy or a toy – and a hand immediately reached out and gave it to him. And it wasn't because he was especially beautiful. Cute, definitely, but not the sort of kid you see in ads. He simply had that elusive quality that makes the world nod. Eitan didn't have it. Neither did Itamar. Naturally, pre-school teachers and sales people in shops handed things to his older son as well. But only after he asked. After he paid. After Eitan drew their attention to the fact that the quiet kid standing there still hadn't received his.

That ability of Yaheli's to charm people surprised him. Perhaps because he didn't think that hiding somewhere in his genes was the same trait that had been entirely Yuval's. (But in fact, why not? Eitan inherited the light-colored eyes and Yuval the brown, and Yuval had cried to his parents that it wasn't fair, why did Eitan get the blue and I got this shitty brown, that's how much it bothered him that he wasn't as good. And Eitan had said to him, you jerk, stop cutting your biology class and learn that even if people see the brown, Mom's blue DNA is still hiding in there, and maybe your kids will have blue eyes. Yuval had laughed and said, okay, I'm willing to settle for that, not knowing that he was going to settle for much less, for nineteen years, five months and two days, and not even a nephew named after him because Eitan wouldn't allow his children to be turned into a memorial for other children. His parents understood that, though they didn't understand much of anything else.)

He didn't remember Yuval as a baby. He was only three when he was born, and that's why it took time for him to understand that Yaheli resembled him. His mother saw it first, but he thought that was because she saw Yuval everywhere anyway. But when Yaheli grew up a bit, Eitan began to see it as well. Not only in that openness of his, but also in the way he wrinkled his nose when he was upset, a perfect copy of Yuval's face after every game Maccabee Haifa lost. It was great to see those flashes of Yuval, but it was also strange. And it was even stranger to look at Itamar and Yaheli and feel that he had to protect his quiet older son from the charm of his younger son. Protect him firmly from what might be taken and what might be given. Even now, Liat didn't understand why he wasn't more dazzled by Yaheli; the entire neighborhood is dazzled by him except for you and those stingy smiles of yours. What could he tell her? That he was saving his smiles for the other child, the one nobody was dazzled by? So what did he think, that smiles were a limited resource? Even if they were a limited resource with his parents, what did that have to do with that child of his, what did Yaheli have to do with the automatic nod, the "yes" that was Yuval's?

And there was that other, magical fear as well, the one he couldn't speak about. The fear that, just as it had been with Yuval, the world would one day grow tired of saying yes to Yaheli, and a huge, resounding "no" would come all at once in the form of friendly fire, of an entire unit firing (by mistake! by mistake!) on that successful, favored brother. Some part of him was jealous of Yaheli, of his small son, and he hated that part. But part of him was also frightened for Yaheli and wanted to protect him from the jealousy of others. Perhaps that was how Jacob felt when he saw Joseph go out into the field with his brothers, the ones who would soon throw him into a pit. And Eitan understood those brothers so well, with their plain clothes, driven mad by the luxurious coat of many colors. Perhaps that was why he always made sure, even on birthdays, to bring presents for both of them. So one would never open the crinkly wrapping paper while the other watched with his hands empty. But he didn't understand that it wasn't because of the coat that they threw Joseph into the pit, but because of the look on his father's face when he put it on him. You can distribute presents equally. Not so with looks.

On the morning they came to tell them about Yuval, his mother had gone out to the yard with a tub full of laundry. There were sheets, towels, Eitan's clothes and his father's clothes, but she foraged around in the pile of wet cloth until she pulled out the jeans Yuval had worn on Saturday. She shook them out and straightened them carefully, then hung them up first. She hung them with the determination of someone stating a fact – no one whose jeans are hanging on the line outside to dry is dead. She managed to hang another few shirts before the army guys arrived. They didn't have to knock. She saw them from the yard. They went into the house through the back door with her, straight into the kitchen. Eitan remembered the taste of the cornflakes in his mouth at the moment his mother came inside with the two men in uniform and began to cry.

But she didn't look surprised. On the contrary. As if something inside her had been expecting this since morning. Eitan remembered a description he'd read in the papers about the tsunami in Thailand. How people stood on the shore and watched the waves coming. They saw them in the distance, saw them approaching. Some tried to run, but there were others who knew there was no point, the water would reach them in any case. So they simply stood there and waited, and perhaps they also hung laundry.

His mother knew even before they came, and perhaps also the Eritrean woman in the garage already knew. Or at least guessed. But even if she knew, her body didn't. It continued to produce milk for a baby who wouldn't be coming. The pituitary gland secretes prolactin. The prolactin sets the colostrum flowing. Eitan remembered how the previous night, a long time before the baby was born, the Eritrean woman's dress had already been soaked with milk. Two large, round, dark stains, one on each breast, grew in size from hour to hour. Her body dripped. Sirkit suggested that she take off her dress. She had so much pain anyway, so why add the discomfort of cloth sticking to her breasts. But the woman refused. Perhaps she was self-conscious in front of him. It was embarrassing enough that he looked at her like that, between her legs; she could at least keep her breasts for herself. Or the milk oozing from her and staining her dress might not have bothered her at all. Perhaps she was glad that the cloth that was meant to conceal was suddenly revealing. The body was speaking to itself with absolute clarity, saying: I'm full. I'm full of bursting life.

It drove him mad to think about the milk. That dress and the round stains expanding on it – he didn't want to picture them anymore. He went into the house and washed his face in the bathroom sink, and then went into Yaheli's room, lay down on the Robots sheet and fell asleep. Toy soldiers watched over him as he slept. A toy tank sat on the rug, and that was enough to keep anyone from stepping over the threshold. Eitan lay on his side and slept, not tossing or turning even once.

*   *   *

She didn't know whether it was sleep or unconsciousness, but she was happy that Semar had finally closed her eyes and stopped screaming. She wiped the sweat from her forehead, straightened her blanket and scrubbed the sheet Semar had bloodied during delivery. She scrubbed for a long while, scrubbed and rinsed and scrubbed again, but she couldn't get it clean. She looked at her phone again; maybe he had called, but there was no call. Not that she needed a call from him in order to know. She'd seen the baby. She knew what that color meant. And unlike Eitan and Semar, she didn't close her ears when death came knocking at the door. She knew it would enter in any case. None the less, she waited. Decided to wash the sheet again. Scrubbed and rinsed. Straightened the sleeping Semar's blanket again. Swept the garage floor. Arranged the bottles of medicine. One, two, three babies, and now four, though obviously it made a difference that this baby wasn't hers, but still.

He didn't call. He might still be trying to save the baby in their hospital. Maybe he never got there. Maybe he'd managed to do something to reverse the clear, unmistakable direction of life emptying out of the baby's face. Maybe he didn't think it was so urgent to let her know, and she wasn't even sure why she had to know so urgently. Waiting was something she knew how to do very well. She was an expert in the secrets of sitting still and silent, waiting for what would come. The total suspension of thought and feeling, until someone else came and decided. "We're leaving," and she'd leave. "We're going back," and she'd go back. "We're getting up," and she'd get up. And now, as always, she had to wait. To hear what the doctor would say. And if he didn't say anything, that was fine too. He didn't call, and from that silence she understood that the baby had died. From that small silence she understood the large, final silence of lungs that no longer breathed. If she were angry at him about anything, it wasn't about the baby – it really wasn't his fault. It was about how unbearably effortless it had been for him to switch their roles. She was waiting and he was deciding; he was the master of time and she was the one sitting on the sidelines, scrubbing a sheet that would never be clean, waiting.

11

H E WOKE UP SCREAMING. Discovered he had slept only two hours, though it felt like much more. He immediately called Sirkit. His voice shook a bit when he told her about the baby, but he didn't care. Your voice should shake when you tell somebody something like that. Even if you're a doctor. Sirkit's voice didn't shake. Eitan had expected nothing else. He almost forgot the tears he'd seen in her eyes when he went out to her after the birth. Now he hated her more than ever. He had to blame someone for what had happened. Babies don't die for no reason. There had to be a reason. Someone had to have screwed up. That chemical transformation of sadness into anger relieves the body and quiets the soul. And Sirkit had delayed him when he wanted to leave with the baby. Had threatened him. Had stolen precious seconds. (Those seconds wouldn't have changed anything, but he held on to them all the same. In Yaheli's room, lying on the Robot sheets, surrounded by toy soldiers, he again realized how good it was to divide the world into good guys and bad guys.)

She asked him to come and check on the mother, who was still bleeding, and he said fine, but he had to shower first. Standing under the water, covered in foamy, almond-and-green-tea-scented shower gel, he read the label on the shampoo bottle. Herbal essence. Natural spring water carried the flowers and essences straight from the field. Who writes that stuff? Who reads it? After stepping out of the shower and drying himself, he went back to Yaheli's room and sat on the bed, then lay down again. Closed his eyes. Waited for the moment when the final thought came, the one after which there was only the endless expanse of impervious sleep. The final signal from the spaceship before you are finally lost in the unknown. But this time, the soldiers and the Robots did not help. He tossed and turned. He sweated. The sheets prickled and the mattress was too small. But he didn't get up. Finally, he fell asleep. An hour later, he woke up screaming.

The woman's bleeding didn't worry him. Given the situation, it was completely normal. What did bother him was her look. At the most difficult moments of the birth, even when she had almost passed out, there was still a distant sparkle in Semar's eyes. Now the eyes were vacant. He looked into them and was shaken.

"Tell her she has to stay in bed for a while. At least two days." Sirkit translated for Semar. The woman did not look at her as she spoke, but when she finished, she shook her head.

She must go back to the restaurant. She cannot stay away for so long.

"Then someone needs to go over there and explain to her boss that she just had a baby. He must have seen that she was pregnant."

A rapid exchange of glances between Sirkit and the woman on the mattress. Silence. Eitan's glance wandered to the pile of clothes on the floor. Skirts and shawls she had taken off when she first arrived, too much for any sort of weather. "Even so," he said, "she's staying here."

Sirkit translated the doctor's words and added some of her own, and Semar shook her head and thought, "I'm not listening to you anymore. I did it once and look what happened. For nine months his baby grew in my belly, laid down roots in my heart, spread branches in my chest. For five days, I have been dripping milk like a cracked jug. And now, who knows where that baby is, that dolphin that glowed in front of me for one moment and then vanished."

Years ago, on that morning on the boat with her father, she had thought that the dolphin symbolized something. Some hidden message from the world. All her life she had believed that if she worked hard enough, if she continued to mend the holes in the net, amazing creatures like the dolphin would occasionally flash by. Appear for a moment outside the field of reach, but within the field of vision. Would let her be dazzled by them, if only at a distance. And then they'd dive back in, leaving behind only gray ocean and hard work. You could do that work if you knew that every now and then the sea would split in two for a second and in the middle would be something truly beautiful. But since that dolphin, there had been no other dolphins. The sea hadn't split in two, and even the ordinary fish had also stopped coming. There was no longer any point in mending the net. It came out of the water empty in any case. And now her belly was empty too. Where the baby had been before, there was nothing now. Even the blood that flowed from her, insisting that yes, there had been something there, even that would stop soon. She'd be empty again, the way she had been before the baby came, but different. Only the sink in the restaurant was always full. Endlessly filling up. Leftovers of unfamiliar food that people had eaten a lot of, or a little of, or hadn't eaten at all, then had stood up and walked away from, leaving the food on the plate. The baby's father didn't care whether people left food on their plates or not. He only wanted the restaurant to be full. And for that, he needed clean rest rooms, a kitchen that worked quickly and an organized storeroom. She'd spent a great deal of time in the rest rooms and the kitchen these last few months, but he hadn't taken her to the storeroom again since *that* time. He took other girls, but not her. Sirkit told her that she had to hide the baby well when it was still in her belly, but the baby's father never looked at her anyway, so that wasn't too difficult. But she hadn't been at work since yesterday, and that was something he'd notice. The other girls had promised to work hard in her place, but still.

Semar looked around the garage. She couldn't stay here and she knew it. That was why she waited until Sirkit and her doctor had momentarily disappeared before she lowered a trembling foot, then the other foot, and stood barefoot on the cement floor. The cold flowed upward from the floor, climbed from her heels to the top of her head. The pain between her legs was still asleep, didn't notice that she'd stood up, didn't understand that she was sneaking outside. But the moment she took a step, it woke up all at once and enveloped her before she could escape, gripped her in a white-hot iron vise. The darkness of the garage was suddenly punctuated by darting colors, and Semar thought she was going to pass out. She didn't pass out, but splashes of purple and blue continued to glow before her eyes, and between them the face of the baby's father appeared suddenly. She told herself it was okay, the splashes would soon disappear along with that face, and a moment later the purple and the blue really did disappear, but the baby's father was still there.

Davidson examined the garage with stunned eyes. He'd had his own thoughts about what he'd find when he entered, but none of them approached this. For the last several days he had been sniffing around the Eritreans, ever since Rachmanov had told him that there was movement there at night. At first, he'd thought the Bedouins who stole the shipment had come back to search for more, but only an idiot would do something like that. Then he thought it was Sayyid's crew. He had even called Sayyid to say he should get the hell out of his territory, and that if he had had his shipment, he would have returned it already. Sayyid said that he hadn't sent anybody to look for it. The person who had to look for the shipment was Davidson. He was the one who'd lost it. "Not to worry though," Sayyid had told him, "I'm a patient man. But you should know that you need to start thinking about how to return the money, because it doesn't look like you're going to find the shipment."

After that conversation, Davidson was so jumpy that he decided to close the restaurant early and send all the workers to the caravans. They went, but there was something in their glance that stayed with him even after he was left alone. A secret. There was a secret there. He wanted to follow them right then, but told himself that it would be better to wait. The next day, he checked them out carefully when they arrived and saw that two of them were missing. Semar, and the one with the big eyes. Now that he didn't like. He looked for the two women in the caravans and didn't find them, so he drove around in the van for a while, but saw nothing. Then he noticed the kibbutz's abandoned garage and the red suv parked at the entrance. It looked like whoever had stolen the shipment actually was stupid enough to come back.

He thought about calling Rachmanov, but he had his gun on him and he was more agitated than he had ever been in his life. The last thing he expected to see was shelves of medications, surgical gloves, and an iron table that had been converted into a treatment table. And Semar, who looked at him with gaping eyes, like a chicken in the kibbutz coop before it was shut down.

Someone like Davidson.

People generally assumed that someone like him had made a choice somewhere in the past.

For example – at a crossroads.

One road turned right. The other left. If he turned right, he'd choose evil. If left – good. The directions themselves weren't important. What was important was the crossroads; that is, the existence of the moment when a person stands before two clear, opposing paths and chooses one over the other. Of course, at that moment he may not necessarily know that a turn to the right will end in a life of evil and a turn to the left will lead to a life of goodness. But he knows he's at a crossroads. He knows he is choosing. And that when he reaches the place he finally reaches after many days and kilometers, he can look back and pinpoint the moment it all began. He can say *there*. It happened *there*.

If not a crossroads, if not two clear paths, if not devastation or salvation, children of light or children of darkness, if not any of those, then goat paths. Anyone who has walked in the desert knows. Elusive lines that have no beginning and no end, and walking along them is as random as the wind. They have no purpose and no direction; sometimes they lead to a hidden spring, sometimes to a steep cliff. Sometimes to both, and sometimes to neither. Clear intersections and paved roads are marked on maps. A person traveling them begins at point A and reaches point B. A person also knows that if he sets out from C instead, he will undoubtedly reach D. Because one ends where the other begins and one begins where the other ends. But a person who begins walking on a goat path doesn't know where he will end up. Even after he reaches the end, he cannot know how he got there. That's why those paths do not appear on maps or in books, although they are infinitely greater in number than the clearly marked paths. The world is full of goat paths of which no one speaks.

A paved path should lead, for example, from Davidson the man back to Davidson the child. It is clear, after all, that a man who assaults a woman in the back of a storeroom assaulted something else when he was a boy. He abused kittens, or intimidated kids in his class. Bad adults were once bad youngsters, and even before that they were children who'd had something bad done to them. You can chart it. You can investigate it. You can walk heel-to-toe along the family tree, either on the father's side or the mother's, until you reach the roots of the evil. Davidson the toddler – you can look into his eyes and see it. A drop of blood in a glass of milk. Anyone tracing it will ultimately reach the drop of blood on the Eritrean woman's underpants. To deny that would mean to toss out all the charts. Obliterate once and for all the assumption that roads lead and do not just happen. But that would be impossible, so a moment of choice is required. A crossroads is required, and a decision.

But the truth is that he had never abused kittens or hit other kids more than was normal. The truth is that he himself had never been hit, at least not an exceptional number of times. The urge to do evil did not arise in him, and so he could neither overcome it nor abandon himself to it. He lived his life totally asleep. In a state of slumber that became a way of life. When he could take something, he took it. When he couldn't, he tried to take it anyway. Not out of greed, but out of habit. He began dealing drugs a short time after his discharge from the army. Everyone was using; someone had to deal. The guy who offered him the job was a kid himself, but he seemed terribly grown-up. He was from Beersheba, that guy, and the whole kibbutz gang called him BS. They made fun of him behind his back but were respectful to his face. When Davidson began dealing for him, they were also respectful to Davidson, and that was nice. But the real kick was the money. Buying what you wanted. Eating where you wanted. In a few years, he had enough for the restaurant. He loved to watch people eat. Even the biggest phonies, the ones who stopped at his place on their way to the jazz festival in Eilat – when they chewed, they were just like any other animal. He'd been to restaurants in Tel Aviv; he knew they ate differently there. With their mouths closed. Eyes averted. Intelligent thoughts in their minds. But they came to his restaurant after a two-and-a-half-hour drive. They were tired and hungry, and thought no one was looking at them. He saw them chew their chicken steaks, ripping them apart with their teeth, their mouths smeared with oil from their salads. He saw them wolf down chocolate cake warmed in the microwave and then leave no tip for the waitress they'd never see again anyway.

He loved his work, but when that guy from Beersheba came to him with an offer to send shipments through him, he didn't need to consider it for long. The restaurant was still full and the Eritreans saved him a hell of a lot of money, but the truth was that he was beginning to feel bored. The bear-like slumber that had made him an easy baby to take care of, a quiet pupil and a definitely acceptable husband enveloped him like a fat tire. Only rarely was the fat penetrated by a flash of genuine desire, of true passion. Even when he was taking a woman in the darkness of the storeroom, he hardly felt anything but a slight ripple in the ocean of boredom. He could just as easily have been grabbing a bag of snacks as the naked ass in front of him. Everything was simply there, waiting for him to taste it.

He thought the shipments might arouse something in him, and in that sense he was quite right. Since the package he'd sent with the Eritrean had disappeared, his senses had become sharper. If he were to wake up several days later to discover that the restaurant had burned down, a scenario Sayyid had hinted at in their last few conversations, he would certainly have felt more alive than ever. But he felt alive enough as it was, more alive than he wanted to feel. They had played him for a fool – this entire time, they had clearly played him for a fool. The medications, the bandages, the antiseptics from the storeroom – those two Eritrean women had set up a clinic for refugees in his backyard. He, who had always been careful not to attract attention, and had succeeded, was now smack in the middle of an illegal route for illegal immigrants. God only knew how many had already passed through there, and who knew what they would say if the immigration police caught them. It infuriated him, and what infuriated him even more was the look in the eyes of that woman, the one he suddenly remembered was called Sirkit. An insolent look. A fuck-you look. She stood in front of him now, holding a crate she'd brought from outside. Looking at him as if he were someone who'd come into her house without permission. And it was *his* house, damn it, *his* territory.

Semar was standing closer, so she caught the first slap. He didn't plan to do more than that, one slap for her, one for Sirkit, and a phone call to that babe from the police to show her what good citizenship was. But when the slap landed on her face, Semar grabbed his hand and bit it as hard as she could, bit it with a strength she never dreamed she had, despite all the hours she'd spent watching people chew. He tried to shake her off, but couldn't. He grabbed her hair and pulled with all his might, but she only bit down harder, and with the last vestiges of clear thought he still had, he was shocked at how that puny woman was capable of such a thing. He let go of her hair – pulling it was leading nowhere – and began to punch her in the stomach instead. That worked. With the third punch, she let go of his hand and collapsed onto the floor. He bent over her, planning to keep punching her with his uninjured hand. He knew he'd have stop at some point – he couldn't take her to the police with bruises that were too prominent – but at the moment, he simply couldn't stop.

Let her go.

If he momentarily let go of Semar, it wasn't because of the order the other one had given him, but because he was so astonished that she had dared to give him an order at all. And in Hebrew. Who would have believed that this quiet girl had managed to pick up the language? He punched Semar one more time, and was intending to teach the other one a lesson too, when he suddenly felt something cold tear through his stomach, through layer after layer of fat and slumber, all the way to his very core.

Eitan was closing the trunk when he heard the fall. He had taken a coat out of it for Semar. It was too cold for the thin blankets they had in the garage, and his down army jacket seemed like a good solution. Another piece of his previous life casually appropriated by his present, different life. Under the jacket, he'd found an old bottle of wine from the time he still believed he would surprise Liat with a spontaneous picnic. It had suited him to think he was the sort of person who always had a bottle of wine in the trunk, ready for a celebration. There were also some of Yaheli's toys. Itamar's books. Charcoal for the barbecue that would never come. Two months earlier, if anyone had asked him, he would have said that his trunk was full of junk. But now he understood that it wasn't junk, but a treasure trove. A time capsule in the back of the car, and he hadn't known.

He closed the trunk with one hand, the jacket in his other, and then heard the noise. Heavy and muted. He dropped the coat and ran inside, expecting to find Semar passed out on the floor. And there she was, on the garage floor, but she wasn't the only one. A large man wearing jeans lay not far from her, a knife in his stomach. Semar held her own stomach as she stood up, shaking. The man remained lying there.

12

T HE EARTH DID NOT WANT to take him back, that filthy man. It made itself as hard as rock. It had rained two weeks earlier and the earth had been soft and slippery, like a sheep's intestines. But now the earth was hard, very hard, and Sirkit was angry at it for not helping, but she also understood why it wasn't willing to have that filthy man pushed into it. Tesfa and Yasu dug like mad with large spoons that Semar had found. They had blood on their hands from the digging, and Sirkit thought that for men, they were really okay. They did what had to be done, didn't speak much and didn't hit anyone unless they were asked to do so. They might have looked surprised when she called them into the garage and showed them that one lying there on the floor, but they'd said nothing. They hesitated for a moment when she asked them to lift him, as if they weren't sure he might not suddenly stand up and shout at them because they were supposed to be cleaning the restaurant now. But in the end, he was a dead white man and they were alive black men, so a moment later they bent down and picked him up, not very gently. But there had been another moment, when they first saw his face and Sirkit saw them waver. His eyes had been open, and their blue pupils looked strangely off to the side.

Tesfa and Yasu looked at the spot that the eyes were looking at and saw nothing, but it still seemed odd to them, seeing their boss wall-eyed like that. Before then, they had never looked directly into his eyes. And now they could look as much as they wanted, and that confused them a bit. But they quickly remembered that a dead man is a dead man, and open eyes that saw nothing was something they knew very well from the desert and the Bedouin camp.

They dug for almost three hours, until they finally cared nothing about the dead man's eyes or his huge feet, which had fascinated them at first. They just wanted him to get into the hole so they could return the earth to where it belonged, cover him well and go to sleep. When they'd gone, she remained standing there. That filthy man was under the ground and she was above it, and that felt good. She was glad they had finally managed to get him in. She had begun to think they'd have to cut him up. That was a terrible thing to see. In the Bedouin camp, she saw how they cut a person's ear off and took pictures of it so that their family could see it, be terrified and send money. It didn't take much time, cutting off an ear, but with bones it had to be different. She wasn't sure that Tesfa and Yasu would have been able to handle bones. About herself, she had no doubt. The doctor, on the other hand, was horrified when he saw the knife in the filthy man's stomach. It was almost *funny* to see his face. He hadn't believed she could do something like that. She hadn't believed it either, until the second it happened. Then it seemed extremely logical, almost inevitable.

She told the doctor to go. She said that if he didn't say anything, she wouldn't say anything either. Now each of them had his own dead man. They didn't owe each other anything. Just silence. But he still asked who the man was. Insisted on knowing. She didn't answer him. What that man had done wasn't her secret. It was Semar's. A few seconds later, she thought he understood. He wasn't stupid, her doctor. He saw Semar's face and the beating that filthy man had given her. And he had seen the color of the baby she had given birth to.

There was a moment of silence, and then he went out and came back with the jacket. For a brief moment she thought he was going to stay. Even though he no longer had to. He put the jacket around Semar, whose entire body was shaking, and then turned to look at her. The filthy man lay between them and there was nothing to say about it. He looked at the filthy man and the knife she had stuck in his stomach. Then he turned around and left.

Now she had to get out of there. Gather everything she had, which was quite a lot, and take off. She turned away from the earth under which the filthy man lay and began walking back to the caravan. On the way, she passed the garage. Two nights earlier a baby was born there. Yesterday morning it died. Then a man was killed there. Then the doctor left. Now the garage stood as empty as it had been on the night she found it. She walked faster.

At the door to the caravan, she stopped to water the roses. Considered taking them with her, but that was stupid. Semar would look after them, or one of the others would. Or maybe they would just wither and die there. They wouldn't be the first. No sound came from inside, and that was good. She didn't have the strength now for the endless chattering of that bunch of cleaners after a day of work. She opened the door and turned on the light.

Three Bedouins were sitting on the mattresses.

*   *   *

Despite everything that happened in the hospitality tent of the people of the desert, when the sun rose on the village the next morning Sharaf's father poured black coffee into a glass and went to wake up his son. He walked into the tin shack and held the glass very close to his son's nostrils so he would inhale it. Sharaf inhaled. But he didn't get up.

Several days later, Sharaf started working with Sayyid. His father didn't know about it. Two weeks later, Mussa went back to work on the kibbutz and told Matti that he appreciated everything he'd done for him, and Matti said, "No problem, Mussa, you and me, we're family." He continued to return every night with 150 shekels rolled up in his hand, and he came home so tired – humiliation is exhausting, Sharaf thought – that he never noticed Sharaf sneaking out in the middle of the night. Sayyid would wait for him in his new BMW, behind the hill. At first, Sayyid didn't want him to bring Mohannad along, said he made a lot of noise, but when Mohannad showed up one day with a rifle he'd stolen from a soldier who was taking a shit in the Beersheba central bus station, Sayyid decided to give him a chance. After Sharaf and Mohannad had scared the hell out of all the dishwashers in the city for him, convincing them that it would be worth their while to pay Sayyid and not only the gangs in Rahat, Sayyid was really satisfied. "Now I can give you both a man's job."

A man's job turned out to be the worst night of their lives. Nine hours at the meeting point not far from the Tlalim junction, shaking with cold in their too-thin jackets and dying of boredom because Sayyid swore that if they spoke to each other he would cut off their pricks. Who knew, there could be a police ambush waiting for them. Not a word. Don't move. Don't even piss. For Sharaf, that wasn't hard – he was used to holding it in from the mornings he waited for his father. But Mohannad was freaking out. Sharaf heard him groaning as the hours passed, sweating despite the cold. Maybe he hoped to sweat the urine out and finally deliver his tormented bladder from its suffering.

The sun had begun to rise when Mohannad broke the silence and rasped in a throaty, tormented voice, "That's it, Sharaf. He's not coming."

"What are you talking about?"

"He's not coming. Sun's out. No Eritrean. Let's go."

"But what about the shipment? What are we going to tell Sayyid?"

"That we waited all night and no shipment came."

"He'll kill us."

"Us? If he kills anyone, it'll be the Eritrean. We have to get out of here before it's morning and someone walks by and asks himself what we're doing here."

So they took off, but not before Mohannad peed for three straight minutes. When Sharaf got home, his father was already sitting outside, drinking coffee. He didn't ask where Sharaf had been and he didn't offer him any coffee. He didn't even look at him. And Sharaf – who was tired and thirsty and still felt the cold of the night in his bones, actually wanted very much to sit beside his father and sip hot coffee – walked inside, lay down on his mattress and didn't wake up until long after two o'clock.

When they called Sayyid to tell him that no one had come with the shipment, he shouted, "What? Are you sure?" Then he told them he'd check on it and hung up. After that, he didn't call them for weeks. He said he believed them and everything, family is family, but he didn't want them to be mixed up in his business anymore. Maybe he thought they'd bring him bad luck. They'd almost started working as dishwashers at the gas station on Kibbutz Beit Kama when he called, almost two months later, and told them to go and talk to the Eritrean's wife.

He was still shaking when he turned the suv from the dirt road onto the main road, and for a moment thought maybe he needed to pull over and calm down before going on. But his desire to get away from there was greater. Four kilometers east, a man in jeans was lying on the floor with a knife in his stomach. When he thought about that, his hands began to shake again. It wasn't that he hadn't seen dead people before. But this time it was different. Because she had *intended* to kill him. He had no doubt about that. There hadn't been an iota of alarm in her eyes after it happened. They might even have held a challenge: look – I did it. So what have you got to say about it?

He had nothing to say. The man lying on the floor had managed to beat the hell out of Semar before he fell, and Eitan had a pretty good sense of how things had played out before that. The thought of the rape nauseated him, but he was honest enough to admit that the nausea he felt was only indirectly related to Semar. First and foremost, he thought of himself. He wasn't supposed to see it. He wasn't supposed to know about it. As if someone had left the cover off a street sewer and the shit had risen and flooded everything. The shit was always there, everyone knew that. But not in their faces, not right in front of their eyes. Eitan was experiencing the same feeling he had when he went into a public bathroom and saw that someone had defecated and not flushed the toilet. A great deal of disgust, a bit of curiosity, and mainly anger at the person who had spilled his shit for all to see, a disgusting public display that couldn't be ignored. What that man had done to Semar was horrible, but it wasn't Eitan's shit. He wasn't supposed to open the door and see it. Not that he didn't want someone to deal with it. He was willing to invest public money and he was willing to vote for someone who promised that such things would not happen. But he wasn't willing to have it shoved in his face.

Not far from the Tlalim junction, the nausea was replaced by something that at first he couldn't define. Relief. Because in fact, if you thought about it, he was a free man. She'd said so herself. She'd understood immediately, even before he did, that the balance of power had changed irrevocably. No longer the extorted and the extorter, but two equals. Each one and his dead person. He thought again about the man lying on the garage floor. He wondered suddenly if he had dared to touch her as well. And was surprised to discover that the thought sent chills of anger through him. But he reassured himself that it wasn't possible. After all, he knew her. Then he gave an ironic laugh.

Knew her?

He didn't even know himself. Two months ago, he had run over a man and driven away. He hadn't known he was capable of such a thing or all the things that came afterwards. Perhaps she too had been completely different until that moment. A Sirkit he couldn't describe or even imagine. That regal stillness, that icy power. Perhaps those qualities had been born there. At that moment. They hadn't been there before and would not have existed if it hadn't happened. (But there had to be something, some seed. In both of them. Or perhaps they might have lived their entire lives without anything growing from that seed. Silent carriers.)

None of that changed anything. He was on his way home. There would be no more treatment in the garage, no more phone calls, sudden visits by her to his home. There would be Liat and Yaheli and Itamar. There would be work. There would be no more nights of silence, no more whistling. And suddenly, after the nausea and the relief, a new, not entirely

318

clear feeling rose in him. Before he could feel it completely, he found himself driving the SUV quickly to the mall entrance, having made a firm decision: he would take home a pizza as a surprise. A large family-size pizza. With mushrooms. And olives. And one of those plastic toys for kids.

*   *   *

On the way to the Eritrean woman, Sharaf sat next to Hisham and thought about the gun Hisham had in his pants pocket. He'd already seen guns a few times and Mohannad had even let him shoot one bullet from the rifle he'd stolen from that soldier, but Hisham's gun was in a different league. Small, elegant, like something you see in an American movie. Before they left, Mohannad asked Hisham if he could hold the gun and Hisham had laughed in his face and said, "Are you kidding? As it is, Sayyid sent me to take care of two babies." Mohannad didn't say anything, but Sharaf knew he was furious. Sharaf was furious too. He played with his switchblade the entire time they were in the car, opening it and closing it so that Hisham would see that even though he had a gun and a driver's license, Sharaf still had a weapon of his own. It didn't matter that the only thing he'd ever cut with that knife was orange peels. Hisham didn't know that. The Eritrean woman didn't know that. He'd give her a good scare and she'd tell them what they wanted to know, and even Hisham would have to admit to Sayyid that those babies knew how to work just as well as the grown-ups did.

They waited a long time for the Eritrean woman. They thought she'd be home at noon and it was already evening. They were edgy, tired. Hisham knew that the night patrol car at Tlalim junction got there around six. Which meant that they'd definitely stop them. Open the trunk. Turn the car inside out. Ask questions. He knew the cops would hassle them a little and then let them go. They had other cars with Bedouin drivers to stop. The cops would let them go right away. They didn't argue. They knew how to sit quietly, answer when they were asked, look down at the asphalt and not into their eyes. But the kids in the other cars, they didn't know yet. They'd start whining. Why are you stopping me, why not them? Just because I'm an Arab? Why are you turning the car inside out? Why are you talking to me like that? They didn't understand that all that would only make it take longer. The kids got pissed off. It's not fair. "Fair" is a word for Jews. In the end, the police would let them go too, and they'd go back to the car, put things back in order, more or less, and drive away. Off the good, paved road onto a dirt road that led to the tin shacks. They'd shout at their mothers to turn on the generator, they couldn't see a thing.

Sometimes at night, one of the guys says they should go back to the junction. Throw stones at the patrol car. Maybe burn it. Others say no, he should calm down. It would just make trouble. He's quiet. It isn't his pride that's injured, it's something else. But in the morning he gets up and goes out again. To the mall in Beersheba, where they need a security guard. To the university cafeteria, where they need a cleaner. To the Bedouin hospitality tent the kibbutz opened for tourists;

maybe they need someone to saddle the camel. Sometimes he gets sick and tired of all that, and then he checks out other things he could do. First of all, they make sure he's stopped throwing stones at patrol cars. Letting your anger out like that gets you nowhere. The fire in your eyes has to turn to ice so you can do something with it. When they see that he's okay, they start giving him things to do. First, small things like waiting at the Kestina junction with a shipment. Then bigger things. For instance, asking the Eritreans if anyone was close to that guy who was killed with Sayyid's package. Finding out if he was married. Then going and checking to see how his wife is doing.

When the woman came in, it was already very late. That had made them edgy even before the conversation began, and the woman's behavior only made them even edgier. Hisham had already opened his mouth to speak when Sharaf interrupted – they don't have a drop of respect, these kids – and asked the woman if she'd been with her husband the night the shipment disappeared. She said no. Her Arabic was different, hard to understand, but it was still clear that they didn't scare her at all. She looked them right in the eye when she spoke, and she kept looking at them right in the eye even when Mohannad told her she was lying and slapped her face. It was too much. It didn't make sense that they had to keep their eyes downcast with the cops, and this woman looked at them as much as she wanted. Everyone had to know when they couldn't look at someone else's face. That rule was very clear to animals; anyone who had a dog knew that. You don't look at someone stronger than you are; if you do, it's like you don't understand that he's stronger. And then he has to explain it to you.

Sharaf stood up and pulled out his switchblade. He wasn't planning to do anything with it, just show it to that woman and enjoy the moment of fear in her eyes. But there was no fear there, and that really confused him. She looked at the knife, and looked at his face, and for a moment it reminded him of the way his unmarried teacher Tamam looked at him, and that made him hesitate. But an instant later, a nasty little smile appeared at the corners of her mouth, the same sort of smile he'd seen on the face of the kid in the hospitality tent. This woman looked at his knife, looked at him and said without words, is that all you have kid? Before he knew what he was doing he had gone over to her, grabbed her chin the way he'd imagined grabbing Tamam's chin so many times, and instead of kissing her, the way he'd imagined kissing Tamam, instead of sticking his tongue between her lips, he stuck the tip of the knife through the soft skin under her ear, and shook as much as she did when the first, large drop of blood welled up in the cut.

13

THE PIZZA WAS STILL HOT when he got home. The smell in the SUV had driven him mad, but he'd sworn to restrain himself. He wanted to open the box with everyone. Miraculously balancing the giant-size box and two bottles of Coke in his arms, he opened the front door and called out twice, "Who wants pizza?" realizing only then that the house was empty.

Their coats weren't there. Or their umbrellas. That made sense. If they'd gone out for supper with friends or something, they'd need them. But even Mr. Bear wasn't there, and that seemed strange. Yaheli never went to sleep without him. Mr. Bear spent his days in the living room, in front of the turned-off TV, watching special programs for bears. In the evening, Yaheli would take him to sleep, once again challenging the limits of his father's patience. Eitan said that the thing should have been put in the washing machine a long time ago. Liat and Yaheli defended Mr. Bear zealously, though each had different reasons. Yaheli claimed that Mr. Bear hated water and he swore that if they put him in the wash, he'd go in after him and take him out. Liat agreed that after a year and a half of being dragged from room to room, the stuffed animal really did look more like a rag than a bear, but she said that psychologically it was very important for a child to have something of his own. "I'm not planning to kidnap the bear," Eitan had said, "I just want it not to be filthy." "If you wash it, it'll stop being it," Liat had said. "Things look different after a washing. And they smell different. It won't be the same thing." Eitan tried to object, but the united forces of a three-and-a-half-year-old boy and his wife were too much for him. Mr. Bear continued to spend his days on the living-room couch and his nights in Yaheli's bed, as grubby as usual.

But now he wasn't there. The couch was empty. Eitan went into the kids' rooms; maybe Yaheli had gone to sleep early with him. But there he discovered that the toy theft had continued – not only Mr. Bear, but also the two plastic soldiers that had always stood beside the bed, fearlessly determined in their war against the dark, had deserted their posts.

But he persisted in believing that everything was fine. They'd be right back. He went into the kitchen and put the Coke bottles in the fridge, where the vegetables were lined up in perfect order. He closed the door and checked the calendar that was hung on it with magnets. No, there was no event scheduled in Itamar's class. Or in Yaheli's nursery school. No obscure agricultural holiday, no birthday. So where were they?

Unconsciously, his gaze wandered over the fridge door: calendar; shopping list. An entire household expressed in banal facts. Liat always wanted to add pictures, hang drawings, but he objected. Told her that he liked his fridge to be business-like. He didn't tell her about his parents' fridge, how all the notes and drawings had taken revenge on them after Yuval was killed. How before, his mother had hung funny notes and poems on the fridge door. Had cut clippings from the literary supplements and hung them on the fridge door among the shopping lists and wedding invitations. The lists changed, as did the weddings. But the notes and the poems stayed where they were. A week after Yuval was killed, a container of cottage cheese was still inside. Its sell-by date was the date he had died. Everyone noticed it, but no one said a word. The poems on the door had exactly the same words as they'd had before. Not a single period had thought it should move from where it was only because once there had been another person in the house and now he was gone. The rhymes didn't change either. But at the end of each poem was a silence that had not been there before.

After two weeks, his mother put a new container of cottage cheese on the shelf. But the dairy products continued to mark the days: the expiry date of the yoghurt was the thirty-day anniversary of his death. The hard cheese had been processed on his birthday. Printed on one of the milk containers was the date of his discharge, which would never come. And then there were the sell-by dates that were unconnected to him. Simply dates. April 7th, for example. Or December 24th. Dates that said nothing except: two months and a week have passed. Or – it's been a year and ten days. Or – he would have had a birthday in two and a half weeks.

Eitan turned away from the fridge abruptly, as if his continuing to stand there would cause the dates on the calendar to disappear right before his eyes. He hurried to the bath-room. A lone toothbrush stood in the glass. An orphan that said everything. He called Liat, vacillating between concern and anger. She wasn't the dramatic type, and that was why he was frightened now. She answered after the seventh ring, and something in her tone told him that she had checked the phone display carefully before she had finally deigned to answer.

"Where are you?!" he exclaimed.

"Where are you?"

"Home. With a box of pizza."

And two bottles of Coke, but he didn't say that because the weirdness of the situation was beginning to paralyze him. It couldn't be that now of all times, when everything had worked out in some twisted way, when he had finally left the garage for good, that Mr. Bear, his two children and three toothbrushes had disappeared.

When Liat spoke, her voice was like stone. After he'd lost it with Yaheli that morning, she had called him in the department. She was furious that he had disappeared the night before, but it was clear to her that they needed to talk. "The nurse said you were sick," she said, "that you'd stayed home." She said that and then was silent. She didn't tell him how she'd hung up, her hand shaking, had left everything and driven home. Told Marciano she didn't feel well. And she wasn't lying. She really hadn't felt well. She was nauseous all the way home. And when she opened the door and went inside and found what she knew she'd find, namely no one, she was so overwhelmed by nausea that she thought she was going to throw up.

She didn't throw up. She went back to the office and told Marciano she felt better. An hour and a half later, the results of the autopsy on the Eritrean came in. They found traces of drugs in his body. Marciano had first thought that the Eritrean was working alone, but Liat knew right away that he was a mule for Davidson. The tough kibbutznik's concern was nothing more than simple greed. Someone had killed Davidson's messenger and he wanted her to catch the guy for him. The new information should have excited her, yet she was anything but excited. Mainly, she was tired. She asked Marciano to send two undercovers to Davidson's restaurant that night to do some sniffing around. On the way out, she saw the detectives' hostile looks. The last thing they felt like doing on Thursday night was work an ambush at some shithole on Route 40. On Thursday nights, you could smell the weekend as if it were a challah in the oven. You wanted to get home early. You wanted it to be Friday. You didn't want a new detective to stick you with an ambush that was like a broom handle up your ass.

She had ignored their looks and driven home. On the way, she'd called her mother. Ignored the surprise in her voice when she asked if she could spend the night at her place with the kids. Ignored the explicit questions that came after she said that she might want to sleep there the next night as well. Her mother wasn't the type who waited quietly with a serene look on her face that said, "You'll tell me when you want to." With her grandmother, it had been different. But her grandmother was lying in the Hadera cemetery now.

In the end, her mother wasn't such a bad compromise. When she arrived with the kids, the house was in tip-top order, nicer than Liat had ever seen it. There were flowers on the table, and schnitzels, and her mother was just making a vegetable pie. Liat thought her mother looked like someone interviewing to be a grandmother because she had been fired from her job as a mother a long time ago.

Itamar and Yaheli were confused at first, but soon enough began to play. Liat and Aviva watched them. That was more or less the only thing they could do together. Aviva tried to ask and Liat said, "Enough Mom, you can see I'm wiped out." An hour later, Itamar and Yaheli finished investigating the house and sat down in front of the TV. That was good, because both Liat and Aviva were getting tired of their running around, but it was also a problem, because they didn't have to keep an eye on the kids if they were watching TV, and that meant they had to find something to talk about. It would have been perfectly fine if the food had been ready. When your mouth is full of schnitzel and cauliflower pie, the silence is legitimate. But the cauliflower pie had just been put into the oven.

"You know what we haven't done in years?"

Liat gave her mother a perplexed look.

"We haven't looked at your picture albums."

Before Liat could object, Aviva leaped up from the couch and pulled a worn album off the top shelf of the bookcase. Then she sat down again, allowing herself to sit closer to Liat, slipping toward her with the album as an excuse. "My God, look at how sweet you are here."

"How old do you think I am?"

"About six, I think. Yes, look at the cake in the picture under it. It was when I still baked them in the shape of numbers."

Liat leaned forward over the album. "I remember that you used to bake them like that. They never tasted good, just the icing on top."

Her mother's laugh was mixed with hurt. "But look at how sweet you are here, with that yellow dress. You look like a princess."

Liat reached out and removed the picture. "She doesn't look like me at all."

A girl in a yellow dress with her hands over her ears. Behind her a pink balloon. She's looking at someone outside the frame. The dress has a fringe. The collar is embroidered. The girl's hair is neatly combed. Further away is a blurred, white brick wall. Her elbows are sharp. Her arms brown. Her hands plump.

"How sad. Look at how I'm closing my ears."

"What are you talking about?" Aviva cried. "You're fixing your hair. You make that gesture to this day when you push your curls behind your ears."

"No Mom, I'm covering my ears. Take a good look."

"I'm looking."

"And?"

There was no longer any nostalgia on the couch, but something else, nameless but very much present.

"If it's so important to you, then okay, you're covering your ears. Even though I think you're fixing your hair here.

329

Why would a six-year-old want to cover her ears at her own birthday party?"

"Maybe she was sick and tired of hearing her parents arguing."

"Your father and I never argued in front of you."

"So maybe she was sick and tired of you not talking to each other."

The smell of cauliflower pie filled the living room. Aviva took the album and continued to leaf through it. "Look here at that big smile. Do you see, Liati, you're really smiling here."

Liat looked at the picture. There was no reason it should make her so angry, but it did. An old, unnamed affront now opened a yellow eye deep down in her stomach. "But it's so typical that, in the first picture in the album, instead of looking forward and smiling like a normal kid, I'm looking off to the side and holding my hands over my ears. So typical, and with that sad look too."

"Why are you so sure it's a sad look? It looks to me like the space between one smile and the next. By chance, they took your picture between smiles and didn't capture the smiles themselves."

"And you don't think that symbolizes something?"

"Why do you always think that something symbolizes something else? Explain to me, why focus only on this picture and not the others?"

Liat didn't reply, and a moment later her mother let the question go, moved it far away, the way she moved the plate with the candlesticks on it on Friday night so that a candle wouldn't suddenly fall and burn down the house.

Liat looked at the picture again. A girl straightening her hair as she looks at her birthday cake. A six-year-old girl covering her ears, already disconnecting from the world.

"Come on, honey," her mother said, "the pie will burn."

And yet, something inside her refused to believe it. Despite the lies piling up one on top of the other, despite the nights she spent alone and the things the secretary had told her when she'd called the department. Despite his strange behavior, the mornings he sat silent and cut off, the nights he came home evasive and guilty, and the terrible, baffling outburst of anger at the kids near the car. Something inside her said it couldn't be. That Eitan didn't do things like that. She had chosen him because he was solid, arrogant, hers. She had checked him out thoroughly from the very beginning, and only when she was sure that he was really head over heels in love with her, completely mad about her, did she give herself license to do something very rare for her: she let herself become attached to him. And that license was not renewed automatically. She continued to investigate the way he looked at her from year to year, listened well to his "I love you," poised to hear every subliminal discordant note. She tested him for three years, and only then did she tell him that she would let him propose to her. He roared with laughter. "It's because of that cynicism that I love you," he had said. But something inside him had understood, because the fact was that when he actually did propose two months later, he

331

said he would have proposed much sooner if he hadn't been afraid she might refuse.

So what, in fact, had happened? she asked herself all the way from Omer to Or Akiva. The kids were sitting in the back, curious and excited about the unexpected trip, and she spoke to them in a calm voice and to herself in a trembling voice, saying I don't know, I swear, I don't know. There were many other things she didn't know. She didn't know what she'd do when he came home and called her. She didn't know whether she'd demand that he leave the house immediately or let him sleep on the couch for a few days. Whether to explain to the kids that Mom and Dad had a little fight, or just act as if it was all part of a spontaneous weekend trip. When she closed the album and sat down at the table in front of the cauliflower pie that was burnt around the edges, she thought this couldn't be her life. Someone had screwed up and woken her up this morning to another woman's life. The other woman also had two children, worked for the police, had an unsolved case and a wrinkle above the corner of her right lip. The other woman had been stupid enough to build her life at the foot of a volcano. She hadn't checked the lay of the land earlier, she hadn't made sure that there was no smoke billowing from the mouth of the volcano. Poor thing, that other woman. Really.

At 8:15, Eitan called. She and her mother were sitting in front of the TV with the kids eating *burekas* and watching an endless parade of auditions. Auditions for the cooking program, auditions for the dance program, auditions for the role of presenter who would preside over the auditions for a singing program. She was thinking about switching channels but didn't have the energy, and it wouldn't really make a difference. So she sat in the heavy, heated air of the apartment, squeezed onto the couch between her mother and her children with the TV wailing like a Greek chorus, and decided she had to go to sleep early tonight.

But at 8:15 Eitan called, and unfortunately she was still too awake to miss it. She waited seven rings before answering. Stared at the flashing display that showed the name: Tani.

Finally she answered. Not because of him. Because of Itamar. He looked at the phone, puzzled, unable to read the name of the caller from where he was sitting, but definitely capable of guessing. A seven-year-old shouldn't have to see his mother screening his father's calls.

"Where are you?!?"

She allowed herself to enjoy the surprise in his voice. The panic. He hadn't expected to come home to an empty house. She waited a moment before responding with a question, although she knew very well what he would say: "Where are you?"

"Home. With a box of pizza."

So she explained it to him. Slowly. What they had told her when she called the department looking for him. What she had found when she got home. What she had decided to do. And he listened on the other end of the line, breathing heavily into the phone, as if the air were too heavy to drag into his lungs. When she finished speaking, he was silent, and she thought about how all relationships are born in silence and

333

end in silence, the silence before the first word and the silence after the last one, and asked herself whether the last-words phase was beginning.

Then he said, "I'm on my way," and hung up. She went back to the couch, ignoring the looks of Itamar and her mother, smiling at the half-asleep Yaheli.

Time began to move slowly. Yaheli fell asleep and she moved him to the room her mother had prepared for the children. It was her grandmother's room, and it still had the scent of her perfume in it. Rosewater and something else. Apart from the scent, everything in the room was different, and Liat thought that if it were possible to pack the fragrance in bags and donate it to WIZO, her mother would probably do it. Now, when she went into the room with Yaheli in her arms, Liat inhaled the fragrance deeply. She could actually feel her grandmother in the room. Her image took shape among the shadows, birdlike and thin, lying on the bed under the blankets. When she was a child, Liat had snuck into her room at night, once with the excuse that there'd been thunder and once that she'd had a bad dream, until her grandmother told her to stop looking for reasons and just come whenever she wanted to. Her grandmother would lift the blanket slightly and she would squeeze in beside her, smelling that rosewater-and-something-else perfume. The frequency decreased with the years, and when she was in high school she crawled into her grandmother's bed only twice: the night before her math matriculation exam, when she couldn't sleep, and the night after she'd had sex with Kfir, and she was in pain. But even when she remained in her room, she still knew there was a birdlike woman lying in the next room, and that gave her peace of mind.

Yaheli tossed and turned in his sleep, and Liat continued to look at the collection of shadows generous enough to disguise itself as her grandmother. How could she accept that she would never, never ever get into that bed? And the scent of rosewater and something else – how long would it take for it to fade away as well? Maybe that was why her grandmother had demanded that they give everything away to WIZO with one sharp blow, the way she'd crack the heads of the carp she bought for the Sabbath, explaining to the horrified Liat that it hurt less that way. And Liat suddenly remembered coming back after the funeral and seeing her toothbrush standing tall and proud in the glass. And her clothes folded neatly in the closet. And her socks. Who in the world folded socks? But her grandmother did. She folded even underpants. She folded tablecloths, papers, bills. Her quick fingers divided the world into squares and put them into the closet. For her grandmother, everything had its place, and everything was folded. One woman's quiet but resolute mutiny against an entire world. Outside there was disarray, wars and *khamsins* and storms. But none of it crossed the threshold of the house. A simple screen door kept the mosquitoes, the flies and the world outside. And inside – perfect order. Life carefully folded. Jars of pickles arranged in rows, prepared for battle. And how quickly they ate them during the shiva, almost without noticing. They ate them with such wastefulness, one after the other, until her mother suddenly appeared from the kitchen, her face pale, and said: that's the last one.

They put it on a porcelain plate and took it ceremoniously to the balcony. There it lay, as damp as a fetus. They waited for the last of the visitors to go and then cut it into three pieces – one for Mom, one for Liat, one for Uncle Nissim. They chewed it slowly, knowing that the taste that filled their mouths and tickled their tongues now was the last. The absolute end. And that their mouths had never been so full and so empty at the same time.

During the shiva, the house seemed graced with benevolence. They treated each other with a gentleness they didn't know they possessed. They forgave each other with the same ease with which, on normal days, they raged at each other. In the evening, after the last visitors had mumbled their condolences, they wandered around the house in silence. Gradually, they gathered in her room. A malicious trick – it looked as it had before. But the pictures on the wall had already begun to hang crookedly, the Persian carpet to unravel, the letters on the pages of the books to disappear. All the folded clothes spread their sleeves and rose skyward with a flutter of cotton and mothballs. A covey of white underpants beside a flock of black socks, woolen swallows, followed by her magnificent, embroidered shawls, rare birds gliding out of sight into the horizon. Or at least, that was what should have happened, because there is nothing more dreadful than an object that outlives its owner.

But they didn't disappear, those objects. They remained folded. And if at first Liat and her mother wanted to go into

336

the room and cherish them, they slowly began to hate them. Because the objects swelled until there was no room in the house for anything but the objects themselves. Liat couldn't identify the moment when cherishing had turned into clinging. When had her grandmother's room turned from a living, breathing place to a mummified corpse? On the second floor of 56 Ben Yehuda Street, time was frozen in the scent of rosewater. But there is nothing deader than a museum and there is nothing more alive than fresh longing that burns your throat like arak.

Now she wanted to break a dish in that room. Deliberately. Turn on the radio to full volume. During the ads. Remove the sesame seeds, one by one, from the *burekas*, and drop them on the floor. And wait. If she didn't come, if she really didn't come, maybe then Liat would finally understand that it was true. That her grandmother truly wasn't here. That Liat could fart loudly or announce that, in the next elections, she was voting for the left-wing party. That she could say, "Fuck it," without her grandmother's birdlike hand slapping her gently on the wrist and admonishing her, "What kind of way is that to talk!" That she could do whatever she wanted without criticism. Without praise. Without. She no longer needed to be a good granddaughter. Because if there was no grandmother, there was no granddaughter. There was just Liat. Alone.

The room was dark and warm, and Yaheli's breathing was slow and quiet. The shadows wrapped Liat in black cotton wool and longing, which was painfully sharp at first, and then took on a sleepy quality. She moved her head close to Yaheli's, inhaling deeply the scent of his shampoo. Why couldn't he always smell like that, even when he grew up? She could cope with his voice changing, with the fact that one day he would be taller than she was, even that one day he'd love another woman more than her. She could accept all of it if at least they left her that scent, that childlike sweetness. But his scent would fade, just as the scent in this room had faded.

The last time she visited her in the hospital, Liat had put bright red polish on her grandmother's nails. Her grandmother had lain on the mattress. Her wonderful hair spread around her head, her nails as red as strawberries. Now, in the dark bedroom, time was untethered from the chains of logic; everything was possible. The old grandfather clock still stood ticking away in a corner of the room, but its hands moved blindly in the dark. Perhaps forward, perhaps back. You know time only when you see it. You can't see it in the dark, which means it doesn't exist. In the dark, you can move things around, mix the future with the past and the present, shift years from side to side the way you shuffle cards in a card trick. Here's Yaheli, three years old, with his child's smell. Here's Yaheli, thirteen years old, with his adolescent disdain. Here's Liat, five years old, fifteen years old, thirty-five years old. Here's her grandmother with black hair, white hair, red hair, with only her nails forever red.

When she woke up, Eitan was standing at the door. The hallway behind him glowed with the bluish light of the TV in the living room. In the darkness of the room, she could barely see his face. He didn't speak, hardly moved, and he looked like another one of the illusory images that room could create so well. But she *had known* he'd come. So she wasn't surprised when he actually appeared.

Since she had known he would come, it was reasonable to assume she'd know what to say to him when he arrived. The traffic jams on the way from Omer to Or Akiva had left her ample time to think. As had the long hours at the table in the living room. And yet, when she woke up and saw him, she couldn't think of anything to say. All the things she had wanted to shout at him earlier had long since faded. And she wasn't especially in the mood for a dramatic silence. She simply had nothing to say. "You lied to me." "Where were you when you told the department you were sick?" "Who is she?" Ridiculous words. Superfluous. The words of women in terrible movies. From adjacent apartments.

She saw him lean forward, clear his throat. If so, he seemed to be planning to speak first. She looked at him with genuine curiosity. What rabbit could he possibly pull out of his hat now?

"Tuli—"

That infuriated her, really infuriated her, because how dare he call her Tuli. How dare he use that private, pet name, *their* name, at a time when everything that was theirs had fallen apart today at one in the afternoon, when she'd walked into the house and found it empty.

He saw her recoil. When she was asleep, her arms had been spread to the side, open and trusting, and now she drew them in close to her body. Her brown eyes assessed him in the dark, and then moved onward. That frightened him. Turning her gaze from him said far more than the hostile words, "I don't want to talk." She stopped looking at him the way people stop looking at an accident on the side of the road. At first they can't take their eyes off it, and then the moment comes when it's too much to bear, and they abruptly turn their heads, drive on and don't look back even once. Because there's nothing to be done anyway.

He should have told her that night. Should have walked into the house and told her. I ran someone over, Tul. An Eritrean. Widespread cortical damage. I left him there. The bright voices of a commercial came from Aviva's living room. Someone was talking about the enormous benefits of whole-wheat grains. She would have listened to him that night. It was doubtful that she would listen now. (But would she really have listened to him then? And what sort of listening? Would she have been able to suspend for even a moment that clear distinction of hers between right and wrong? Let go, for a moment, of that eternal I-always-do-the-right-thing of hers, which was even greater than his? The thing that stood between them also had a mother, not only a father. A secret like that required two people. One who doesn't want to tell and one who doesn't really want to hear.) And there was another, not much more pleasant possibility. It hadn't been his fear of her harsh criticism that had kept him from telling her that night. Or the admonishing speech she would give him and the self-righteous looks lurking in the corner of her eyes. It was because he knew that if she had hit the Eritrean, she would never have driven away and left him there. Not because of her

I-always-do-the-right-thing, but because of who she was. She wasn't a person who did such things. He, it turned out, was.

Eitan had no intention of telling Liat the truth. It was too complicated, too dirty, too covered in blood and brain matter. On the other hand, he definitely couldn't leave things as they were without saying anything. That privilege was reserved for men who came home at normal hours. Men who didn't stay out all night and weren't caught in a series of embarrassing untruths and inaccuracies. Liat would not forgive him if he maintained his silence, but she certainly wouldn't forgive him if he told her the truth. In a world of two terrible options, the lie shone like the sun. Filled everything with color.

Extortion for malpractice. That was the best he could come up with, and considering the circumstances, it wasn't bad at all. The wife of a man he had operated on. He died, she threatened to sue. She still hadn't filed the suit, but if she did, he would undoubtedly be ruined. He'd tried to meet with her over the last few weeks, convince her to drop the whole business. She was middle-aged, pretty crazy. Called him at weird hours. Demanded that he come. Gave wild, accusing speeches. But today she had summoned him urgently and said she was dropping the whole matter. Tore up the legal papers right in front of him. She was going back to her family in South Africa. "I haven't told you until now because I didn't want to worry you. Maybe I was also afraid that you'd be ashamed of me."

There it was. The lie was out, smooth and glistening, like a hippopotamus emerging from a river. Huge. Almost monstrous. Born from him all at once, gigantic and perfect, like

Athena emerging from Zeus's brain. As he spoke, Eitan saw no difference between medical negligence during surgery and running over the Eritrean. In the end, both had occurred at work, both accidentally. And the extortion at the heart of the story was no different from the extortion that had actually taken place. And the happy ending was ultimately the same. As was the shame.

There were also differences, of course. Medical negligence was embarrassing, even disgraceful, and yet the consequences for a doctor who errs at work were not the same as those for a doctor who hits and runs. The first would probably be fired, that was all; the second would certainly be sent to prison. And if we're already nitpicking, there was also quite a substantial disparity between the middle-aged crazy lady and the tall, slim woman whose velvet eyes still glowed in his memory. But Eitan ignored the differences. Had to ignore them, just as the pilot of a Boeing 747 steers the plane away from any obstacles on the runway during takeoff. The lie could not take off any other way. Liat, sitting there with her arms folded, looked at him as he pushed his hippopotamus along the runway, up into the sky. In some twisted way, it was very beautiful.

"Daddy? You're here?"

Yaheli raised his sleepy head from the bed. Eitan stopped speaking. He didn't yet know whether his hippopotamus would ultimately take off and remain in the air, or crash to the ground. Liat was looking at him again, and that was a good sign. She no longer looked like a passer-by who had just happened to meet up with him in an elevator. But he still couldn't figure out the

342

nature of her glance. The room was too dark and he was too anxious to grasp the subtleties. Usually, he could recognize the rapid blinking of impatience, her back tensing with disbelief. He had studied her face for fifteen years. But now he was entirely focused on the lie, and any distraction might end in disaster. Yaheli's words were that sort of distraction, because even if he had managed to bring himself to tell such a despicable lie to his wife, he wasn't willing for the lie to reach the ears of his small son. So he stopped speaking, and a moment later, when Yaheli repeated his question, he replied, "Yes, I came to put you to bed." Now he felt completely comfortable because he knew for certain he wasn't lying. He really had come to put him to bed. And in a moment, he would put Itamar, who had fallen asleep on the living-room couch, to bed as well. He'd tuck them in and tomorrow morning he'd take them all back home. To their lives. That crazy lady, middle-aged or not, would never appear again.

Yaheli waved him over with his hand. A small, commanding gesture that could not be denied. Liat moved aside, making room for Eitan. Even if she was thinking about telling him to leave, demanding that he go and come back tomorrow, the three-year-old's demand was stronger. She couldn't send the father away in front of the child.

Eitan hesitated for a moment before sitting down, examined Liat's face and waited for her permission. She nodded and said nothing. He sat down beside her and ran his hand over Yaheli's silken curls, which had been responsible for the surprising permission he had been granted to sit. Yaheli

343

asked him to sing to him, and he whispered a song about two little girls and one umbrella, smiling when Yaheli demanded, "Mommy too! Sing together!" They sang together. It was funny and ridiculous and sad, depending on how things would end. If they went home together tomorrow, they would certainly laugh one day about the night they sang children's songs in harmony, despite themselves. If Liat continued to be angry, that song would become a grotesque memorial: mother, father and child singing all the way to the divorce court. Eitan didn't know which possibility was the right one. Neither did Liat. With his child's wisdom, Yaheli held both their hands, held them tight and didn't let go.

Six songs later, Eitan's phone rang. He and Liat had just finished the *la la la* of the second chorus of "The Sixteenth Sheep". Yaheli lay between them, overjoyed. They had never indulged his whims with such devotion. Both of them together, singing above his head, and no one said it was late, no one announced that it was enough. They sang to him so he would fall asleep and they sang to him to put their guilt to sleep, because they had told him that everything was fine when everything was not fine at all. Liat listened to Eitan, his bass voice slightly off-key, and thought that at some point our child will fall asleep and then our problems will begin. But she also thought that anyone who could sing to his child like that couldn't be a liar. Which, by the way, was not accurate because people are definitely capable of singing charming songs to their children and telling terrible lies to other people, and sometimes to the children themselves. Liat knew that, though at that moment she clearly did not feel like knowing it. She felt like believing him. Like ignoring the strain she heard in his voice when he spoke, the strain she recognized from endless hours in the interrogation room. In the end, telling a story that differs from the reality is quite tiring. Unless you're well practiced at it. You have to invent details, synchronize facts, fill holes. You never understand how complex reality is until you try to create a replacement for it. Nevertheless, there was something to the story, something that removed it from the typical territory of a lie. An alloy of a pure metal and another metal. A certain percentage of truth, a certain percentage of lie, melted together into a mixture. Who could tell?

She could. She had no doubt that she could. A brief phone call to the crazy widow. She wouldn't settle for less than that. She'd verify that the woman was indeed a widow, indeed crazy, indeed middle-aged and on her way to South Africa. If all the answers were correct, they could begin to rebuild. Slowly, carefully – the sword would not be removed from the neck immediately. But if he opened his eyes in fright when she demanded to make that call, a short time after the curly-haired child in the bed fell asleep – if he refused her, then she would rid herself of him that very night.

The incoming call surprised them both. The ring cut through the lullaby they were singing to Yaheli. They were silent. Eitan was intensely aware of Liat's glance. He would have loved to screen out that call. Let it sink into the well of forgetfulness. But he couldn't. Wasn't capable of it. Because there was a woman on the other end who needed to speak to

345

him. He understood that from the urgent ringing, which went on for quite a while.

Yaheli turned over on the mattress, half-asleep. It was actually because of those soft curls, those clean cotton sheets that he had to check whether the world on the other end of the line actually existed, if it could possibly exist at the same time that his world existed.

He whispered to Liat that he had to take the call. Her reproachful look followed him out of the room. In the hallway, her heard Semar whisper in broken English. "Sirkit need doctor. Sirkit very very bad. Need doctor." He didn't say a word. What could he say? He hung up, and after a brief hesitation put the phone on mute. He went back into Yaheli's room. Tried to sing "Lightning and Thunder", but the thunder stuck in his throat and the lightning exploded inside his stomach. *Sirkit need doctor. Very very bad.*

14

WHY WAS HE GOING BACK THERE?

If there were an answer, the sort composed of ten words or 10,000, the sort that began with "because" and ended with "that's why", the sort in which things began at point A and therefore had to reach point B – if there were such an answer, Eitan Green didn't know it.

Thursday night, and the road from Or Akiva to Beersheba was deserted. Occasionally the face of a Russian child selling flowers appeared at a dark intersection. Eitan didn't slow down, but settled further into his jacket, though the temperature in the car remained the same. After twenty or thirty minutes, another intersection, another child, and again he pulled his jacket tighter around him without thinking about it, without remembering.

He asked himself why he was going back, and had no answer. From the sides of the road, gas stations glowed at him in shades of yellow and orange, like a controlled fire. Maybe he was going back now because he hadn't stayed then, that night. Maybe he was going back because of her. And maybe he wasn't going back at all and would take the next exit, turn around and drive straight back to Or Akiva.

But no. He continued driving. And when the lights of Kiryat Gat disappeared behind him, he thought this was the first time since that thing had happened that he was *choosing* to do something and wasn't being forced to do it. In some strange way, that made him feel good.

But when he exited onto the road that bypassed Beersheba, he already felt different. He turned on the radio, and a short time later turned it off. After a few moments of driving he turned it on again, turned it off again, then angrily turned it on again, this time leaving it on even though he wanted to turn it off again. Possible flooding in the Negev hills, the news said. Then music came on, the bouncy sort they played on Thursday nights. Party music. Eitan wondered how many people were driving in their cars now, listening to a party they were not part of. Not that it bothered him very much; thinking about it was simply preferable to wondering why he was in fact going back there. He had already passed the Shoket junction when it suddenly occurred to him that he was going back there to search for someone who had once been and was lost. He had lost him on the night he ran down the Eritrean. Actually, he might have lost him a long, long time before, but on that night he had discovered that he was lost. The child who had burst into tears the first time he saw a homeless person on the street – a story his grandmother, who had been there, reminded him about to this day. When had he stopped looking wonderingly at homeless people and begun to avert his gaze at any cost? When was the moment he had stopped being saddened at the sight of a person sprawled in the middle of the street and had begun to quicken his steps?

And yet he wasn't going back only to find that child. No less importantly, it was to show him to *her*. To stand before her and say: I've come back. And not because she had commanded him to. She'd be shocked, he thought, utterly shocked, and was surprised to discover how much pleasure he derived from the image of that moment, the moment of his return. (He didn't ask himself whether he would have returned if she hadn't been beautiful, if she hadn't possessed an icy calm that bordered on indifference. If she hadn't had those unique aristocratic eyes, an African queen with a human bone stuck in her hair.)

As he approached Tlalim junction, his hands began to sweat, the way Itamar's did the night before a dictation in class. He had already memorized the words, had practiced them, tested himself once with his mom and once with his dad. And yet when he climbed into bed, rivers of sweat flowed from his hands. Eitan told him it was fine, it was the way our bodies drained out pressure, but Itamar wasn't persuaded. It drove him mad that his body did something like that without being told to do it, without taking him into consideration at all. As he wiped his hands on the steering wheel Eitan thought about his older son, about how justified the mind's complaint against the body was, against that unruly child who trembled and sweated, paled and blushed, always at the wrong time, always when it should be doing something else.

He turned the suv onto the dirt road leading to the garage. Tried unsuccessfully to remember how many times he'd made that turn. But he felt the confidence of his fingers on the wheel, the way his body remembered the place. Here was a pothole, there was a depression on the side of the road, here you had to stay to the right and there, left was better. He knew the road by heart, even if he realized it only now. Suddenly, he thought about the house in Haifa, the fact that although he hadn't called it his parents' house for years, it insisted on still being his house. Several years ago, during a winter storm, he, Liat and the children were having Friday night dinner with his parents when there was a power outage. The darkness was absolute. Dense and thick. Yaheli was still too young to be afraid, but Itamar grabbed his hand and wouldn't let go. His mother asked him to go and get some candles, and at first he'd wanted to tell her to go herself – what were the chances that he'd find anything in the dark, in a house he hadn't slept in for ten years? But his parents were already at the age when it was a bit scary to send them anywhere alone in the dark, so he had stood up and begun groping his way. It was incredible how easy it was. Here was the dining-room wall. If you walked along it, you reached the kitchen wall. A great observation post for him and Yuval when they were trying to discover, once and for all, where the chocolate was hidden. You had to be careful at the kitchen wall; the heavy cabinet was still standing there, as nasty as always, just waiting for you to stub your little toe on it. He hadn't known that he remembered that, but it was still all there, exactly where he had left it. So were his mother's candles, on the second shelf, way back behind the tea service that came out only on special occasions, and which he actually hadn't seen since the shiva. He went back with the candles, and shortly after that the electricity came on again and he could tell himself once more that it wasn't his house, that he had built himself a different house in which he didn't feel like an outsider. But he still remembered how his body had navigated it so confidently in the dark and wondered whether he would ever be able to move that way in any other house.

Now it seemed that not only the house in Haifa was burned into his memory. This road was also imprinted on his neurons. Two and a half months ago he hadn't known it existed, and now he drove along it almost as if he'd been doing it for ever. There was less than a kilometer to go before he arrived and he still didn't know why he'd come back. And maybe that made sense, because he didn't really know why he'd driven out here the first time. Perhaps the question of why he was coming back was merely the little sister of that bigger question: why hadn't he stopped that night. For weeks he'd avoided it, but couldn't help circling around it. And perhaps there was no reason why he hadn't stopped. Not because that man was black and he was white. Not because of Liat. Not because of the kids. Perhaps he'd never know why. And the only thing left for him to do was to keep asking. That was his atonement.

They had broken her nose, two teeth and two ribs, and her left eye was ringed in bright purple. Her goddess's face now looked like a shattered mask. She was lying on the mattress, her eyes closed, breathing slowly between her broken ribs and then through her broken teeth. She didn't open her eyes when

Eitan came in, nor did she show any sign that she was aware of his presence, even when he bent beside her and took her pulse. He looked at her wide-eyed because despite the great number of faces he'd seen in that condition or even worse, he had never believed he would see *that* face looking like that.

Nevertheless, even now, with that shattered face and all the blood, she still possessed the nobility that had disturbed him from the beginning. Her silent lips looked a thousand times more silent. In some way, she was still brazen, provocative, still could drive him mad with that waiting of hers. Because he suddenly realized that she was indeed waiting. Not sleeping, not semi-conscious, but lying there with closed eyes, waiting. (But he didn't realize that she wasn't waiting in an effort to be provocative or contemptuous, but because she knew that if she opened her eyes now, she would do what she had not done earlier and would not do later – burst into tears.)

"Who did this?" The words came out matter-of-factly, quietly, and he was surprised at how hard his voice was. He hadn't come here to be hard. He hadn't left wife, children and mother-in-law at home in Or Akiva only to be cold and callous when he arrived here. Just the opposite. He wanted to help her, to feel pity for her. Wanted her to open her eyes and look at him differently. Or perhaps, see that he was different. And now, without even beginning to understand why, the anger rose in him once again. She must have felt it, because when she did open her eyes, there was no trace of the tears she had held back only a moment ago. Scorched earth. It had all been absorbed into the blackness of her pupils without leaving a sign. Her left eye was half closed from the blow, but her right eye was functioning properly and saw clearly: her doctor had returned and he was full of questions. He needed things to be put in order. She almost laughed, but restrained herself. It wasn't his fault that for him, everything was ordered, explained. It wasn't his fault that he had no idea what to do with stories that had no order or explanation, stories that swept in like a sandstorm and departed like one. Dust wandering from one country to another. He couldn't understand her story, just as he couldn't eat her African food or drink her African water. Because it would make his stomach turn. Because his body wasn't built for the sort of things they had there. So she remained silent, as did he, and as the moments passed, the anger in him grew larger and larger. Her insolence. Her arrogance. He had driven all the way here, had dropped everything and come, only to discover that a broken sphinx is still a sphinx.

He barricaded himself in his silence and she barricaded herself in hers, and the barricades grew higher. In another moment, Eitan and Sirkit would have completely disappeared behind them, would have vanished from each other's sight, if a drop of blood hadn't suddenly oozed from Sirkit's ear.

Eitan saw it and was horrified. He hadn't even examined her yet, hadn't yet understood the depth of the damage. And a drop of blood like that could definitely be the harbinger of catastrophe. A cracked skull. Cortical hemorrhage. Increasing intracranial pressure, and the brain, in a final attempt to halt collapse, drains the liquid through the ears. That nightmarish scenario filled his mind for a few seconds before he noticed the

353

cut right under her ear. That was where the blood was coming from, not from her brain. But he had to be sure, so he bent over her, looked and touched her ear. Gently. Without asking. Without explaining. She trembled. Perhaps from pain. Perhaps from pleasure. Either way, her look changed abruptly. There was no longer any insolence or arrogance in it, no trace of the sphinx. (And there was no denying the possibility that, from the beginning, she had demonstrated none of those qualities, that people found riddles only when they were looking for them, and the real sphinx might have rolled around on its back like a kitten if only someone had dared to come close and pet it.)

"Does it hurt?"

Yes.

She replied so simply, so acceptingly, that Eitan felt all the anger that had accumulated in him against her suddenly turn into anger against them. Against the ones who had come here and shattered this woman with their blows. He began to sterilize the wounds. Saw her cringe. Thought of saying, "It'll be over in a minute," but stopped himself. How do you know it'll be over in a minute? You don't even know why it had begun. You say it'll be over in a minute to a child who has scraped his knee, to a person slightly injured in a motorcycle accident when he's brought into the emergency room. But what do you say to this woman lying here and looking at you with eyes so black that the darkness outside looked bright in comparison?

So he was silent. But this time, it was a different kind of silence. And it was because she felt that this silence wasn't demanding or probing that she began to tell him. She told him there had been three of them. That they had been waiting for her in the caravan and had asked about Asum, becoming angry when she hadn't answered. She began to describe what they did and how they did it, but that appeared to be too much for her doctor, because he interrupted her, asking emotionally, "But why?", not seeing that she flinched again now, even more violently than she had when the antiseptic had burned her, and he persisted, "How could they do something like this?!"

Then she laughed in front of him for the first time. Out loud, her mouth open, despite the flashes of pain every facial movement caused. She laughed and laughed, and saw the surprise in his face, then the confusion, the anger, and finally the concern. He seemed to think her laughter was a side effect of what the Bedouins had done. Hysteria, a touch of madness. He didn't know that it wasn't because of the Bedouins that she was laughing, but because of him. And perhaps not because of him, but because of herself. Stupid woman, how could you even think he would understand?

They knew what they came for, she told him. *Asum was supposed to deliver a shipment that night. They thought I knew where it disappeared to.* And when Eitan continued to stare at her with confusion in his eyes, the eyes of a good-natured dog that had to deal with something other than herding sheep, she added, *And they were right.*

"A shipment?"

That's what they call it, don't they?

"Of... drugs?"

355

She burst out laughing again, but this time less loudly, and with her mouth opened less widely, not only because of the pain in her face, but also because of his face. She had already seen him upset and furious, nervous and smiling, fascinated and excited, but she had never seen him disappointed. And his disappointment angered her more than anything she had seen before. More than *that* night. How dare he be disappointed by her? How dare he expect her to be different?

"What did you think you'd do with it?"

She shrugged and said, *Sell it.*

He straightened up and stood over her, agitated. He paced the garage, shaking his head in some kind of internal argument she didn't hear but could definitely guess at. "Do you have any idea what it means to sell?" he suddenly blurted out. "Do you know how many people get into trouble because of that? Do you even know how to do it? You need people, you need…"

I have enough people who owe me a favor.

He froze in the middle of a step. Turned around, looked at her. That witch knew exactly what she would do. Every cut she had sterilized, every wound she had bandaged. The grateful faces of dozens of Eritreans and Sudanese. World champions in the 500-meter run. At her command.

He wanted to yell at her, but even before he opened his mouth she laughed for the third time. She should have known that he'd prefer her to be the victim and not the victimizer. Her doctor loved saintly people, and he didn't care how often they were trampled. On the contrary, that only made them saintlier. But she had no desire to be saintly. She wanted to be the one doing the trampling. And it seemed as if even God had wanted her to do a bit of it because he had dropped that shipment right into her hands, and he'd also dropped this doctor right into her hands. The doctor could go now if he wanted. But the shipment stayed with her, and she didn't care how many of her teeth they broke.

Eitan looked at her and said nothing. A moment later, he saw another drop of blood ooze out of the cut under her ear. But he didn't go to her this time. Didn't touch her. To keep from catching that blackness, that filth of hers. She was wrong. He didn't want her to be a saint. All he wanted was for her to be human (and it never occurred to him that there were times when being human was a privilege).

The blood, which at first had made him feel sorry for her, now seemed like a cheap trick to him. Another manipulation in an endless chain. Now he was definitely ready to believe that he had never run over that man. That the entire accident had been nothing but an illusion, a bloody, terrifying magic spell orchestrated by the witch with the broken nose. That possibility seemed much more reasonable than the more solid, silenced one: that the corruption, if indeed there had been any, had occurred gradually. That the woman lying in front of him hadn't planned anything. Hadn't schemed in secret. But at every step along the way, had chosen the possibility that seemed best to her. When she had first come to his house many days ago, she had wanted only to see his face. To look into his eyes and see whether her husband's face a moment before the accident was preserved in them. But when he opened the door, she saw nothing but panic and suddenly realized that she could definitely turn that panic into money. She had told him to come to the garage and went back to the caravan, her brain as white and airy as flour all the way. When she arrived, everyone already knew about Asum, and she had to look as surprised as she could. No one asked her about the shipment. No one but that filthy man had known. And he didn't know she'd been there that night. He'd paced around his restaurant, looking upset, and spoke to no one. She'd gone into the caravan and sat down on her mattress. After a while, people began to ask why she wasn't crying. Gently, at first. Then less so. It angered them that she didn't even look sad. Mostly the men. A man needs to know that his woman will cry for him after he dies. There were so many ways you could be screwed here. Thirst. Hunger. The Bedouins' beatings. The Egyptians' bullets. Now the Israelis' cars. You needed to know that if something happened to you, your woman would take the trouble to squeeze a few tears out of her fucking eyes. But Sirkit's eyes had remained dry and open, and two hours later they saw the new man who had come from the border.

They put him on the mattress next to hers and fussed over his wound all afternoon. In addition to the genuine concern for the man, there was also a great deal of anger toward the woman on the adjacent mattress. Her refusal to cry turned her tragedy from mutual loss into a personal enigma. Her dry eyes were more than an affront to her husband. They were an affront to them as well. She was denying them the pleasure of offering consolation to another person. At a certain point, they left the man who had been wounded at the border. With all due respect to wounded hands, people had to go back to work. He remained lying there with closed eyes. Every now and then, he moaned in pain. Sirkit's eyes darted over his wound. The infection was as fascinating as it was repulsive. The people who had examined the wound earlier said the Egyptians had started to put poison on the fences. There was no other explanation for that hideous cut. How stupid, she had thought, as if the Egyptians cared enough about them to bother to poison them. His hand looked that way because that's what happened to a wound that wasn't treated.

It was more or less then that she had decided to take him with her to see the doctor. She hadn't been thinking about money yet, hadn't even guessed that the illegal hospital would be set up. She had simply known that she couldn't sleep at night if the man kept up that moaning. The noise would kill her. Maybe she had even wanted to feel benevolent and compassionate. Maybe she *truly was* benevolent and compassionate. At least then, before everything became complicated.

That night, in the garage, she had understood for the first time how much power she had. The package the doctor had given her contained more money than she had ever seen in her life, and his eyes told her that if she demanded it, there would be more, much more. She hadn't demanded it. She'd ordered him to go into the garage and treat that man, and meanwhile her brain was working so fast it hurt. A moment before the doctor went inside, the man had offered her money. At first, she hadn't understood what he wanted and thought it was his fever talking. But the man had said again that a real doctor cost a lot of money, and she realized that it had never occurred to him that she was helping him free of charge. She was about to correct him, but stopped herself.

When she was six, her father had given her a goose. He'd brought it from town one especially yellow morning. All the chickens in their village were sick and scrawny, and the new fowl, with its beautiful white feathers, looked like the cleanest thing in the world. They put it in the yard and Sirkit went to visit it every few hours. She opened the gate to give it seeds, stroke its white feathers and check to see which of them was taller. Most of the time it was Sirkit, but when the goose was excited, it stood on its legs, spread its wings and stretched its neck so that the tip of its beak was a full centimeter higher than Sirkit. It was impressive. A few months later Sirkit was already taller than the goose, but she still went to visit it every day, and may even have loved it more now that it was smaller than she was.

One morning, people hung flags because it was a holiday, and her father told her mother that the next evening, they would eat the goose. Sirkit didn't say anything – her father wasn't the sort of person you argued with – but that night, she got up and sneaked into the yard. She opened the gate to let her goose escape. In the morning, she'd blame it on thieves. Maybe they'd believe her. Maybe they'd suspect she'd been careless and would hit her. Either way, the white feathers would remain in place. She hugged the goose and kissed her goodbye, surprised at how efficiently the feathers absorbed her little girl's tears. Then she untied the rope that kept the goose from flying, left the gate open and went back to sleep. How shocked she was when she went back in the morning and saw the goose pecking away peacefully exactly where she had left it. The gate was open, the rope untied, but the goose hadn't even contemplated an escape. The thought had never entered the goose's mind simply because geese don't do things like that. The white feathers were plucked a short while after, when the morning coolness still stood in the air like a false promise.

The man who had come from the border kept talking about money and she began to wonder whether she should really refuse him, set him straight. She hadn't considered asking him for anything. Simply because people don't do such things. Even if you open the gate for them. Even if you untie their ropes. Even if you can hear, in the adjacent yard, the crackling of the fire that has been lit for your flesh.

She still hadn't decided, but that night she told the doctor that when he finished, he should come there again. So furious was she about the expression of refusal on his face that she added a brief, spontaneous speech about her people and their needs. It had felt good, standing in front of him like that, although she knew very well that if he asked her more about "her people," she would not have been able to answer. What actually made them hers? What made her theirs? The fact that they had stood together in line for water in a Bedouin camp? That together they scraped leftover food from plates in the kitchen? That they looked into each other's eyes to see which deaths caused tears and which ones didn't? They were from different villages, different tribes, different paths. If they had anything in common, it was the name given to them by others who were of a different color. What did she actually owe them, apart from the metallic rattle of the chains of the journey that bound them together? To emigrate is to leave one place for another, with the place you've left tied to your ankle with steel chains. If it's difficult for a person to emigrate, it's only because it's difficult to walk in the world when an entire country is shackled to your ankle, dragging behind you wherever you go.

That night, when she finished talking to the doctor outside and went back into the garage, the man who had come from the border was sitting on the table and looking at her. His shoulders were broad, and somehow, despite the journey, still not stooped. It had occurred to her that being alone there with him so late at night could easily have become danger- ous. But when she looked into his eyes, she saw something she had never thought she'd see in the eyes of a man looking at a woman. The awe of a person looking at someone stronger than he is. His broad shoulders and great height could not heal his injured hand, which was now clean and sterilized under a bandage as white as that goose's feathers. The man reached into his pocket and took out a wrinkled note. If there had been a moment when she thought of telling him to leave his money in his pocket, it vanished when the awe in his eyes made her skin glow.

In the days that followed, the people began to look at her differently. And when they looked at her differently, she began to be different. The way she walked. The way she stood. There was even something different about the smell of her body. While her gait and posture were visible, no one was aware of the different smell of her body. Since the doctor had run Asum down, no one had been close enough to smell it. No one had gotten very close to her at all since the doctor hit Asum. They looked at her from a distance. Spoke to her from a distance. That "from a distance" had a name – respect. The people's awe of her wafted around her like perfume. She immersed herself in their submissive glances as if they were a milk bath. An outsider would not understand it. Certainly not Eitan. Awe, respect and submission were not words Eitan concerned himself with because he took their existence for granted. Just as people pay no attention to the miraculous flow of electricity through the wires of their houses until the flow stops.

At the end of every night in the garage, when she walked to the caravan, exhausted, Sirkit stopped to water the rose bush. In the depleting blackness of the night, the scent of the roses was strong, almost mystical. She was careful not to inhale too deeply. Two-thirds of her lungs was fine, but more than that might intoxicate her. Might make her forget other smells. And she must never forget that even if that breath was all roses, the next one might be all something else. Or might not be at all. And also that bush, which was here now, could so easily not be here in another week. It might dry up and wither or be torn out and moved to different ground, leaving only the earth gaping in shock to suggest that there might have been something there previously, a fullness that had been plundered. The roses reached up to the sky and under the ground, the roots reached out as well, but not to the sky – to something different, yearning for some mossy, muddy truth the desert sky did not know existed. Above the roots, under the roses, lay a package made by human hands. Ants scurried along its outer sides. Damp earthworms rubbed against its corners. Blind worms bumped into it as they slithered along, and hurried to dig themselves another path. And the package stayed where it was, unperturbed. Three kilograms of white powder, carefully wrapped. Resistant to dampness, mustiness, worms' anger and people's investigations. The roses reached to the sky, the roots clutched the ground, and the package lay quietly, as packages do, indifferent to whether it would lie there for eternity or be pulled out to have its insides cut to pieces.

At the end of each night she spent in the garage, Sirkit would stop at the bush, water the roses and ponder the package under her feet. A great deal of money. Perhaps too much. Perhaps it had been a mistake not to take it to Davidson's door that night. If she'd had a plan when she dug under the bush, it was a mystery even to her. It had been almost dawn when she decided that the hole she had dug was deep enough. Her body shook, but her hands were steady. She placed the package in the hole and it lay there, as plump and relaxed as a baby. And with that baby, as with any other baby, you had to wait to see how it would develop. Even if she never came back and squatted beside the bush, if she never dug out what she had put there in the depths of the earth, the pleasure of knowing the burial place of something everyone was searching for would be hers alone.

The days had passed, and with them the nights in the garage. The roses continued to reach to the sky, and from day to day their reaching became more daring, more brazen. Now they no longer bent their heads before the moon and the sun. They looked straight at them. And if the roses allowed themselves that, it was no wonder that the roots also became greedy. They demanded greater and greater depth, and the roses reached higher and higher. Sirkit watered the bush and listened. She heard the package which, until then, had lain as quiet as a sleeping, good-natured baby, begin to writhe. She lay on her mattress, tossing and turning when she should be sleeping. Trying to decide whether to dare to look around for buyers. To shed once and for all the dust of the woman she had been and expose the royal armor of glittering scales under it. As she tossed and turned, scores of people she had known crowded onto the mattress beside her. Her mother, her father, people from the village, the dead children, the goose that was all magnificent white feathers. She didn't drive them away. On the contrary, it was amidst the din of their chatter that she managed to fall asleep. And then – white, dusty dreams visited her.

She was edgy and exhausted in the mornings. Stumbled out of the caravan and looked at the bush. Through the earth, the labyrinth of roots, the damp web of earthworms, the package hummed to her.

From one night to the next, the scent of the roses grew heavier. Now everyone was talking about it. Even when the caravan door was closed, the fragrance crept in through the cracks. Devouring people's dreams. It might have been nice if it hadn't been so aggressive. The bush demanded that its presence be recognized, forced you to inhale its scent deeply. If you could inhale it all, you shouldn't dare to settle for less. Otherwise, you were just as stupid as that goose with the open gate, the untied rope and the feathers that had been plucked one by one before noon.

In the end, the Bedouins found her. Perhaps they had asked in the restaurant about Asum and someone had pointed to her and said: his wife. Perhaps someone had approached them at his own initiative. There was no lack of people who would snitch on you if someone convinced them there was a reason. It didn't really matter. What did matter was that they came, and when they came they broke her nose, two teeth and two ribs and left her with a shiny purple ring around her left eye. But even through the broken nose, she could still smell the roses. In fact, their smell was even stronger than before. The scent faded only in the garage, when the doctor came and drove away the roses with the strong smell of his antiseptic. He spread it on her nose. Around her eye. Along the length of the cut under her ear. Her face burned, and even more, thoughts of the package burned in her mind. But all of that passed when she told him about the shipment. His disappointment infuriated her so much that nothing burned anymore but her desire for him to leave.

*

366

Eitan also had a burning desire to leave. So he stood up and left. The simplicity of his steps boosted his spirits. This is where the garage floor ended. This is where the desert earth began. Here was the SUV. With every movement of his muscles – intoxicating freedom. To drive away from there and never see her again. Ever. He punched in the code. Buckled his safety belt. His brain was filled with pleasant emptiness. Not a single thought passed through it as he drove along the dirt roads except, perhaps, for the strangely persistent image of the purple stain around Sirkit's left eye. A hand he did not know had aimed an accurate punch at it. Blood vessels tore. Capillaries burst. The purplish fluid had spread under the delicate skin, a glass of wine spilled on an embroidered tablecloth. And now it was that closed eye that stayed with him as he turned the wheel. What lived there, behind the lowered velvet curtain? If she had any tears, regret, question marks, even the possibility of compassion, then that was undoubtedly where they existed. For a moment, he allowed himself to roll up the purple velvet curtain and look into her closed eye. What he saw there, what he *imagined* he saw there, made him tremble.

A long moment later, he averted his gaze. Angry, almost furious. He was once again being drawn in. He turned on the heater though there was no need for it. Turned on the radio, though there was no real need for that either. He took a deep breath of the artificially heated air. He listened intently to two artificially produced songs. In another minute, he'd reach the main road. A female singer – he wasn't sure of her name – moaned that they were meant for each other. He listened closely

367

to her. Ready to believe. But by the second chorus, it was clear to Eitan that even the singer didn't believe. Her voice was metallic and hollow, and Eitan thought she wouldn't recognize love even if it punched her in the left eye. He switched to a station where female singers knew what they were talking about when they sang, "Baby, I need you". It was Billie Holiday, and he believed her in a way he didn't believe any other singer. Perhaps because she died a long time ago and her love was no longer something that could be measured, only sung about. Old songs about old stories. That was what he needed now. Even the story of that night would one day be an old story. It was definitely a comforting thought.

Right near the main road, a battered van passed the SUV. It drove off the asphalt just as Eitan was about to turn onto it, and the turn was so wild that he was shocked when there was no collision. Since he'd hit the Eritrean, he no longer considered himself a model driver where safety was concerned, but he was nevertheless stunned to see that it never occurred to the driver to stop and apologize. The van raced forward along the dirt road and Eitan muttered to himself, "Crazy Bedouins," as he was about to drive onto the main road. Suddenly he braked. As the van moved further away, he followed its progress through the rearview mirror. Three hundred meters from where he stood was the junction where the dirt road that led to the garage met the one that led to the kibbutz. He prayed silently that the van would turn toward the kibbutz, although the voice in his mind was absolutely certain it would not. The van reached the junction and drove straight toward the garage as fast as a battered van could drive on such a rocky road. They were going back to finish what they had begun. They would get the shipment from her or kill her, or they would get the shipment from her and kill her anyway.

He turned the wheel some more before realizing he was doing it, and as he drove along a side road to the garage, he didn't think even once about what he was doing. If he had, he wouldn't have been able to do it. He would have sat there thinking, considering, debating, deliberating, agonizing, philosophizing, wavering – and meanwhile, the people who had broken Sirkit's ribs, her nose and two of her teeth would break everything else that could be broken. (As a doctor, he was intensely aware of the myriad possibilities.) The side road was faster, and he had no doubt that he would arrive in time. The only question bothering him was what would happen afterwards. He couldn't plan very much beyond going inside, grabbing Sirkit, putting her in the suv and getting the hell out of there. It might not be an especially clever plan, but it was the best he could come up with, and in many ways it wasn't a bad idea at all.

He stopped the suv with a squeal of brakes in front of the back entrance to the garage and ran inside. She was lying where he had left her. Her left eye was even more swollen and purple than it had been earlier, and her right eye looked at him with such awe and astonishment that if he'd had the time, he would have been thrilled. But he had no time, so he roared at her,

"They're coming, get up!" and bent to pick her up himself. She didn't protest. Perhaps she understood what he wanted, or perhaps she was just too surprised to object. He carried her as quickly as he could to the door, and then realized that although he'd managed to get there before them, that didn't mean that he'd manage to get out before them. The sound of running and voices shouting in Arabic came from outside the garage. They were surrounded.

They didn't look like bad people. Their faces were totally ordinary. Quite different from each other, as you would expect people's faces to be – here a pointy chin and there a broad one, deep-set eyes in one face, protruding eyes in the other – but they shared the characteristics common to all members of the human family. The guy who blocked the back door of the garage reminded Eitan of his medic course commander, only younger. And the guy who blocked the front door looked like (and maybe he actually was) the security guard at the entrance to the Negev Mall parking area. There was something surprising about that, at least for Eitan. After the wild car race, he had expected something more impressive. More frightening. Muscular arms, thick eyebrows, the hate-filled expression familiar to him from images of terrorists on TV. The two young men at the doors and the one who came running a few seconds later reminded him more of high-school kids racing into class late, panting and stressed.

But they had a gun, and that changed the picture. When the kid who resembled his medic course commander pulled a switchblade out of his pocket (he did it with the practiced movement of someone taking out a pen to sign a receipt), Eitan understood that they were indeed in trouble. Because the people who didn't look like bad people did look like working people. Their job was to get the shipment and apparently to kill the person who had ripped them off. And that someone, based on the conclusion the three had certainly reached, was Sirkit. And him.

The guy who looked like the security guard shouted something in Arabic, and the other two began to search the garage. Eitan wondered how much time had passed since he'd come in and sent away Semar and the other two Eritreans who had been staying with Sirkit, and what the chances were that one of them might decide to return to check on her. Not that they could do much, what with that gun the Bedouin was pointing at both their faces. He gestured for Eitan to put Sirkit down, and he put her gently on the floor, not convinced that she would be able to stand. She was able to stand, but her body shook from the strain, and perhaps also from fear. When Eitan saw that, his body began to shake as well. Uncontrollably. Because if Sirkit was afraid, then there was evidently a good reason to be afraid. The guy who looked like the mall guard noticed the shaking and laughed. He said something to his younger pal with the knife, who also laughed. Maybe they weren't bad people after all. And maybe anyone would react the way they did when he finally caught someone who had evaded him for so long, someone who had stolen from him, got him into trouble and made his boss yell at him so loudly that he went deaf.

The younger guy who looked like his medic course commander asked Eitan where the shipment was. He had almost no accent, and Eitan recalled that, to break the ice, the commander had done fantastic imitations of Arabs speaking Hebrew.

"I don't know."

He guessed that the punch was coming even before it hit him, but nothing prepared him for its power. The last time he'd been hit was sometime back in the ninth grade. He'd already forgotten the taste of blood in his mouth, the explosion of pain into a multitude of small pieces. He almost fell onto the cement floor, but steadied himself at the last minute. He tried to open his left eye, only to discover that he couldn't. Perhaps it had been the same Bedouin who had smashed Sirkit's face because he always aimed at the same eye. And now they had twin black eyes. Their faces, so different from one another, now had an identical swollen, half-closed left eye, and maybe a broken nose as well.

"Where's the shipment?"

Eitan didn't answer. It wasn't that he was trying to act tough. He truly didn't know what to say. The only person who might know was standing beside him now. Barely standing, but bravely silent. Eitan wondered if it was that insane composure of hers or actually a crazy sense of pride, the sort that would rather die here than give them what they wanted.

It was neither composure nor pride. She was silent because she knew that if she told them where the shipment was, they'd kill them. Or at least him. No one would believe that she was the one who had organized it all. Too stupid. Too black. A woman. Her doctor stood beside her wiping away the blood that had begun to flow from his nose. His movements were shaky, confused. He was undoubtedly more skilled at cleaning up other people's blood. The guy with the gun lit a cigarette and said they had plenty of time, then gestured at the kid with the knife, who went over and punched Eitan again. Sirkit wanted to avert her eyes, but forced herself to keep looking. It was the least she owed him.

Eitan was already on the floor. He looked small. It was incredible how small he looked. That was why she couldn't believe it when he suddenly straightened up and told the guy with the gun that he'd give him the shipment. The guy with the gun looked pleased. He took another drag of his cigarette, only to show Eitan and Sirkit that he wasn't the least bit stressed and had all the time in the world. Then he said to Eitan, "*Ya'allah, habibi.* Where is it?" Eitan got up from the floor gingerly. She watched him walk toward the door. There was no way he could know about the roses, so what the hell was he doing? She watched as he stopped near the crate of medical supplies.

The Bedouin with the gun took a step forward. "No tricks, okay?"

"No tricks," her doctor replied, "I hid it here, inside the tank." He took the oxygen tank out of the crate. Sirkit looked at it, astonished. Two punches must be all it took to make a white man lose his mind completely. Unless she hadn't been updated and oxygen tanks could shoot.

It turned out that they could. Because when Eitan said he was just going to open it, and aimed the pure oxygen straight at the face of the guy with the gun. The oxygen caught onto his cigarette like gunpowder. It was only for a moment, but that moment was enough to burn half his lip and the entire mustache above it, and maybe much more if he hadn't dropped the gun to slap out the fire on his face. The kid with the switchblade ran over to help him put it out. In that sense, they really weren't bad people. Mutual aid and all that. In another sense, it was very much in Eitan and Sirkit's best interest to run.

They ran. And they weren't alone. The guy with the gun continued to writhe in pain on the floor, but the other two did a fast priority check and took off after them. The kid with the switchblade made a quick stop on the way out to pick up his pal's gun. That held him up in the short term, but opened up many more possibilities in the long term. Because when they got outside, the two escapees were already in their suv, halfway out of there. The kid with the switchblade and the gun knew how Sayyid would react if those two got away from him again without a trace of the shipment after all the efforts they'd made to catch them. He knew that Sayyid would have to vent his rage on someone and that without those two, he would most likely vent it on him. He knew that he had no real choice but to stand in front of the SUV, aim the gun straight at the asshole and his Eritrean whore and shoot.

The bullet shattered the windshield of the SUV when it entered and the back window when it exited. It didn't hit anything on the way, but it passed so close to Eitan's ear that the whistle was truly unbearable. Sirkit screamed. Or perhaps he was the one who screamed. He wasn't sure. Just as he hadn't been sure about the business with the oxygen a few moments earlier. Because yes, he, along with everyone else in the chemistry classroom, had seen what happens when pure oxygen and a lit cigarette come close and he had memorized words like "explosive" and "combustible" for the exam. But there was a hell of a difference between the white pages of his exam booklet and that guy with the gun, mainly that the exam booklet didn't shoot you if you made a mistake. On the other hand, there was a good chance that the guy with the gun would have shot him in any case, and if that was true, there had been no reason not to try. When he'd bent to pick up the oxygen tank, he felt Sirkit watching him and gave a silent prayer that if it worked, she'd be smart enough to run straight out of there. Obviously she was. In fact, she had begun to run even before he did. If it hadn't been for her, he might still be standing there, as stunned by his success as a student who is surprised to discover that he'd earned a 90 on an exam he was convinced he'd failed. But she had started running, and a split second later he was running after her, and two moments later the kid who looked like his medic course commander was hot in pursuit, along with another guy who must have resembled someone, though not someone Eitan knew.

He got into the SUV, planning to race forward, and he most certainly would have done so if the kid with the gun who was standing in front of them hadn't started shooting. The first shot split the windshield and exited through the back window, leaving him with the vague question about the source of the scream that reverberated through the SUV. The second shot hit the baby seat in the back, leaving behind the smell of burnt plastic. The Bedouin shifted the gun in his hand in preparation for the third shot. Eitan looked him right in the eye and drove straight ahead.

The blow shook the SUV slightly, but to Eitan's ears the collision of body and bumper was as thunderous as an atomic bomb exploding. He knew that sound. He remembered it very well from *that* night, from the last time he'd driven the SUV into what a moment before had been a human creature. He knew what would happen if he stepped out of the SUV. And this time, it had been no accident.

How had that night been different from all other nights? A huge moon was shining on both nights. Perhaps even the same moon. And on both nights, a sharp, guttural scream had filled the SUV. Then, it had been Janis Joplin, and this time, Sirkit, or him, or a combination of both of them – EitanSirkit. SirkitEitan. On that night, each of them had been alone, and on this night, they were together. And apparently they were about to die together, because after it hit the Bedouin, the SUV was heading straight for the concrete barricade at the entrance to the garage. Eitan braked. Sirkit screamed. The SUV veered sharply and stopped right in front of the two remaining Bedouins.

At that moment, he wanted more than anything to take her hand in his. But that seemed desperate, sentimental. He was prepared to die without a hand to hold, without a finger to stroke just to avoid being considered desperate, or even worse, sentimental. He censored himself even then, at that last moment, because even at last moments he could not shake the fear that if he extended a hand to the world, it would remain empty.

Through the shattered windshield of the SUV, Sirkit looked at the two remaining Bedouins. If she pulled out a shard of glass, she could at least try to cause damage. She had no idea how lethal a shard of glass could be, and she knew that the two furious men would pull it out of her hand very quickly. But she couldn't just sit there waiting to see what they would decide to do to her. She had waited in the camps in the Sinai. She had waited in the desert, in the village. She had waited enough. The only thing she felt bad about was her doctor, who was sitting white-faced at the wheel, the whitest white she had ever seen in her life. He was looking at the Bedouins in silent shock. She sat beside him in his red SUV, enveloped in its pleasant air conditioning, its pleasant music, and its seats so comfortable you could call them beds. A red SUV that enabled you to go from point A to point B without thinking for even a moment about all the points along the way or the people on the sides of the road. And that suv, that wonderful isolating machine, was broken. The windshield was gone. And the back window. The collision with the concrete barricade had finished off the hood and who knew what else. And worst of all – through the broken windshield, the real world was now terrifyingly real.

The hatred in the eyes of the guy standing in front of them was real. He had just wiped the blood flowing from the head of his run-over pal on his pants. And also real was the rage of the guy whose lip had been scorched by the oxygen Eitan had sprayed at him. There was great pain on his face, but the rage was greater. It was the rage that had forced him to get up from the garage floor, stumble outside and see the suv hit his friend, who had the gun. Now he had the weapon in his hand again. Trapped in the suv in front of him were the man and woman he had been sent to kill. If he had been indifferent about the job earlier, he approached it now with a profound, almost religious commitment.

From where he sat, Eitan saw the Bedouin advancing toward them. He wanted to think about Itamar, about Yaheli, about Liat, but the only image that came into his mind was that of his mother hanging laundry in the yard when someone opened the gate. "You're not serious," she'd tell him. She always responded that way to announcements that surprised her. "You're not serious" to the spontaneous airplane tickets to Greece his father had bought for her birthday. "You're not serious" to the soldiers who came to inform her about Yuval. As if a low wall of disbelief separated her from the spoken words, a you're-not-serious wall which those speaking to her had to climb over in order to get inside and say yes, they were very serious.

The Bedouin shouted something in Arabic, and aimed the gun at him. Eitan wondered whether he should close his eyes. Then he heard the siren, and at first he too wanted to say "You're not serious," because there was a limit to how many times a person could teeter between life and death in one night. The Bedouins shouted at each other in Arabic and began to run, and Eitan and Sirkit looked at each other without the slightest idea of what they would do now. Not that there was much they could do – the undercover police cars shot forward from the curve in the road and stopped in front of them, brakes squealing. The sirens were deafening. Three detectives jumped out and began pursuing the Bedouins. Three more detectives surrounded the suv and shouted, "Hands in the air."

So they put their hands in the air.

15

H E DIDN'T KNOW how many hours he'd been in the
cell. The clock at the far end of the corridor showed
ten minutes to three, but the hands clutched the 3 and the
10 and didn't let go, no matter how much time passed. Eitan
wondered whether someone had deliberately sabotaged the
clock. When your perception of time is broken, other things
tend to break as well. Cover stories, for example. But none of
the prisoners at the station looked important enough to warrant
sabotaging the clock for. There were two pimply-faced young
guys who reeked of alcohol, a rather amiable junkie who kept
asking Eitan if he had a cigarette, and a Russian guy with a
Mohawk who cursed constantly. He pictured them waiting for
the nurse at the entrance to the department at Soroka. That
made it all nicer, mainly because it blurred the fact that this
time, he wasn't watching a group of waiting people from the
sidelines. He was one of them. In the hours that had passed
since his arrival no one had asked him why he was there. No
one had tried to start a conversation. In that sense, they were
all as polite as if they were enjoying an evening at the theater.

The patients at Soroka actually spoke to one another quite
a bit. Perhaps it helped them ease the tension. They griped
about the vending machine that swallowed coins and refused

to respond with coffee. Complained to each other about the snooty doctor or the stuck-up nurse. They exchanged names of rabbis and kabbalists, holistic therapists and acupuncturists. In fact, they were willing to talk about anything from politics to Sudoku, as long as they didn't have to sit on the waiting room bench and listen to the sound of the Death stepping across the linoleum floor. The corridors of Soroka Hospital were filled with astonishingly friendly people, friendlier than they had ever been. Like sheep crowding together on a cold night, one trembling body pressed up against another – that was how those patients clung to one another and to their small talk. But here, in the jail cell, the prisoners kept to themselves. Not even their glances met.

Eitan sat in the jail cell and waited. Looked at the clock that showed ten to three and spoke to no one. The young guy with the Mohawk stopped cursing and began to sing a song in Russian. It was a nice song. Kind of gentle. It made Eitan wonder what the guy was doing there. Or maybe that was easier than asking what he himself was doing there. Alice had fallen into the rabbit hole. Ali Baba had sneaked into the cave. But he – he'd just been driving home after a day's work. How had he suddenly entered this dark and twisted wonderland that already had three dead people and one blue baby in it? He himself had killed two of those people, one by accident, the other deliberately, and in between there had been cut, shot, bleeding Eritreans, guns and knives, and one shipment, whereabouts unknown. All of that in the light of an enormous white moon, which might not have been a moon at all but his home planet, the one he had been abducted from into this horror story, the place he was supposed to have driven to that night without hitting anyone. Where he was supposed to have gone to sleep and woken up as usual. As usual.

The other possibility flowed through Eitan's body in surging waves of "what if". What if he had simply gone home that night? Finished work and driven straight home. Kissed Yaheli and Itamar, lain down in bed beside Liat. The picture was so clear, so vivid that it was almost impossible to believe it hadn't happened. He hadn't driven home. He had driven *there*. And now *there* was going to swallow him up, had already swallowed him up, in fact, and now all that remained was for it to finish chewing him up and spit out the bones.

The guy with the Mohawk continued singing. The junkie fell asleep with his head against the wall. The two pimply-faced kids smelled less of alcohol now and more of fear. Sweat had a different smell in a jail cell. Eitan smelled it on both kids and knew that they smelled it on him as well. He tried to remember whether he'd sweated like that earlier, in front of the Bedouins, and couldn't. But he did know that in that clash he'd been all adrenaline, and now the adrenaline had evaporated, leaving room for thoughts of what was to come. Earlier, he'd faced a tangible external threat, and now he was facing all the threats and scenarios he could imagine. His mother's face. His father's disappointment. Reproachful looks from Liat. Poignant prison visits from Itamar and Yaheli. And that didn't even include the imagined faces of patients, nurses, fellow doctors, department heads. Prof. Zakai.

Prof. Zakai. How horrified he had been to discover that the much admired professor was an aficionado of not only wine and Russian literature, but also of envelopes fat with money. How angry he had been when it became clear that Zakai collected them with the same devotion he collected antique *dreidels*. How he loved those spinning tops with a letter on each of their four sides. Arranged them neatly in his office at the university, reprimanded the Ethiopian cleaner for changing their positions even slightly. There they stood, on his monstrously large glass desk, and Zakai forced every student who came in to bet which letter a *dreidel* would fall on before he spun it. The students didn't care about the *dreidels*; they were there to complain about an exam grade they'd received, but Zakai cared very much. "Bet on miracles. That's what the Jews have done from the time of their exile to this very day. And that's what every doctor does, even if he doesn't want to admit it." As far as Zakai was concerned, all doctors were gamblers. Perhaps that was why those envelopes of money seemed so logical to him. Or perhaps it was much simpler: he took better care of people who paid more. A basic economic principle that controlled everyone. Even Eitan would never have considered spending entire nights treating Eritreans without remuneration if Sirkit hadn't paid for it with her silence.

None of that made any difference now, but he thought about it anyway. It was ten minutes to three, eternally ten minutes to three, and Eitan's brain had begun to tire. His thoughts sprang from one subject to another in an endless zapping of channels. The alternative was to think about where he was now, and that option was inconceivable. So he thought about Zakai, about Prof. Shakedi, about the song the kid with the Mohawk was humming, about a TV series that had been broadcast recently. He would think about anything, as long as he didn't have to think about the moment when the time would stop being ten to three.

In the end, someone came and opened the door. Eitan wondered whether the policeman was really looking at him curiously as he led him into the interview room, or it was only a trick of his imagination. The junkie was still sleeping when he walked out of the cell, but the guy with the Mohawk stopped singing for a minute in what might have been a goodbye. The two pimply-faced kids had been taken out a while ago, though the smell of their sweat still stood in the air. Three turns away along the corridor, Commander Marciano was waiting for him. He knew it was Commander Marciano from the tag on his shirt. But not only. Also because of Liat's imitations of him, which had been spot on, as all her imitations were. And because he knew that the station commander would want to talk to him himself. It wasn't every day that they had a murder suspect who was married to a senior detective.

The clock in Marciano's office didn't think the time was ten to three. It showed 8:30 in the morning, and Eitan believed it. He was much less inclined to believe the friendly smile on Marciano's face or the surprising, awkward handshake he gave him as he sat down.

"Sorry you waited so long. I had one detective on the Eritrean, two on the Bedouins, and one female detective who bailed early yesterday because she didn't feel well." The smile waited at the corners of Marciano's mouth like a fat cat, and Eitan understood that the fourth detective was none other than his wife. Marciano was really enjoying this whole business.

"Which story should we start with, the Eritrean's or the Bedouins'?"

Eitan said nothing. Marciano's joviality annoyed him. For him, the disparity between Sirkit's and the Bedouins' stories was a minor detail – it might add another few months to his prison sentence or not. Among the ruins of his previous life, it really didn't make much of a difference. In the end, there were two dead people here. And both had been struck by his SUV.

"The Bedouins say you're the drug lord of the southern district. You finished off the messenger, stole their shipment and wasted anyone who tried to get it back. Guy Davidson, who was the middleman for the shipments, has been missing for twenty-six hours. They figure that's your doing. Sharaf abu Ayad died two hours ago at Soroka. In his case, they saw with their own eyes that it was your doing. What can I tell you? As far as those people are concerned, you're more lethal than Saladin."

Marciano stopped speaking. He was hugely pleased with himself for that Saladin. Eitan would bet unhesitatingly on a master's degree in Israeli history, a quick-track degree that required no thesis-writing and added a few hundred shekels a month to Marciano's salary. Police commanders flocked to that program. He wasn't quite sure why he was thinking about Marciano's academic pretensions or his salary just then. Since he'd come into the room, his brain had been wandering in the most remote alleyways. Dead-end thoughts. Winding roads. And yet everything was really terribly simple: what had been secret was now exposed in the sunlight. Even if they hadn't yet told Liat, his department or the media, from this point on it was only a matter of time.

None the less, he found himself curious to hear exactly what Sirkit had told them. Because there was still a difference between the premeditated murder of one person or two. He had hit Asum by accident and had run, while he had hit the Bedouin intentionally ("But ladies and gentlemen, he had no choice!" shouted the defense attorney. "It was self-defense!" The jurors would nod because that was what jurors did in TV shows, but the judge of the Beersheba Magistrates Court would not nod at all. He would ask when Eitan had first learned about the drug shipment. Why he hadn't reported it immediately. Why he hadn't called the police when he saw Sirkit bending over the body of a man who apparently was Davidson. Why he had driven away that night after hitting the Eritrean. The judge would ask and Eitan would remain silent, because the replies that came to his mind were all false. As if all his life he had memorized a misleading, distorted multiplication table and all the multiplication he knew how to do was fundamentally biased. This was a different sort of mathematics: not the geometry of flat surfaces, but the geometry of gaping pits. Of sand dunes. Try explaining that to someone who has never seen an enormous moon over the desert).

Marciano leaned back on his chair. "She's something else, that Eritrean. First I thought we'd need an interpreter for her, but her Hebrew is better than the Bedouins'. You ever see anything like that?" Eitan shook his head. He had never seen anything like that. "Gifted with languages. Some people are like that. My grandfather, for instance, knew how to curse in nine different languages and order boiling-hot coffee in five others." Eitan looked at Marciano. Either the precinct commander was one hell of a clever strategist or he was just a bullshitter. It was definitely a very strange way to extract a confession. (And maybe, Eitan thought suddenly, maybe he doesn't need a confession at all. He has Sirkit, he has the Bedouins, he doesn't really need me.) Marciano looked at him from behind two framed pictures of his children at a swimming pool. Eitan asked himself whether Liat had put pictures of the kids on her desk. Funny that he didn't know something like that about her. On the other hand, maybe it was logical, given all the things she didn't know about him.

Marciano's children smiled at the camera in their bathing suits, holding ice pops, and it was obvious from their faces that they hadn't the slightest idea what their father did for a living. If they had known that he spent hours in his office in the company of murderers, thieves, drug smugglers and paedophiles, their smiles might have been less broad. Why the hell did he have to expose their faces to all the scum Israeli society is capable of producing? Only to broadcast to the world that he'd managed to reproduce? That his genes were walking the earth, splashing in the country-club swimming pool? The photos weren't a warm reminder for Marciano of the intimate space waiting for him at home at the end of a work day. Eitan knew that for a certainty, because the pictures had been placed facing outward. It wasn't Marciano who looked at them, but the visitors to his office. He knew his children's faces – he wanted others to know them. And by doing so – they'd know him. A solid member of society. A man of law and order. Of signed confessions and exact bedtimes. Lights out at 7:20. No games.

"I'll tell you the truth, Eitan. I'm not crazy about this story. I realize that for you, it's kind of holy work, Hippocrates and all that, but I'm telling you, a country can't exist like that. You can't let everyone in. Ongoing medical treatment, welfare – if we give all that free, then half of Africa will be on its way here."

The precinct commander gave Eitan a serious, understanding look. Eitan gave the precinct commander a totally uncomprehending look.

"Don't get me wrong," Marciano said, "I appreciate what you did. Not every doctor would go there voluntarily, in his free time, to treat those illegal immigrants. That's what they call a Jewish heart. But look at what all that compassion has got us. Not to mention that sometimes things get complicated, like they did in your case. If we hadn't had an undercover cruiser near Davidson's restaurant, that gang would have slaughtered you in that garage. You think they would have stopped to find out if you were a drug dealer or David ben Gurion? Guys like that, as soon as they decide to make you a target, they don't ask questions. If you hadn't run over that abu Ayad, he would have shot you full of holes. You think I don't know that? Hell, even your Eritrean knows that, and that's without twelve years of schooling."

Marciano spoke for another several minutes. Apologized for the night in jail, which must have been hard, and explained that he'd really had no choice. "True, the Eritrean woman cleared you completely in the first minute, and the CSI crew found all the evidence of the clinic being operated in the garage, just like she said. But Doctor, you still ran someone over and killed him, and even though that someone had a gun and was a piece-of-shit drug dealer, it doesn't mean I can let you out of the station the same night. It wouldn't look good. But now that everything's been checked out and we have signed witness statements and bagged evidence, you can go home, take a shower and go to sleep in your own bed."

Marciano stood up and walked Eitan to the door, complaining about the Eritreans, the Bedouins and the reporters, who were always on his back. "Prepare yourself," he told Eitan, "they'll call you. It's not every day a story like this comes their way. Secret medical treatment, drugs, murder. You want to talk to them, be my guest. But we won't say anything. Case still under investigation. We still have to find the asshole who ran over that Eritrean and took the shipment. We have to find that Davidson. Let's just say your wife's going to be working hard this week. If you ask me, it's all the Bedouins. This whole business, one gang against another. You know what they'd do to them in an enlightened country?"

He stopped talking. Maybe he was waiting for an answer. But Eitan just stared into space, as indifferent to Marciano's silence as he had been to his words a moment before. There was only one thought in his mind: she hadn't given him up. Other thoughts were eclipsed now. Liat, Yaheli, Itamar. Work. The media. They were all waiting in the darkness as one gigantic moon shone in his mind: she hadn't given him up. She had turned him into a hero.

How stupid she felt now. The stupidest woman in the world. She felt so stupid it actually hurt her body. The pain was between her shoulders and in her lower back, on the side of her stomach and in her temples. (Although maybe it wasn't the stupidity that hurt her, or the humiliation, but the insane drive from Or Akiva to Beersheba, two and a quarter hours without a break, cramped muscles and racing thoughts.) Liat stood in the hallway of the precinct and massaged her shoulders slowly, as if that were the only thing bothering her at the moment. As if it weren't her husband sitting there, on the other side of the door at the end of the corridor. She massaged her shoulders and knew that Cheetah and Rachmanov, Esti the emergency phone-call operator and Amsalem from the patrol unit were looking at her from behind. Even if they weren't actually standing there and looking, they were looking. They all knew. From the precinct commander down to the last prisoner. Everyone had seen what she hadn't seen. What had been right in front of her eyes, and she hadn't noticed.

The call from Marciano had come at three in the morning. She answered immediately. She didn't have to wake up. As if she'd been waiting for that call. After that, things happened very quickly. She woke her mother and asked her to take care of Itamar and Yaheli. She got into the car and reminded herself that a senior detective can get into real trouble if she's caught driving way over the speed limit. She drove the two and a quarter hours to Beersheba without stopping, asking herself all the way if it was possible. Two people live in the same house. Sleep beside each other. Fuck each other. Shower after each other. Cook, eat, put kids to bed, pass each other the remote, the salt, a roll of toilet paper. And all that time, they're not really living together. Not even in parallel. They have been separate the entire time, and she had no idea.

Two and a quarter hours and she still couldn't make sense of it. What had he been doing there, in the middle of the night, with Bedouin gangs and drug shipments? What the hell did any of it have to do with him? Her astonishment was so great that it left no room for anger. An enormous, swollen question mark had obliterated the face of the man who was her husband. His name – Eitan Green – suddenly stood outside the house, outside their common memories, like the first time they met, when she hadn't yet known anything apart from his face, and the name was still an empty container waiting to be filled. Eitan Green, a stranger.

By the time she reached the station, Marciano could already tell her what had happened. But that only made everything more complicated. She read the Bedouins' statements. The transcript of the Eritrean woman's interview. She closed herself in her office (the corridor was too exposed to probing glances) and went over the material again. Something did not add up.

"Do you mind if I go in to talk to the Eritrean woman?"

"I thought you'd want to talk to your husband, who's been cooling his heels in a jail cell."

Liat listened to Marciano through the internal phone receiver and felt her stomach clench. It was a good thing she'd called instead of going into his office. A punch in the diaphragm is easier to take when you're sitting down.

"So I'm going in to talk to the Eritrean."

"Should I talk to your husband in the meantime, let him know he's free to go?" Marciano sounded quite amused and Liat thought he might not really understand. Perhaps that punch to the diaphragm wasn't gloating or derision. He might actually think it wasn't such a big deal. A half-funny marital spat. A sitcom conflict between a husband and wife. The husband does something without telling his wife, the wife gives him hell, makes his life miserable at home, and in the end it all works out.

"Don't release him yet." And she hung up before he could say anything else. Before he could say with a smile, someone screwed up, or suggest sarcastically that she come into his office to get a pair of handcuffs. Before he had time to wonder whether there was something more than a power struggle going on here, more than a small, pathetic bit of revenge being taken by a small, pathetic woman who didn't know anything.

The Eritrean woman glanced at her when she opened the door. Her face looked terrible. A blackened, swollen left eye. A nose that was definitely broken.

"Hello Sirkit."

Sirkit.

The Eritrean woman gazed at her silently. Liat looked her over carefully. Outside the interview room she wouldn't have dared to look at anyone that way. An open, shameless glance. A brazen, direct look that didn't shift when the person in front of you became aware of it. But here, inside, there was no need for politeness. People walking in the street have the right to demand they be looked at surreptitiously. For periods of time that do not cause cheeks to redden or knees to tingle. But a person sitting in an interrogation room is denied that right. So Liat allowed herself to relax in her chair and scrutinize the Eritrean woman's face. Slowly, with the calm of someone who has all the time in the world.

Several moments later, the Eritrean woman looked away. Liat wasn't surprised. Most people did that. Not only petty criminals, but the serious ones as well lowered their eyes to the floor after a minute at the most. Or they looked at another corner of the room. The more brazen among them stared at her breasts, deliberately. But the Eritrean woman didn't look at the floor or at another corner of the room. Nor did she stare at her breasts. She closed her eyes.

"Sirkit? Is everything okay?"

Only after she had spoken the words did she realize that she had mispronounced her name again. This time the Eritrean woman did not correct her. Maybe she didn't notice. Maybe she had given up the hope that anyone there would pronounce her name properly.

Everything's fine.

Her eyes remained closed, and Liat didn't know whether she should feel sorry for the woman who'd had her face battered like that, let her sleep a bit because she really looked wiped out, or insist on asking her what she'd come to ask (she never thought for a moment that eyes could be closed not only out of tiredness, but also out of defiance. It never occurred to her that such a woman could be defiant at all.)

But she asked all the same. Requested that the Eritrean woman repeat her version of events. She heard what she had read in the transcript of the interview: how Davidson had demanded that the woman's husband deliver a shipment. How the Eritrean's body had been found the next morning and the shipment gone. How the Bedouins had beaten his wife mercilessly because they thought she might know something about the gang that had taken off with the package.

"But the doctor," Liat asked, "what about the doctor?!"

The woman suddenly stopped speaking and opened her eyes, which had been closed until then. As if she felt that the question was different from the previous ones the detective had asked her. Liat waited for a moment, then repeated the question. Slowly, evenly, with all the inner quiet she could muster.

"How does the doctor come into all of this?"

He was driving around in his SUV one night and saw us. Saw that we needed help. He wanted to help.

She asked her several more questions, and she got several more answers, all of them identical to the transcript of the interview and the evidence. There was a clinic in the garage, and the person operating it was her husband. Though there was no reason for Liat to be in that room, she couldn't leave. Not yet. Once again, she examined the Eritrean woman's face. A broken nose. A blackened left eye. A spot of dry blood under her ear. Before the Bedouins had surprised them, Eitan had gone to treat her injuries. He'd left Yaheli's bed and driven two and a quarter hours to get there. Only an angel would do something like that. (But her man was no angel. So what happened here? She hadn't let him be a hero and expose Zakai, so he went off to be a hero in the dead of night?) Maybe he did, she thought, suddenly straightening up. Maybe that's exactly what happened. And she could already feel the tension in her shoulders and the pain near her stomach ease slightly. Felt her body being released from the tight grip of doubt. She grew more relaxed as the story became clearer, her relief increasing with each additional detail: he felt guilty about the silence she had imposed on him concerning Zakai's bribes. He wanted to atone. That fit right in with his rigid morality. His damaged ego. And it was just like him not to tell her. After all, she would have stopped him. It was illegal. And dangerous. What about all that stuff you make me read about those refugees? he would have asked her. And she realized suddenly why he had been so interested in the investigation of that Eritrean's death. Those people weren't just a newspaper article for him. He knew them. He was helping them.

She still hated him. Was still ready to hang him upside down. Still intended not to talk to him for quite a few days. Even weeks. But when she went out of the interview room, leaving the Eritrean woman behind, she knew she had to thank the black woman for her ruined face. The broken nose. Blackened left eye. Spot of dried blood under her ear. Eitan had treated her. Her husband.

And he was a stranger to her no longer.

16

NOT FAR FROM THE REFUGEE DETENTION CAMP, he stopped the SUV and bought an ice pop. The gas station was full of families on their way to a weekend of fun in Eilat. Several people frowned at him, trying to recall where they knew his face from. One little boy asked if he was in the Children's Song Festival. He almost said yes, but decided against it. He'd eaten his way through half the ice pop when a woman with a baby carriage came up to him and said, "You're that doctor with the refugees. Your picture was in the paper." He didn't reply because she hadn't actually asked him anything. "That's nice, what you did," she said. "We need more people like you in this country." He thanked her. She seemed to be expecting it. Other people came over to them. They asked the woman what he'd done and she told them. The little boy who had asked about the Song Festival listened and asked for an autograph for his collection. "But I'm not a singer," Eitan said. "I know," the little boy agreed, looking disappointed, "but you were in the papers." Several people began arguing. We can't have all of Africa coming here. If those bleeding hearts have their way, we'll end up without a country. The people saying those things looked at Eitan. They seemed to be waiting for him to speak. The woman with the carriage answered them. She too was looking at Eitan. Maybe she was also waiting for him to say something. He finished the ice pop and got into his car.

At the entrance to the camp he was met by a representative of the administration. A cheery guy of twenty-seven who was going to be married in a week and was constantly texting his girlfriend. He looked like a kid dressed up as a policeman. "They're all in the yard now," he said. "I'll take you there." As they walked past the high fences, the guy told him about their problems with the wedding hall. "Believe me, I had no idea that napkins came in so many colors." They stopped in front of a large area full of people. "Okay, bro, here's the yard. I'll open the gate for you. You see her? What am I saying, they all look alike."

Eitan went inside and scanned the bustling yard. They really did look alike. The same dark, deadened faces. The same slack expression of apathetic boredom. Any one of those people could be Sirkit. Brown eyes. Black hair. Flat nose. Black Eritrean African women refugees. Identical. They looked as alike as a herd of sheep. Of cows. Several years ago, when Spencer Tunick was in Israel to create one of his large-scale nude photographic installations, Eitan looked at the resulting pictures and was horrified. The newspapers talked about the liberation of the body from the tyranny of thinness. About pornography being transformed into intimacy. But he had looked at the naked bodies, the parade of nipples, navels and pubic hair and thought something had been stolen from those people. Not modesty – that had never bothered him. If each one had been photographed separately, stark naked, he would not have been repelled. But when he looked at them together, a crowded collection of bodies, he felt that they had lost every drop of selfhood, and all the small differences that made each of them who they were had been eclipsed by that large mass of identical flesh. The women in the yard were not naked, but the identical conditions and the overcrowded space stripped them of their personalities and made them a single entity – Eritrean women. The generosity of one or the meanness of another, this one's sense of humor or that one's shyness were of no value. They were Eritrean women waiting to be deported, and he was an Israeli looking at them.

(But there was one here who'd had an effect on you. There was one here whose body, whose specific body haunted your dreams. There was someone named Sirkit, and her voice was icy cold, her skin velvety soft. You hate her and you love her, and now she's standing in front of you and you can't see her.)

A few moments later he did see her and at first didn't realize that he was seeing her. She was leaning against the fence with a group of other women, her long hair coiled around the top of her head. For a moment, his eyes passed over her just as they passed over all the others, and the next moment stopped abruptly. He knew that look. Knew that body. Her body. Feet in plastic flip-flops. Hips drowning in wide, shapeless pants. Blue shirt printed with the logo MY NETIVOT, words that the woman wearing the shirt couldn't read. Her body. Fingers with bitten nails holding the gate. He hadn't known that she bit her nails. Perhaps she'd started here, or perhaps the proof had always been right under his nose and he never saw it. Unequivocal proof that even Lilith was a mere mortal. They called her a devil because she was awake when upstanding women were asleep in their beds, because she rode a man when he should have been riding her. Because she kidnapped babies. And all that time, she had been biting her nails. Unconsciously, Eitan felt his own fingernails. Clean. Carefully cut. Growing at the average rate of four centimeters per year. (Not only his, but all the fingernails here. An average of four centimeters per year. For a moment, he could see them all, the residents of this place, dozens of black women, the Russian guard at the entrance, the jailer who was about to be married, even his future wife. All of them at the rate of four centimeters per year.)

She still hadn't seen him. He stood there looking at her. Who is she when I'm not looking at her? When I don't feel guilty about her or don't want her? Who is she when she's alone, as she was a moment before I arrived, as she will be a moment after I leave?

The women standing around Sirkit spoke, and she might have been listening or simply staring outside, beyond the fence. At any moment, an enormous tiger might appear from the desert, leap over the concrete and barbed wire and land at her feet. The other women would scream, the Russian guard would run for his life, but she would reach out and pet the striped fur of its forehead. The tiger would purr its consent. It would lick her face like a puppy. She would climb onto its back, it would leap once again, and they would gallop off into the distance until they disappeared.

It was because of the tiger that he recognized her, that he picked her out from all the others. Many women were staring through the fence that morning, but only one summoned a tiger with her glance. Eitan was almost saddened that he was about to deliver a poor substitute for that beast of prey – himself – and leaping over fences was something he did not know how to do (and if he did know, would he leap?). He looked at the fence. Horizontal and vertical metal wires dividing the world into squares. The desert outside, the sky and the horizon, all partitioned into identical, iron-framed squares.

When he turned his glance from the fence, he saw that she had been looking at him for several moments. That made him uncomfortable. It was one thing for him to look at Sirkit without her knowing it, and something else for Sirkit to look at him. It made no difference whether the glance was critical or favorable. Generous or judgmental. The very fact that you don't know you're being looked at gives the observer the upper hand. One is looking and the other is being looked at. One scrutinizes and the other is under scrutiny. Sirkit looked at him without his knowing it, which meant that she had been close to him without his knowledge, had been inside him and hadn't told him. That night as well, the first night, she had looked at him without his being aware of her. Hidden by the night. It was that first look that had given her possession of him. And only because she had taken possession of him had he begun to look at her. But even then, he hadn't seen her bitten nails.

She left the fence and walked toward him. The other women followed her with their eyes. Suddenly Eitan was very much aware of the sweat that had gathered in his armpits.

You came to visit.

He nodded. All the things he wanted to say to her, all the words that had filled his SUV on the drive there, everything vanished when she stood before him, as if he were a scolded child. But behind the scolded child was a sketch artist. And he used every moment to examine her features, to memorize them, to keep her from vanishing into the sea of years as she had vanished into the sea of faces a few moments before. Nose. Mouth. Forehead. Eyes. Sirkit.

Suddenly he realized that she was sketching him as well, standing there and sketching him in her mind. Nose. Mouth. Forehead. Eyes. Eitan. Her doctor. She had already done it before. The night he hit Asum. She had lain on the sand after that vicious punch in the stomach. Asum was good at punches like that. If you angered him at noon, he didn't hit you right away. He waited patiently. An hour, two hours, a day. And then when you thought it had passed, when air entered your lungs without that smell of fear, he'd punch you. Quick and smooth. He never spoke when he did it. Didn't shout or explain. He punched you and moved on, the way someone hits a cow that kicked or a goat that insists on drifting away from the herd. Without emotion, simply because it had to be done.

The night she had lain on the sand and thought that one day she would kill him, the way the cows would if they had the intelligence. But she knew she wouldn't do it, just as the cows and goats didn't. Sometimes bulls raise their heads, or dogs. They have pride, those animals. That's why people smash their heads with stones if they're dogs, or slit their throats if they're bulls. No one wastes a bullet on them; it's too expensive.

That night, Asum had stood there with the shipment in his hand and told her to get up, they were late, and then the car came out of nowhere and hit him. For the first moment she thought it was because of her, that her hatred had been so red and so strong that it had come out of her and turned into a red SUV moving at 100 kilometers an hour. But then a white man stepped out of the red SUV, and she took a very good look at his face. She saw the fear on it when he realized what he had hit, and the repulsion on it right before he placed his lips on Asum's. Even before he stood up and drove away, she knew he was going to get up and drive away. She had seen that on his face as well. Then he really made her angry. Not because of Asum. She didn't shed a single tear for Asum. But because the man got into the SUV and ran his hand over his face as if he were trying to rub away a bad dream, without understanding that it was someone else's bad dream. The cows drove me mad today, her father used to say; my hands hurt from hitting them.

A moment later, the SUV wasn't there anymore. She stood up. The moon in the sky was the most beautiful she had ever seen in her life. Round and perfect. He was still breathing, her husband. His eyes looked at her evilly. He hadn't let her pee before they went out, wanted her to come right away. She hadn't known where they were going, but she understood that

Davidson had given him a mission, and he was going to take advantage of it to punch her or smack her around without anyone hearing. The caravans were too crowded for beatings or moaning, and now Davidson had given him an excuse to get far away from them. She ran after him in the sand even though she had to pee, until he turned around and gave her that vicious punch without saying a word, and a moment later the suv hit him. She took off her underpants and stood over him. A hot, yellow stream flowed out of her, down her thighs and onto the evil eyes beneath her. Urine that had been accumulating for hours burst out freely. A pleasant, satisfying flow. And the smell that rose from it was incredibly beautiful.

Later, she saw the wallet that had been dropped next to where the man had knelt. His picture on a card: serious, confident. The complete opposite of the man who had been there a few minutes ago, who had stumbled out of the suv on shaky legs. She looked carefully at the picture. Since that night, she had already learned to know that face. His smile, his anger, his scientist's excitement and his white man's righteousness. But in the days she had spent here, behind the fence, his face had become blurred in her mind. Not only his. The whole garage. The treatment table. The people waiting in line. They disappeared because there was no point in remembering them. She had to think about other things; for instance, about looking carefully into the guards' faces to see which of them she could have sex with. Which of the older, heavy men or the younger ones who still had pimples on their faces. Checking out breasts, evaluating asses, pointing out to each other that the one over there was actually pretty, don't you think. But she needed more than their looks. She needed a heavy body to lie on top of her, a pimply face that would contort when he came so that she could utter the one word that would get her out of there: rape. They didn't settle for anything less than that here. Less than that, and they might even send you back there. Although she missed her village, and even more the sea beside her village, she knew that there, the land of the dead children, was not a place she wanted to go back to. She only had to look carefully, find the right guard. Then there would be a trial, and when it all ended they wouldn't dare send her back. She'd stay here and make new children in place of the ones she'd had, and they'd look like all the previous babies in every way, except that they would be alive. One of those new children would be a girl. She would comb her hair and braid it. The last little girl – her hair hadn't grown long enough for braids. The new little girl would reach the age when she could talk to her as if she were a big girl. A person. None of her previous children had reached the age when you could talk to them as if they were people. Yamana and Miriam had still spoken the language of babies when they took sick, and Goitom had already spoken the language of grown-ups, but he had never really understood – he didn't stop when that soldier told him to stop. The new children would never know what she'd had to do to bring them into the world. They would be proud and stupid. Not like the women here, who were smart and understood how the world worked, and that was why they didn't have a single drop of pride. Unlike her.

Sirkit wasn't waiting for a tiger to leap over the fence into the detention camp. The tiger was already inside her, lying in wait, quiet, watching. Or maybe there was no tiger at all, but a crazy, hallucinating antelope that kept insisting on being something it was not. She didn't know, and didn't want to know. Such thoughts could only hurt her. If a bird asked how it could fly, it would fall immediately. That was her mother's answer to every question but the simplest. For instance, you could ask where the flour was, but if you asked why the soldiers took all the flour, she'd explain to you that if a fish asked how it could breathe underwater, it would choke. So she had stopped asking questions and did what the birds and the fish did: she moved forward. From the village to the desert, from the desert to the border, from the border to a different desert that was actually the same desert, but someone had drawn a line and called it Egypt. From the Egyptian desert to the Egyptian Bedouins, the ones her memory had to pass over very quickly, without stopping, because if she stopped, she really wouldn't be able to push onward. And from the Egyptian Bedouins to that country where the people were white and the roads were wide and the houses had red roofs that slanted at a strange angle. Here she stopped. From here she would not move. If she had to stand at the fence all day and look at the faces of the guards, she'd stand and look. Sooner or later she'd find the dark glint in the eyes. It was always there, that glint. You just had to know how to look.

And suddenly her doctor appeared out of nowhere. She had almost forgotten him. Or at least, wanted to think that she had forgotten him. When she first saw him, she wanted to punch him and slap him. Scream "Get out of here. What are you doing here!" Because if he was here, then it wasn't all in her mind. Those things she had felt, had pushed away, maybe they had really existed. Maybe dark, heavy water had flowed between them the entire time, though they never spoke of it.

She looked at him, stuck in the sea of black women, a white sailboat in dark waters (Asum's sailboat, she thought suddenly, recalling how she had watched as it moved out to sea, and how disappointed she had been when it reappeared with the other sailboats in the evening. He hadn't drowned.) A moment later, she saw that her doctor was standing in front of her, but wasn't looking at her. Was thinking of other things at that moment. Maybe his wife, his children. Funny, she had no idea whether he had boys or girls. Whether he'd ever tried to braid a tangle of hair. Whether they were at the age when they still had to be carried, or they walked beside him, heads held high. One thing was clear to her: they were stupid and proud. Like him.

He finally looked at her, that gray look of his. She walked toward him and he stayed where he was.

You came to visit.

"Yes."

Then he was silent. So was she. Her brain was suddenly empty of thoughts, like that well near the village that one day, simply had no more water. The silence grew larger and thicker, like a swelling elephant, reaching truly huge proportions. Finally he said, "I wanted to say thank you," and regretted the words even as he spoke them because why in the world did he owe this woman thanks? He could have died that night. One good shot and the whole business would have ended completely differently. She listened to his thank you and thought that if he wanted to, he could fight for her. Send letters, make calls, bang on desks. When people like him bang on desks, the world listens. But he wouldn't bang on any desks. It might hurt, might cause damage to the joints. And suddenly she knew that he hadn't come there to thank her, and he certainly hadn't come to secure her release. He had come to say goodbye. With a sad look, a wave of the hand, a hope that remained hidden even to him, that he would never see her again. He had come to end the whole dark story that had upset him and threatened his family, even his life. But no matter how much that dark story had upset him, it had been fascinating and seductive, and had aroused him to the depths of his soul the way such dark stories do. But stories must come to an end. Life must continue along its sure, quiet paths. Even if he looked at her with eyes that caressed the features of her face, even if you could actually see him making room in his memory for her image, in the end he wanted nothing more than a picture on the wall. A memory to ponder. And to move forward. Like the birds and the fish. For even he, were he to stop for too long, if he were to ask why, would fall and choke.

It's okay.

Two people stand facing each other with nothing left to say. The woman wearing flip-flops, too-wide pants, a MY NETIVOT shirt. The man wearing jeans, a shirt and running shoes with orthopedic insoles bought in the duty-free shop. The words they have spoken and the words they could have spoken become superfluous all at once.

Fifteen minutes later, when the red suv turned onto the road leading to Omer, Eitan Green kept carefully to the speed limit. A person gets up in the morning, leaves the house and finds that planet earth is back in its orbit. He says to his wife "See you tonight," and they do indeed see each other that night. He says "See you later" to the grocery store clerk, knowing that they'll see each other again the next day, knowing that the tomatoes, even if their price goes up tenfold, will always be within reach of his hand. How beautiful the earth is when it moves properly. How pleasant to move with it. To forget that any other movement ever existed. That a different movement is even possible.

PUSHKIN PRESS

Pushkin Press was founded in 1997, and publishes novels, essays, memoirs, children's books—everything from timeless classics to the urgent and contemporary.

Our books represent exciting, high-quality writing from around the world: we publish some of the twentieth century's most widely acclaimed, brilliant authors such as Stefan Zweig, Marcel Aymé, Antal Szerb, Gaito Gazdanov and Yasushi Inoue, as well as compelling and award-winning contemporary writers, including Andrés Neuman, Edith Pearlman, Erwin Mortier and Ayelet Gundar-Goshen.

Pushkin Press publishes the world's best stories, to be read and read again. Here are just some of the titles from our long and varied list. For more amazing stories, visit www.pushkinpress.com.

TRAVELLER OF THE CENTURY
ANDRÉS NEUMAN

'A beautiful, accomplished novel: as ambitious as it is generous, as moving as it is smart' Juan Gabriel Vásquez, *Guardian*

THE WORLD OF YESTERDAY
STEFAN ZWEIG

'*The World of Yesterday* is one of the greatest memoirs of the twentieth century, as perfect in its evocation of the world Zweig loved, as it is in its portrayal of how that world was destroyed' David Hare

WAKE UP, SIR!
JONATHAN AMES

'The novel is extremely funny but it is also sad and poignant, and almost incredibly clever' *Guardian*

BONITA AVENUE
PETER BUWALDA

'One wild ride: a swirling helix of a family saga... a new writer as toe-curling as early Roth, as roomy as Franzen and as caustic as Houellebecq' *Sunday Telegraph*

JOURNEY BY MOONLIGHT
ANTAL SZERB

'Just divine... makes you imagine the author has had private access to your own soul' Nicholas Lezard, *Guardian*

ONE NIGHT, MARKOVITCH
AYELET GUNDAR-GOSHEN

'Wry, ironically tinged and poignant... this is a fable for the twenty-first century' *Sunday Telegraph*

KARATE CHOP & MINNA NEEDS REHEARSAL SPACE
DORTHE NORS

'Unique in form and effect... Nors has found a novel way of getting into the human heart' *Guardian*

RED LOVE: THE STORY OF AN EAST GERMAN FAMILY
MAXIM LEO

'Beautiful and supremely touching... an unbearably poignant description of a world that no longer exists' *Sunday Telegraph*

THE PARROTS
FILIPPO BOLOGNA

'A five-star satire on literary vanity... a wonderful, surprising novel' *Metro*

SONG FOR AN APPROACHING STORM
PETER FRÖBERG IDLING

'Beautifully evocative... a must-read novel' *Daily Mail*

THE RABBIT BACK LITERATURE SOCIETY
PASI ILMARI JÄÄSKELÄINEN

'Wonderfully knotty... a very grown-up fantasy masquerading as quirky fable. Unexpected, thrilling and absurd' *Sunday Telegraph*

STAMMERED SONGBOOK: A MOTHER'S BOOK OF HOURS
ERWIN MORTIER

'Mortier has a poet's eye for vibrant detail and prose to match... If this is a book of fragmentation, it is also a son's moving tribute' *Observer*

THE BRETHREN
ROBERT MERLE

'Swashbuckling historical fiction... For all its philosophical depth [*The Brethren*] is a hugely entertaining romp' *Guardian*

BARCELONA SHADOWS
MARC PASTOR

'As gruesome as it is gripping... the writing is extraordinarily vivid... Highly recommended' *Independent*

THE LIBRARIAN
MIKHAIL ELIZAROV

'A romping good tale... Pretty sensational' *Big Issue*

WHILE THE GODS WERE SLEEPING
ERWIN MORTIER

'A monumental, phenomenal book' *De Morgen*

BUTTERFLIES IN NOVEMBER
AUÐUR AVA ÓLAFSDÓTTIR

'A funny, moving and occasionally bizarre exploration of life's upheavals and reversals' *Financial Times*